ANNA UNDREAMING

BOOK ONE

The Metiks Fade Trilogy

Thomas Welsh

OWL HOLLOW PRESS

Owl Hollow Press, LLC, Springville, UT 84663

Anna Undreaming

Library of Congress Cataloging-in-Publication Data
Anna Undreaming / T. Welsh. — First edition.

Summary: When Anna learns she's an Undreamer with powers to alter worlds constructed by Dreamers, she must travel through their strange and treacherous creations, her existence spiraling into wonder and danger, to face the horrors of her past and save her old world as well as her new.

Cover design: Les Solot
Images: Depositphotos
ISBN 978-1-945654-08-4 (paperback)
ISBN 978-1-945654-09-1 (e-book)
LCCN 2017963796

Nana,

This story is for you.

I can't paint, draw, sew or sing.

But you seem to like my stories

And from now until I leave this world

All my stories are yours

Both the stories I write for you

And the stories we make together.

PART ONE

A Girl Dreams of Fire

one

Anna rocked the candle back and forth, examining the wax as it thickened and set around the edges. The blackened wick, now extinguished, puffed out little coils of gray smoke.

"Why do you always do that?" asked Sue.

"I just like playing with the flame. Sometimes it lights itself again…"

Sue wrinkled her nose and shook her head. "No it doesn't. Sorry Dean. She's in one of her moods again."

Dean smirked and fingered his well-groomed beard like he was about to say something clever. It was a practiced affectation. Sue looked at him with wide eyes and left a long space in the conversation, but no one filled it. Anna winced as her friend coiled a lock of blonde hair around one finger while staring at Dean's lips. Forcing her gaze away while maintaining as neutral an expression as she could manage, Anna turned her attention back to the candle.

The bar was busy, but they huddled intimately around a small table in a quiet corner. Anna wondered what they must look like to an outsider. The soft orange light might hide each of their flaws. A stranger might think Dean's smile looked friendly rather than predatory. Sue might seem serene rather than desperate. Anna knew she looked tired, but from a distance, the dark circles under her hollow eyes might seem to disappear. From far enough away, she might even look happy.

Although she looked at their faces, in her peripheral vision Anna saw Dean's hand sliding up her friend's thigh. It made her uncomfortable. Sue was right; she was maudlin tonight, but she was also wary. Dean's words were honeyed but too-smooth. Too sincere. In the spaces between the jokes, he would look directly into Anna's eyes. There was an implicit challenge. He wanted Sue. Anna didn't want him to have her.

Dean gave Anna a wink before turning to face Sue. "Did you know that if you tell a lie, there's a way your body gives it away? And *I* know what to look for. It's a little thing you absolutely cannot hide. Should I show you?"

Sue nodded eagerly. Her eyes shone.

"It probably wouldn't work on Anna. We all know she's a robot."

"Never mind her. Do me!" said Sue. She laughed too hard, but Dean gave her a serious look.

"Okay, now look straight into my eyes. I'm going to ask you some questions. Okay? You have to keep looking into my eyes."

Sue sucked her lips nervously and gave him a short nod. Anna glanced around the bar, looking for a distraction. Her gaze rested on the barman at the other side of the room. A young, nervous looking boy with a wispy moustache, he was leaning on the bar and frowning. When she caught his eye, he gave her a tiny, conciliatory nod. She gave him a little thumbs-up in return, then looked back at her two companions and wished she hadn't.

"You're not going to hypnotize me to…do things, are you?" asked Sue. She used a tone of voice Anna had never heard her use before. Childlike. Baby-talk.

"Oh for fuck…" Anna caught herself too late.

Sue shot her an angry glance. "What? What's your problem?"

"It's fine, it's fine," said Dean. "Anna's too clever for my tricks. Isn't that right?" Dean turned his whole attention to Anna. He was waiting for an answer.

She raised her head, put the candle to one side and looked back at him flatly.

"Yes," she said, keeping her expression neutral.

Dean leaned back in his seat, ignoring Sue now and addressing only Anna. "You're the smartest person here, right? Real clever. What is it you're studying again? Feminism?"

Sue picked up her drink and sipped as she tried to look nonchalant, but her leg shook nervously under the table.

"No," replied Anna.

"You're writing a thesis though right? 'The Benefits of Celibacy'? Based on personal research?" Dean's clear blue eyes shone. He was loving this. Sue laughed for a fraction of a second then stopped when no one else joined her. There was a sliver of concern in her conflicted expression. But not enough.

Anna didn't look away. "I've heard people talking about you, Dean. I've heard rumors."

"Anna!" snapped Sue. "Why do you always do this? We're having a nice time. Why do you always have to be like *this*?"

Dean's smile widened. "She's been like this since 'the accident,' right Sue? People talk about you, too, Anna. People spread terrible rumors. I think it fucking sucks. They say it was your fault he died. Why would they say that?"

Anna almost flinched, but though her stomach twisted in knots, she willed herself to stay calm. He wanted a reaction, and she refused to give him that. She nodded nonchalantly.

Dean leaned his big hand across the table and touched her arm. She forced herself not to yank it away. "We're here for you

Anna. It wasn't your fault. Okay?" He flashed her a tiny smile, then squeezed her arm hard. It hurt.

"See." Sue grinned, oblivious to the tension. "I told you he was okay. I told him everything that happened to you, and he doesn't mind. We're all here for you, Anna."

Even after Dean let her go, her arm throbbed.

Anna's head spun. She forced herself to calm down. She wouldn't storm off or shout or scream. That's what he wanted. If this escalated into a full-blown argument, Sue would be in trouble. She was enthralled by Dean, and he was trying to drive a wedge between them. To protect her friend, Anna had to assuage Dean's suspicions while placating her friend. Taking one long breath, she centered herself, settled back into her seat and gave them a smile so good it was almost real.

"Thanks, guys. I'm just touchy, you know? Just ignore me."

Sue smiled with relief. "Oh, don't worry. We don't mind. Anyway, why don't you tell us about that mystery man of yours? Your internet guy. Teej?"

"Who is this then?" asked Dean with a sickly-sweet smile. "Teej? Is it another gamer nerd? Or are you a cam girl now. Stripping your way through college?"

Relieved that the focus was moving away from Sue, and glad that Dean was no longer touching either of them, Anna relaxed a little. She shook her head. "No, he was...that was a mistake. He was someone I met online. He was an expert on...well, he seemed to be an expert on everything. He knew a lot about the philosophy I was reading for my thesis: Absurdism and Albert Camus. But I haven't spoken to him since I graduated."

"He turned out to be a major psycho!" interjected Sue with relish.

"Like what?" asked Dean. "Obsessed stalker?"

"No, not that kind of psycho," said Anna. "Kinda worse. He told me he knew Camus. Personally."

"But he's been dead for hundreds of years," said Sue. Anna and Dean shared a look but neither spoke.

"Anyway," Anna went on, "I don't talk to him anymore. He got very *weird*. Maybe he was weird from the start. He had a lot of ideas about the world that were…look, it doesn't matter. It was never going to work out."

They shared an awkward silence. Anna opened her mouth to speak again, but Dean broke in, "You just need a good man."

"Sure, that's what I need."

He smirked in response to her sarcasm but went on. "And not one you meet online. That's not working. You know what Einstein said: *Insanity is repeating the same actions and expecting different results.*"

Sue nodded thoughtfully like this was sage wisdom, but Anna smiled broadly.

"Einstein? Einstein didn't say that. And even if he did, it's fucking stupid. I mean it literally makes no sense. Do you roll dice over and over and expect to get the same number every time?"

For a moment, Anna was genuinely happy at Dean's furrowed brow. Sue waited for him to retort. Instead, he pushed Anna's drink across the table to her. "Drink up, smart ass. You win this round."

She smiled and finished her rum and coke. Even if the company wasn't good, she was happy she could still amuse herself. Her head spun a little from the drink. She let herself enjoy it.

"Well, I have to go to the ladies," said Sue. "You kids chat amongst yourselves."

Sue unsteadily clambered over the low stools as she left, and Anna mused that her friend seemed more drunk than she should be. Anna rubbed her ring finger absent-mindedly while

13

Dean watched Sue go. He rubbed his biceps unconsciously, forcing Anna to notice the definition of the man's upper body in his tight shirt. He was broad and powerful. She brushed a red curl from her face and waited for him to meet her gaze. She tried to sit up straight and appear as tall as she could, but still, he loomed over her.

"I *am* too smart for your tricks," she said.

"Not all of them," he replied without looking at her. He picked at his beard absent-mindedly.

"What do you mean? She won't go home with you. She's not like that."

He turned to her, and for a moment, he looked almost hurt. But when he answered, there was a sense of the inevitable in his tone. "It's already decided. I'm an alpha, Anna. I get what I want. I'm not a bad guy, but in life when you really want some-thing, you have to be brave enough to go take it. There's no point denying what you want. And I want her."

Anna shifted in her seat and considered chasing after Sue. Perhaps she could make an excuse for them to both leave now. She had to get away from Dean.

"We should play a game," he said, changing the subject. He rubbed his hands together with nervous energy. Anna shook her head, beginning to suspect something was seriously wrong, but he went on.

"So, you think you're pretty clever. That you're a good judge of people? Well let's test that. I've put a little pill in one of these drinks." He slid two identical glasses across the table, leaving one slightly closer to Anna than the other.

"A little pill that would help anyone chill out. Even you. If you choose the wrong one, me and Sue go home, and you have a little nap. Maybe some kind gentleman will escort you home. If you get the right one though—and drink it down—I'll make an excuse and go home and you can have your friend back for the rest of the night. What do you think?"

Anna's mind raced. Time slowed to a crawl. The music in the bar seemed to fade. Had Dean planned this all along? Was this a joke? A trick? She felt the blood pumping in her ears.

"So, if I say to you that this one on the right—" he pushed the drink toward her "—has the pill, will you believe me? Am I lying, Anna? Why don't you look in my eyes? Look in my eyes, and tell me if I'm lying."

Obeying him, Anna looked into Dean's eyes and saw the truth. This wasn't the real game. The real game had already taken place. She had already lost. Anna debated stepping away to call the police or signal for help, but he'd revealed his hand, and there was no way he was letting her get away. She was trapped here with him in this quiet corner, and he counted on her complicity. He was controlling everything about this situation, and she had to take that control back.

It all happened so fast. She flipped the table. Or tried. It was heavy, but urgency lent her strength, and she pushed with enough force to topple the drinks, glasses clattering and shattering across the wooden floor. Dean shouted something unintelligible, and everyone in the bar turned to them. *Good.* She had to make a scene. She had to get to Sue.

Legs of lead, head filled with fuzz, the stumble was almost a fall, but she pushed through it, getting as far as the bathroom door before she stopped to steady herself with both hands. Her legs felt like they were already asleep. The drug was fast. People got out of her way, but she was barely aware of them. Behind her, Dean might have shouted but the sound was muffled, like she was underwater.

Her mouth felt like it was stuffed with cloth. Gagged. A calmness was falling over her mind like a shadow, dampening her panic and fear. It lied to her that everything would be okay.

15

It robbed her of the anger and desperation she needed to fight. She raged against it. She might have screamed.

Pushing through the heavy door, she almost fell down a set of stairs. Both arms shot out to grasp the walls on each side of the stairwell. She stumbled downward, battering her way into the bathroom and past a woman to collapse into the bathroom stall. Barely aware of what was happening, Anna stuck two fingers down her throat as she leaned over the toilet bowl, her other hand instinctively pulling her long hair back behind her head. When the vomiting subsided, there was dry heaving that seemed like it would never end.

Eventually, her gagging ended, and all she felt was pain. On her knees on the cold floor, arms out to steady her, Anna's head pounded with every thudding heartbeat, and her throat and mouth burned. In the distant background, she was vaguely aware that her phone was ringing.

Unable to do anything but breathe in and out, Anna desperately tried to clear her head. No doubt he had slipped them both a pill, but she wouldn't let him do this. She would get to Sue. She had to give herself a moment. Just a moment longer. As soon as she caught up to them and could tell the police where Sue was, she would call them.

Steeling herself to face Dean, Anna tried to catch her breath. She recited that old mantra in her head. The mantra she repeated for every man she ever met.

Never play their game. Their game is always rigged.

two

The streetlights became long, hazy streaks as Anna pushed herself through the dark, wet roads. Panic and desperation fueled her steps, impelling her forward so she was half sprinting, half falling. The ground was unstable and rumbled under her feet, like she was at the epicenter of a tiny earthquake. As she stumbled through the rainy night, the moon was the only constant; everything else morphed and twisted and shifted, as if reality itself was reflected in a melted mirror.

Trees. Trees all around her. Anna struggled to comprehend why the buildings on either side of the street sprouted long, gnarled, black branches. The city was becoming a forest, and she was running deeper and deeper into its dark heart.

Maybe she ran past people on the streets. Maybe they turned to look at her. She couldn't tell.

She wondered where the wheezing, ragged breath came from. It took her long minutes to realize the sound came from her. Still, she pressed on.

Over the sound of her own breathing, her phone continued to ring in her pocket. She'd been ignoring it for a while now, but suddenly, a flash of insight hit her: what if Sue was calling? Leaning on a nearby wall, she fished it out of her jacket with numb fingers. Confusion tipped over into frustration as she struggled to process what she was seeing on the bright screen.

There were flashing symbols and shapes, but she didn't recognize them.

She closed her eyes. The world thrummed around her, but she forced her concentration to focus on where she was right now. Her current location. Outside a nightclub. She'd run down Mitchell Street. For five...no, ten, minutes. She was almost at the big crossroad with Dunmer Avenue. Without opening her eyes, she tried to reconstruct her reality. The drug Dean had slipped her was very strong and it affected her senses, but her thinking was beginning to clear. She could intuit where she was. She could force her perception back to where it needed to be. She could still help Sue.

Anna cracked her eyes open and looked at the screen. She could make out an outline of the letters. "Teej." He was messaging her. She had told him never to contact her again. Why was he trying now? It was just two words:

Look left.

What was that supposed to mean?

Unable to ignore the message, Anna turned to her left to look down Miller Lane. At the end—perhaps a hundred feet away—she saw two figures: a woman leaning heavily on a much taller man. Illuminated by a streetlamp that shone on them like a spotlight, Anna took a moment to realize who she was looking at. It was Dean and Sue.

Anna found herself running again.

The lane was narrow, and as she splashed through puddles and past dumpsters, old boxes and piles of trash, the world began to morph and change around her once more. Each step seemed to take her further from reality. She ran deeper into the dark woods, the long, twisted oak branches clawing at her as she scraped through. The passage narrowed as she pushed on. It seemed for a moment that the woods might swallow her completely, but she cleared the periphery and broke through into the city again. She knew it wasn't real, but she had no time to think about it. No time to process the effects the pill still must be having.

Unable to mask her ragged breath and faltering footsteps, she couldn't sneak up on Dean. As she approached, he turned to face her. She squinted to see him more clearly. He glowed with a sickly green patina, a greenish-gray aura that made him stand out from the environment. She rubbed her eyes with the heels of her hands, trying to physically scrape away the illusions the drug imposed on her senses.

He smirked at her. Sue hung from his right arm, her body limp in his grasp. Her head lolled back and forth as if too heavy for her neck. Still, he held her easily, his broad arm locked tight around her waist. The rain beat down on them as the winds whistled through the night. The streets were deserted. *Where was everyone?*

"You asshole. Let her go!" shouted Anna.

He laughed. "You are fucked up! Look at you. Your eyes are like saucers. You can barely stand. It's *supposed* to make you chill out. It's *supposed* to make you relax. Nothing works out for you, does it? It always has to be complicated with you."

A rumble of thunder shook little ripples through the puddles. In a few minutes, the storm would be on them. If Anna looked past Dean and Sue, all she saw were dark trees and shadows, so she focused her gaze on him. The drug would fade. This feeling wouldn't last forever. Right now, no one could help her. She had to push through this. She just had to get Sue to safety.

Anna's tongue felt fat in her mouth. She struggled to get the words out. "I won't let you do this. You're...you're not taking her home."

He rolled his eyes. "Don't be so dramatic. It's just a joke, Anna. It's all just a *joke*. I didn't even think the pills would work. I'll get her home, okay. I'm sorry you had a weird reaction. Maybe you are, I dunno, allergic. They're supposed to make you relax. I mean, I take them sometimes. It's always fine. Just calm down."

His words came in low, soothing tones as if he was speaking to a mad woman. But she wouldn't let him talk his way out of this. Anna steadied herself and took two steps forward. She tried to look sober and serious, but her legs betrayed her. She swayed.

"You let her go right now!"

"Let her go?" he laughed. "Why? Are *you* going to carry her home?"

Dean slid his arm down Sue's body and lifted her so she stood up straight. Wet hair ran across her face. Her bare legs were pale, and she'd lost a shoe somewhere.

"Where do you want to go tonight, hunny? Back to mine? Or should I leave you? You don't want to be alone, do you?"

Sue's head rolled across his shoulder and flopped forward again. He pulled her chin up so she could speak. "Not alone. Don't want to be alone…"

Anna, now close enough to touch them, reached out to grab Sue's arm, but Dean pulled her away. Off balance, Anna almost fell but righted herself at the last moment.

"Dean, if you rape her…"

"Oh, fuck this!" he screamed. "You bitches. You spend all that time trying to turn us on, then when we react, you scream rape. Rape! I don't need this. Fine! You get her home yourself. I'm out."

Sue's limp body fell like a doll, and she flopped to the ground. Anna tried to catch her, but her own legs gave way, and they both ended up in a tangle on the ground. Anna fell heavily, her hip crunching down on the sidewalk and sending a jolt through her body as she cushioned Sue falling into her lap. The drug anaesthetizing her, Anna felt shock rather than pain.

Anna cradled her friend's head and looked down at her with concern. Sue was moving her mouth but no words came. Sitting on the wet ground, arms around her friend, Anna looked up at Dean.

He took three steps away from them. Then just when Anna thought she was safe, he turned on his heels and came back. He loomed over them. Anna looked up in defiance as he deliberately and slowly leaned down. He raised a hand, but she didn't flinch. His face twisted in rage, unsure how to react to her defiance, he spat in her face.

"You should've drowned in that river with him. Bitch!"

Anna forced herself to remain completely still. Her eyes locked him in place. For a moment, he looked embarrassed or confused. Because she didn't look away. She didn't wipe her face. She didn't respond. No crying. No tears. *No way I let you win. No way.*

He turned and strode off, pulling the collar of his shirt up as he stomped along the street, around the corner and out of view. And just like that, he was gone.

Anna fingered the wet strands of hair out of Sue's face and checked her pupils and breath to see if she was lucid. Her friend mumbled under her breath.

"Ruined it. You ruined everything. I hate you…I hate you so much. I hate you…I hate you."

Sue repeated the words over and over. In the heart of the dark woods, Anna just sat and listened.

three

Long hours passed, but Anna couldn't find a route home. She'd managed to get Sue to safety, but after leaving her friend at her mom's house, Anna wandered deep and far into the night. Sue's parents lived in the city center, but Anna's apartment was miles away on the east of town. At first, the route had seemed straightforward, but the farther she went, the less familiar everything looked. She tried to look at the map on her phone, but it was a smear of color and symbols her brain didn't comprehend. *Where was she? Why did the streets keep flickering and bending? Why was the ground beneath her constantly rumbling?*

Somehow her condition was worsening. Though her mind was clear, her senses were clouding over. The buildings wobbled up and down in waves, and the streets flickered between bright, blinding light and all-encompassing darkness. As the rain fell heavily on the wet road, Anna felt like she was floating off to sea. Lost. Drowning.

The streets felt unfamiliar, and the alleyway she'd followed led to a very definite dead end. When she turned, her escape was blocked by a wall of utter blackness. Beyond the buzzing strip lights that illuminated the dirty back entrances in the alleyway, clogged with rubbish and battered and boarded up windows, there seemed to be an impenetrable black nothingness. The streetlights, the shop fronts and even the moonlight seemed to stop at the end of the alleyway. Turning away from the darkness and holding her aching head in one hand, Anna turned her attention to her phone. It was ringing again. The cheery tone she'd selected was so incongruous in her current situation that she almost smiled. *Marimba.*

With Sue home safe, she faced her own predicament with disinterest. With a heavy resignation—and lacking any hope that it might be a good decision—Anna touched the green icon on her phone and lifted it to her ear. She had no idea what she would hear, but with her reality still impaired, and unable to dismiss the illusions that plagued her senses, she decided the phone call couldn't make her night any worse.

"Anna, it's me. You are in trouble. Remember what I told you before? In the messages? You've gone too far and too deep. I can't get to you in time. Do you remember what I told you about being in a Haze?"

Haze? It was the first time she had heard Teej's voice. It was clear and resonant and not nearly grim enough for a night like this.

"Yes. I mean no. I remember you sent me *lots* of messages. They were all crazy. I told you we shouldn't talk any more. You know what? Could you just go away? My night can't get worse, but it definitely doesn't need to get any crazier."

Anna felt like the words came directly from her thoughts; the normal filter between her brain and mouth was gone. Meanwhile, all around her, the alleyway seemed to be getting darker and darker. She jumped as a high, nasal moan pierced the stillness of the night. The sound continued, wheezing and creaking and getting closer. Anna's hands and arms began to shake.

"What is this? I can't handle anything else. I'm done—"

"Listen to me," he cut her off. "Just do what I say. Do you see them yet?"

23

Panic rising, Anna glanced around the darkness closing in on her. She was in a little island of light, and the fear was rolling toward her in waves.

"See what? None of this is real. I should just stay here in case I do something stupid. Wander across a road and get hit by a car. Are you real? You can't be. You couldn't know what was happening to me. This is all in my head…"

Anna heard her own voice drone on and on, justifying and explaining. The moaning closed in on her. She saw something reach out of the shadow at the end of the alley; monstrous blue-gray arms, far larger than a human. Nightmares made real. Her whole body went rigid, her fingers curled into claws as she froze in place.

"Anna, it's not in your head; you're in a Haze. The Doxa are after you. Didn't you read my warnings?"

She frowned. Huddling down, she tried to ignore the movement in the shadows. She closed her eyes. "The crazy stuff you sent? I'll be honest, I stopped reading when I got to the bit about super powers."

The noises were getting louder. She clung onto the phone tightly.

"Super powers? No, listen, you have to—"

"Can you just get me help please? In the real world? Some-one gave me a drug or something. I'm seeing things. I can't even dial my phone."

She rubbed her head with the sleeve of her cardigan, closing her eyes tightly and trying to dismiss the incoming horrors by disbelieving them.

"You *have* to listen carefully," he replied. "There's a door to your right. You can burst through it if you hit it hard. Run in-to it. Go now. You can do it."

Anna found herself moving. He was right—she was in trou-ble here. The writhing shapes in the shadows forced her to look for any escape she could find. She was running, discovering energy she didn't know she had. No longer numb and acquiescent, her body and mind entered a kind of panic. She had to get out of this place. She had to get home.

Both feet leaving the ground, she launched herself into the door shoulder first, and it buckled but didn't break. Rattling on a deadbolt, the rotten wood bounced her backward. She almost dropped the phone, but she heard him shout something so put it to her ear again.

"What do I—"

"Hit it again. With your hand. The palm. Just think of the wood splintering. Picture it in your mind. Quickly!"

He sounded calm, but she felt something drawing nearer. The alleyway was filled with the reek of dampness and rot and something worse. A tang in the back of her throat. Like metal. Like blood.

As she pressed her hand into the wood, she felt heat spread across her palm, into her fingers and up her wrist. A swelling as something within her pushed outwards, past her own skin and into the wood. It buckled, although she didn't put much pressure on it. She felt a momentary burst of strength, as if temporarily imbued with the power to smash through any barrier. The door crunched off its hinges, collapsing inwards, and she was inside.

Anna ran into what looked like a dark storeroom and pushed through another door. Momentarily blinded by sudden light, she held the phone to her ear and heard Teej speak again. It took her a moment to understand the words.

"…I said get down. To the right. Behind the shelves. Go now."

She obeyed. Stumbling down onto her hands and knees, she saw cereal boxes. She was in a convenience store. Scrambling along the aisle, she kept her head down and moved toward the exit. Her shiny black shoes clacked on the tiled floor, so she kicked them off. The bright ceiling lights made her conspicuous and vulnerable. She huddled in on herself as she moved, sure something or someone would spot her any moment.

"No, go back," said Teej on the phone.

She froze and glanced up. Ahead of her, towering above one of the aisles, she saw the head and shoulders of one of her pursuers. Bizarrely tall. Filthy gray-blue skin pulled tight over a stretched, ridged skull. A wet, twitching snout for a face, mostly hidden beneath a long black hooded cowl. No eyes and no ears, just two wet nostrils that trembled and wheezed. No mouth to scream. The cowl only covered the upper arm—the rest was a sickly mass of slick sinew and muscle. The creature carried a large gray sack over one shoulder while the other hand rested loosely on top of a shelf. The three fingers were each as big as her arm. It was a wretched, crooked thing, but if it stretched to its full height it would exceed eight feet.

Anna huddled in close to the shelf to hide. Behind her—her back to the boxes—she heard another creature plod down the aisle. Each percussive footstep shook the ground, knocking loose items from the shelves. From the other end of the store, she heard someone scream.

Scurrying to the end of the aisle, she crouched low and looked around the corner toward the deli. One of the creatures had grabbed an old man around the waist with a single hand. He screamed and fought, but the creature slowly and carefully lifted him up, held his wriggling form over the sack, and placed him inside.

As he fell into the bag, it constricted tightly around his body, shrinking, and wrapping the man. She could see his face moan and gasp beneath the tight material, struggling for air, fighting to escape. His movements got smaller and more desperate as he kicked and twitched in the dairy aisle, till eventually the shrink-wrapped victim was still, and the creature pulled another sack from beneath its cloak to plod off in search of its next victim. For a moment, it seemed it might come Anna's way, but a young girl ran between them, and the creature plodded after her toward the back of the store instead.

Anna dropped low as she heard the creatures methodically gather up each and every person in the store, their immense size and strength making any attempt to fight pointless. She glanced over the shelves again, but it was clear running was not an option. One of the creatures resolutely blocked the exit, its huge gray body as broad as both doors.

The place was filled with screams, but one by one they died out. Once inside the sacks, the victims' screams stopped. They struggled and fought for long minutes in silence before falling still.

Anna squeezed into a space between an ice cream freezer and a drink machine. Her arms pressed tight into her body and her knees drawn into her chest, she made herself as small as she could manage. It was over. It was all over. They would get to her eventually, too.

Cupping the phone close to her face so they wouldn't hear Teej's voice, she whispered, "There's one near the door. I can't get out. What are these things?"

She felt herself curling tighter into a ball. Over her head, the shadow of the creature sniffed the air above her. She held her breath, and after a long moment, it moved on, leaving her momentarily safe.

"The creatures you see in a Haze are called Etunes, and the particular Etunes the Midnight Man commands are called Night Collectors. These ones are just nasty little foot soldiers. You could just…well, I guess you don't know how yet. Just wait five seconds, and run for the door when I tell you."

She didn't start counting. She had too many questions and was too paralyzed with fear and disbelief and confusion. She realized he was still speaking.

"Are you counting? Now, Anna, now!"

She saw the thing in her peripheral vision as she pushed her feet under herself and started to run. Her legs felt heavy and slow, and the creature reacted instantly. It was far away but abnormally tall. Stretched out, like a long shadow. A huge gray hand reached for her, and the arm grew along the length of the aisle. Five, six feet long. It grasped her cardigan, but she shed it as she ran, twisting out of the sleeves and sprinting for the open doorway. To her left another one of the tall creatures turned to her. Its long black cloak fluttered in the air as both huge arms groped toward her.

Anna tucked her legs in and jumped through the space between them. It was an acrobatic feat she wouldn't have attempted had her life not depended on it, but it worked.

She was out, into the black street once again. Behind her, the creatures moaned and screeched and followed her outside. Pure adrenalin fueled her steps as she ran to freedom.

Beyond the entrance of the store there was inky darkness so thick Anna stopped dead in her tracks. The shops and bars were all closed, the streetlights were all out, there were no cars or people and no one to help. Only the moon offered any succor, its light cold and distant and faint. She stopped and turned, facing back toward the shop entrance as she lifted the phone to her ear.

"Teej, what is this? Are you doing this to me? There's nowhere left to go. I want to go home. *Please* just let me go home..."

"I'm sorry. I'm...I'm so sorry, Anna. You're in a Haze. You're trapped there; I can't get through to you. He is resisting me. I can't find a way in. I can see this world, but I can't touch it. It's all I can do to get these messages to you. You're near the periphery. Help me find you. He is making you feel more lost than you really are. Resist him."

She beat her head with one fist while holding the phone with the other, her eyes closed in momentary rage. When she opened them again, the creatures were snaking out of the shop and approaching her. Long baggy sleeves held gray, slick hands that groped the air in her direction. They grasped and gestured with the heavy sacks as if they offered her something. They writhed toward her, their wet noses sucking in air and her scent.

"I don't know how to resist him. I don't know what to do!"

"Listen to me! There's always a way through a Haze and out the other end. I can't help you find it. I can only tell you that it's there."

She wished anything he said made sense. He made it sound so easy.

Two of them were close and moving toward her faster than she could back away. The nearest suddenly loped forward, momentarily falling to all fours before leaping at her.

"You just have to…"

She dropped the phone, and it clattered across the ground as a muscled gray hand grasped her ankle, each finger as thick as her wrist. With beastly strength, it tugged and she fell backward heavily. Cracking her head on the concrete, her vision swam and filled with stars. The Night Collector pulled her across the ground with ease. Looking straight up, she watched the distant stars as the world slid by above her. There was nothing else she could do, so she stopped struggling and surrendered.

Then something flashed. A deep anger rose in her. Fireworks in her head, Anna's mind lit up. A spark caught, and she felt something awaken. Something angry and defiant. She scrambled and struggled, trying to turn over. The thing started to lift her. Her world tipped around and up again.

"No!" she screamed. As the words came out, Anna felt like the whole world shook. The air cracked, the sky trembled, and the monster froze in place. Her voice held a primal power. In this world, she could command these creatures, and they were compelled to obey. That was *the Word*. It extended beyond sound, penetrating the creature like a shockwave. It wasn't what she said, but the force behind her command. An instinctual, deep and resonant blast, it twisted and warped the reality of the Night Collector. Instinctively she realized her word was a weapon. She felt its power flow up from her bones, rise in her chest and warp the air it touched. The creature recoiled, dropping her and retreating with both arms held up in a defensive stance. She pulled herself up, barely aware of the cuts and bruises and the throbbing pain in her ankle. She faced them.

"No. You will not!"

They huddled low and retreated farther, her words anathema to their very nature. A great understanding started to come over her. This type of nightmare—this type of monster—held no threat for her. She did not know how or why, but she was not in danger here. Not unless she allowed herself to be.

They recoiled, pushed back by an invisible barrier they could not cross. Anna wanted to chase them. Grab them and crush them with her bare hands, but she was exhausted. As she took a step, her knees started to buckle. Her will was still strong, but her body was failing. Beaten and pushed to its limit, she felt her legs give way under her, but she didn't fall. Someone caught her. He had come through that door to help her.

"Easy, Anna," the voice said. "I heard you use *the Word*, and that's how I found you! You see? In a Haze, your Word carries power. The Word protects you, and it commands those within the Haze, but it's also a signal flare that helped me find you. I just followed your flame."

Anna tried to speak again, but the words came out as a low moan. Teej nodded as if he understood her.

"You're Behind the Veil now," said Teej. "And Undreaming is hard when you haven't fully awoken."

She collapsed backward into his arms and fell from consciousness into a deep, black sea of nothingness.

four

Rain and wind rattled the window, but it took the distant rumble of thunder to wake Anna. She lifted her head from the desk, wiping a patch of drool from the corner of her mouth with her sleeve, and looked up at the computer screen to see how long she had slept. It was dark again. Seven o'clock. She'd lost most of the day.

Stretching, Anna rubbed her eyes with both hands then leaned over the desk and pulled the window shut. It was warm in her apartment, but the wind had blown her papers across the floor while she slept. Picking them up and piling them on her desk one after another, she read the notes she'd written last night. Etunes, Night Collectors, the Midnight Man, the Doxa, the Word. What had she hoped to achieve by recording it all? Maybe some measure of control, or maybe she thought it would all fade like a dream when she woke. But it hadn't. Instead, she could remember every detail. The dark trees, the creatures that hunted her, the screams.

The only thing she couldn't remember from yesterday was how she'd gotten home. She'd woken up in bed, still wearing her clothes, dirty and sore and confused. Her phone was in her pocket. Her body was a pile of aches and pains.

She pulled her hair out of its tight bun, stuck the hair tie in her mouth, scraped it back into a ponytail, then tied it again.

She'd showered last night, but she already felt dirty again. Somehow the dirt clung to her, especially her hair. The musty reek of the creatures was in her mouth and nose.

Anna's flat was messy. Her laundry lay across the floor, her notes were scattered across every surface and her desk was buried underneath piles of paper, plates of half-eaten food and empty bottles. She felt a moment of shame as she looked on her mess with fresh eyes. She picked up a half-finished glass of wine, swirled it around then put it down. No. This had to stop.

She pushed the glass to the other side of her desk, rubbed the sleep out of her eyes and tried to decide what to do next. She could message Teej. Flicking through her phone, she saw the logged calls from the night before. She'd talked to him for twelve minutes. So that part was real at least. But one thing troubled her: he had called her.

Dropping her phone on the floor, Anna pushed the notes and folders off her desk and cleared some space, pulled the keyboard close and opened her email. She scrolled through the long list of deleted emails—from her mother, from Sue, spam about health supplements, bank statements, mobile phone bills—till she got to her last message from him. From Teej.

She let out a long, low breath to mentally prepare herself. This had been the one. This had been the message that convinced her he was crazy. She'd only read the first three lines then deleted it and forced it to the back of her mind. That had been three months ago. Now she would comb through it for clues.

"Hi, Anna."

Well, it started innocuously enough.

"You are in danger."

Yup, this was when the alarm bells had first gone off.

"I know this might seem a little strange—"

Yeah, I'll say.

33

"—but you need to listen closely. The Doxa are after you. They are a group of Dreamers that have a vested interest in making sure they eliminate any new Metiks. I know I told you about Dreamers before, and I know that when I told you they could change reality, you thought I was being metaphorical. I was not. Dreamers can literally rewrite the rules of reality. With their Art, they can paint, dance, sew or sing whole new worlds. And within the Hazes they create, only Metiks can stand against them."

Anna pushed her chair backward and put both hands behind her head. This was a lot of crazy to take in one dose. She needed a break.

Did this mean she had been attacked by a Dreamer? Was Teej a Metik? Was she? Or was she combining the ramblings of a crazy man with a bad trip? Whether she chose to believe him or not, this felt like a bad path she was going down. She was curious to read more, but she had to keep some distance. She would analyze the message to understand exactly what was wrong with Teej. Paranoid delusions, schizophrenia, split personality—whatever.

She rubbed her eyes again, stretched, wheeled her chair back under her desk and went back to the message.

"We should meet, so I can convince you I'm telling the truth."

It was a bit late for that.

"I can track you now. Your powers shine like a beacon in the night."

Not creepy at all.

"But that means the Doxa can track you, and they might try to recruit you, intimidate you, or kill you. Either way, you need me."

Anna snorted. She didn't need him, and she didn't need his paranoia. This kind of man could draw her into his madness.

Clever, charismatic, charming and completely deluded. *Never play their game…*

She closed the message at the exact same moment her phone rang. Anna glanced at the screen, and her stomach dropped. *No. Not now.* This was the absolute worst thing that could happen. Well, maybe not the worst, considering what happened last night. Still, with absolute horror, Anna answered her mobile.

"Hi, Mom."

"Have you tidied your apartment?"

She wasn't messing around this time. Straight on the attack. Anna lifted a nearby Chinese food container, sniffed it cautiously, then threw it to the other side of the room as she stifled a retch.

"Yup. Uh huh."

"So, it's been a month since you handed in the thesis. Did you look into those research fellowships I emailed you?"

Anna stood and kicked dirty clothes across the floor as she paced back and forth.

"Sure, Mom."

"No, you didn't."

Anna wouldn't be able to deflect her today. This would take her full attention to endure. "I only had a quick look, but I'll send for them later today."

"You didn't look at them at all," said her mom flatly, "because if you had, you would be mad at me. Those research fellowships are at the college back home. I think you need to leave the city, Anna."

Anna knew this was coming. "Mom, I've told you. I like it here. I'm not coming back."

Her mom tutted. "You have no friends in the city. No family. I know you tell me you're fine, but…don't you want to talk about what happened? Just a little. It doesn't have to be with me. You can talk to Dad."

"Dad doesn't care."

"Your father does care. He—"

"No, I don't mean it like that. I know he is happy as long as I am not in trouble. And I'm not. I'm okay, Mom. Really."

Her mom was silent for a moment. Anna flopped on the sofa and waited for her to start again.

"I know the life insurance was generous, and you don't *need* to work for money, but you need to keep yourself busy. If you don't find something to do, then you'll end up…"

"End up what?" said Anna with a tremble in her voice.

"Oh, I know you miss him terribly, honey."

"Do not start with this again," Anna snapped. "You know what I told you. We've been through this before. When I'm ready. I'll talk when I'm ready!"

"I just want you to—"

"I'm going to go."

"Don't go! Honey, I'm sorry."

Anna pursed her lips to stop the trembling.

"You know we're here for you. Your dad…well…you know what he's like. He seems fine, and he doesn't talk much and watches the old black and white movies, but he *is* thinking about you. And I know I fret and nag, but it's because…well, you told me you won't talk about it, and I respect that, but if you change your mind, you know I am here."

"Uh huh."

"You understand what I'm saying, Anna? You're far away, but you're still close. To me, you are still close."

"Yeah."

"You're young and clever, and this isn't the end. All that time and no work, no friends…that's a lot of life to fill up. Fill it with something good, okay?"

"Sure, Mom."

Anna looked over at the computer.

"Honey, I want you to know that *darkness* you feel. It doesn't go away, but eventually, you see it as just a different kind of light. Do you hear what I'm saying to you? I love you. I don't think I say it enough, but it's always been true."

"I have to go, Mom," said Anna as she hung up the phone.

She put the phone down on her desk, walked across the room to the cabinet next to the television, put her hand on the top-drawer handle, and froze. This was where she kept the letter. And the ring. She'd stuck both in the drawer after the accident and tried to forget about them, but her mom had a way of getting to her. She couldn't move forward till she decided what to do with them. She had to choose now. She had to read his letter, or burn it and forget about it. And the ring…it didn't mean anything now. He was gone.

The rattle of the letterbox made Anna jump.

Sliding the half-opened drawer closed, she went to check on her mail. As she walked down the hallway toward the front door, she noticed how sore her ankle was when she moved quickly. She lifted the leg of her jeans and saw a huge bruise extend almost the whole way from her knee to her foot. It looked like a hand mark.

"Jesus. That's not good…"

So, her delusions had some basis in reality. When she imagined a monster holding her leg though, what had *actually* grabbed her? Frustrated that her mind clung so resolutely to the illusions the drug had shown her, Anna limped to the end of the hallway. Expecting a flyer, she tensed when she realized someone had slid a letter through her door's mail slot. Quickly, without questioning the wisdom of the move, she unbolted the door, stepped outside, and looked both ways along the corridor outside her flat. Whoever had delivered the message was already gone. Closing the door and double bolting it, she picked up the plain white envelope and turned it over. In calligraphy, someone had written: "To the girl who got away."

Her stomach turned. Limping back to her desk, she sat for a few moments looking at the letter. Her hands trembled. Seeking some anchor to reality, she turned on the little transistor radio her dad had given her. She hoped it would deflate her fear.

"The storm front that's built this week shows no sign of abating as—"

She didn't want to listen to the news; she just wanted some background noise. Tearing open the envelope, she pulled out the stiff white card. It was like a wedding invite, blank on one side but on the other there was a poem.

"The Midnight Man is at your door,
The Midnight Man has been before,
The Midnight Man comes every night,
The Midnight Man comes after light,
The Midnight Man says the hour is nigh,
The Midnight Man says it's time to die."

Anna placed the note down carefully on her desk, smoothed it flat, and read it again. Breathing deeply, she bit her bottom lip and tried to think calmly. Within a few moments though, she felt the anger rise.

"No. No, no way!"

Was this Dean? Or some other joke? A viral marketing stunt or a prank, or just a coincidence? She knew she should talk to the police. Sue told her not to contact the authorities, but this had to be reported. She found her thoughts drifting to Teej. Could this be his doing? She leaned over to turn the radio off, but as she did, something caught her ear.

"Three people were found dead in a convenience store on Mitchell Street this morning. A statement from police suggests there was a possible gas leak in the 24-hour shop, as all three victims suffocated. The incident is not being treated as a terrorist attack, although the environment hazard team at the scene has yet to find the source of the leak. Police are keen to contact anyone with any information—"

Something really *had* happened. Anna knew what she had to do: call the police. Tell them about Dean and how he spiked her drink. Explain as much as she could about what happened that night. That would be the sensible thing to do. That would be what her mother would tell her to do.

What would she call the monsters when she called the police? *Giant faceless creatures* or just *creepy guys that were ten feet tall?*

Anna found herself holding her mobile phone. She didn't remember picking it up, and she typed the message without thinking. She refused to second guess herself. This wasn't what she *should* do, but it was what she *wanted* to do.

Teej, we should talk.

For a moment, there was no response. Anna held the phone in front of her face, examining the screen and willing it to respond. She bit the skin at the bottom of her fingernails—a horrible habit she had managed to suppress for months.

The phone flashed and his message appeared.

15 Dunmer Gardens. 8pm.

That didn't give her much time. Anna stuffed the letter into her backpack and ran for the front door.

five

Anna attempted to fold the umbrella, but the wind had blown it inside-out so many times the metal spokes were ruined. She splashed her way to a nearby trashcan and shoved it inside with some vigor, then went back to the cross-roads to look at the street signs again. She was completely lost.

Dunmer Gardens was a short side street in the industrial East of the city. Close to the river and surrounded by old, abandoned factories and steel works, it was a rundown area most sensible people avoided. The apartments were cheap, but even students and drug dealers didn't want to live there. Every second doorway she passed was boarded up, and she couldn't seem to find number fifteen. She read the numbers aloud as she walked past them again. "19A, 101, 17, 6, 21D."

Pulling her phone from her pocket, she considered calling Teej. It was the sensible thing to do, but then, none of this was really sensible. *Why was she here? Why wasn't she calling the police? Why would she come to this part of town to see a man she had never met?* This was exactly what her mother would be asking right now if she knew what Anna was doing. None of this was a good idea, but she'd chosen the path, and now she had to push onwards through the madness. Through and out the other end.

Anna walked back along the deserted street, zigzagging between piles of trash and huge puddles, till she got to number 16B. Climbing three steps, she approached the doorway, perched on her tiptoes, and looked through the small window. There was a buzzer, but inside, there were no signs of life. Turning around to go back, she noticed a low gate in the fence. Pushing it open cautiously, she descended four more stairs and found a narrow path between the apartment buildings. Feeling like a trespasser, she took a few steps along the path. It was dark and narrow, and she was sure it wasn't the right way, but it sheltered her from the rain.

She looked back and, for a moment, was stung with a twinge of déjà vu. If she chose to go back now, it would be the end of this journey. If she took a single step backward, she would come to her senses. Call a taxi, go home, call her mother, report this all to the police, make a mug of tea, turn on the television, fall asleep on the sofa, wake up the next day and…no. That wasn't what she wanted. She'd been down that path before. She turned back into the dark passageway and pushed onwards.

Her shoes already soaked, Anna tried to avoid the massive puddle at the end of the path. Taking a few steps backward, she ran and jumped and splashed down to find herself in a fenced-off garden area. Little rocky trails led off to meander around bushes, flowerbeds and neatly planted trees, and behind her and around the corner, beneath two hanging baskets filled with flowers, was a clean white door labeled "Number 15: Lady Almeria Braddock."

"Well, shit…" Anna exclaimed under her breath, surprised, relieved, and unnerved all at once. She'd found the door. There was no excuse to give up now.

She cautiously approached the entrance and took a moment to compose herself. *What would she say? What did she hope to find?* She was still debating what to do next when the door opened inwards by itself. Startled, she stepped back and almost fell. Brushing the wet hair out of her face, she looked up to see him.

"Come in out of the rain, Anna," said Teej.

six

Lady Almeria's ground floor apartment was a tight, cluttered space filled with knick knacks, potted plants, old paintings and tapestries, framed photographs, neatly piled hardback books and loudly ticking antique carriage clocks. The place smelled of floral perfume and home baking. On a medical bed in the corner and connected to a drip but sitting up with alertness, the lady stared off into the middle distance. Moving to sit next to her was Teej. He reached out to hold the old woman's wrinkled hand and rubbed it gently with his fingers. His posture was relaxed but his eyes were focused and intent. He gave Anna a small smile then turned his attention back to the old lady.

Anna sat across from them on a too-soft sofa. Next to her were a steaming pot of tea and a stack of sugar cookies on a floral plate.

"We don't have much time," said Teej without turning.

Anna, unsure where to begin, waited for his full attention. She had come all this way. She would have answers. Patting the lady's hand affectionately, Teej laid it on her chest, breathed in deeply then turned to Anna.

"It is nice to meet you. Properly."

He sounded sincere, his voice clear and low. His eyes were blue-green and kind and there was an openness to his face that was impossible to dislike. He could be any age between thirty and forty, but the laughter lines around his mouth and eyes and his fuzzy stubble made him look both older and gentler. His smile—which she saw only a glimpse of now—was playful and infectious, but his cheeks were unnaturally gaunt, and his skin was sallow. Anna felt a sharp pang of sympathy as she noted how his clothes hung loosely on his boney frame, and he sat hunched, as if in pain. Illness haunted him. He was not well, no matter how reassuringly he smiled at her.

Strategically ignoring him, Anna said to the lady, "Thank you for the tea. My name is Anna."

For a moment, embarrassment flashed across his features. He had manners, and she had caught him forgetting them. "I am so sorry! This is Lady Almeria Braddock. I'm afraid her words don't come easily any more, but I assure you, we are welcome here. She's an old friend."

Anna nodded, then remembered his earlier warning. "Why don't we have much time?"

He brushed back his messy brown hair with one hand and smiled with his mouth but not his eyes. "The Night Collectors must practice their art, and death is coming to eat your heart."

She frowned. "So it was you? With the poems. You did all of this."

"No. Those words are not mine. They weave an incantation that brought your attackers to life."

He spoke plainly and she wanted to believe him, but it was all starting to make sense. This was all some scheme of his. He was a madman.

"You have a pretty face. An autumn face." They both turned to the old lady, surprised she was interrupting. "But you are an ignorant girl. You won't believe until you see, but you already see and still you doubt."

Lady Almeria shuffled discontentedly, but Teej put a hand on her shoulder.

44

"Shush, my old friend. Worry not; we will lead them away from here. When we go, they will follow us. Away from you."

"Who will?" interjected Anna. "Why are we short of time?"

Teej ignored her questions and instead asked, "Do you have a timer on your phone?"

"What? Yes. Why?"

"Twelve minutes," he said. "That's how long they will take to find us. Set it for twelve minutes. Then we have to go."

"I…fine." She set the timer for eleven minutes then turned back to him. "Okay, answers. I want answers."

"Yes…" he stalled, rubbing his forehead as if lost in thought. Anna held her hands out in frustration. Aware that he could stall no longer, Teej went on. "The Dreamer who is after you is called Mott. Or he was. He calls himself the Midnight Man now. He's been killing young women. You might have seen him on the news? He's lost his mind—"

"He's not the only one," Anna said plainly.

"I'm not crazy, Anna. Neither are you."

Teej gave her a look of concern, but it made her angry.

"I know *I'm* not crazy. I was drugged!" she snapped back.

"And that's what opened your eyes. That's what brought about your awakening. You're Behind the Veil now. With us. Now you see what they can do. Mimesis—"

"The Art," interrupted Lady Almeria. "No one calls it Mimesis any more, Donnel. It's called the Art."

Teej nodded.

"The Art?" asked Anna.

"Yes. It's the ability held by the world's greatest artists to create a new reality. These artists, or Dreamers, use their ability to create Hazes. Within a Haze, that Dreamer is God. They can dream *anything* into reality. They can change the rules of existence, and they can make and unmake life itself."

Anna rolled her eyes and flopped back on the sofa. "This conversation!" she said to herself. "This is what I get. This is what I get for being so gullible. Nonsense. Just like your emails. Total nonsense."

"It's not nonsense, Anna. There's truth in it. In all of it. You feel it."

"Don't tell me how I feel," she snapped back. She started to get to her feet. "Start making sense. Or I won't listen to any more of this. I'll leave."

He sighed heavily, his furrowed brow showing his frustration. Gently touching her arm, he gestured for her to sit and waited for her to calm down.

"Look, I know it makes no sense right now."

"Or ever."

He looked upward, his brow furrowing deeper, and he frowned as he spoke.

"You know that feeling when you see a painting or watch a film or read something that really moves you? Your favorite song, how it feels inside your bones. A turn of phrase in a poem or book that makes you shudder, like the air is crackling around the back of your neck. When art makes you feel a...a transcendence. You feel like you're moving *toward* something. You feel like you're *almost* on the edge of another place, a truer place. When you experience art that touches your soul, and when you're communing with something powerful and mighty and *true*, well, when that happens, you're skirting the periphery of a Haze. You almost cross over, but not quite.

"But for a small number of people—people like you and me—we *can* cross over. We go Behind the Veil. We can experience a Haze. We are aware. Awakened."

Anna couldn't look at him. She stared at the cookies, listening, holding in her frustration. She didn't know what she wanted to hear, but it wasn't this.

When she spoke, she felt like the words came from some-one else. "That doesn't explain anything. It doesn't prove anything. That night with the…that night when I was lost. What did I see? If the hallucinations I saw were real, tell me what they looked like."

Teej stroked the short stubble on his chin distractedly. He seemed agitated. "Night Collectors? They're just Etunes. Ugly creatures created by the Midnight Man inside his Hazes. Gray skin, big, no faces, a bit slimy. You defeated them with *the Word*, yes?"

Anna narrowed her eyes. How could he know that? He looked back at her simply. She'd dealt with people who were delusional before. People who had lost their grip on reality. They weren't normally so forthright, but it didn't make her trust him more. Instead, it made her think he wasn't insane. Maybe he was just a liar. A very good, very imaginative liar.

He went on: "The Dreamers, sometimes we call them Aes-thetes, can change the world through the Art. If they have the ability and the Will, they can change the rules of reality. They can create little pockets of Dream. They remake the world and become the author and the director and the conductor and the architect of the metaphysical space they inhabit. The truest real-ization of all art is its ability to change and reshape reality. Not in a metaphorical way, *actually* change the world. The Art is a way to shape existence through pure creativity. Thought and willpower become tools to bend and mold the physical world."

"Show her," interrupted Lady Almeria. "All these words! Just show the girl."

"How much time?" Teej asked again. Anna sighed then looked at her phone.

"Six more minutes. Six more minutes until this train wreck of a conversation ends."

"Okay," he said. "Lady Almeria, I'll need your help."

47

She nodded. "Some water please?"

Teej walked across the room, filled a glass from the water jug on the table, then came back and handed it to Lady Almeria carefully with both hands. Lady Almeria shook as she held it for a second, then when Teej stepped back, she immediately threw it across the room into the middle of the floor.

"What…?" said Anna.

The old lady laughed. "Now listen here girl and pay attention! *See* for yourself."

At first all Anna saw was the water slowly sinking into the thick carpet. But then movement. The fibers seemed to twitch and shift and the ground seemed to rumble, just for a second. Little green shoots climbed, twisting left and right as they surged upward. One burst into a yellow bloom. A pink flash of color followed a splash of purple as two more flowers popped into existence. Within a few seconds, there was a garden growing in the center of the room.

"Did you notice my flower bed on the way in?" asked Lady Almeria wanly. "The one you saw looks small, but it is not small for the paths go very far. You see, I am a fine Gardener, and this is my Art. This is how it looks when I create a Haze; impossible, infinite, beautiful gardens, all of them with fairies at the end. Do you see now?"

Anna nodded slowly. "No."

As Teej walked across the room to the flowers and plucked one, he asked again, "Time?"

She stared at the flowers.

"Anna, time?" he repeated.

She looked at her phone. "Three minutes."

"Okay, we have to go soon. Do you understand now? Lady Almeria is an Aesthete. A Dreamer. Both words mean the same thing. She uses the Art to remake our world. Mott—or the Midnight Man as he calls himself now—is another type of Dreamer.

The things he makes are *darker*. He was a writer and a poet, but now he's written so many monsters that he's become one himself. The monsters don't last for long, but he is always creating more, and they hunger. His Art is a bitter and hopeless thing. It *consumes*."

Momentarily caught up in the story Teej was telling, Anna forgot she didn't believe any of this. He brought her a flower and held it up as Lady Almeria smiled serenely.

"How did you do that?" asked Anna. "The flowers are made of the same *stuff* as the Night Collectors? These Dreamers can just make things they imagine? That's genuinely, committed-to-mental-hospital crazy, you know?"

Teej nodded as he lifted the flower in front of her face. With a flick of his wrist he turned the stem of the flower around. It seemed to blur and shift in front of her eyes. And she felt something. A twinge went down her back and along the base of her spine. It felt familiar and new at the same time, and it resonated with his trick. The flower had changed somehow. It was stiff and solid and shone in the light. He handed it to her.

Heavy, smoothly polished and perfect. A long, green stem leading up to petals of blue and purple and red, made of solid glass. She turned it over and over in her hands. Numbly, she said "Um, thank you."

"Time?" he prompted again.

She looked up at him and noticed the slight glow of pride. He was showing off.

"Is this how you get all the girls? Parlor tricks?"

"It's not a trick. Are we out of time?"

She looked at her phone again and showed him the screen. There was one minute left, but she was nervous about what happened when the time ran out. Was she free to go? Did he want her to come with him? Should she?

"We have to go."

"Wait…" said Anna.

As Teej stood, the glass suddenly shattered in her grasp. She dropped the pieces and pulled away. Rubbing the palm of her hand in shock, she felt a line. A second later the skin split and the bleeding began. A deep, ragged cut from the base of her thumb to her wrist.

"I didn't mean to. It just broke in my hand."

"That won't be the last thing she breaks," said Lady Almeria.

"Here," said Teej dismissively. Before she could pull away, he had a firm grasp on her wrist. She was about to resist, but he quickly laid a hand across her palm and held her firmly. There was a warmth, almost too hot to bear, but his grip was solid as rock. When he released her, she rocked backward, flopping into the sofa. Looking down at her hand, Anna saw the cut was healed completely. There wasn't even a mark.

"What is this?"

It was too much. She must be drugged again. *Could it have been in the tea?* She hadn't drunk any. *Something in the air, or was she hallucinating?*

Teej grasped her firmly by the shoulders. His gaze held her.

"Listen to me," he said. "You have a power. I do, too. That doesn't mean you're safe. It doesn't mean you'll make it. They'll kill you for it. This isn't a trick. For your whole life, you've known something was happening just beyond the horizon of your own senses. Now you can see it. You don't have to learn from me. You don't have to trust me. But you absolutely cannot go back. These are things you can't un-know."

When he spoke, his voice trembled. His eyes were wide, pupils dilated. Every muscle in his body was tense. He believed what he was telling her. He was not a liar. He believed it so intently that she had no choice but to go along with him.

But there was something else. She was feeling that twinge again. The same feeling she'd experienced last night, when they came for her. And she could hear them. Distant, but coming closer. The high wail of the Midnight Man's Night Collectors. Whether nightmares from her own subconscious or monsters-made-real, she had to get away from them.

"Let's go," she agreed. Teej grabbed her hand, and they both ran for the door. As they were about to leave, Anna turned to the old lady and stopped him. He continued to tug at her arm.

"What about—"

"Go!" said Lady Almeria. "They don't care about me one bit. My dueling days are long gone."

"Well...goodbye then," said Anna meekly as Teej pulled her away. The old lady gave her a slight nod.

They hustled out the back door, splashing through the rain puddles outside. Along the wet garden path Anna stumbled as Teej pulled her fast enough to make her nervous. Behind them, an encroaching dread closed in faster than they could run.

The narrow garden path opened out into a grand, wooded maze, then green hedges gave way to orange and red and yellow leaves, both on the forest floor and in the canopies above. The geography of this place made no sense. Teej had taken Anna into a different world. Again.

Ahead of her he ran, darting left and right through the towering tree trunks, pulling her along till her arm ached, her lungs burned, and her head spun. All she wanted in the world was to stop, but he scrambled onwards across the uneven forest floor, pulling her the whole way.

Grabbing hold of a broad branch, she stopped to catch her breath. He tugged on her arm, but she refused to go any farther.

"What is it? We need to keep going. We are on the periphery of Lady Almeria's Haze. There is safety inside the woods, but Mott can block all our exits with his own traps. Our window of escape is closing, Anna."

Teej looked ill, but he ran like an athlete. His lithe frame was perfectly adapted for moving fast, so he hardly seemed to breathe during their wild sprint through the woods. Anna, meanwhile, hadn't been to the gym in months and had always hated running. Seeking an excuse to delay a moment longer, she asked him a question.

"Why did she call you Donnel?"

That unnerved him. He winced, his green-gray eyes looking distant in the low autumnal light that broke through the dense canopy of leaves above them.

"Sometimes you change so much your old name doesn't fit you properly any more. When that happens, you choose a new one."

"And the guy who's trying to kill us? His name is Mott *and* the Midnight Man?"

"Yeah," said Teej as he scrambled around the edge of the clearing looking for the best path.

"Is that because Midnight Man makes for better rhymes than Mott?"

"It does not," said Teej with a half-smile.

"How old are you?" she asked. She was stalling, but after she asked the question, she realized it was a good one. Again, he took a while to answer.

"Older than I look."

"That's a bit arrogant, isn't it?"

"I can see how you might think that."

She pushed off the tree to start moving again, but when he offered his hand, she refused it.

"I can't. One second more, please."

Teej glanced back and forth, scanning for she-didn't-know-what, then nodded briefly.

"Okay. Catch your breath. When we go again, though, we don't stop. One long sprint."

"Where are we? I don't know this forest. It doesn't make any *sense*."

"We're in a Haze," he replied simply. "Lady Almeria's. She stretched this desire path out as long as she could to help us outrun the Midnight Man. Hazes can't overlap and—"

"What am I supposed to do with that information, Teej?" she challenged him. "These explanations. I don't believe any of them. I don't believe you."

"Believe your senses," he shot back.

"I've been drugged. Something is wrong with me. That's why I see all *this*."

"Look with more than your eyes. Beyond the smell of the leaves and the sound of the wind. You have Haze Sense now. You have the Sight."

She sighed and pushed herself off the tree, stumbling across the uneven forest floor toward him. "Okay, we might as well keep running. None of your answers make any sense anyway. Let's go." She walked ahead of him. "My mom would kill me if she knew I was following a lunatic into the woods. This way?"

He didn't follow. "You *do* feel it, Anna. I know you do. The *fidelity* of this place. The *vibrancy*. It's more real to you than anything else. This moment, right here, in this Haze. Tell me you don't know what I'm talking about."

For a moment, Anna opened herself up to the place. Her eyes scanned the environment, and with a tremor, she realized he was right. The edges of the leaves were crisper and more distinct than any she had ever seen, and the smell of the moss on the trees came to her in waves. Her skin felt warmth where the sunlight burst through the canopy. This place felt more real than

53

reality. It made her feel a longing for something she couldn't quite identify.

"I don't know what you're talking about," she said flatly.

He nodded as if he hadn't heard her words. "This way" he said, running off in the opposite direction and leaving Anna to follow as fast as she could.

They ran for ten more minutes—between trees, across rough ground, under dappled sunlight breaking through the dark canopy—but to Anna, it seemed much longer. The forest became denser and colder. As they neared the edge, Anna felt like she was back in the dark woods. The circle of her nightmare complete; she felt sure they would emerge back into that store and the creatures would be waiting for her, faceless and giant and unstoppable. In nightmares, running away from monsters always leads you back into their arms.

"Through here." Teej motioned as he bent down and squeezed into a narrow gap in a hedgerow. The branches scraped and snapped as he forced his way in.

"Teej, I can't—"

He had already disappeared inside, but Anna delayed. Trying to discern a path she could follow, she kneeled outside the crawl space. *How had he squeezed into the gap?* It was dirty and dark and narrow and seemed impenetrable.

She was about to stand up again when she heard the high-pitched moans. The Midnight Man's Night Collectors were closing in.

"I didn't expect quite so much crawling in the dirt," she complained as she dropped to her hands and knees and pushed her way through the undergrowth.

seven

"Teej," Anna shouted. "Teej, I can't see anything!" There was no response. She continued to crawl in complete darkness, and after a few minutes, the dirt and grime beneath her hands and knees gave way to a smooth, chalky surface. The branches and leaves disappeared too, but still no light found her. Eventually, she found she could stand up, so she got to her feet and pushed her hands out in either direction trying to find something to hold onto. A smooth, flat wall to her right guided her, so she followed it until her eyes adjusted to the darkness enough to perceive the thin sliver of light ahead. With no choice but to walk toward it, she stumbled onwards through the shadow.

The darkness was so complete that she walked into a wall. Sliding her hands across the surface in front of her, she felt a piece of cold metal bathed in a thin sliver of light. A door handle. She pushed it down and light flooded in, blinding her. Confused and unsteady, she squinted in the brightness, and when her vision cleared, she found she had stumbled into a shopping mall.

"What?"

"You're filthy," said Teej with a hint of amusement.

"I…that's your fault!" she snapped.

He was right. Her tights were ripped, and her hands were caked in mud. Running her fingers through her hair, she realized with mild annoyance that it had leaves in it.

"Didn't you have a backpack?" asked Teej.

"Shit. I must have left it in…shit!"

"We can find another one here," he said gesturing at their surroundings. "And get something to eat, maybe?"

Anna looked back at the door she'd just come through. It was the disabled toilet on the ground floor of Millie's Mall. She'd been here many times before, but at this time of day it was closed, and the lights inside the mall were turned down low.

She turned to Teej, and he gave her a comical look and a shrug.

"I dunno what to tell you. Almeria created a route to the mall. Perhaps she foresaw the state of your…"

He pointed to her filthy clothes. Meanwhile, his light cotton trousers, smart shirt, and hoodie were all spotless. Even his hair seemed tidier than before.

She frowned at him.

"You know you have leaves in your—"

"I know!" she snapped as she ran her fingers through her matted hair. "You know you're too old to wear a hoodie?"

"Girl," he said with a mischievous smile, "I'm too old to wear pantaloons!" He walked across the forecourt of the mall and sat down on the edge of a water fountain next to a donut stand. Numb from so many revelations in such a short period, Anna wandered over and sat beside him. She found her mood was stabilizing quickly. From confusion to fear to anger, the simple comfort of a seat in a warm place was enough to make her feel almost normal again.

"A dragon used to live in this mall," he said as he gestured up to the rafters where rain battered the high glass windows.

"That must have been quite a shock for the kids in the soft play area. Did they put up a warning sign?"

He laughed. It was a warm sound, and Anna couldn't help but join in.

"People *experience* Hazes—monsters and dragons and ninja-pirate cyborgs—but they don't *see* them. The mind rationalizes it all away. That's how it used to be for you too, before you joined us Behind the Veil."

She nodded as if that made sense. "So I would have walked right past the mall dragon?"

He nodded, and they sat in silence for a moment. The low lighting felt almost peaceful, if a little surreal. The storefront mannequins sat in silent vigil. Every movement she made echoed in the emptiness, and behind her, the fountain gurgled and splashed serenely. She replayed events in her head, trying to piece together how she got here and why this was all happening. For a fraction of a second, she considered accepting his explanations. Surrendering to his imagination. If she wasn't so steadfastly opposed to flights of fancy and wishful thinking, she might just go along with him. She knew though—from bitter experience—that wishing for things didn't make them real. Reality was cold and impervious to the hopes and desires of people like her. And him, no matter how enchanting a tale he spun.

"I'll come to my senses eventually," she said matter-of-factly. "And then you'll disappear. Or become a *sane* person. So why don't you tell me more nonsense? Tell me about your super powers."

"Enough rope to hang myself with, eh?"

She laughed a little.

"Tell me something nice. Tell me everything will be okay."

She was teasing him. Though she toyed with the idea that this was all a game, he answered her question thoughtfully and with care.

"It *will* all work out in the end, but nothing will ever be quite the same for you. Do you…do you want a donut?"

"What?"

He jumped to his feet boyishly, swinging his legs around and skipping to the little donut stand off to the side.

"We're stealing food now?"

"There's no one here to buy from," he complained. "I'll leave them money. Well…actually, do you have any money?"

"I lost my bag," she reminded him.

"These ones are all dried up anyway. They would probably get thrown out by tomorrow."

She watched him with detached fascination as he examined the glass case holding the donuts. He reached under the counter, pulled out a pen and flicked the lid off, then jammed it in the lock and popped the case open with a strange twisting motion.

"You should have opened with that trick," she said.

"Oh, that wasn't a trick. Although I *am* showing off. When you're as old as me, you have plenty of time to learn lots of useful skills. Fighting, juggling, oboe, donut stealing. I'm not great at anything, but I'm pretty good at almost everything."

"Except maybe modesty?" she said.

"Never saw the point in it."

He hopped over to sit next to her again, two donuts in hand. She reluctantly took one from him. It wasn't stale at all; it was sticky.

"Would you set a timer on your phone again?" he asked.

"Why do you make me do that? If you can *feel* when the…Midnight Man has almost caught us, why do you need a timer to remind you?"

"I can only *feel* when he becomes aware of us. From that time, he takes twelve minutes to manifest his Art. And I get *distracted*. I'm not myself right now. I'm fuzzy. Still recovering. There was a big fight, not just me and him. But he was there, and I was there, and it all went sideways. And when things go wrong in a Haze, your body takes a beating, but your mind is the part that goes—"

He made a wobbly hand gesture that she thought she understood.

"You beat him?" she asked, but he shook his head.

"There were no winners, but that's a story for another time, I'm afraid. I...can't really talk about it right now."

"But you admit you're not thinking clearly right now?" she said. "You're messed up in the head?"

He nodded. "Yeah, you got me there, but everything I told you is true. Even if I'm not telling it very well.

"Set it for twelve minutes again. He just got a reading on us."

Anna nodded and set her phone again, then looked back at him. If he really was some sort of sociopathic master manipulator, he didn't fit the type. It felt more like they were both caught up in a tornado together, flying from place to place, not sure where they were or why.

Anna took a bite out of the donut. Cinnamon with apple. It was glorious, and she devoured it in seconds. She had no idea how hungry she had been. Looking around for some way to clean the sugar—and dirt and muck—from her hands, she decided to wash them in the fountain. The water was very cold, but she felt better afterwards. Balling up the napkin and throwing it with a perfect arc into the nearby trashcan, Teej rubbed his hands together and stood up.

"Let's go for a walk. Walk and talk?"

He offered her his hand, but she refused it and stood up by herself.

"Sure," she said as she followed him. They wandered through the deserted shopping mall, past clothes stores and accessory stores and mobile phone stores. As they went, Anna felt a strange déjà vu. She'd been through the mall many times before, but this echoing twilight world with Teej still felt strangely familiar.

"You'd look nice in that. Classy," he said, pointing to a short, shiny, tight blue dress in a cheap boutique clothes store.

"Don't be creepy," she said. "How about instead of changing the subject, you tell me what will happen next?"

They walked through the central area of the mall, and the shadows all around them started to feel more threatening. He turned to her to continue talking while walking backward.

"Well, you have to make a choice."

She grabbed his sleeve to make him stop walking. "What choice? To come with you?"

"Yes. Or go back to your flat on Albert Street."

"So, I can just…Wait a minute. How do you know where I live?"

"I've been there," he said simply. "I carried you up the stairs. Past the green flowers outside your neighbor's door. Into your bedroom. Light blue bed covers, really messy. Notes and books everywhere. Lots of little penguin plushies on your bedside table."

"That's correct," she said curtly. Inside her mind, a battle raged between three different thoughts: this was all a game played by a madman, this was all a hallucination, or this was—most terrifyingly of all—real.

She looked at her phone screen to give herself time to think.

"Seven minutes. When the time runs out, do we have some other secret path to run through?"

"No," he said seriously. "When time runs out, we face him. Here. On this spot. Before he gets too strong."

"We?"

"Yes. If you choose to stay."

"What am I supposed to do?" she asked. "I can't help you."

"That's the thing; you can help me. Do you remember how you stopped the Night Collectors?"

"I shouted at them."

"Yes. That's 'the Word'"

"What's 'the Word'? What word?"

"Not a specific word. *The* Word. You know how to use it. Even though no one ever taught you. *'The Will, the Word, the Sight, and the Sword.'* That's what it takes to be a Metik. You already know one of the four. You're a natural. These are four different aspects of what we call your Praxis. They are your powers, and they are what you will use to help me fight him."

"I don't want to fight anyone. This has nothing to do with me!" Anna grimaced. He was pulling her in again. Making her forget that she didn't believe any of this.

He looked conflicted; his jaw was set, and the easy smile was gone from his lips. "It's your choice. I won't *make* you help me, but I can't protect you if you dismiss me. Your abilities are obvious to anyone Behind the Veil now. That's why he comes for you. That's why the Doxa will come for you. They hate us. Especially Mott. He will take any opportunity he can to crush one of us before we are strong enough to face him. To extinguish your fire while it's still kindling. And even if I stop him here and now, the rest will still come for you. There is no way to hide what you are. You're a beacon now. They won't struggle to find you."

She obviously didn't look convinced, because his voice was almost pleading now.

"Anna…in a world of dwindling light, you're a bonfire in the night."

"I…Teej, I just want to go home."

When she said the words, tears came to her eyes. She didn't want them to. She fought them back, but they came anyway.

61

"Let me go. I want to wake up in bed and have this all go away. All of it. I want *you* to go away. Do you understand?"

He nodded slowly.

"Okay… Okay, then. That's enough. Enough from me."

He almost looked relieved.

"Time?"

She didn't answer him. She wanted him to argue with her. She wanted an answer. Something that would explain all of this. Some closure. Anything.

"Time?" he repeated firmly.

She looked at her phone.

"Three minutes."

"You should go. Take the door, over there." He pointed to a fire exit in the corner of the atrium.

"You can get out that way. When you push through, the alarm will sound and the security guards will come, so you must go fast. Head straight home."

She nodded once and walked toward the exit. *Was it that simple?*

"Anna," he called after her. "From now on, you have to be careful around people. When you feel you're in a Haze, just remember to…well, just look after yourself."

She tried to smile and walked on. She felt her left hand shake and held it with her right, trying to steady herself. *Was this a good choice?* It didn't feel good. At the door, she turned back to him.

"Teej…" She didn't know what to say.

"The world is not so complicated, Anna. Only two things ever happen. Things change or things stay the same."

She nodded, not sure what to think or say. The shadows started to creak and moan. She felt the Night Collectors pulling their way into the mall. Forcing themselves into existence. Hungering.

Pushing through the fire exit, she took one last look at him before she left. He gave her a wave and a small smile. He didn't look frightened. He didn't even look that sad.

Anna felt terrible, but she didn't look back again. She ran.

eight

The red wine stained the sides of the white sink as it sloshed little blue pills down the drain. Anna clicked open another bottle—the last one—and three more handfuls of antidepressants and painkillers rattled out of existence. She rested her hands on the counter top and waited to feel something, but there was no accompanying sense of satisfaction. No release.

She had to decide what to do with three remaining items: the letter, the ring, and the final bottle of wine. She started with the last one. Unscrewing the lid (it was a very cheap bottle of wine), she poured it down the sink, too. Throwing the bottle into the trash, she wandered back into her now tidy and clean living room and dropped onto the sofa. She picked the ring up off the clear coffee table and slipped it onto her finger, then placed the letter carefully in the center of the table.

Tired of living her life like an open wound, she had made some big changes. It had taken her three weeks. Three weeks to get to this stage. Three weeks since she had finally met Teej, the catalyst for all of these changes. Three weeks to fix the mess she had created in the previous six months.

She'd started with the drinking, cutting down little by little. When she decided to do something, she did it properly. Although each glass tasted bad now, she knew that cutting herself off completely would be too difficult. So she was patient, and she did it slowly. Methodically. A bottle a night. A couple of glasses. A single glass. Then none.

Same with the painkillers. Same with the junk food. She weaned herself off each of her vices. And even the friends. The destructive ones. One by one, she cut them out of her life. And that included Sue, who had gone into her own self-destructive spiral. She was, Anna now realized, a grief tourist. Attracted to Anna's tragedies, she fed on sorrow and drama. A stormy-weather friend. Anna didn't blame her friend for her nature, but she knew Sue couldn't help her. No one could.

But now there wasn't much left to fix or give up. Anna's dissertation was written and submitted. She wasn't a PhD student any more, though she found her success brought her little satisfaction. It was just one more thing off the list.

Now the writing was done, and she had little else to distract herself. She'd applied for jobs, but the money left from the insurance policy meant she wouldn't have to work for a very long time. And although she wanted to keep busy, the thought of starting some new career didn't feel good. It felt cold. No matter how hard she tried to move forward, the future still felt like it held no hope for happiness. No matter how carefully she organized her life, it still had no direction. Fixing the mess had felt good, but now she had nothing to look forward to. Nothing left to repair.

That word came into her mind once more. That word came to her when she had nothing to distract herself any more. When her mind drifted back to the accident. The river. His death. *Desolation.*

She adjusted the letter on the table once more, eyeing it like it was a bomb. Her name was written on the front in an almost-unreadable scrawl. Scribbled in green ink, the letters were chicken scratchings. *What now?* She wasn't ready to decide.

Seeking a distraction, she scrolled through the messages on her phone and saw several from her mom and one from her dad. Each week they sent less than the week before. They had stopped asking her to come back "home." They saw the change in her attitude and in the choices she was making. Everything was getting better, at least as far as they could tell. From the out-side, it might seem like Anna was healing. For all that work though, she didn't feel any better. She didn't feel anything at all.

Surprisingly, she found escape from her lethargy came each night in the form of vivid dreams of Teej. They offered her a respite from the perpetual nightmares she used to have. Her sleep was now filled with color and light. She dreamt of travel-ling to places and running with him and joking and flying through the air. Silly, wonderful dreams that prodded at her to think about the mysterious stranger, even when she tried to sup-press her memories of that crazy night when she left him to fight the monsters creeping out of the shadows. Left him to fight them alone.

She thought of his fuzzy stubble and his serious gray-green eyes and his messy hair and his easy smile. Either he was insane and a master manipulator, or they were both crazy. Or there was a third option. He was sane and everything he said was true.

No, she couldn't handle that. Thinking that way wouldn't help her. She couldn't let herself escape into fantasy just now. She had real decisions to make before she pursued flights of fancy.

Anna shifted the letter on the table, pushing it to the right so that it was perfectly in line with the edge. Frowning, she bal-anced on the precipice of a choice. *Read it? Burn it?* Either option might change everything. Or nothing.

She'd waited this long, so she could put it off a little longer, but was there any point? What did she have left to do? The real choice had come the night after the accident, when she'd decided she would numbly continue, even if she never felt anything ever again.

Pulling the metal waste bin close, she dangled the letter over it for a second before dropping it inside. Was this what moving forward looked like? If anyone else in the world knew about this letter, they would tell her to read it. But how could she when she felt nothing? No sorrow, no pain, no anger at his death. All she felt was numb. Nothing could change that. Not alcohol, not drugs, not hallucinations and not Teej.

With the old coldness falling over her once more, she opened the little drawer in the coffee table, pulled out a match, lit it and dropped it into the waste bin. The letter burned quickly and completely. When it was too far gone to recover, she did feel a twinge, but it disappeared in a second. Still no sorrow, still no pain. Anna realized, with an emotionless resignation, that she had absolutely nothing left to do now. Nothing else to discard, nothing else to burn, nowhere else to run. *Desolation.*

Fishing her phone out of her jean pocket, she looked back through her messages. Scrolling past the recent ones, she moved down the list till she reached Teej. She'd typed the message before she realized what she was doing.

How are you?
Why not?

nine

After several hours of checking her phone, pacing from room to room in her apartment and glancing out her window looking for who-knows-what, Anna was unwilling to wait any longer for a response. Agitated inaction gave way to feverish planning. *Why hadn't he messaged back?* She refused to wait around. She would do something.

Lacking a better plan, Anna decided to go out for a long walk. Grabbing her coat and wrapping a warm scarf around her neck in preparation for a long, cold night, she dashed out the front door to explore the city.

The cars and buildings seemed to rush past her, like the lights in a train tunnel. Anna walked for hours, wandering past all the places where she'd met Teej. She didn't mean to walk in that direction when she left her apartment, but her feet carried her to those places. The mall, Lady Almeria's house, the garden. She didn't know what she was looking for, but there was nothing to see. No sign of him or the creatures from the "Hazes." She still had no reply to her message, and she was wet and tired.

Anna arrived outside The Gisborne Hotel at 2 a.m. Certain that she was making a bad decision, Anna pushed through the swinging door and stepped inside.

Opulent but archaic, the Gisborne was an unfashionable building in an unfashionable part of the city. Once the premier location for wealthy tourists and business luminaries, it was now the personification of faded glory. It was also where Sue worked as the night manager, and it was where Anna hoped she might find one more thing to fix: her relationship with her friend.

Anna tiptoed through the gloomy hallway and stepped out into the lobby. Lemon and vanilla carpet freshener masked the staleness and damp. Although it was brighter than outside, it was dimly lit. Little lamps around the lobby sat next to brown leather sofas and green-topped oak coffee tables. There was dark wood everywhere, and the place made Anna feel small and out-of-place. Her footsteps echoed loudly as she walked. The only other sound was the heavy clack-clack of a grandfather clock. She felt like an intruder.

From an armchair next to the bar, an old, gray man looked at her suspiciously over the top of his small round spectacles before disappearing once more behind his giant newspaper. Approaching the empty reception desk, Anna looked all around for signs of her friend. On the counter were an open magazine, a guest book, a bell, a pen, and a mug of tea, but no Sue.

"Hello," she said far too quietly for anyone to hear. There was an eerie stillness that she felt powerless to break. Time seemed to freeze. Her hand hovered over the bell for a moment, but before she could work up the nerve to hit it, she saw someone moving around in the back room.

"Sue?"

"One moment please."

Sue walked toward the desk holding a stack of folders. When she saw Anna, she stopped in her tracks.

"Anna? What a nice surprise."

It was as if she wore a mask. Dressed in her smart suit and wearing her reading glasses, she looked serious and officious. She flicked her long blonde hair back over her shoulder, dropped the folders on the desk and opened one, making a show of how busy she was. She didn't look at Anna.

"I'm on my own here tonight. Lots to do."

"I need to talk to you. About that night."

Without looking up, Sue said, "Maybe I don't want to talk. Maybe you did enough talking. Don't you think? Mm?"

Sue's hand shook, and when Anna noticed and reached out, Sue placed the pen on the counter, closed the folder and stepped backward. Anna pulled her hand away when she saw how upset her friend was.

"What are you doing here?" demanded Sue, arms crossed.

"I need to talk with you. I've made some changes in my life. I'm trying to *fix* things. Maybe...maybe you need to talk, too?"

Sue's tongue pushed up against her cheek as she shook her head and leaned both hands on the counter. She gripped the edges tightly, her fingertips turning white.

"You need to talk? Do you think that's what I need? Do things get better when we talk about them? You and me?"

Anna frowned.

"Well, I think—"

"I think," Sue interrupted, "that we bring each other down. I think I was happier when you were ignoring me."

There were tears in Sue's eyes, but her jaw was set. Her mouth was pursed, her arms crossed defensively as she spoke.

"But..." said Anna.

Sue cut her off again. "You haven't called me in weeks. And you know what? It's been better. Do we help each other? All those awkward meetings where we stare into our coffee, neither of us knowing what to say? Until the tears start. Competing over who is the loneliest? Or the saddest? Well you win, Anna. You are the most miserable, so you win a fucking trophy."

Anna shook her head. She was getting annoyed too, but she knew where this was going. If it devolved into an argument, then she would be in the wrong for bringing that fight into Sue's workplace. Her friend would blame her for instigating this all. Anna wouldn't let that happen.

"Let's not talk like this. Can we go somewhere? Can you take a break? I'm not…I'm not judging you for who you date or sleep with. I don't think I'm better than you, and I don't want to unload on you. I'm not here asking for anything. I just want someone to talk to. I just…I need a friend."

Sue rolled her eyes and sighed heavily.

"Okay, if it helps you, then I can take a break. I don't have much time though. Go wait near the bar, and I'll come over."

Anna nodded and walked through the hotel lobby, mentally preparing herself for the conversation ahead. Again, the man with the little round spectacles looked up at her. She almost apologized, her footsteps seeming unreasonably loud. She walked past him to the bar where a wall of multi-colored bottles stretched upward to infinity. High above them, the ceiling was so dark it was like a starless night sky.

As she perched nervously on a creaky bar stool waiting for Sue, her gaze wandered up the tall hotel lobby walls. Huge paintings looked down on her. Her eyes lingered on one in particular. A gaunt man in an ill-fitting suit looked down on her with cruel eyes. In faded black letters on a gold plate beneath the portrait was the name "Ichabod Gisborne."

Her eyes scanned downward. Below Ichabod's portrait was a framed quote. Anna heard Sue walk up behind her, but she felt compelled to finish reading the words in the frame.

"Spend the hours of the day well, because Midnight comes for us all."

Anna shivered. Suddenly she felt the fear rise once again. Oblivious, Sue scribbled noisily with a pen, her heavy strokes scoring the paper with blue ink.

"Well? What did you want? I need to finish the guestbook records, so I'm going to keep working. If you wanna talk, then talk."

Ignoring Sue's passive-aggressive demeanor, Anna tugged on her sleeve.

"Do you see that quote up there? The one about midnight?"

She pointed at it, and Sue looked up with a sigh.

"Yes. It's been there forever. What's wrong with you?"

"I thought it was…"

Anna calmed herself.

"It's just—never mind. Since that night, I've had some weird experiences. I'm a bit jumpy now. You know the drug that Dean gave us? Did it do the same thing to you? Have you been *seeing* things? Did you lose some of your memories?"

Sue looked at her flatly. "I remember everything."

Anna pushed her for more information. "So it didn't have any after effects? Nothing…strange has happened to you?"

Sue shook her head dismissively then exhaled, going back to her writing. "No. It just makes you relax. Don't make this into a big thing. It was just a joke. You didn't have to overreact like that. And you don't have to make all this drama *now*."

Anna frowned. This wasn't how she wanted the conversation to go. Sue went on scribbling and talking,

"Look, he shouldn't have done it. I know that. I know that since the accident anything can…set you off. But it doesn't have to be this big drama. So, you got a bit lightheaded! You got home fine. No one got hurt. I just don't think we *help* each other. You know? You need to get to one of those support groups. I don't know how I'm supposed to help someone like you. I'll probably say the wrong thing to you and make you worse. You need to see a professional."

"Maybe," Anna conceded as she leaned back in her chair. She bit the skin at the corner of her nail nervously. "But I want to make things right with us. And I need to make sense of some stuff I saw."

Sue looked up at her critically. "I'm not sure what you really want from me. I don't think you know, either."

They sat in silence for long moments. Anna felt despondent. She had no messages from Teej and was getting nowhere with Sue. She put her head in her hands, rubbed her brow and tried to think of some way to reconcile with her friend. *What could she say to fix this?*

"Oh, what is this now?" Sue complained. "You ask people to do one simple thing!"

Confused, Anna leaned across to see what was bothering her. Sue turned to her and almost smiled.

"Look at this joker. All they have to do is write their name, and this guy has written a poem."

Again, Anna felt a twinge. Static across the skin, a sinking in the pit of her stomach.

"What does it say?"

"It's nonsense. I can barely read it."

"Show me."

Sue tipped the big notebook on its side and turned it in Anna's direction. Sue's finger rested under a scrawl of dirty black writing. "Here."

Anna read the words with mounting dread.

The Night Collectors come for your heart. They tear your flesh to feed my art. My words come real, your journey is done. Nobody can save you; no man, no one.

"Hey," Sue shouted. "Hey, you! Look at me."

Anna tore her eyes away from the script to see Sue screeching at the man hiding behind the newspaper. He seemed to be ignoring her. Anna grabbed at Sue's arm as a low thrumming noise started to fill her ears. The ground rumbled like it had before. Anna struggled to speak. She couldn't get Sue's attention.

"Sue…"

Her friend ignored her, obviously angry now.

"You can't write stuff like that on the guest book. What's wrong with you, you fucking weirdo?"

"Sue, get away from him!" Anna cried, but it was already too late.

The newspaper came down and a flat, featureless gray face came up from behind it. The man was gone. In his place, the Night Collector swelled and grew before their eyes, splintering the chair it sat upon. Its hooded, long-limbed, stooped form loomed upward as it got to its feet. Hump-backed and squat, it nonetheless stretched to over eight-feet-tall. Slickly smooth, muscly arms quivered with excitement as they gestured wordlessly, motioning for Anna and Sue to come closer. With a barely repressed hunger, it stomped toward them, the padded foot softly thumping the ground and shaking their bodies. Above them, an antique chandelier swung precariously with each percussive movement the creature made.

"Not again," Anna muttered.

She grabbed Sue's hand and tried to run, but her friend was frozen in place. The creature was maybe twenty feet away, but it could cross that distance in a few steps.

"Sue! We have to get out of here."

They exchanged glances for a moment. Anna somehow felt like she was seeing her friend for the first time. She gave Sue a nod, trying to get some acknowledgement that she was all right and understood what was happening. After a second, Sue returned her nod and they both ran for the door.

Sue's high heels slowed her down as Anna pulled her across the lobby toward the revolving doors. She almost fell, then bent down to take them off.

"We have to—"

Anna's words died in her mouth as she saw another of the Night Collectors climbing down from the ceiling, its large, flat hands and feet sticking to the wall. It dangled a huge, heavy arm loosely across the doorway, daring them to try to get past without being caught.

"Fire exit?" Anna asked in desperation.

"In the back," said Sue, gesturing past the reception area. Anna grabbed hold of her arm and dragged her along again. Sue was slow, and Anna pulled her lumpen form as the Night Collectors closed in on them inexorably, stomping over and crushing sofas and tables. Two more of them had joined the chase, loping out of the dining area and into the main hall.

Anna and Sue clambered through the lobby toward a prominent sign for a fire exit ahead. As they entered a tight corridor, they turned a corner and ran straight into the path of another Night Collector. Bent low in the narrow space, it bounded forward on all fours like a giant animal when it sensed them. Anna turned on her heels, almost falling before switching direction. Still, Sue was stiff, and Anna had to drag her as they ran.

The cramped hallway flew past in a blur. The thudding steps of the creatures closed in on them, but Sue's paralyzing fear was now giving way to blind panic. She started to run, too. It was what they needed to have any chance of escape.

Aware that they were heading toward a dead end, Anna scanned the paths ahead for any way to evade their pursuers. Her heart beat heavily in her chest and thudded in her ears as she looked left then right. There was an elevator, but she couldn't decide whether they should stop and call it or keep running. The sliding door was closed.

Betting that it might be on the ground floor, she hit the button as she ran past. A second later it opened, and Anna skidded to a stop.

"Sue, back here. The elevator!"

Sue kept running without looking back.

"Dammit."

Anna turned to see the creature bear down on her. Over its shoulder, it carried one of the huge, heavy sacks she'd seen them use before. She remembered the smothered faces of the victims. That would *not* happen to her.

"Stop!" she commanded the creature.

As soon as she spoke, the creature turned its sickly gray head in her direction and started moving more quickly. She breathed out slowly, steadied herself and tried again.

"Stop!"

The creature slowed its advance. It was like Teej said: *the Word.* The creatures had to follow Anna's commands when she used the Word. For just a moment, she would have complete power. She could compel them to obey her. In this world, her words were made real; their effects were as solid as the ground she stood upon.

"Anna," Sue shouted as she ran back from the corridor, another creature chasing her from the opposite direction. Together they bundled into the elevator, and Anna's hand shot out, hitting the nearest button.

It was the one labeled *open.*

"Dammit!" Sue snapped and pressed the button for the second floor. The doors started to close, agonizingly slowly. They stood together arm-in-arm watching the panels gently slide together.

They almost made it. A second before the doors closed, a giant, dirty hand shot through the gap and reached for Anna's throat.

Instead of cowering backward, Anna shot forward, both her hands pressing against the doors on either side of the creature. Against all sense and logic, she pushed her hands together, and the elevator doors crunched shut. They slammed together heavily, eliciting a wet snapping sound as the creature's arm was sheared off just below the elbow. The twitching appendage fell to the floor as clear, viscous blood pooled in the middle of the elevator.

"How did you...?" muttered Sue. "That's not possible."

Anna looked at the palms of her own hands in disbelief. "I think I can do things here that aren't possible. That's what Teej said."

The elevator pinged to the next floor. The doors started to open again, and Anna and Sue looked down the long, empty corridor.

"Let's go back up," said Sue as she pressed the button for the top floor.

"No, we need to get out!" said Anna, but it was too late. The doors closed again, and they started to ascend.

"There must be an exit in the basement. We should have gone down!"

Sue didn't respond. She was looking at the creature's massive arm—as big as her own torso—as it melted into translucent slime on the floor.

"When we get to the top—"

The elevator fell.

Anna and Sue felt a moment of weightlessness before they had a chance to panic. Long moments passed as the elevator fell and their bodies floated upward. It seemed bizarre rather than frightening to Anna. She had enough time to realize she might not survive this fall. In that moment, she felt the weight of her regrets. *Why had she burned the letter? Why didn't she go back to her mom?* She missed her terribly. She was so frightened, all the time, but she just kept running and running. Killing herself slowly.

When they hit the ground, the lights went out.

Anna's head smacked the floor hard enough to knock her unconscious.

ten

Anna awoke to the smell of burning in her nostrils and the taste of blood in her mouth. She was tangled with Sue, who was still unconscious. It was dark, so with no idea how badly hurt she was and unable to see her friend, she crawled to the sliver of light and managed to push her fingers through the gap. Although the doors were battered and buckled from the fall and made of solid steel, she somehow pulled them apart and was momentarily blinded as she escaped the gloom.

"I should have stayed in that mall," Anna muttered under her breath as she surveyed the landscape ahead. If she was going to get sucked into this world anyway, it might as well have been with Teej. Now she had to fight alone.

She stepped out of the elevator and into a desert. Purple sands stretched in every direction, amassing in mighty dunes that rolled all the way to the horizon. Above the sands, a sickly green-gray sky completed a landscape of pestilence and wrong-ness. The warm wind blew a miasma of decay into her face and the setting sun—a bright green semi-circle squatting on the sky-line—licked the landscape with a slimy, iridescent light. The air was raw and abrasive.

Anna stood at the crest of a dune, and in the valley below sat a calm lake. The water looked black and rancid, and around the shore sprouted diseased yellow and orange trees. The only other familiar object was the moon high above, faint and distant; the rest of the sky was a blend of green and blue lines and swirls—like a painting by a madman.

The bright purple sand swallowed her feet up to the ankles, and she stepped gingerly, aware that a slip could easily send her sliding down the steep dune.

Behind her, Sue stirred. Anna turned to see her friend crawl unsteadily out of the elevator toward her. She'd smashed her nose in the fall, and her face was bloodied, but otherwise she looked unhurt.

Anna took a moment to look at the elevator from the outside. It wasn't connected to anything, just two broken, freestanding doors floating in space.

"Anna, where are we?"

"In trouble," said Anna simply. "Are you okay? Can you walk?" Sue limped forward into the nightmare landscape, blinking at the light. It took her a few moments to react.

"This isn't right." She started to sob. "What have you done to us? I want to go home."

"Let's keep *calm*," said Anna, her voice trembling as she spoke.

Mott had brought them here. The Midnight Man. He controlled everything about this place, but Teej had told her there was always an escape route. There was always a way *through and out the other end*. She just had to find it and get them both to safety.

To her own surprise, she found she could push panic out of her mind. She was frightened, but it wasn't overpowering her. They weren't dead yet. Perhaps her enemy underestimated her.

"Listen to me," said Anna, filling her voice with as much conviction as she could muster. "We can get out of here."

Sue's eyes looked wild. They darted back and forth desperately. Sue needed some anchor to reality, and Anna had to be that anchor. There was no one else.

"This is just a hallucination," Anna lied to her friend. "It's not real. You're only in trouble if you panic. If you panic, your heart rate will go up too high, but if you keep calm, then this will all go away. Can you do that?"

Sue was shaking her head, but she didn't look at Anna. Perhaps it was enough to calm her friend for now.

Squinting against the malignant light of the green sun, Anna looked down at the lake. There was something by the water. Something manmade, angular and out of place in this environment. With no other options, Anna resolved to move closer to the object.

"Can you see what that is?" she asked Sue as she pointed ahead, trying to involve her in the decision. Sue didn't look up but shook her head, so Anna grabbed her by the arm and together they started to work their way down the dune.

They weaved a long, winding path through the sand as Anna tried to navigate a route that wasn't too steep. Twice they almost fell, but eventually they made it to the bottom. As they got closer to the lake, the surface appeared slick, as if coated with oil, and the object on the shore emerged as three: a table, a chair and a child's tricycle. She decided not to think too much about their incongruity until they got closer.

As they approached the bottom, Anna felt a mounting unease in the base of her stomach, as if the air was making her sick. The longer she spent here, the further she drifted from her own world. It was as if a door was slowly closing behind her, and she wouldn't get back through it in time. She hustled to the table, pulling Sue along as best she could. It was an old-fashioned writing table, leather topped and made of dark, solid wood. It looked just like the tables in the hotel lobby, and although its heavy wooden legs sunk into the purple sand, the surface was clear and clean. On top of the table, a chunky old dial phone and a single fountain pen sat next to a heavy, leather-bound book. Nearby, the child's tricycle was rusted and dirty, covered in corroded, metallic abrasions.

Anna eyed the book cautiously but didn't open it. She remembered Teej's words. *He was once a writer.* That was how Mott created this world. Through his words. Whatever might be written in that book, reading it would do her no good.

Anna checked on her friend. Sue's gaze was locked on the horizon. Her arms were pulled in tight to her body, and she shivered. Her pale face, dilated pupils and appearance worried Anna, but she realized she probably looked just as bad.

"This place," said Sue, her voice distant and faint. "It's bad. How can it be here in the hotel? This is the basement..."

Anna shook her head. "Not anymore."

She held the back of her neck as she debated what to do. A thick bump rose at the base of her skull where she'd hit the elevator floor. Her arm ached at the shoulder, and a small cut on her forehead had already started to crust, sticking her hair uncomfortably to her face. She brushed it away irritably and was about to lean on the desk when the phone started to ring. It startled her, and she took a step backward, almost falling.

Anna and Sue looked at each other for a moment, frozen in place. The phone rang three times. Four. Five. It was loud and insistent, rocking violently on the cradle with each ring.

"I think I should answer it." Anna wanted to prove to her aggressor that she wasn't frightened, but she also didn't want to make a mistake. *If he planned to kill them, why were they here? What method could the Midnight Man employ to destroy them?* Surely a phone was far from an optimal weapon...

Anna reached out to answer it, but when her fingertips brushed the phone, Sue cried out to stop her.

"No! We shouldn't…"

"It's going to be all right," said Anna.

She took a deep breath, brushed her hair away from her face and reached down. She grasped hold of the phone, then picked it up and held it to her ear. She was brave enough to pick it up but couldn't manage to speak, so instead, she waited.

"Anna?"

Teej. She recognized the voice instantly.

"Don't read the book."

"I didn't. How do you always find me? And why are you never actually here to help?"

"I can sense you. And him. You used your powers, right? They make ripples. But when he creates a Haze, he hides the entrances and exits. It takes time to find a way in. I can see you, but I won't get to you in time. Where exactly are you?"

She looked around and shrugged. "A desert. But the sand is purple, and the sky is green."

"No, no! I told you I can see you. I mean, how did you get there? Where did you come *from*?"

It took her a moment to understand what he meant. Sue was tugging on her sleeve, but she ignored her.

"Where did I— Oh, I see what you mean! Gisborne Hotel. We went down in an elevator and—"

She didn't know what else to say. There was a moment of silence, and Anna licked her lips nervously. Sue whimpered and pointed at something, but Anna didn't know what. They still seemed to be alone.

"I'm not close," said Teej. "You need to know something about yourself, Anna. You're an Undreamer. These worlds you find yourself in, you can change them. You can unmake them. There's a way out."

"How?" she snapped. "I don't know how to—"

Anna trailed off as she suddenly noticed what Sue was pointing at. Footprints formed on the sand. Hundreds of them. Coming from every direction. And they were getting closer.

"What are they? Why can't we see them?" asked Sue between tears.

Teej spoke through the phone again.

"He's coming for you. When you see him, you have to hurt him. He's focused on keeping you there, but when he's hurt, you'll have a window. Use it. When you can, run to the elevator. That's how you got in; it should get you out. You just have to *make* it work. But only if he is weakened. Only if he is surprised. Remember to—"

The line clicked silent.

"Wait, Teej! How do I hurt him? How do we get to the elevator? There are...there are things in the way. Teej?"

There was no answer. He was gone.

The footprints stopped about ten feet from where they stood, but Anna and Sue were surrounded. Anna could feel the presence of something all around her, but she couldn't tell what. Whatever it was—whatever *they* were—they blocked the wind and somehow diffracted the light around them. Although she couldn't see them, she felt their shadows resting across her.

There was one gap in the circle, and it led to the dirty lake. Both Anna and Sue turned at the same time to see a creature rise out of the water.

The monster broke the surface slowly, rising from the slime and filth. His face emerged first. Pale, gray skin and two small, pure black eyes looked out from under a black hood, a sick grin painted from ear to ear. The smiling mouth was full of teeth like broken glass, shattered and sharp and bleeding. He wasn't as tall as the Night Collectors, but he was still larger than a man. Stooped with elongated arms and legs and huge, three-fingered hands as big as a human's torso. He dripped and shambled in their direction, walking out of the water and onto the shore smoothly, like oil on glass. He smiled at them, a monstrous combination of childlike curiosity and pure malice.

So this was the Midnight Man.

Sue screamed, but Anna didn't allow herself to be gripped by panic. This creature was trying to frighten them. Perhaps it needed to frighten them. Perhaps it used their fear. Everything here was intentional. He wanted this reaction, and whatever the Midnight Man wanted from her, she would resist. If he needed her to be afraid, she would be strong. *Never play their game. Their game is always rigged.*

"Get back," she shouted at the creature.

He tilted his head to one side as if he didn't understand, but he kept coming. He was too strong for the Word. She might be able to command the Night Collectors, but the Midnight Man was too powerful. He spoke back without moving his mouth, the words seeming to come from every direction. A chorus of wailing childlike voices said:

Across endless purple sand
'Neath an azure sky
The formless legions marched
Just to watch you die

Teej told her the Midnight Man had been a poet once, before he lost his mind. That was how he formed and exhibited his power. How could she use that against him? How could she fight him?

Anna was reaching for the book before she knew exactly why. It was heavy and bound in brown leather, with a title across the front that she refused to read. Instead of opening it, she spun around and threw it as hard as she could. It arced over the Midnight Man's head, and he turned in bemusement to watch it splash into the slimy water. There was a moment of awkward silence where Sue and the creature both looked back at Anna in confusion. She shrugged.

A split second later, the smile changed to fury, the features of the Midnight Man's face distorting into feral rage. He bounded toward them on all fours like an angry ape. Anna and Sue turned in unison and started to run toward the high dune and the elevator at the top.

When they came to the heavy footprints in the sand, there was a moment of hesitation, but with Mott closing in, they had to keep moving. Anna felt her hand coming up in front of her. As they threatened to collide with the invisible line, Anna spoke.

"Get out of the way."

Again, her words held power, for this task, at least. She saw the footprints shuffle aside as they barreled forward. There was a space in the line. They shambled on through the sand, and as they passed through the space, Anna felt sure some invisible hand would grab for her. She felt something like hot breath on her shoulder as they pushed through, but they cleared the barrier and continued. Ahead, the high dune looked much steeper than before.

Anna risked a look behind her. She pushed Sue in front first and then turned to see the Midnight Man bearing down on them. His bloody mouth snapped at the air, his long, muscular arms impelling him forward in great leaps. He seemed to glide over the ground, while each step they took was heavy and plodding, their feet sinking into the soft sand. Their pace was too slow. They wouldn't make it.

Anna pushed Sue ahead of her. Her friend started to turn, but Anna shouted, "Just keep going! Don't turn around."

She didn't know what else to do. They ran and ran. Anna's back ached as she pushed on, each step heavy and leaden. At times, she fell onto all fours but still she scrambled upward. The elevator didn't seem to be getting any closer. Lungs burning, legs aching, she refused to look behind her. Her back felt exposed, like the creature's fangs would sink into her skin at any time and pull her down the hill. Maybe he would drown her in his swamp, or maybe he would consume her where she stood. Regardless of his intentions, there was nothing she could do to save herself. All she could do was push Sue ahead and hope that when he grabbed her, her friend might still escape.

They climbed and climbed. As desperation gave way to exhaustion, Anna began to wonder why they were still alive. They should have been caught by now. The Midnight Man was so much faster than them. She dared to quickly look back, and found to her relief and confusion that he was gone. They were alone.

Sue slowed ahead of her, but Anna pushed her to keep going. "Don't stop," she said between gasps. "We're almost there. We can get out…with the elevator. That's what Teej told me."

Sue didn't turn, but she gave a tiny nod. They were both out of breath, but Anna allowed herself a moment of hope. Perhaps throwing the book in the water had really hurt the Midnight Man, or perhaps he could only maintain his form for a limited time. Whatever the reason for their reprieve, it didn't change their course of action. *Keep. Climbing.*

Finally, they crested the summit, and Sue broke into a full-on sprint to the elevator. Anna felt the change in the air, in the ground and in the sky. He was waiting.

Out of breath, Anna cried after Sue. "Wait. It's a trap. Stop!"

Her warning came too late. He was ahead of them. *In nightmares, you always run into the thing you're trying to escape.*

The elevator doors opened slowly, and the Midnight Man stepped out. He bounded forward, a hideous smile across his face as he snatched Sue with one hand, his three huge fingers

87

clamping around her waist. His massive paw grasped her like a baton. He lifted her up and examined her like a toy. Sue screamed and turned to Anna, her arm reaching out. Anna tried to grasp her hand, but the Midnight Man pulled her away jealously and clutched Sue to his breast.

Seemingly on a whim, he lifted her high over his head, and his sharp, broken teeth clamped down on her right thigh. Sue let out an inhuman sound—a deep, resonant, echoing screech. When he pulled his mouth away, a chunk of flesh was torn clear. Anna screamed and shouted, but it made no difference. Blood sprayed furiously from the wound, staining the sand, and covering the creature's face in crimson gore. Sue twitched and writhed, clawing at him, desperate to free herself. Ignoring her struggles, Mott lifted her to his mouth once again and bit off her right leg, swallowing it whole from the knee down.

The horror paralyzed Anna. It was beyond terror. Beyond disgust. She fell to her knees in desolation as the creature continued to slowly consume her friend. It looked into Anna's eyes with each bite, and Sue's screams became gurgles as she struggled and wailed into the night. Anna found herself looking beyond the creature, over its shoulder at the sky. She couldn't bear to witness what was happening to her friend, so she locked her gaze on the moon. A strange thought flickered through her mind—how beautiful the moon was. She had never realized before. *Why wasn't the moon helping her now? Why wasn't anyone helping?*

No one would help her. No one ever helped her at times like these. She had to fight it. Even now, when she had no weapons and no way to win, she would fight it. She was going to die anyway, best to die on her feet, fighting.

Anna turned back deliberately to look at the Midnight Man. Sue had gone limp in his hand. He lifted her body up, tipped his head back and let the blood run into his mouth. One of his dark eyes continued to glance at Anna as he drank deeply of the last of her life blood. He seemed to be swelling larger as he consumed Sue, his gray arms and legs flexing and straining as if they would explode outwards in sudden growth.

As Anna ran toward the Midnight Man, memories flashed through her mind. Thoughts and feelings she had locked away came back to her one last time. Her mother, the accident, a thin red line marked across her wrist and sudden sharp pain and panic, the water closing over her head, her husband's breath on her cheek when they hugged close, Teej. She blinked tears out of her eyes and closed out the memories. The pain, the pain was all that mattered. She converted that pain to raw hate, and that hate became fuel. Fuel that would burn her up and take her enemies with her.

That fuel was real here. In the Haze, all that pain and rage was made physical, and though she couldn't focus it or use it properly, it impelled her forward. As she ran at the bloody creature, it took a step backward and to the side. The Midnight Man lined up to face her, one hand ready to strike as the other dropped the pieces of Sue's lifeless body. Anna's arm went up, and she felt a heat build within her. A fire had been lit. She prepared to strike, some buried instincts within her guiding her movements. *In a world of dwindling light, you're a bonfire in the night.*

Then she saw it. A tiny window of opportunity. A glittering golden path that led to survival. She adjusted in a flash, ducked her body and shimmied, darting to one side. The Midnight Man instantly realized her goal, but he reacted too slowly. She could make it into the elevator. She could make it through the doors.

The Midnight Man had expected some sort of attack. He moved to intercept her, but she had wrong-footed him. He tried to adjust his position, but he slid and stumbled, one mighty hand coming down to steady himself before he leaped forward.

The heavy sand kicked up in clouds behind her with each step. She felt like she was gliding across the surface, driven by her own will to live as much as the energy of her body. It would be close. Desperately close. Either she would dive into the elevator, or he would intercept her at the last second and snatch her away.

Time slowed, almost stopped. She leaped forward. He leaped too.

She tucked her legs in and went between his outstretched arms. The toe of her shoe brushed one of his massive fingers as she slid away from him. His leap sent him past the elevator and past her. She hit the floor heavily and time seemed to return to normal. Everything happened at once. She hit a button, and the doors started to close. He leaped at the door; she fell backward as she stumbled away from him; his arm reached out, thudding against the closed door. The light in the elevator came back on.

There was a long moment of silence as Anna listened to her own ragged breathing, then the doors opened a moment later with a ping.

She had escaped the Haze.

Back in the hotel, everything was just as it had been. The lobby was empty; the only noise, the ticking of the grandfather clock.

Stunned and confused, Anna stepped out and looked down at her sneakers, noting with detached fascination that they were stained and ruined.

Purple sand and blood.

eleven

Anna didn't dream. Instead, she skirted the edge of nightmares, not quite awake and not quite asleep. Her exhausted body forced her mind to drop out of consciousness, but each time she felt herself drift off, she came up again like a drowning woman: desperate, gasping for air and terrified. She saw that monsters face no matter how tightly she closed her eyes.

Outside her bedroom window, the rain rattled the glass. It was still dark. The sun should have come up by now, but the dark gray clouds held firm against the breaking light. The curtains flapped in the cold, morning breeze.

She'd existed in this state for hours now, tossing and turning, the blankets twisted around her feet. She was shivering and sweating at the same time, her back sticky and wet, but her shoulders and hands and feet were cool. Her thoughts looped around and around, replaying the same moments over and over. Her conversation with Sue, stepping across the purple sands, the blood.

It took Anna a long time to realize she was no longer alone in the room. The large shadow in the corner hadn't been there when she came to bed. Sitting on the chair next to her dresser, she thought she recognized the shape, but it took her several long moments to react. Still half asleep, she wondered if he was real. Was it Teej? She closed her eyes, too tired to react. Whoever it was, they could do anything they wanted, as long as they let her lie here and drift off. Eventually, she slipped into dreams again.

She stirred six hours later, slowly coalescing into conscious thought. Her senses came back to her by degrees, and she watched the still shape in the corner of the room in the pale early-morning light. Outside, the rain came down in sheets, and he watched it through the window in silence. His face was set. His green-gray eyes looked desperately sad, his cheeks gaunt, his skin sallow, and his demeanor was defeat. She knew her reaction should be shock, confusion, fear or even anger, but all she wanted to do was lie for a moment more and sleepily watch him before he noticed she was awake. He already knew though.

"It takes two of us," he said sadly. "We have a saying—*Two Metiks make a team; two Dreamers make a mess.* It takes two Metiks to fight a Dreamer."

She took long moments to understand what he was saying. The words echoed in her head, but she had to decode them. Eventually, they clicked in her mind. He had tried to fight the Midnight Man too and failed. He couldn't beat him on his own.

"Dreamers are the only ones that can create Hazes, but Dreamers can't oppose each other. Their powers cancel out, and when they fight, it always leads to disaster. It takes a Metik to stop a Dreamer and Metiks' powers are limited to adapting what has already been dreamed. We can adapt Hazes…or destroy them. But one is not enough. It takes two Metiks to face a Dreamer in their own Haze. One to control the Haze, and one to find and fight the Dreamer.

"When Metiks fight Dreamers, it's like two songs are playing, yours and theirs, and they're competing. You have to match the tempo, and then make your melody catchier till only one song remains. And I'm no soloist. On my own, the result is always the same. Stalemate. And each fight takes a toll."

She sat up slowly, examining him as she pushed the blankets off her chest. She was still wearing her clothes from last night. Even one of her shoes. She kicked it off unconsciously as she turned to face him. She was glad it was dark in the room. She must look terrible. Her hair was a mess of tugs and curls and every inch of her skin felt dirty and grimy. Still, she pushed all of that from her thoughts and focused on him. He gave off an aura of failure. She might be tired and dirty, but he seemed completely broken. He needed her.

"I'm...sorry. I'm sorry I didn't believe you."

She said it directly and deliberately. She had to say it. She thought she might never get to say those words. It was important that he knew, but now that she had apologized, she found there was no lightening of her load. No weight off her shoulders. No less guilt.

He nodded a little but didn't turn to her. He remained silent, so she asked the question she felt she had to. "How did you get in here?"

"I'm good at a lot of things," he said. "Picking locks, climbing drain pipes—"

"Being creepy. Some women don't like it when you sneak into their bedrooms and watch them sleep," she chided.

"Some women." He tried to smile but it was a sad, broken thing. She felt immediate pangs of sympathy. He was not himself.

"Are you okay?"

"It doesn't matter."

His gaze drifted back to the window and the rain. "You can go back to sleep. You're safe."

"I don't feel safe, Teej. Sue is really dead, isn't she? In the real world."

He sighed heavily. "Yes. Hazes aren't separate from the *real* world. Everything that happens in a Haze really *happens*, and when the Haze is over, everything knits back together. The Haze is gone, but the effects remain and the outcome sticks. If someone dies in a Haze, they're dead."

"So why don't people know about all this? Why can't other people see it all?"

"The Veil. The Veil hides everything that happens from them. When a Haze occurs then Basine—that's what we call the real world—frays. Suddenly, all sorts of possibilities open up, but when the Haze fades again, every strange thing gets rationalized away. People's memories are rewritten in a way that they can accept. But the Metiks and the Dreamers remember. The Haze is like a tributary, but it always flows back into the river. It always flows back into Basine, and Basine flows on forever. And so the world goes on. Oblivious."

When he'd spoken like this before, Anna had tried to shut out the words. Even now, her mind railed against what he was saying, but she needed to know more.

"Basine?" she asked.

"The real world, or what you thought of as the real world before you joined us Behind the Veil.

"Teej…I don't believe in God or spirituality. Or crystal healing or chem trails or lizard people or Thetans or Chi or spells. I don't talk about how jet fuel can't cut steel beams, and I don't go on meditation retreats to get in contact with my Menstrual Goddess."

"Me neither," he said, and his smile seemed a little lighter this time.

"How am I supposed to process all of this?" she asked plainly. "I don't need you to convince me. I've seen these things now. I just need to know how to…accept them."

94

"You just keep going forward. You question everything, and when the answers satisfy you, you accept them. And when you see someone do something wrong, you use what power you have to stop them."

"I don't know how to fight monsters like you do. My friend just died right in front of me, and I was powerless. That *can't* happen again."

He was about to interrupt her, but she held her hand up.

"I don't blame you for it. I know you won't always be able to save me."

He let out a brittle laugh. "Save you? You have entirely the wrong idea about this."

"What do you mean?"

"Anna from here on, you'll be the one that saves me."

Anna didn't know what to say.

"Remember I said it takes two Metiks to fight a Dreamer? One controls the Haze and the other one fights? You're the fighter. You fight because you're stronger than me. Or you can be. If you let me teach you, I promise you that you'll never be powerless like that again. I'll teach you how to stop anyone who hurts you or your friends."

Anna nodded. He seemed to know exactly what she needed to hear.

"All right, but promise me one more thing?"

"What's that?"

Though he might not see it in the gloom, she gave him the sternest expression she could manage. "Don't sneak into my bedroom ever again."

He gave her a look she couldn't decipher, but his voice was full of mischief. "Understood. By invite only."

Suddenly aware of just how much she didn't know about him—including whether he had somewhere else to go—she said, "You can stay now, though. If you want to. Just till morning."

"Thank you," he said simply. He leaned his head back and closed his eyes. "We can start tomorrow."

"Start what?" she asked.

"Training."

Anna sat upright as she watched him. He seemed to be thinking deeply, but after a few awkward moments waiting for him to speak, she realized he had fallen asleep. She lowered herself quietly back to the mattress and pulled the blanket up to her eyes. Glad that he was there, she tried to sleep. Her toes and legs shook restlessly. Despite the horrors she'd just seen, she felt a strange, unfamiliar spark of excitement.

When sleep finally came upon her, it was deep and dreamless.

twelve

axine's Bar was hard to find, not because it was hidden, but because it was veiled in banality. Huddled near a quiet corner of a quiet street, a dirty sign hung over a heavy door with a food menu printed outside that door. The prices were all wrong and the food descriptions partially worn away. The stairway descended to an entrance that smelled of stagnant water and rot. It was unpleasant enough that the only people who went beyond the stairs were those who already knew what was inside.

Anna followed Teej toward the stairs, taking a moment to look nervously around at the damp, empty street before she descended. Trash cans and candy wrappers clogging dirty drains—it all looked so mundane. Tugging on the soggy sleeves of her sweater, Anna mused that it was strange to see how little the world had changed.

She considered running.

She didn't know why or where she would go, but her mom would have told her to run. Her mom would tell her this was *all* a bad idea. They'd had disagreements, but in moments like this—when everything seemed to be getting out of hand—her mom's calm, reasoned advice had always been something she could fall back on. Even if Anna couldn't speak with her now, it was easy enough to call to mind what her advice would be. *Don't follow the strange man into the underground bar.*

"It's safe here, Anna. Really, completely safe. The safest place you can be right now."

She nodded and followed him down by taking small steps. *Where else could she go?*

As they stepped inside Maxine's cool, gloomy interior, Anna glanced around at the shadowy corners, looking for threats or danger. Teej put a gentle hand on her shoulder. He directed her to the bar where a balding, chubby man wearing a loose-fitting t-shirt and a lukewarm smile cleaned the coffee machine.

"'Lo, Donnel. I'll go get him for ya."

The man waddled into the back room behind the bar, leaving them alone. She sat on one of the high, red leather stools and leaned on the bar, and Teej sat next to her.

This was a strange place. Disarmingly plain, boring even. At one time, it might have been a trendy bar—a shabby-chic hangout for students and smart office types. Vinyl records hung on the walls, and the beer mats were old CDs. The floor was crusted with dirt, the glasses were cloudy, and the "specials" board was dusty and faded. The bar had transitioned from rustic to run-down, and most of the leather seats were split open to show tufts of yellow, foam sponge bursting out. The place smelled of stale spirits, and the windows, which were below ground and looked onto dark passageways, were thick with dust and dirt. This made the bar overwhelmingly gloomy, and even in the early afternoon, she was barely able to see if anyone was skulking in the shadowy corners. It certainly didn't feel like the safest place she could be.

"Is Donnel your real name?" she asked.

"Just a name. No more real than any of the others," he replied.

"Should I call you that?"

"No, I'm Teej."

He smiled like he thought he was in trouble, but she didn't mind him having more than one name. Everything else in this crazy world seemed to have more than one name anyway.

They were here to see Teej's mentor. His name was Garret (although he probably had a million other names, too). Now retired, he used to be the best at what he did—whatever that was. And Teej needed advice. Anna hoped Garret would speak more freely than Teej. When they met, he wouldn't know anything about her. He might assume she was already working with Teej rather than "auditioning." He might let crucial information slip that Teej wasn't yet ready to divulge. She had to play this smart.

As they waited in the murky bar, Anna noticed that Teej seemed calmer and more at-ease now. She took a moment to examine him, eyeing him from his messy hair to his battered sneakers. There was still a strangeness to him she couldn't identify. Certainly, he was eccentric, but he was charming, too. Old fashioned, but boyish. She got the impression that he was not quite himself now, although she hadn't known him before. The fight with the Midnight Man had affected him. Damaged him. Sometimes she saw him grimace, like he was in pain, but he didn't want her to notice. And, like her, he felt guilt over what happened to Sue. Part of Anna's mind still wanted to blame him for what had happened. None of these horrors existed in her world *before* him, but she had to confront the fact that they didn't come *from* him. And she'd seen plenty more mundane horrors in her life.

Sitting at the bar, she tried to force her nerves to settle. During the walk, their brisk pace had let her burn up adrenaline, but now that they were waiting, she had to accept his reassurance that they were safe and let her guard down a little.

"Why is he called the Midnight Man?"

Teej leaned low on the bar as he spoke, resting his chin on his hands as he shuffled restlessly. "He became obsessed with one of his own poems, and it drove him mad. The poem was about the Midnight Man. And now he *is* the Midnight Man."

"Sometimes our old names don't fit us anymore?" she said.

He smiled broadly. "So you were listening? Even when you thought this was all nonsense."

She couldn't help but smile back, but she checked herself instantly. She was accepting this new world, but she had to keep questioning it. She had to be wary of what he told her and why. *Never play their game...*

"Who are you? Who are you *really*?" she asked.

"I'm Teej," he said neutrally.

"You know what I mean. How old are you? What do you do? Where are you from? Do you have family? All those questions."

He shrugged. "You know all that already."

"No," she said firmly. "I know what you told me before I found out about...all this. When we spoke online, you didn't tell me about Hazes and Metiks and Dreamers."

"Yes, I did."

"You did not!" she protested.

"You weren't listening."

She gave him a look that made him physically back away.

"Okay, okay. Maybe I left stuff out. And maybe I wasn't always totally forthright about...myself. What do you want to know?"

"How old? What is your job? Where were you born? Do you have family?"

"One by one, then. I don't know, but this is as old as I want to look. I'm going to show you what I do, but you'll learn to do it, too. I was born near Nottingham in England, I think, but no one really knows. I don't exactly remember, but listening to my accent you'd think I was—"

"From nowhere," she interrupted. There was a moment's silence.

"Exactly. And I have no family. Left. Only a few *good* friends."

Anna turned her stool to face him. She swallowed hard.

"And do you want to ask me anything?"

"Do you want a drink?"

She frowned. "Nope."

They sat in silence as she tried to decide what she wanted to hear him say. The empty bar creaked and groaned like an old wooden ship, and she jumped nervously, half standing up and scanning the shadows for danger. Teej didn't budge, though, so she settled down again and turned to him.

"What was that noise?" she asked.

"Nothing."

"Are we in danger right now?"

"It takes tremendous Vig to create a Haze like the one he attacked you with. Mott must regenerate that Vig, and it will take him a day at least. He has to harvest. Those little poems don't write themselves, and he has to write more. Those are the source of his power, and without them, he can't do anything."

"Vig?"

"Yeah. It's the fuel the Dreamers use to create Hazes. It comes from people or places that inspire them."

"And how did he find us?"

"We shine like beacons, especially when we use our powers. That's how I could always find you when you were in trouble. But we can hide. Like fireflies, we can fly close to the sun."

"Is that what we're doing now? Does this place hide us?"

"Exactly!" He seemed pleased with the direction of the conversation.

"And why didn't he find me before?"

"That—" he paused for dramatic purposes "—is a good question."

"And can *we* find *him*?"

"Hmmm, tricky. We can try, but Dreamers aren't easy to locate when they're not using the Art. Mimesis burns brightly, but without the expenditure of Vig, there's really nothing for us to track. We struggle to follow the smoke when the fire burns low."

"And Vig is...physical? Or like an energy?"

"That's a hard philosophical question. Some Dreamers believe it's the distilled essence of the leftover stuff that created the universe, and they reshape it to create Hazes. Others believe it's the qualia that's generated from—"

"Teej," she cut him off. "Like I'm a slow child. Or a very clever dog. Where does it come from, and what does it do?"

"Yes, yes of course," he said. "Vig comes from all of us. And sometimes it accumulates in places. You can't see it or touch it, but you feel it. When you're behind the Veil, you can feel it in everything. You'll learn that. Dreamers use it to fuel their Art, and some people create more of it than others. Those people are called Muses. Some *places* produce Vig in greater quantities too, and they're called Idylls."

"I have trouble believing in things I don't see or experience," she said honestly.

"Like Lady Almeria said, it will make more sense when I show you."

"Is that why we're here?"

"One of the reasons."

"Teej, I have to ask you, how often do you win against these Dreamers? If it's your job to protect people, why are they still dying?"

It was a hard question to ask, but she had to know the answer. She didn't understand what he was supposed to do, and she didn't understand the rules he followed. Teej looked conflicted, but before he could respond, the back room door opened and Garret walked in.

Anna didn't know what she expected, but what she got was different. Garret's wavy, gray, shoulder-length hair tangled through his gray-black stubble, making him the untidiest looking man Anna had ever seen. A tight-fitting black t-shirt clung to his wiry frame, and as he walked to the bar, she noted the litheness and length of his figure. He was tall and stringy, wrinkled, and a little tired looking, but at one point in his past, he would have been ruggedly handsome. He flashed a smile in her direction, and somehow his whole demeanor changed from weariness to laconic charm. He winked at her and smiled at Teej. She would have guessed he was in his fifties but wouldn't have been surprised if he were much older.

"Hey, Donnel. And nice to meet you, young lady. I'm sure you'll make a great Metik."

"What? How do you know I'd be great? You haven't even heard me speak yet," she said.

"And now I have, and I am even more sure you are the right choice," he replied, flashing her a cheeky smirk. Teej grinned, and the two men shared a brief, strong embrace.

Teej said, "I'm glad to see you, Garret."

Garret smiled but didn't look at him. Instead, his eyes were locked on Anna. He brushed his long, gray hair back to see her better and extended a hand in her direction. She shook it. His hand was warm and strong and much bigger than hers.

He looked down when he spoke. "Don't worry, hun. You're safe, and we're gonna have some beers. Don't fret about what this guy has been telling you. Things aren't so bad. He tends to overcomplicate the world."

There was a twang to his accent she didn't recognize. A roundness to his words that made him sound vaguely Southern. It was warm and inviting and charming as hell. He gestured to a nearby table, and they went over to sit together. Garret stretched out and spread his arms over two nearby chairs, while Teej and Anna sat opposite him. Anna looked at him intently, hands on her lap, ready to take in everything they said. Teej was distracted and fidgeted as he tried to get comfortable.

"So, *the Midnight Man?*" said Garret. "That's his name now. I know what he's been up to. Seems like it took you a while to figure this one out, Don...Teej."

Teej scowled a little. "I'm still not really back to full strength, yet."

Garret nodded, his expression neutral. Anna found herself starring at Garret. He was fascinating. The kind of man who couldn't walk into a busy room without everyone turning to look at him. She bit her bottom lip and waited to hear what he had to say.

"Well, at least you're both safe. You'll be back to full health in no time. Should we be talking about training soon?" Garret eyed Anna as he spoke, trying to gauge her reaction, even though he was speaking to Teej. They both turned to look at her.

They were quiet for a moment, and Anna felt herself shrink under their gaze. She was starting to feel self-conscious, until Garret leaned in close, like he was telling her a secret. "He's judging you. Look at him, with his little judgy eyes."

She laughed a little. He did look like he had small eyes, but through fatigue. He looked exhausted.

"We can train later," said Teej. "We need to talk about Mott. And the Doxa. There was a fight. The Haze Spiraled. It collapsed in on itself, and we were trapped. It was like being in a hurricane and an earthquake at the same time. We didn't have a chance. Linda..."

Who was Linda? Anna didn't fully understand what they were talking about. It seemed that Teej had faced Mott before their conflict at the mall, and it hadn't gone well. She could at least surmise that when Hazes Spiraled, it was bad.

"I heard," said Garret. "Linda knew what she was getting into. You woulda managed if Wildey hadn't been there. I know it shook you up, son, but you gotta get yourself together. You've been through worse. Why do you need me now? I'll help any way I can, but you know I'm all washed up."

Teej didn't say anything, but he looked at Anna.

"Oh, so it's you two?" said Garret with a smile she couldn't read. "This is the new team."

"You want to take him on before he gets too strong?" said Garret as he pointed in Anna's direction. "With her."

"I almost took him on my own," said Teej firmly.

"But you didn't."

Teej looked like he would protest, but then he stopped himself. Garret turned to Anna and went on. "I see you know how to do this already, don't you? You're a natural. Your friend died. So, do you want revenge? Or answers? Or are you running?"

Anna shrugged noncommittally. She would have answered him if she knew.

"You ran away at the mall. Something changed your mind."

She looked at Garret skeptically. "How did you know all that? Is it a Metik thing?"

"No, he texted me this morning."

She almost let out a laugh, and both men smiled easily.

"Okay, we got some work to do," said Garret. "Why don't you go grab some food from behind the bar, hun? We'll lock this place up, so we don't get disturbed. Go ahead. We won't talk about anything important without you."

Anna was going to refuse his offer, but with perfect comic timing, her stomach let out a loud, long, low grumble. Garret laughed, and it was so warm and infectious that Anna found herself laughing, too.

thirteen

Anna snapped awake with a gasp. She had dreamt of her mother stroking her hair, but she awoke to a world that was dark and unfamiliar. Looking around with sleep-swollen eyes, she started to figure out where she was. Sitting alone, memories drifted back. Exhausted, after eating half a tuna sandwich—the other half was still sitting on a plate next to her—she had put her head down on the bar and passed out. Although Teej and his old friend Garret had said it was completely safe here, she still chided herself for letting her defenses down so thoroughly. Even tired and strung out as she was, she had to be more careful. The Midnight Man probably didn't sleep.

Anna looked into the dark corners of the bar, but there was no one else around. It was completely silent. No sign of the chubby bartender or Teej or Garret. She was alone.

Unwilling to sit around while everyone else debated what their next step would be, she got unsteadily to her feet and wandered around the bar looking for any sign of where Teej and Garret had gone. She wanted to hear everything they had to say, especially if they were discussing her abilities or how she would fight Mott.

Anna moved around the side of the bar toward the back room. It was dark, and as she stumbled past a dusty sound stage and a mountain of tables and chairs haphazardly stacked at precarious angles, she felt sure this part of the bar was rarely used. The dust lay heavy and thick on the floor, but she could see footprints and she followed them. Each step she took led her further from the light, and a cold draft blew from the shadows.

There was something about the dark corner that made her want to retreat to the comfort of the light, but she forced herself onwards toward a door. It was made of wood, but it was perfectly flush with the wall, so it looked like it was painted on to the bricks. A heavy round brass knob, cold and unfriendly to the touch, made it feel like something she should stay away from. But she experienced that familiar tingle when she approached it.

With a shiver, Anna turned the handle and pushed open the door.

A cold wind slapped her face and forced her eyes closed. The ground rumbled beneath her feet, twisting her stomach in knots. When she managed to open her eyes again, she found herself looking out into a snowy blizzard.

Anna turned from the wind and started to close the door. She stopped herself. This was where she had to go. This was a Haze. Not malevolent like the Midnight Man's. This felt old and a little worn and a little melancholy. Teej and Garret were in here. Without her. She had to show them she was ready to join them. She had to go into the Haze.

Slowly turning back into the face of the wind and snow, she realized this was a portal of sorts. In this dark, basement bar, she had opened a door onto what looked like a Himalayan mountain. White flakes blew past her, settling on the wood floor and red leather seats in Maxine's Bar. Through that door, the white landscape stretched out to infinity. Huge mountains dominated the skyline through the drifting, swirling storm. The ground was mostly covered in snow too, but here in the valley, the coverage was lighter and she could make out loose brown patches of rock and dirt. The cold was biting, and as she considered what to do next, every part of her screamed to close the door and get back to the warm bar.

Stepping gingerly through the door, Anna saw an indistinct building at the foot of the nearest hill. Perhaps a wood cabin. Although obscured by the blizzard, it seemed like she could make it.

As she stepped past the doorway, she was startled—but in some ways not surprised—when it closed behind her. When she turned, it had disappeared completely. *If this was a movie, that's exactly what I would expect to happen.*

The door, and any trace of its existence, had been erased. Anna stood alone in a mountain valley, her frozen toes curling inside her sneakers. She wished she had her gloves with her. They had panda faces on them.

Trudging toward the cabin, she glanced backward once to see if the door would reappear. It did not. In its place, the valley spread as far behind her as it did ahead. She was in a whole other world. And she could feel the excitement again.

She had felt like this before; she recognized that peculiar tingle now. Her skin felt more sensitive; her cheeks were pinched, but the sun, though filtered through fog and snow, felt glorious on her face. The crispness of the environment made her feel cleaner, and the soft white snow was like powder, engulfing her feet with each step in a way that made her senses tingle.

The cabin wasn't far, but her progress was slow. Still, she was surprised by how much she didn't mind the journey. As she pushed on, the snow thinned a little and her steps lightened. By the time she got to the cabin, there was only an inch or two and patches of dirt and shoots of grass poked through the carpet of white. She walked up a few wooden steps and stood in front of a huge door framed by dripping icicles.

The windows were steamed with condensation, but she could see a warm, orange glow flickering from what seemed to be a fire. The snow outside the windows reflected the warm colors within.

She knocked on the door, but it was so solid that she barely made a sound. She knocked again harder, little flakes of black wood sticking to her red, frozen knuckles. A rustle of movement came from within.

Warmth and light flooded over her as the heavy door swung inwards. Without even looking at her, Teej walked back to an overstuffed armchair in front of an open fire.

"Well, come in then!" he called over his shoulder.

Closing the door behind her to keep the cold out, she stamped the snow off her feet onto the woolly rug and peeled off her cardigan. It was stiflingly warm inside, and the change from snow to extreme heat was making her hands and feet feel like they were burning. It felt amazing.

"Not cool. Making me walk through the snow was not cool."

Garret, reclining lazily in a seat opposite Teej at the fireplace, said, "Yeah, this asshole could have edited out the walk; made the cabin closer to the door."

Teej looked at him with exaggerated shock, as if he had been betrayed. "The walk through the snow is what makes the warm cabin at the end worthwhile!"

"No woman needs to first walk through a blizzard to enjoy an open fire," said Anna.

Garret clapped his hands together warmly. "That, my dear, is the smartest thing anyone in this room has said so far. Drink?"

She walked across the room and flopped onto a big, soft chair by the fire. The whole cabin smelled like cinnamon and booze and rosewood. On a small table by their side, a decanter with rich, golden liquid shined in the light of the open fire. She suspected it was whiskey, and when Garret passed a glass to her, the smell told her immediately that she was right. It smelled strong, and though she didn't normally drink spirits, she much preferred wine, she suspected this one time she might enjoy it. Taking a sip of the husky but surprisingly smooth liquid, she was happy to learn that she had been right.

Gazing around the cabin as she sipped the warming drink, she noticed how prosaic the decor was. It literally had a bearskin rug in front of the fire. The walls were bare wood, adorned with hunting trophies and heads of stuffed animals. A higher mezzanine area held a large double bed and—other than a door at the back that probably led to a bathroom—the cabin was open-planned. It was cozy, despite the gawping animal heads with black, beady eyes that made her mildly uncomfortable. It felt more like a film set than a real place. It was inauthentic in a way that was somehow comforting.

"Kill many of these animals yourself, Garret?" she teased.

"Not one, my dear. Wouldn't hurt a fly. I'm a drinker, not a fighter."

"And they were never really alive anyway," Teej interjected somewhat stiffly, deflating the joke.

Garret still smiled, but Teej frowned a little.

"So, what have we decided then? Do we have a plan?" she asked. She was keen to get started on something. Anything. Waiting seemed like torture. She wanted to go after the Midnight Man and the rest of the Doxa, even if it was dangerous.

"Oh, he has a plan," said Garret. "He just doesn't think you're up to it."

She snapped a look at Teej that made him put his hands out in supplication.

"It's not that I don't think you can do it," he placated. "It's just that I think it's too dangerous."

"What is this plan?" she asked.

Teej looked away. Garret turned to her and said earnestly, "The plan is that he uses you as bait, and you just kill the Midnight Man yourself. The plan is that you're ready for this and Mott thinks you're not. So, that gives you the upper hand."

"A *plan* must mean something different to you people," said Anna.

Teej was about to respond, but before he could, Anna said, "But, I'll do it."

Garrett smiled. "That's my girl!"

Teej looked worried. "Oh, why did you have to say yes so fast?"

fourteen

In the secret cabin behind the secret door in the nondescript basement bar, the dancing flames of an open fire flickered across three faces. Anna and Teej and Garret talked all night long, drinking slowly, listening intently. When Anna spoke, her words were slow and deliberate, her revelations tightly rationed. She didn't want to give away more than she had to. Why did they care about her past? It was irrelevant.

While she parried their questions, they were forthright with their own answers. Teej and Garret explained so much. They explained how this little cabin was a remnant from a Dreamer's Haze made long ago that hadn't faded because it was small and few people knew about it. They explained that by letting her come here, the Haze would collapse sooner and they would be left with a simple storage room in Maxine's Bar instead of an enchanted portal to another world. And they discussed how they only came here when they needed to talk seriously.

As the fire burned down to embers, the moments of silence between them grew longer. Each of them lost in thought. Garret rested his head on one hand and wore a wan smile. Teej swirled his whiskey, the flickering shadows highlighting the frown lines around his mouth. Anna perched on the end of her chair and fidgeted with her ring, unsure where the conversation should go next.

"I like it here," she said finally.

"Me too," replied Garret. "I've brought lots of nice ladies here."

"Ewww," said Anna.

Teej rolled his eyes. "He hasn't. He's just trying to get a rise out of you."

Garret chuckled.

"Remember last time we met here?" asked Teej.

Garret nodded slowly. "When the Doxa first formed."

"Who are they?" asked Anna.

"They are a problem," replied Teej. "The Doxa is a loose coalition of Dreamers aligned by their similar ideologies. They all want to *birth* a new god or make someone *into* a new god or *elect* a new god. Always with the gods. They think a new god will fix everything: create new Dreamers, make more Hazes, fix world poverty, make internet commenters be nice to each other. They're insane."

"So after we face the Midnight Man, then what?"

Teej frowned but didn't answer.

"Problems for another time," interjected Garret. "These Dreamers wax and wane in power and influence. Right now, we worry about Mott because he's the one that's after your pretty little head."

She shot him an angry look but it evaporated when she saw his smile. He was teasing again. She rolled her eyes and smiled back.

As the firewood crackled and popped and burned low, Anna felt ready. "Do we go now?"

"No," said Teej. "You need to rest. Then tomorrow we need to train."

"I slept at the bar."

"That was…" He checked his watch. "Almost eight hours ago."

The time had gone too fast. Anna wasn't tired. Not at all. She just wanted to get home and confront her enemies. The Doxa and the Midnight Man. She folded her arms across her chest.

"Well, you can do what you like," said Teej, "but I need to sleep."

He stood, and as he walked up the creaky wooden stair to the mezzanine above them, he called back, "Don't stay up all night listening to his old man stories. Big day tomorrow."

"Night, night, insane person," she shouted after him.

Anna put her head down for a moment to think about what to say. When she looked up at Garret, she was struck by how old the man looked in the firelight. The dying flames cast long shadows over his face and made the wrinkles around his eyes deeper and darker. He looked grizzled, and he was looking at her intently. He seemed to be waiting for Teej to get out of ear-shot before he spoke.

"Well, lady," he said. "You have some big challenges ahead. And you're ready for them; I can see that. I just wonder why you're so ready."

She opened her mouth to say something, but he spoke over her.

"I can tell when someone is keeping secrets. Oh, I don't need to know what they are. Don't say anything to me. I doubt you would tell me the truth, anyway. But there's a reason you're so keen to go into danger. Right? There's a reason you're so ready for your old view of the world to be ripped away. You're trying to escape. From some…pain or other."

He slowly swirled the whiskey in his glass as he spoke, and she was happy to listen. She looked deeply into the flames and refused to think about the burning letter. She was glad he wasn't pressing her. There was a distance in the way he spoke. Like he was reading a story from an old book about someone else. It put her at ease.

Rubbing his eyes, Garret went on. "I guess Donnel knows that. He either knows what pain you have and why, or he doesn't care. Hope it's the first one. I hope he believes that being Behind the Veil will help you, because going into Hazes is a great way to forget, but it only makes you forget the details, not the pain. The pain stays.

"It's not as complicated as it seems. You know? That's what I told him and what I'll tell you. Only two things ever happen in this world. Things change or things stay the same.

"You're a good girl, and you're strong. You'll see that tomorrow. When he trains you to gauge your strength, he's going to be surprised. In your bones, you know what you can do. Sometimes the ash catches a spark and sometimes the flame splutters back to life."

Garret was lost in his own reverie. His eyes were closed now, and he spoke like she wasn't there. Like he was reciting the lyrics to an old song. She guessed he enjoyed the sound of his own voice.

"We're all embers now, Anna. The time of Dreamers and Metiks is running out. All the big battles are over. But even embers can burn up.

"I can tell you what will happen next. Listen to me closely now, hun. You're going to learn a lot. He's going to tell you more about the Metiks and Dreamers—about being an Undreamer. He's going to prepare you for the things you'll face. You're going to learn so much after this point. And go to places beyond your wildest dreams.

"But it doesn't matter where you go or who you fight. Even if he doesn't see it in your eyes, I do. We both know what's really happening here. You don't care about me or Teej or Dreamers. You're just running. You think because you're not looking backward, you're going forward. But you're still killing yourself; you're just doing it slowly. Instead of jumping out a hundred-story building, you're jumping out the first story a hundred times."

Anna shook her head. She didn't want to talk about her past. It made her feel that cold dread again, stretching across the small of her back and up over her shoulders then curling around her neck. As if the coldness was coming from inside her, and spreading out, because inside she was already dead. *Desolation*.

"And the thing no one is telling you is how dangerous *you* are. Neither a Metik nor a Dreamer, none of them can cause as much damage to you as you can to them. You think your pain burns you? Your pain will burn *them* and burn the *world* and burn us *all*. Burns us out."

Garret opened his eyes and looked right at her and said, "What nonsense, eh? Just tell me to shut my trap when I ramble on like that. I am quite drunk...Anna. Yes, that's your name! You see, I don't normally allow myself to indulge in front of others. It's my weakness. Now, I must get some sleep. And I'm going to sleep right here, in this chair, right under your pretty nose. Whether you sleep or not is none of my concern."

He was smiling again, and she realized he really was rambling, but there was truth amongst the nonsense.

"Good night, Garret. I'll go sleep on the sofa in the back."

"You do that, girl. Leave an old man to his dreams."

He closed his eyes, and in seconds, he seemed to be asleep.

Gathering her jacket, Anna moved to the sofa and pulled a soft brown blanket from the back to cover herself. She didn't feel tired, but within moments of laying her head down, she was fast asleep.

fifteen

She awoke gently, her eyes opening by degrees. It took Anna a few moments to realize where she was, but her sleep had been restful. She'd dreamt of floating along.

As she stood, she noticed that her blanket seemed more threadbare and frayed than the night before. Lifting it to her face, she could see it was full of holes and was falling apart. It had grown thin, and the sofa was falling apart, too. Last night in the light of the fire, it had seemed plump and soft, but now it was patchy and the cushions had burst and split. She could see through the stuffing to the rusty, metal springs.

Walking to the blackened, dead embers of the fire, she sensed the whole cabin had changed around her. Everything was in the same place but faded and layered in dust. The whole building looked dilapidated. Even the animal heads that hung on the walls were emaciated—rotten patches showed the skeletons beneath the skin. The comfortable armchair that Garret had fallen asleep in was veiled in cobwebs, and the rotted wooden legs looked ready to collapse.

Anna stumbled to the back of the room then to the front again, noticing the rot and decay as she went. Mustiness and mold filled her nostrils. Was this because of her?

She decided to look for Garret and Teej outside.

The door creaked open on rusted hinges. The wood was heavy with damp and rot and almost fell out of the frame. She maneuvered it slowly and closed it carefully after her, moving outside into the gloom. The chill hit her immediately. She saw Teej sitting on the wooden steps, looking out into a sea of impenetrable mist.

The snow had melted, and the cloudy sky now resembled a solid sheet of gray concrete. The crispness of the air and the fresh wind were long gone. In its place was an uncomfortable humidity that saturated her, as if she were *inside* a raincloud. The air smelled stale, like an old garage or storeroom. The mountains in the distance were no longer visible. In fact, very little of the beautiful landscape from the day before could be seen now. In its place was an oppressive fog that hung like a heavy wet blanket. In any direction, Anna couldn't see more than a hundred feet.

"What's happening, Teej?" she asked.

"It won't last long now," he replied. "Every Haze must fade, and this one's time is long overdue. Did you sleep well?"

His gray-green eyes looked out at the grim horizon. He seemed sad.

"Yeah, I did. Weird dreams, but why is everything changing so fast?"

Words hung on his lips for a second. "It's because of you. Well, because of the three of us, but mainly you. All these Hazes get broken down by Banille eventually. This one was very strong, and it lasted a long time because it was hidden. With only me and Garret coming, it faded slowly, but with three of us, it accelerated. And you're an Undreamer, so the Banille you exert is very high."

"Banille?"

"It's the force that erodes the Haze and brings us back to Basine."

119

"And is it like a *gas* or something? Tell me what it's made of!"

"It's nothing. I mean it is *literally* nothing. You know when there's a vacuum and that creates low pressure and the high pressure pushes against it? Banille is like that. It's the push back from Basine. It makes the Haze collapse, and then Basine takes over and that's it. Unless you're Behind the Veil, you don't even notice, but for us, we feel the weight and we are affected by it."

"So, why do I exert more Banille than you?"

"You are an Undreamer, and I'm going to show you what that means right now."

She was ready. The oppressive fog and the fading beauty of this Haze had brought her mood down a little, but when Teej spoke about testing her, she felt her resolve harden again. She was ready to face his challenges.

"Where's Garret?" she asked.

"He had to go. Probably for a long time. It's just us now."

She walked in front of Teej and breathed deliberately and slowly. She nodded. "I'm ready."

He sprung to his feet and clapped his hands together eagerly, startling her. "Okay, then! Look behind you."

Anna turned to see nothing, then the nothing was replaced by outlines and shadows in the mist. They swirled to form human shapes, tall and indistinct. They weren't people.

"Uhh, Teej…what are these? More Night Collectors?"

He snorted. "No, these are much older. And fainter. Leftover Etunes from a long dead Dreamer. Dangerous, but vulnerable to our abilities."

The creatures were getting closer now. Anna wanted to hide behind Teej for protection, but that wasn't the point of this test.

Through the cold mist, arms and legs formed from wisps and whorls of fog. She could see the creatures more clearly now. The first thing that she noticed was their knees bent the wrong way, like animals. They walked upright, but their gait wasn't human. Lumbering and heavy, their upper bodies were huge and heavily muscled. Long arms scraped the ground even when they stood. And they were fuzzy, or more like hairy. Their faces were elongated and...

"Teej..." Anna's voice rose in her chest, "are those wolves?"

She wanted to say "werewolves," but the word wouldn't come out of her throat. It sounded too ridiculous.

"Le Meneur de Loups. With the cabin and the mist, they just...made sense. And they were present here when the Aesthete made this place. Among many other creatures. And now they're coming to kill us, so how will you stop them?"

She sensed eagerness in his voice. He had been looking forward to this, but she could also hear the tension when he spoke. To test her, he had put them both in danger. With growing dread, Anna realized the swirls in the mist *were* werewolves, whether the term seemed silly or not. Prowling and slavering as they came, the pack closed rank and advanced. The closest ones were almost completely visible now, while more formed in the distance.

She turned to face the nearest one. Red eyes, a long, hairy snout and teeth. So many teeth, long, sharp and dripping with clear saliva. They snapped and clacked at the air. Suddenly, her peril started to feel very real. These creatures were about to rip her apart. Huge claws swung loosely at the side of the closest wolf, ready to tear open her soft belly and eat whatever spilled out.

Anna had to do something. Some instinct in her head said "weapon." But what weapon? Could she make one appear? Was there one nearby?

There was no time. The closest werewolf was on her. She tried to back away and bumped into Teej behind her. Coming toward him from the opposite direction was another wolf. It was a single leap away from them. Any second now, both wolves would jump forward, and their dirty yellow claws would open her up and her wet insides would splash on the ground. They snarled and spat at her. Pure terror weakened her knees.

Why had Teej done this to her? He hadn't given her enough time. There was no plan. She was going to be killed right here before she even knew what was happening. She didn't have time to look at him. The moment she looked away, the creature would attack. An intense desire to curl into a ball swept over her, and for a moment, she felt like she might give up.

As the nearest wolf crouched low to pounce, she made her decision. She would do something—anything. She allowed her instincts to take over. Anger and defiance built inside her. If she was going to die here, it was going to be walking forward. Walking *into* danger, not backing away from it like a frightened little girl.

She stepped forward and held her arm out, not as a blow, but as a gesture. As her hand came up in front of her face, she saw her silver ring. It glinted in the low light, hinting at its hidden potential; a potential that she recognized instinctively but didn't yet understand. She walked two more steps toward the beast, pushing through her own fear and pain, and for a moment, their gaze locked. As she stared into that red, glassy eye, she hit upon a revelation: there was no life in this thing. No mind behind the eyes and no heart within; it had no soul. The creature was all exterior, and its existence required her acceptance.

And now it was standing still. In fact, as she continued forward, the creature was starting to pull away from her. Instead of crouching, it was cowering; ears down, eyes wide with its face pulled back. She skipped forward—her steps light and swift—and caught it off guard. Her hand hit wet fur. She wanted to recoil, but she didn't. As her fingers brushed the wolf's maw, she said plainly, "Fire."

It took a second, and then the flames sparked and burned quickly, like a flash of gunpowder, accompanied by a lick of black smoke. There was a howl of pain—a monstrous, inhuman sound that startled her. She had caused that pain. That both frightened and exhilarated her.

The beast scrambled back, a small patch of fire spreading across its face. Pawing and scratching at the flames, the wolf seemed confused at first. A rush of heat and light bounced off Anna as the creature conflagrated suddenly, and within seconds, its whole head and shoulders were ablaze in a bright orange-blue flame. It danced in the flame, casting ghastly, flickering shadows as it clawed at the air and the sky uselessly. Thick, black, sweet-smelling smoke rose into the night, swirling and mixing with the mist, obscuring the raging beast.

On the ground, it thrashed and howled, struggling to put out the flames. It burned steadily; the flames were inexorable. Though horrified, Anna watched silently, unmoving.

The wolves formed a circle around Anna and Teej, but the circumference was widening. They backed off now, giving out low moans of sadness and confusion, their heads bowed low. They wailed and wailed into the night. Anna turned quickly to see that from behind Teej, two more closed in. They no longer looked like werewolves though. They sunk back into themselves, their pelts shrinking as their spines snapped forward so they were no longer upright. They fell to all fours as their faces stretched. Shorn of their supernatural forms, they had become simple wolves once more. Still terrifying, but vulnerable and manageable and something she could fight.

With a surge of adrenaline, Anna ran at the wolves. Reveling in her newfound power and wanting to protect Teej, she accepted that she had nothing to fear from these creatures. Her fear gave way to elation.

"My fire burns!" she screamed as her arm shot out, her will focused and magnified through her ring. A faint aura of blue-red light seemed to engulf her hand, and an old wooden tree stump next to the nearest wolf burst into flames. The wolves backed off with their heads bowed. The pack let out a low moan in chorus, then one by one, they turned and fled. Their tails bobbed as they lopped into the mist. They looked almost comically small as they ran off into the night.

Her body filled with righteous fury as she screamed, "I am not afraid of you!" They were gone in moments, the mist swallowing them completely.

Teej gestured for calm. "Anna, they're gone. You can stop."

His voice cut through her screams. Had she been screaming? She hadn't realized. He walked slowly toward her and touched her shoulder. "They're gone. We're safe now."

She slowly lowered her hand, and though the ring glowed warmly on her finger, the flame inside her was cooling. She'd never felt anything like this before, but she remembered the feeling. It was like he was teaching her lessons she already knew.

All around them the world was fading. The color was draining—desaturating—and it was getting darker. It was like all the stars in the universe were blinking out one by one. As she turned to look into Teej's gentle eyes, the light faded completely. She could see nothing at all now. They stood together in the empty blackness, Teej's hand on her shoulder. Anna wanted to put her arms around him...but hesitated.

Instead, she looked up at the black space where she guessed his face was. She tried to make sense of his words and articulate her own discovery, her mouth making shapes but no sound. But before she could voice her thoughts, the door slowly fell open. Light flooded in from Maxine's Bar, stinging her eyes. As An-

124

na's sight adjusted, she looked around the cluttered storeroom, so normal after everything she'd seen and done. Reaching out to steady herself, she knocked over a mop that clattered across the floor. Teej reached out to support her, and they stepped over the mess in the doorway and back into the bar.

"Well, I would call that a passing grade," he said. He seemed calm and was trying to reassure her, but she noticed his hands shaking.

Meanwhile, Anna shivered from head to foot. Exhilarated and terrified, she still managed to reply, "B Minus?"

He smiled in relief. In a mock teacher voice, he said, "Anna's work shows promise, but she tends to be overdramatic."

She managed a little laugh. "What? That was…effective. Right?"

"'My fire burns?'"

"It…seemed like the right thing to say at the time."

He laughed. "Okay, let's go get some breakfast and a coffee. Then some feedback."

She nodded. "I'll work on my one-liners."

Behind the bar, Teej meticulously leveled off the coffee with the back of a spoon before setting the filter on the machine. Turning away from him, Anna looked out the high window as the morning sun peeked through in thin shafts from the outside world. Commuters hustled past on their way to work, casting long shadows across the room. She was glad the doors were locked and no one else would walk in. She was also glad the barman from earlier seemed to have left. They had a lot to talk about.

"You're one of those guys, aren't you? You're one of those guys that are really fussy about coffee."

"Life is too short for drinking bad coffee, reading bad books, and sexing bad sex."

"Could there be less philosophizing and more coffee please? I need it to human."

He brought two steaming mugs over, carrying them carefully and setting them down in front of her. Walking around the bar, he sat next to her. She took a sip and immediately spat it out.

"Jesus, Teej! What's your secret ingredient? Lava? This is hotter than the sun."

"Oh, you're one of those," he responded.

"One of those what?"

"People who drink cold coffee. Also known as *monsters*!"

"Well, I like coffee that doesn't strip the flesh from my mouth, yes!"

He looked like he was going to argue with her, then changed his mind, gave up and sighed. She cupped the mug in her hands to keep her warm even though it wasn't cold in the bar. The memory of the gray, fading Haze she had just escaped still chilled her.

Teej looked like he didn't know what to say next. He started to talk, stopped himself, and then started again in a conciliatory tone. "When you've experienced a lot of Hazes, tasted every amazing food, drank every legendary drink, and experienced just about every sensation a person can experience, you get picky about stuff. Stuff like coffee. And where you go. And *who* you choose to go with you."

She nodded and smiled. He went on, "So I guess we should talk about what happened in that Haze. About what you can do. I should tell you how you can help me. What you actually *are*."

She tried to hold back her questions and let him talk, but she couldn't help herself. "Was all of that *real*? Could those wolves hurt us?"

He sighed, but his weariness didn't seem to come from her question. Rather, he didn't seem to know where to start with his explanation. He stroked his fine stubble as he answered, "Yes. Absolutely, yes. That's the thing about Hazes, Anna. They're not separate from reality. They *are* reality. Everything that happens in a Haze is *real*. Everything that happens in a Haze actually *happens*."

"Hazes are essential. They are as fundamental an element of nature as clouds or the sea or air. Hazes give Basine light and life and fill it with possibility. And no matter what type of Haze is created, whether it's full of joy or some horrifying thing made of nightmares, it will *cleanse*. Hazes aren't by definition happy or sad, dangerous or safe, good or evil. They're like nature. Savage and cruel but also beautiful and essential. Without Hazes, possibility and imagination and eventually, even life would fade. Well, that's what I think anyway."

"You're a romantic," commented Anna, "but I don't see the world that way. This all seems so pointlessly dangerous. Werewolves and Midnight Men and all sorts of monsters don't need to exist. They don't make the world better. They certainly haven't improved *my* life."

"It must seem that way," he admitted. "And when Hazes go away and we go back to the world without werewolves and Midnight Men and secret passages to fairytale lands, the changes don't go away. They're re-assimilated. If someone dies in a Haze, they're dead. If a house collapses or a car crashes, well the house really *did* collapse and the car really *did* crash. Maybe when Basine reestablishes itself some details will be different, maybe not. The change between the Haze and Basine can cut and shape reality with no consideration for the damage caused.

"And no one can protect you from that. You're not going to get help from the police. When Hazes take away someone you love, the world doesn't care. There are no Dreamers in jail. Aesthetes don't go on trial. That's why Hazes that Spiral out of control are so dangerous. Many people can die."

Anna listened intently. Some of this was making sense, but so much was still unclear. She asked, "So, if I'm killed in a Haze…like Sue…there's no way to come back?"

"No. It's all *real*. If you get shot or stabbed or strangled in a Haze, then you're done. You're still thinking like Hazes are dreams. They're not. They're just possibility spaces. They're moments in time and space where things can happen that normally can't.

"In a Haze, most people's fate lies in the hands of the Dreamer. Their Art—whether sewing, singing, painting, dancing, writing, sculpting, acting—creates the Haze. And that Haze is a whole world *they* control. Unless you are Behind the Veil, there is nothing you can do to protect yourself in there. Nothing.

"But the rules are different for us. For me and you. You have a power inside you that's connected very closely with Basine. You can break down Hazes. We both can. But Metiks abilities are focused on change. Adaptation. Metiks can take command of the Haze and bend it to our will. Your abilities are more…destructive."

Her mind struggled to take in everything he was saying. She sipped her coffee. He waited for her next question. She considered for a moment what to ask.

"So, can I create Hazes? How do I use my powers? What is my art? I can't even draw. Even my handwriting is terrible."

Teej shook his head. "Anna, you're not a Dreamer. You can't make Hazes. You're a Metik like me. And something more."

She waited for him to explain.

"I thought maybe Garret told you last night. Do you understand what a Metik can do? You've heard the word a few times now, right? We can't make Hazes, but we can change them.

Adapt them to suit our own needs. We shape other people's dreams. Reconfigure the worlds they make. Sometimes we break our power down into the four elements: *the Will, the Word, the Sight, and the Sword.* In time, you will learn all four.

"But you're a Metik and something else, too. You're an Undreamer. You don't adapt or create things in Hazes. You break them down. You destroy them."

An Undreamer. She was an Undreamer. "I'm not sure I want to be an Undreamer, Teej."

"Too bad. You are one. No one knows how Undreamers come to be or why some people have those powers and others don't. Certainly there are theories, but those are for another time. For now, all that matters is there are very few Undreamers in the world. Maybe just one. And you're a threat to a lot of Dreamers. They'll hate you for what you are, and what you can do to them.

"Together we can achieve so much. I told you before that Metiks always work in pairs. One to control the Haze and one to fight the Dreamer. Attack and defense. Sword and shield. And an Undreamer is…well an Undreamer is a really sharp sword.

"You have to understand, Anna, the time that I saved you wasn't normal; it was all backward. I won't be the one that saves you. You'll be the one that saves me."

So, she was an Undreamer, a destroyer of Hazes and a protector of Teej. A knot twisted in her stomach. "Am I just supposed to fight the Midnight Man? That's the whole plan?"

He tried to protest. "No, it's not just that. I stabilize the Haze so you can face him on even footing. Then when it's just you and him—"

"That's fine," she cut him off. "I'll fight him." Anna stood up. "Now? Should we go now?"

He waved at her to sit down. "Easy there, little warrior. Drink your lava. I still have more to explain. The better prepared you are, the better our chances."

She sat down. "Just tell me how to fight him. How to hurt him."

He nodded resolutely. "I will teach you how to survive."

They sat in silence for a moment, and as he sipped his coffee she worked up the courage to ask him, "Teej, do you want to know anything about me? About my past?"

He paused for a second. Taking a sip of his own coffee, he shook his head. "No, I don't need to know anything."

She nodded expressionlessly. Garret had been right. He didn't care.

sixteen

Teej and Anna walked through the quiet heart of the city, two twilight ghosts, unseen and untouched. The morning was solemn, the sky and the buildings and the streets all shaded from a gray palette. The rain had stopped for now, but the clouds threatened more any moment. Anna's skin bristled in the cold, and she thrust her hands deep inside her pockets to protect them from the chilly morning air.

They walked past the bars and clubs and through the park toward her apartment. As they walked through trees and past fountains, the streetlights started to go off one by one. Anna stopped next to a heavy iron park bench and waited for Teej to realize he was walking alone. He turned and waved at her to follow, but she didn't move.

"Sit. Talk to me." She didn't like following him. She didn't like that he knew what was happening all the time, and she didn't like how few decisions she was making. So, she decided they would sit.

"We don't have time."

"Why not?"

He looked up thoughtfully. "Well…"

"You have nothing."

He shrugged. "Okay, I guess you're right. There used to be a troll that lived in the park, but it's long gone. We should be safe here."

Anna narrowed her eyes as Teej sat next to her. "When you say things like that, are you teasing me or teaching me?"

"Absolutely both."

They sat in silence for a moment. Teej shuffled closer to her. She thought for a moment he might put an arm around her, so she slid away. Rubbing her hands together, she pushed her shoulders up to her ears to try to keep the cold out. She wanted to get walking again, but having made them stop, she didn't know how to say it. Instead, she quizzed him some more.

"The Word, the Will, the Sight and the Sword. Tell me about those."

He coughed nervously like she had put him on the spot. "Yes. Yes, of course," he said stiffly, his voice changing subtly. His teacher voice.

"Well, you already know about the Word. The voice of a Metik carries weight inside a Haze. It can accomplish much when it is augmented with the Will. If you are resolute enough, you can command those within a Haze to do your bidding.

"And the Sight will come with practice and time. Haze Sense lets us differentiate real people from Etunes and Basine from Haze, and it helps us find The Dreamer. Their appearance inside The Haze is obfuscated. Only a Metik can locate them when they are hidden.

"And your Haze Sense will help you greatly outside Hazes, too. You will be able to sense and detect the afterglow of Hazes and spot Dreamers and Idylls and Muses and Vig. By tuning in your senses, you'll be able to determine where Dreamers are using the Art. You'll sense what they've touched and changed. It will help you find truth. You already use it more than you know.

132

It must become more than intuition though. In time, it will supersede your eyes or ears."

"And the Sword?" she asked. "I would like a sword."

"It's not an actual sword," said Teej with a smile. "Or not for most Metiks. It's a… thing. A tool. It's different for everyone. Sometimes it's a weapon, but it's always something simple. And we focus our will through it. The proper name for it is our Periapt. Every Metik needs one."

"And what's your Periapt?" she asked.

"When you see it, you'll know we're in trouble."

Anna nodded slowly. They sat in silence for a moment as she looked across the park. The rain was starting to fall again, and an old woman hustled past them with her dog, struggling with an umbrella. As Anna watched the old woman fight her way through the morning gloom, she came to a realization.

"I believe you, Teej. I think…I believe you. But even when I decide to accept all this, none of it *feels* real. I don't feel like Sue is really dead. I don't feel like I'm about to fight a monster called the Midnight Man."

"That's good," he said, surprising her. "Disbelieving Aesthetes is the first step to fighting them, but reality isn't consensual. You can't fight a Dreamer by disbelieving them. You must make a new reality then believe in that new reality more. Your abilities work best when they begin within the narrative of the Dreamer, then diverge as you wrest away control. The effects you achieve are based on the setting of the Haze, but then you rewrite their narrative. That's how you beat them. That's how you win."

"Well, that sounds just great," she said with a shrug. "How do I actually do that?"

He turned and looked into her eyes. "You already know. You've already done it. Twice. You've used the Word. You've set a wolf on fire. You have the skills. You just need to develop

133

them. You need to learn those lessons so well that your bones remember."

Anna put her hands on her thighs, pushed herself to her feet and stretched out. "Okay. Let's go then."

As Anna unlocked her apartment and pushed the door open slowly, she was unsure what she expected to find. Once she was inside, the first thing she thought about wasn't the potential danger of being there, but the mess she had left when she had run out. Rushing into the bedroom to tidy away some clothes and make the bed, she shouted to Teej:

"Make yourself at home; sorry about the mess! I've actually been really tidy recently."

She heard him walk into the living room as she scooped up armfuls of laundry and threw them in the wardrobe before slamming the door closed. She quickly spread the bed, and as she was about to return to Teej, she spotted some of her underwear on the floor. She grabbed it in a panic, threw it in the wardrobe, too, then came through to see if he was okay.

"So, what's the plan? Oh, can I make you another coffee?"

"Yes, coffee would be great. The plan? Well…"

She darted into the kitchen, brushing bread crumbs off the counters and rinsing out two cups. A sickly-sweet smell wafted from the trash, which had been sitting in the apartment for too long. Tying the bag off, she ran into the corridor and out the front door to throw it down the trash chute. "One second!" she called as she dashed past him.

"Relax, Anna, no need to panic. It's much tidier than last time."

Sure, she was a slob sometimes, but she also never let anyone in her house to see it. She was back in the kitchen in a flash, and as she filled the kettle, she shouted questions at Teej sitting nervously on the edge of the sofa in the other room. "Are we safe here? I mean, he's calling himself 'the Midnight Man.' Does he *have* to come at Midnight? He won't suddenly become the Five Thirty-five Man, will he?"

"No, he can come at any time, but he won't. He'll come for you tonight. It's how his power works. If he doesn't live up to his name, he will lose his momentum. He generates his Vig by writing about murder at midnight, so he needs to stick to that, or he won't be powerful enough to face you. Hey, Anna, can I use your bathroom?"

"Yeah," she called back "The first door on the right."

She heard him close the door, and as she waited for the kettle to boil, she turned the radio on. She grimaced, cycling through the channels trying to find music that didn't put her teeth on edge. Eventually, she settled on the news. She was amazed at the inane headlines. *How could the world go on like normal after everything she had seen?*

"I can't find a towel," shouted Teej from the bathroom.

"They're in the cabinet above the sink," she called back.

She turned up the volume on the radio so she wouldn't hear him splashing around and went back to chewing her nails as she waited for the kettle to boil

"*MIDNIGHT MAN CLAIMS TWO MORE VICTIMS,*" the deep voice echoing through the speakers pulled her from her reverie.

"Oh, God," she whispered. She picked the radio up and held it to her ear.

Teej came through a few seconds later, throwing his jacket on the sofa and rolling up his sleeves as he walked. As soon as he saw her, he stopped. "What's wrong?"

"I checked the news. It's just a habit."

"What happened?"

135

"Twice more."

He looked shocked and saddened. "Oh, no. His Hazes are getting more powerful. His legend is bleeding into Basine. Fame and renown in the real world will make him more dangerous. We have to stop this."

Anna felt breathless. Her head was spinning. "Stop it? Why didn't we save those two women? Instead, we were hiding out in a bar."

He turned away from her, and for some reason, it made her angrier.

"Can you explain to me again why I'm the one who has to stop him? I didn't ask for any of this!"

Teej rubbed his chin and looked off into the middle distance. Lost in his own thoughts, she felt her rage build. He wasn't even listening to her.

"Teej! What is happening?"

He shook his head and walked away from her toward the window. Leaning on the sill, he stared out.

Anna swallowed the lump forming in her throat, finally ready to ask a question that frightened her. "Where is your partner? Metiks fight in pairs, so why don't you have a partner already?"

He shook his head again but didn't turn.

"Teej…who is Linda?"

He turned to her now, his eyes glassy. "I could…I could tell you the truth, or I could tell you a version of the truth that would make me sound better."

"The truth," she snapped. Two more women were dead, and she and Teej were drinking coffee and joking around. And Teej still wouldn't give her straight answers.

Teej looked down as he spoke. "The truth is, I can't help you. When I faced the Doxa last time, I lost someone. My partner. The Haze Spiraled, and she was…gone. I can't go into a

Haze and fight again. Not him. Not so soon. The ghost of that loss—he would use it to control me. That's what happened at the mall. I couldn't stop him. I'm tired and *beaten*. You are the one that must stop him, because he doesn't expect *anything* from you. He is still weakened from our fight, and he's not thinking straight. He will misjudge you. It will throw him off."

Anna took a moment to process what he had said. He had thrown her off balance. "He killed your partner? Was this not something you perhaps could have *mentioned*?"

His head was still down. She pressed him, "Am I just here to help you get back at someone? Is that why you found me in the first place? You want me to kill your enemies, and you won't even help. Is…is this just about revenge for you?"

He looked up thoughtfully for a second, then said carefully, "Not…only revenge."

She shook her head. She understood. "You should have told me this, Teej. If he has killed your partner, what chance do I have? She was trained. I have no idea what I'm even doing."

"You're more ready than Linda was. He took us by surprise. And he wasn't alone. He wasn't the one who killed her, but he *contributed*."

"Who killed her then?" Anna asked.

"There are three main members of the Doxa. And we were betrayed by another Metik, too. He was supposed to help. Or stay out of the way. His name was Wildey. But that's not important right now."

Anna's hands curled into fists. "Not important right now? Teej, there is so much you don't tell me. Even now. Isn't there? Isn't there?"

Heat spread across her face. He had said he wouldn't lie to her, but he left so much out. He didn't trust her with the truth. Even now, even with her friend dead, he wouldn't be honest with her. He would always hold things back from her. *Never play their game…*

Anna could see her words stung him, but she hardened her heart. She could do that. He wouldn't help her anyway. He would leave her alone. It was what always happened. She was always the one that faced her problems alone.

"I don't want it to be like this, Anna. I don't want to leave things out. I just—"

"Maybe it would be better if you left. I have to do this myself anyway. I must fight him. You said yourself that you can't help me. I don't want you to save me. I never want *anyone* to save me."

He put his arms out in exasperation but couldn't find any words. He was ashamed, but she was furious. Two more women: dead. Her friend: dead. Linda: dead. And now she was next, and he couldn't even help her. Couldn't even tell her the truth.

"Get out, Teej."

He tried to protest, "Anna, we need to—"

"OUT!" she screamed as she fought back tears. Sue was gone. Those young women. She didn't even know their names. They were gone forever, and Teej had done nothing to stop this killer. *Desolation.*

He walked to the front door, and she followed him. He turned back to her. "I'll give you some time. You're safe for a little while. I'm…sorry."

He waited for her to say something, but she wouldn't look at him. As he left, Anna closed the door behind him. She stomped back into the kitchen. His coffee sat steaming on the counter. She poured it out, then when the mug was empty, she smashed it into the sink. It broke into three solid, chalky segments. Anna stormed into the living room, lay on the sofa, pulled a blanket over herself and started to cry.

seventeen

When the Midnight Man came, self-pity wouldn't help her, so in the late afternoon Anna crawled from under her blanket and tried to prepare. She wandered listlessly around her apartment for hours, looking into the corners of every room for some sign of an imminent attack. Teej had said she would be safe till midnight, but he had also said he would be back soon, and there was no sign of him. More lies.

She had to do this alone.

During the long evening, she had plenty of time to kill. The internet hadn't helped—searches for Undreamers and Metiks didn't return anything meaningful. Meanwhile, searching for the Midnight Man returned far too much information. Grisly photos of victims and lurid descriptions of his methods only served to unnerve her. She had gone from nervous to anxious to terrified to bored. Now she just wanted the fight to be over. The tension of waiting here helplessly was killing her. She needed something—*anything*—to happen.

Anna checked the clock. Eleven forty-seven.

Weapons were stashed all over the apartment in places where she could get them if she needed them. A kitchen knife under her mattress, a hammer between two books in the bookcase. She had even swung the hammer around, pretending she was fending off an invisible attacker. She'd watched a few videos online about self-defense and had perfected her technique for gouging eyes, pulling hair and kicking accurately and powerfully into an opponent's groin. She had no idea if any of this would help her, but she wanted to be prepared. And now he was due to arrive in just fifteen minutes.

Anna was boiling the kettle for her eleventh coffee of the day when the heavy thump on the door caused her to drop and break another mug. She jumped back from the broken pieces on the kitchen counter and froze in place. She wasn't ready. *He's early!*

She suddenly realized all her preparations had been for nothing. She had no idea what she was doing.

Skipping into the corridor, she stopped a few feet from the front door. She heard the thumping again, heavy and irregular.

"Anna, it's…me."

It was Teej, but he sounded strange. Anna rushed to the door and opened it, and he collapsed inwards. She tried to catch him, but he was too heavy and they fell together. He must have been leaning his whole body weight on the door.

"What happened?" asked Anna as she wriggled out from under him.

He groaned and rolled over, then went still. As Anna tried to rise, she put a hand to the back of his head and recoiled as her fingers touched something wet and sticky. She cautiously touched him again, her hand moving across the back of his skull. With horror, she felt something come loose. Blood ran through the spaces between her fingers as she cradled him. He started to twitch and spasm.

Struggling to her feet, Anna supported his head as best she could and turned him over. She stood and managed to get him to lie in the recovery position—or something like it. As she crouched over him, she realized that outside the front door and across the hall there was another man. Not a man, a boy in a tracksuit. He was shouting to her in a frantic voice.

"Miss! Hey lady! He got attacked. These three guys came at him, and they pushed me down the stairs. They were from the gang that hangs out at the park. I thought they wanted money, but they just started beating on him. I tried to help him fight, but I was hurt. So he punched one, then the other came behind and he punched that one. Then they all jumped on him and got him up, then he knocked one down. And then he was up again, and he beat them up really bad, then they started to win again, then—"

"Shush!" she chided the boy. His rambling helped her come back to her senses. "Are you okay?"

The boy looked himself up and down. "Yeah, I'm fine. I deliver menus, and I was just here and—"

"Okay, go home kid. I'm glad you're okay."

"Please help him, lady."

"I'll help him; don't worry. I'll get an ambulance. Now you get back home."

The boy ran off, and she was left with Teej in a collapsed heap in her hallway. She didn't know what to do. Surely, she had to call an ambulance? She tried to look at his head wound, but all she could see was blood. Too much blood. He could die from this wound.

As well as the sticky, gory mess on the back of his head, his face was swollen and bruised. His nose was bleeding, and one of his cheeks was cut. He was dirty and mangled and some of his clothes had been torn. He looked like he'd been run over. The knuckles of both his hands were badly bruised, too. It must have been a hell of a fight.

"What should I do, Teej? We need to get you help. What happened?" She didn't expect him to respond, but he did.

141

"No time. He's….coming. No Wildey, not soon…Linda's dead? Rayleigh's…can't remember."

He was delirious. Anna dragged him away from the door as best she could, closed it, then grabbed him again below the arms and pulled him into the bedroom, surprising herself with how strong she was. The adrenaline must have kicked in, because she managed to pick him up from the ground and dump him limply onto the bed. She knew she shouldn't be moving him, and she knew he needed an ambulance, but she wanted to get him away from danger. As she laid his hands on his chest and pulled out her phone, he managed to look at her. This time when his words came, they were clear. "No time…He was so scared of you…he sent them to burn the building. Hoped they'd…kill you in Basine. I waited outside the apartment. Did I do….okay?"

He had saved her.

After she sent him away, he had stayed the whole time. Mott had sent thugs to kill her rather than face her in a Haze, and Teej had fought them off. Now, because of that choice, he might die.

"Oh, Teej." Her heart was breaking. "You did great. You did amazing. Don't speak."

"Fought them off…All seven of them."

"Yes, you…The kid said there were three, Teej."

He chuckled, his chest rattling and a bubble of blood on his lips. "Felt like seven."

Grimacing in pain, he closed his eyes and was gone. She brushed the hair away from his face and looked at him gravely. He hadn't left her after all, and because the Midnight Man had come for her outside of a Haze, he had almost died for her.

Knock….Knock….Knock….Knock….Knock….Knock….

He was here. Anna had already dialed the number for the ambulance, but now the phone was dead in her hand. The outside world seemed to fall away. The edges of the room bled

142

color. She felt that faint glimmer—the shimmering, falling sensation that signaled that the Haze had begun.

It was him. It was midnight.

eighteen

KNock...Knock...Knock...
Knock...Knock...Knock...
Knock...Knock...Knock...Knock...Knock...Knock...

What if I just don't answer the door? Anna paced back and forth. She didn't have to play his game. She didn't have to be like the other women. This wasn't his world; it was hers. Her home. Anna didn't have to let him in.

There were about two seconds between each knock, and after each six knocks, there was a break of about ten seconds. Just long enough to make her think he had stopped. That he had gone away. Then it started again.

Knock...Knock...Knock...Knock...Knock...Knock...
Knock...Knock...Knock...Knock...Knock...Knock...

She found herself frozen in place, looking at her own front door, willing the monster outside to go away. He wouldn't stop knocking. Now, each time he knocked, the floor rumbled, too. Like an earthquake. That tremor that always came when a Haze began.

He would never go away. He was there to kill her, and he absolutely would not stop.

She shouted directly at him this time. "No more!"

The knocking stopped. Anna took a step closer to the door, waiting for it to start again. Was that it? Had she stopped him in his tracks? Was it so simple? Maybe he was like a vampire; he couldn't come in unless she invited him.

From the other room, she heard a phone ring. The old-fashioned dial type of phone. Anna didn't have one of those.

Slowly backing away from the front door while keeping her eyes forward, she walked into her familiar living room and saw next to the sofa an unfamiliar, chunky, red telephone. The kind you would see on old TV shows. The kind she had seen in the purple desert. And it wasn't just the phone that had changed. Though her apartment looked the same, everything *felt* different. The air was cool and dry. The colors were more vibrant. She felt exposed.

The ringing echoed around the room, and the sound was more clear and resonant than anything she had ever heard. As though her ears had been stuffed with cotton wool her whole life, and she was hearing clearly for the first time. And she understood now. She was in *his* Haze. In *his* world.

She ran toward the bedroom, partly to see if Teej was still breathing and partly to see if the bedroom was still there. The phone continued to ring in the background as she ran through the hall and back to him. When she came through the bedroom door and reached out to touch him, she ran straight into something soft and impenetrable and almost invisible. It bounced her backward, almost knocking her over.

Approaching gingerly, she squinted to see what she had hit. Across half the room stretched a huge sheet of thick, clear plastic film. It split the room in two, and it ran from wall to ceiling to floor with no gaps. It separated her from the bed and Teej and was easy to see now that she was looking. Anna walked cautiously toward the barrier and pushed her hand into it. She pressed the plastic lightly and found that, while she could push it back, it was completely solid and impermeable. She pressed her whole weight into it with both hands, and it was pliable but remained completely intact. It bulged inwards, but stretched and held firm. She couldn't get through.

Anna looked around the edges of the mysterious barrier and found that it seamlessly connected with the floor and walls. Even at the ceiling it was firmly connected. Not glued or stitched, it seemed to be melded to the room. Around the border, it was impossible to separate it from the walls and floor. She couldn't find an edge no matter how hard she scraped and clawed at it. She pushed her hand into the middle, trying to pierce though, but although it stretched, it would not split. Even when she tried to poke a finger through, pushing as hard as she could, it resisted. It was too heavy and thick. She would have to try and cut through. She was about to leave the room when Teej shouted out, his voice muffled through the barrier.

"Anna...go with it. Wear him down. He's in here. Wait for him to...reveal...He is not as strong as he seems."

He was lapsing in and out of consciousness again. Running through the hall, past the ringing phone in the living room, and into the kitchen, she knew something was wrong. It took a moment to realize what had changed.

Her curtains were closed in the kitchen. In the living room, her curtains were closed, too. Only she didn't have curtains. They must be part of the Haze, made of heavy red material with gold tassels along the bottom. They were heavy and thick and looked like the kind you would see in a cinema or theater. The phone continued to ring. Anna hesitated for a second, then pulled the curtains open to let pale green light flood into the room.

Oh no, not again.

Her old world was gone. The trees and the parked cars and the houses and the street. Gone. In their place a green sky stretched over those familiar, endless purple sands. Surreal light shone into Anna's kitchen—light from a different sun in a different sky. She was in his world now.

And he was there.

Hunched on a purple dune loomed a large, wretched creature with black, empty pits where his eyes should have been. His dark outline stood out on the bright landscape, and a body was at his feet. A girl with long hair that covered her face. Her blood was smeared around his mouth, on his hands, around his feet and all over the body. Splashed on the sand like it had been poured from a bucket. So much blood.

Standing scarecrow still with a dimwitted smile on his clown face, his mouth curled at the corners into a rictus grin. Long, blackened teeth contrasted with his bone-white flesh. His head tilted loosely to one side and his eyes tracked her as she moved. The wind blew through him while the swirling sands swept past but didn't touch him.

She heard a voice from the living room. It was muffled, but it sounded like a hundred children speaking all at once, all saying the same thing:

"I smell the fear,

Your hope is gone,

No friends left,

You are but one."

His voice reverberated like a chorus of nightmares. She looked back into the living room and noticed it echoed through the phone that hung off the hook. It had answered itself, and now Mott spoke through it to her. She turned back to the window, and he was gone. The girl and the blood remained.

Get close to him. Pretend to be afraid. Never play their game.

Anna grabbed a long, sharp knife from the drawer and backed into the living room. She would try to get to Teej. Make sure he was safe. She moved away from the window, but the door to the hall was gone. Now, in its place, was a painting of a door. She was trapped.

"Oh, come on!"

He hands scrambled across the surface, but it was smooth and seamless. Her mind reeled, and her heart thumped in the back of her throat. *This couldn't be happening.* Her only escape route had become a pattern on a bare wall.

Struggling to take it all in, Anna concentrated on holding the knife in her trembling hands. The mutability of reality was straining her mind and forcing panic into her chest. How could she protect herself here? She was supposed to stay strong and fight him, but he controlled every aspect of this world. Anything was his to meld and bend to his will. Everything in her own home, each part of reality, was a weapon he could use against her.

She looked around the vivid, bright living room that was no longer her home, trying to spot what else had changed. What would he use against her next? Would the Night Collectors appear here? Slowly exhaling in an attempt to calm herself, her breath came out as a gasp at first, but she pushed the panic down. Tried to regain her composure. She would play along. Goad him into attacking her and exposing himself.

What about Teej though? Was he in danger? Surely he was. If she wanted to save him, and her own sanity, she had to force the Midnight Man's hand. Make him focus on her. In a moment of defiance, she picked the phone up from the table and said, "I'm here. Come for me." Without waiting for a response, she slammed it down so hard she hurt her wrist. Impressed with how assured she sounded, she waited. It didn't take long. The Midnight Man spoke again, and his voice seemed to come from the walls this time.

"Open your veins to me. Cut deep. Just a tassssssste. Drink it up."

His voice made her stomach heave, like the sound of his voice was damaging her insides. His threat seemed to grow as he spoke, his words the weapons. Was this how he killed the others? Did he need her to hear him and be afraid?

Well, Anna was different. She could fight back. Her mind raced as she tried to decide *how*. She could try commanding him, or she could use her ring again, perhaps. She also seemed stronger in a Haze. She was able to break solid objects like the door in the alleyway or the elevator. Teej had told her the best way to fight a Dreamer was to use their own narrative against them, but if she couldn't see Mott, she couldn't hurt him.

He also said fighting an Aesthete took two Metiks, one to control the Haze and one to find and fight the Dreamer. She had to do both and didn't know how to do either, and she was sure that facing him would be harder than facing the wolves. They were the remnant of an Aesthete that was long gone, and the Midnight Man was still here, working his will against hers. She had to choose her moment. She had to provoke him.

"Why don't you stop *talking* about killing me and just come do it?"

When he replied, his words were like oil. "Soon enough. Just playing, just playing. Just playing some little gamessssss. We can play for years."

"Bullshit!" she called back. "You didn't torture the others for years."

There was a long silence. "Not by your watch."

She rocked back on her heels. *Years*? Could he really keep her here for that long?

"Shut up!" she shouted. And there was silence. It wasn't just that he stopped talking. Everything went silent. It was as if they had been on the phone before, but now the line was dead. With one command, she had silenced everything in the Haze, and now all she could hear was her own shallow breathing. Had she compelled him to stop, or was she just moving into the next stage of this nightmare?

Anna waited to see what would happen next, but there was nothing. No sounds, no sign of movement. The stillness was more unsettling than his voice. She went to the large window and opened the curtains to look out at purple sands, green skies and hazy sunlight. Something was changing. Static crackled across her skin, and she dug her fingers into the palm of her hands as she strained to feel where he was. She pushed her senses outwards, trying to follow Teej's instructions. Trying to find where Mott was hiding.

Out of the corner of her eye, Anna thought she saw something. Turning away from the window, she noticed with confusion that the sofa was full of water. Where the cushions had been before, there was now just a deep, clear pool. Like a bath. She walked toward it, hesitant but too curious to stop. The black leather sides and sofa back remained, but now it was hollow and looked like—

Someone pushed her from behind.

Anna turned as she fell and saw his face, just for a second. Those black, empty eyes— then she was underwater.

The pool was shallow—only a few feet—but Anna fell heavily and it went over her head. Swallowing water, she closed her eyes and mouth tightly and struggled to rise. She tensed every muscle in her body and pushed toward the surface, but as she lifted her head, it hit something solid. Anna had never been able to open her eyes under water, but she managed to force them open now and saw glass. A solid sheet over the pool and over her. She was trapped. Again.

She pushed against it with her palms. She kicked and punched, but underwater, her fists made soft, slow muffled bumps against the barrier. She lifted her legs and pushed her feet against the glass, but it only pushed her body into the ground

150

harder and a stab of pain shot through her back. Her lungs screamed for air, escalating her panic. She was going to die. She was going to drown inside her own sofa.

Her panic was short lived. It wouldn't help her. She had maybe half a minute before she was gone. Before she would lapse into the physiological drowning response: twitching, gulping in water, flailing and then death. She knew about drowning. She had seen it before.

As her hands and feet slapped at the glass with less power, her mind freewheeled. In a sealed tank of water designed to imprison her, she struggled in the soundless void. Cold and muffled inside her tomb, her body screamed for air.

Anna started to drift. She was looking down on herself. She saw her own panicked eyes and twitching limbs. The hair and clothes floating in the water as her hands pawed uselessly on the glass surface. The palms of her hands pressed flat against the barrier, pale and growing paler.

She calmed herself. Stopped struggling. Lay still in the water and pushed her arm out. Like she had with the wolves. She slowly put her hand in front of her face, and pressed it against the glass. The ring on her hand clinked against the glass surface holding her inside. She opened her mouth and tried to say, "Crack," but water flooded into her. She pushed against the glass as hard as she could, even as the water came into her lungs. She gagged.

Her back arched and spasmed, but Anna pushed her hand as hard as she could into the glass. Then she heard it. A tiny, almost imperceptible creak. A noise like ice sliding on ice. Where her ring touched the glass, there was a hairline fracture, but even as it appeared, it started to fix itself. As if some force was fighting against her, undoing her work.

She stopped pushing with her body and focused all her thought on the glass. Every ounce of will went into that glass, imagining it was thin ice. In her skull, something seemed to pop, and she felt wetness and warmth inside her head, like an artery had burst in her brain. Her eyes rolled into the back of her head, and she felt her consciousness slip away. Her toes curled into her feet and her spine twisted. A few more cracks, and a creaking noise echoed dully through her watery prison.

Exploding outwards in a scattered shower of shards and water, Anna crashed to freedom. Gasping and coughing, she came out of the water with a jump before falling down again. Her vision, which had narrowed to a pinprick, started to slowly come back. She lay across the edge of the sofa for a long moment, gasping and struggling to move. Eventually, she coughed up enough liquid to take in some air. Pushing soaked strands of wet hair out of her face, she climbed out, rolled onto her side, and tried to breathe normally. She had been a half second away from drowning.

Still on her hands and knees, Anna looked up to see if he was there. To see what he would throw at her next. Before she had a chance to prepare, the Midnight Man was on her television screen. Just his face, up close and distorted, like the camera was inches from him. His empty eye sockets transfixed her. She stood and faced him.

"Licking blood off my fingers—"

Before he could finish another of his rhymes, Anna put both her hands firmly on the sides of the coffee table, picked it up, and flipped it into the television screen. It smashed spectacularly, showering sparks and a brief lick of fire into the air. The table was solid oak, and she couldn't believe how far she'd thrown it. A ragged, rasping sound made her turn to find its source before she realized it was her own breathing. She shook her head. "No more rhymes!" She coughed. "Come out!"

There was no sign of him, but he had stopped talking. Stopped goading her. She shook the cold water off as best she could, wringing her hair out till it stopped dripping.

Teej said Dreamers would fear her. Fear her because she was so powerful. Well, she didn't feel powerful at this moment. She felt trapped and isolated. And wet. All her bravado disappeared when she realized she was a pawn in his game. Shivering with cold and building rage, she tried to keep her focus. Another attack like the last one would finish her off. What options did she have? She couldn't escape out the windows. Even if she survived the fall, the purple sands outside were his world. She remembered the sound Sue made when the Midnight Man killed her in that endless desert. No, it was better to lure him here if she could.

Anna walked over to the wall where the door had been, trying to rub heat into her wet, cold arms as she went. Looking at the painted outline of the door, she traced the edges of the solid mural with her fingers to see if there was some way to restore it to its former state. Maybe she could force it with her powers somehow; she just had to find a way to leverage them.

Anna imagined the door was back and closed her eyes, trying to picture what it had looked like. She rubbed her hand against the wall and pushed on it, then opened her eyes again. Nothing. Trying something different, she pointed her ring at the wall and thought of fire. She imagined flames appearing on the wall, burning a perfect circle for her to escape. Like an invisible blowtorch. Still nothing. Her ring started to feel warm against her finger, but the heat died when it left her body. Something was pushing back against her. This was harder than before. He had grown stronger.

Exasperated, she stood back and gave out a frustrated sigh. *What now?*

She thought back to how Teej had described her power. An Undreamer. She broke down Hazes and destroyed them. Maybe she couldn't just change the things she saw. Her powers seemed to work best when they were used destructively: burning werewolves to ash, breaking glass, smashing through doors. Every time she had managed to use her power, it had been to break things down. To smash them or dissolve them or burn them. She could take their component material and create more disorder, like a force of entropy.

Yes, that was it! As soon as she thought of the word, she felt the epiphany. Entropy. She could break down Hazes. She had read about entropy before. Entropy was the amount of disorder and chaos in a system, and she was that force embodied. Anna was the personification of entropy in the world of Aesthetes, and she could break that world down. She realized now that Banille was the destruction of the Dreamers' world through loss of information. And if she followed the rules of the Haze, it would be easier to manifest that entropy.

Anna didn't know if this was insight or madness, but maybe as long as she believed it, that would be enough. She had an idea. Rushing through the kitchen, she opened the bottom drawer under the sink. It was her DIY drawer, full of tools and random screws and wrenches and dirty cloths. Looking at it closely, she pictured what she would do. If she was a force of entropy, then she could take anything apart. She could take this world apart if she needed to. She could strip back the layers of this reality till she got to its core, and got to him.

She grabbed a screwdriver and ran back to the living room. Looking around for a second, not quite sure what her plan was, she tried to identify where she would start. She examined the corner of the room. Her eyes rested on the skirting board that ran between the floor and the wall. That was where she would start.

Getting down on her hands and knees in the corner, Anna slid the screwdriver between the wall and the wood panel. When she managed to pry a gap for the metal tip between the wood and the wall, she slammed the palm of her hand down on the top of the screwdriver to push it in farther. As she did it, there was a loud creaking noise. The whole skirting board came away in her hands. She squatted on her knees, pulling the three-foot piece of wood back to see purple sand seep in.

Anna stepped over the wood and put it behind herself, looking out through the space she had made. She could see the ground a few feet below her, which made no sense, because her apartment wasn't on the ground floor. But this wasn't her apartment anymore. If she wanted to escape, she had to break it down. She had to dismantle this reality to get to its core. To get to him.

Sitting back to plan her next move, Anna reflected on how easy that had been. She could literally pull the house apart with her bare hands. She guessed that any action she took that involved breaking things down or dismantling things would help her. That was her power, and if she complied with the laws of this Haze, it would be easier. Like Teej had said, she was stronger than Mott, but only in certain ways. Only when her power was properly harnessed.

Interrupted by a noise behind her, Anna turned and looked at her television. It was whole again. An ancient, black dusty thing that she had inherited from her parents, behind it were huge twisted coils of black cables for her speakers, old VCR, and PlayStation. Rustling and movement came from behind the console; a slithering, grinding sound.

The television tipped forward and slowly fell to the floor, brushed aside as the cables behind it coiled and twisted upward. They coalesced into a roiling black mass that tangled and curled around itself. More and more cables shot out from the wall, and in a few seconds, a creature as big as a person formed.

Horrified, Anna crawled away from the monster—the latest in the series of household items that was going to try to murder her. She had to get away from it, but she couldn't squeeze through the gap she had made. There were no doors, and the windows still showed that she was too high to jump out, even if she could open them.

Jumping to her feet, she ran past the growing mound to the bookcase and grabbed the hammer she had hidden, and then ran back, jumping over the cables now spreading in a network across the floor and starting to slither menacingly in her direction.

She stood in front of the wall, breathing in deeply and holding the hammer in both hands in front of her like a sword. Twisting her body to the right, she swung the hammer back with all her strength and struck the wall.

The hammer went straight through, smashing a hole in the bricks and plaster and sending up a cloud of dust into her face. She coughed, rubbed her eyes, and looked at the damage she had wrought. She had smashed through the wall like a small wrecking ball, bursting a hole about the size of a foot. Her grip had loosened as she swung the hammer, and it was now outside in the sand where it had sunk soundlessly into the purple landscape.

Sliding her hand through the hole, Anna reached for the hammer. Her fingers grasped frantically at the edge of the handle when the creaking behind her began again. She turned to see the cables had piled into a beast about twice her height. It shuffled closer. Two large, knotted arms reached for her while the massive, gaping mouth opened and closed. It was like a huge, blind amoeba, sniffing the air for something to absorb, and it was moving toward her. The black heaving mass of cable lunged forward.

Thin cords shot out like grasping tentacles, and before she could react, they were in her face. Sliding over and around her head, they reached and grabbed for her like a blind animal trying to consume her. Constricting and coiling, they squeezed. She tried to brush them away, but more and more tightened around her face and neck. She pulled away, but they curled around her eyes, strategically blinding her. Pulling taut, they prevented her from seeing where the creature was, and she stumbled toward it rather than away. She struggled to pull the binds from her face, but they wound around her hands.

The cables spread web-like over her shoulders and arms, and as they wrapped around and around her, Anna's world went black. Sound was muted as they engulfed her face and head completely. She couldn't hear it or see it, but the tightness around her was suffocating. She pulled back as hard as she could, and some of the cable stretched and loosened, but even more enclosed her. Leaning her whole weight into pulling away, she started to fall.

No! She was not going to let this happen again. Even as the creature closed off all her senses to make her vulnerable, it made a mistake. Her arms were still somewhat free, and she wasn't panicking this time. She couldn't see or hear, but she could *feel* it, and she knew how to fight it. She had to let it take her.

Anna eased off her struggle and let the creature pull her closer. She wiggled down onto her knees, and as it pulled her in, she reached her hand out to where she thought her backpack should be. At first, she couldn't feel anything as the tentacles continued to wrap around her, engulfing her, but she stretched her arm farther, straining against the ever-strengthening cords, and felt the bag brush her elbow. Plunging her hand inside, she fumbled through the contents. The monster wrapped her tighter in its cocoon, until it was hard to breathe. But even as the creature lifted her and heaved her across the floor, she held onto her bag. Seconds crawled by, and she found what she was looking for.

Pulling her hand from the bag with the body-spray can in her grasp, she pressed the nozzle. She pulled her arm closer to her body and turned the can as best she could, spraying where she thought the monster was. Muffled by the constricting coils around her head, she thought she heard a groan. Was it working? She felt the creature's grip loosen for a second. Imagining the monster melting away to dust, she turned the spray toward herself, clenched her eyes shut, and pressed the nozzle. Instantly her face was free. The spray blew the grasping tendrils away from her head as if they were leaves in the wind, and suddenly, the darkness was gone and she squinted in the light.

As her eyes readjusted, Anna was startled to see that the creature had swollen to take up most of the room, and it had been pulling her into its gaping maw. Although the can had blown part of the tangled cables into dust, most of her lower body was still wrapped tight. The creature's monstrous, bulbous head turned toward her. A cavernous mouth came at her, but she reacted instinctively, spraying the canister directly at it. Every part of the monster that the spray touched fell apart. Fell to pieces. To ash. It was as if she was rapidly ageing the plastic material of the cables and transmuting it to dust before her eyes.

She kept her finger on the trigger, spraying until the whole room smelled like vanilla and honeysuckle and musty old plastic. As she pushed the creature back, she imagined her improvised weapon was an anti-monster spray. A can of acid. Anything that would defeat a creature like this one. And it worked. Its body broke down completely, and by the time she finished the can, the room was full of dust and flecks like fine black snow. And she was free. Catching her breath, she put her hands on her thighs and bent over.

"Every time you try to kill me, I get stronger!" she shouted as she rubbed her face and arms clean. And she believed it. This time she hadn't panicked. She was learning.

Picking herself up, Anna went over to the hole in the wall, stretched as far as she could, and finally managed to grab the hammer from the sand. Pulling it back with all her strength and grasping it firmly this time, she smashed the wall above the hole she had already made. Instead of creating another hole, this time it knocked the wall over entirely. Like it was part of a studio set, the wall fell onto the sand with a muffled thump.

Sweating, dirty, bruised and cut, Anna walked out of her ruined apartment across the purple sands of the Midnight Man's world. She felt like she'd left her old self behind. Something had changed. All her fear and doubt had turned to mist. She willed herself to be dry, imagining the water on her skin was evaporating into the air. And it did.

Her clothes became clean, her hair fell into place, and all her aches and pains healed themselves. She was untouched by the chill of the wind. Beneath the green sky, she walked away from the shell of her house as it collapsed and fell in on itself. The desert howled, little dust storms twirling around her without touching her.

Ahead of her lay the dead girl. Deep red blood on the sand. As Anna got closer, she realized it was Sue. Or a version of her made by the Midnight Man and put there to frighten her. Strands of blood-soaked hair lay across her face like scars. Anna hardened her heart and walked toward the body. If he put Sue here to frighten her, he had made a mistake. It just increased her resolve.

Beyond the body lay a stagnant pool of water. Though it remained ominously quiet, she could feel the presence of the

Midnight Man. The footsteps of the invisible army surrounded her as they shuffled in from all directions.

"Show yourselves!" she demanded.

And they appeared, shimmering into form. Hundreds of them. Thousands. Filling the landscape as far as she could see, the Night Collectors stood atop the purple sands. Their hooded, stooped forms still and resolute, and their gray snouts sniffing the air nervously. They did not approach her. The Night Collectors were no longer a threat to her, instead they were an audience. Dominion of this world was no longer assured. Anna was challenging the King of this Haze, and it was not yet clear who would win.

The ground rumbled around her feet. Mini earthquakes shook the sand as little mounds began rising around her, almost as if something was pushing from underneath.

Anna laughed. It seemed like the only logical response.

She had survived each attack, and each seemed weaker than the last. With each new threat she got stronger, and now she realized, she was going to win. "You didn't kill me with my sofa or my television, you will *not* kill me with sand castles!"

She acted on instinct as some ancestral memory unlocked inside her. She was confident and secure, and she knew how to fight this monster. Her instincts told her what she could do and what his limitations were. As he used up his Vig, his power was waning. But more than that, she could *feel* him weakening. Some sense was developing in her. She was learning how to interpret the world of Hazes like Teej could. She was mastering each in turn—*the Will, the Word, the Sight, and the Sword.*

The mounds of sand grew and started molding into a humanoid shape. Anna held her hand out to the nearest one. Her palm pointed at the creature, and she said in a firm, authoritative voice, "No."

They stopped moving. Not only that, they started to fall apart. As if embarrassed, the aspiring sand creature simply ceased to exist. Whatever force created them was dismissed, and one by one they disintegrated.

Across the purple sands, she walked slowly and calmly, approaching the shore of the murky lake where her enemy lurked. When she got to the edge, Anna looked straight down into the deep, black water. Before she really knew what she was doing, she bent and plunged her hand into the depths. Up to the elbow, she held herself there.

The bubbles rose to the surface slowly, just a few at first, then more and more. Steam began to rise. The radius of the frothing, bubbling water grew and grew. Anna's mouth and nose filled with the fumes of the rancid steam, but she didn't stop. Hotter and hotter. She might have felt searing and scalding across her exposed face and arms, but her frustration and rage blinded her to the pain. The burning felt good. Like she was scratching an itch. Her eyes rolled back in satisfaction and pleasure. Her head swam.

She felt him before she saw him. A mighty swelling as she pulled the Midnight Man out of his sanctuary. He broke the iridescent, oily surface of the water and leaped into the air. She opened her eyes to see him above her, his black form casting a long shadow across her body as he blocked out the blue sun. His long, ape-like arms over his head, his gray-blue legs drawn up, he glided over and above Anna. The air filled with the scent of his scalded flesh, and she almost lost sight of him in the clouds of vapor.

He came down behind her, falling into a crouch. Gravity seemed sluggish around the Midnight Man as his long cloak flowed downward in slow motion. She spun to face him, ready for his next attack. He remained squat, head down, steam rising from his body, trembling. He was in pain. "Now, you will face—"

"No more!" she cut him off. "I don't want to hear it. You murdered my friend, and you murdered those other women, too."

"Even if you defeat me, my brothers will come for you. The Doxa do not rest, and they will avenge—"

"Let them come!" she snapped. He didn't speak again. Twitching and trembling, his body raw and scorched, he tried to reach out a hand in supplication or surrender.

"Stop," she commanded, and her voice conveyed her power. He had tried to take that weapon from her every chance he could. Gagging or choking or drowning her, but when she commanded him to do something, he could not resist.

Mott bowed lower in front of her as a gesture of submission. He was beaten. The purple sands blew around him, resting on the shoulders and head of his black cowl as it blew around and past Anna. Surrounding them, the Night Collectors stood in a broad circle, but in unison they had turned their backs on the scene. They had abandoned him.

Anna walked forward, slowly and steadily. Mott held both hands in front of his demonic face, attempting to create some thaumaturgy to protect himself. He struggled and grunted, as if trying to lift something too heavy to move. All that came were mewling, sniveling noises.

As she got close to him, he fell backward. His boiled flesh, gray and weeping, seemed to shrink before her. With each step she took, he looked more human. He glanced up, and his eyes held intelligence rather than malice. They were human eyes, and they were afraid.

His black cloak fell apart before her eyes, and his sharp teeth broke and crumbled in his mouth. He spat them out in a flow of blood and mucus. Behind the mask, a human mouth and face revealed that his real form was coming through. He was, after all his threats and attacks, just a terrified little man. His long, thin arms danced in front of his face as if deflecting invisible blows.

She leaned over him and said, "For every woman you killed or hurt."

She pointed her ring at him and willed the fire she had used before. Was he still strong enough to stop her? Could he end this Haze early to escape her wrath? No, he had already invested too much Vig, and now he would not survive to see the end. A voice in her mind whispered, *let him burn.*

All around them, one by one, The Night Collectors turned their backs and winked out of existence. As she pointed the ring at the Midnight Man and imagined raging fire, his clothes began to singe and crackle with kindling at the edges. Smoke and steam came from his sleeves as his wet clothes dried, then caught the flames. The bright, burning fire exploded all over him, and she had to jump back as the flames flashed into a conflagration. Thick, orange fire lapped him as he rolled in the sand and screamed. Choking black, bilious smoke drifted up into the green, roofless sky.

He was saying something over and over, as if he were pleading with her to stop the burning. As if he could give her information. All she could make out were cries of "Rayleigh" and "the blood" and "Doxa." But she didn't relent. She didn't think she could stop the flames, nor did she try. She burned him till he was gone.

Alone now, Anna tied her hair back, dusted herself off and sat in front of the embers to watch them burn out.

nineteen

White ceiling, white walls, white beds, beeping white machines making white noises to attract the white-clad nurses, running back and forth across gray floors. For Anna, the true horror of hospitals was how routine the suffering and death became. She knew that waiting for someone to die wasn't just painful, it was boring. Not that Teej would definitely die. Not definitely.

Back and forth they scurried, holding charts and wheeling patients past the white room where Anna sat on an old brown chair next to his bed. Nurses, doctors, porters, cleaners, visitors, more nurses—none of them looked into the room. Anna felt invisible. Running her hands over the coarse hospital bed sheets, Anna shuddered at how terrible they felt on her fingertips. She wished she could cover him with a warm, woolly blanket and make him a cup of coffee and have him come to life. That way she could pretend he was just sleeping and he was going to wake up soon.

He would not wake up soon. The doctor's prognosis was bleak. Swelling in the brain and a cracked skull. The smaller injuries, like his fractured cheekbones and broken ribs, were barely worth mentioning. He might not live long enough to feel their pain.

When Anna had finally defeated the Midnight Man, she had been drained and traumatized, but relieved. It seemed like she had saved people and prevented more deaths, but she hadn't realized the damage he had already done to Teej. Mott was gone, but not before causing irrevocable harm. Looking at Teej connected to these machines, Anna didn't regret what she had done to Mott or how he'd died. Not one bit.

Her bedside vigil drained her. All day long she watched him, and every night she went home and fell into a deep, hopeless sleep. In the first week, she had to deal with police, telling lies and making excuses. She had feigned surprise and pleaded ignorance when they talked about murders. She told them he was an old college friend, and she didn't know anything about his family or friends (that was true), and she expressed confusion when they couldn't determine his identity (she wasn't confused). Now, he was just another random victim of street violence, and she was a mystery to them. With a murdered friend and an unidentifiable victim almost killed on her doorstep, they had asked her a lot of questions, but she had held her nerve. The encounter with the Midnight Man had forged her in flames. When she thought about the rest of the Doxa coming for her, she felt no fear.

The thought of losing Teej frightened her though. He was her guide into this strange new world, and he was already a victim of it. Together they had thwarted one member of the Doxa. She had prevailed in the world of Hazes, and he had stopped an attack in the real world, but at great cost. Thinking back to her battle with Mott, Anna found it hard to comprehend everything that had taken place. If what Teej told her was true, it really had happened, even if it all seemed so ridiculous now.

There were blank, fuzzy spots in her memory about those final moments. How had she gotten back home? How had she arrived at the hospital? She could remember snatches—her face on the cool tiles of the bathroom floor and staring out the window of the ambulance at the lights reflected on the wet road—but most of it was a blur. Perhaps it was what Teej had called Banille: the sometimes-cruel force that reknitted reality with the Hazes and brought everyone and everything back to Basine.

Or maybe she had been through so much stress and strain that her mind was taking some time to organize the memories. Whatever had happened to her, it had taken her days to recover and tiredness had seeped into her bones.

Each time her mother called, Anna had pretended to be at home. She fabricated events and activities with surprising ease. "I was at the cinema." "I haven't seen Sue for weeks." "I'm happy." She had gotten better at lying.

Anna held Teej's hand from time to time. She didn't know if that would be what he wanted. She didn't know if he felt it, or if it helped, but it made her feel better. His fingers were callused, but his palms were soft. They were always warm, but he gave off few other signs of life. His chest barely moved and the tube in the corner of his mouth kept him breathing. His face was black and purple, and a bandage around his head was pristine white, except for a tiny red smudge.

She had been to the city hospital many times before this. Anna's life was always punctuated with painful, life destroying visits to emergency rooms. They would typically occur when things were going too well. That's when fate would drop the hammer on her again.

Caught in a daydream, it took several long moments for Anna to escape her mid-afternoon musings and realize the machine next to her had started to beep: a protracted, piercing noise. Teej breathed out slowly and steadily one last time, then he stopped.

No. Please, no. Anna jumped to her feet and as the ground shook and the bed rattled, and as she ran to get help—

Anna wheeled Teej's chair to the window. Smiling broadly, she realized how handsome he looked in the bright sunlight piercing the gaps in the blinds. There was barely a mark on his face, and she couldn't believe how much he had recovered in just a few short days. He opened the window, and she was shocked to see the countryside speed past. Anna and Teej were on a moving train. The ground shook under her feet as they rumbled across the rails.

"Where are we? Did, uh, did something change?" she asked Teej.

"What do you mean? I don't know where exactly, but it's very exciting. It looks like we have our first Haze to explore together."

Anna nodded. His smile comforted her. As long as they were together, no one could hurt them.

"Are you ready?" he asked.

She hesitated for a second, then nodded. "Yeah, I can do this."

She went over to stand next to him at the window. The sunlight felt good on her skin. Her memories of the hospital faded away.

twenty

Anna pressed her head against the cool glass of the train window as a new world slid past. A green water tower pockmarked with gaping, rust-orange holes through which she could see the blue sky. A dilapidated library— collapsed under its own weight—with dark green plants and trees growing out the windows. The shell of an old pickup truck with a loose bumper hanging downward in a frown. Burned out cars. Dead trees. Dust.

And they chugged through collapsed train stations, too. Anna had been looking out the window for what seemed like hours, and in that time, they had passed four or five of them. They were all rotten husks. The posters were faded, the signs bleached by the sun. It was as if they had been left for hundreds of years to fall apart. "This is all so sad."

"But beautiful too, right?" replied Teej.

"Yeah."

He was right. It was beautiful. There was a melancholy to the landscape, but everything was tinged with the now-familiar aesthetic of a Haze. Everything had an almost-neon glow. An over-saturation. Anna was in no doubt she was in a Haze again, and it felt good. Although they were still in a hospital room, the smell of bleach and medicine was gone from the air now. It was the same but completely different. She was happier here. She hoped they'd never go back.

They looked out together in silence. The staccato *tatatata tatatata* of the track was constant, interrupted only once when they crossed a long metal bridge over a dry riverbed. The creaking and groaning of the old metal was ominously louder than any other sound the train made, but the bridge held, and the journey across the desolate landscape continued. From overgrown countryside to soporific, empty ghost towns, they saw no sign of life. It was a wasteland, and Anna wondered if this Haze had any people in it at all.

Interrupting her reverie, Teej subtly gestured to the doorway, suggesting they explore the rest of the train. The door was closed, and where before she had seen doctors and nurses rushing past through the glass, now the glass was opaque. She had no idea what she would find on the other side. Wheeling ahead of her in his chair, Teej motioned for her to follow.

"Why are we here?"

"Good question. When you're in a Haze you didn't create yourself, you're there for a reason. Now we must figure out who brought us here and why. In case it wasn't obvious before, Dreamers don't often welcome people like you and me. We're not often invited, but this time, they came looking for us."

Teej put his hand on the door and struggled to push it open, so she put her hand over his and helped. Together they turned the handle until the door hit the opposite wall without fully opening. Anna pushed herself into an impossibly narrow passage, but Teej's wheelchair was too big. She peeked both ways. Nothing. The corridor itself was almost featureless. The walls were paneled in rich wood, maybe mahogany, and the doors at either end had ornate brass handles but no glass. It was dim, but little lights along the ceiling showed the way.

"What now?" she asked.

"Help me," Teej replied as he put his arm out to her. Holding his ribs gingerly he grabbed her shoulder with a firm grasp, and she pulled him out of the chair. He didn't feel heavy, but he was unsteady. Stronger, but still in pain. Grimacing slightly, he pushed the wheelchair backward into the room, and as it rolled away, he closed the door behind them. They had to pick a door.

"You choose," he said.

She walked to the door to her right and, supporting himself with one hand on her shoulder from behind and one hand on the wall beside him, Teej followed. Anna put her hand on the brass doorknob, then paused for a second to listen to the rolling wheels below her. She was on a train. *A train.* She repeated it over and over to give herself an anchor. She breathed out and pushed the door open confidently, eager to show Teej that she was not afraid.

They passed into a bright passenger carriage. Wooden seats on either side of the cabin were overlooked by large windows which focused the bright sunlight and made the cabin hot and stuffy. The seats were separated into groups of four with two facing two, and above them were shelves for bags to be stowed. It looked like an old steam train interior—like something Anna had seen in a movie. She knew that notions of past or future didn't mean anything in a Haze, but she felt like she had travelled back in time. With Teej still holding onto her shoulder, she walked slowly into the cabin, and he stumbled along with her.

She wanted to ask if they were in danger, but she didn't want to appear too anxious. "What should we do?" she asked.

According to him, she was an Undreamer. She was the one who had to be most ready for a fight, and more so now that he was injured. He seemed to be able to move, but he was weak. Anna vaguely remembered that at one point, it had seemed like he might not make it.

"There on the seat," Teej pointed to something Anna hadn't seen. Sitting on a bench in the middle of the cabin, an old, heavy book was suspiciously prominent. Perfectly positioned for them to find. Anna walked over and picked it up, leaving Teej to flop down on the wooden chair next to her. She turned the book around to face her and tried to read the faded, golden writing on the cover, but it was written in Spanish. Teej motioned for her to pass him the book, and she placed it carefully on his lap.

Struggling with its heavy pages, Teej thumbed through while Anna went back to looking out the window, noting how mountainous and rocky the scenery had become. Green and yellow scrubby vegetation grew over a network of old train lines. There were so many crisscrossing tracks that it seemed like they must be approaching a major station. All around, looming mountains crowded around like curious giants. The train seemed to be slowing, and Anna struggled to read the sun-stained signs they passed on either side of the track.

"What's it about?" Anna asked. "It's not from the Doxa, is it?"

"I don't think so. I can't read Spanish. Can you read any of the signs?"

"I was just trying, but it's really tough. They're so faded." She squinted as the train passed another sign. This one was recognizably a train station name, and it almost seemed like the train slowed just enough that she could make out most of the letters.

"Canfrance? Canfranc? Something like that."

Teej looked up at her suddenly. "Canfranc?" he repeated. She nodded.

"We might be in trouble." Teej struggled to his feet while Anna pushed her head against the window, trying to see farther. The train made a broad right-hand turn that allowed her a view of the track ahead, and she saw the problem.

"There's a blockage on the track. Will we stop?"

He frowned. "No, maybe not."

Looking closely at the blockade ahead, Anna noted with growing panic that the wreckage around the mountain was made up of other crashed trains. Lots of them. She strained to get a better look, but the train turned left and blocked the view. The blockage was only two or three minutes away at this speed.

"We have to get off," he said, and she was already moving. Anna put her arm around Teej and lifted him, hustling for the exit and pulling him along as best she could. Opening the door into the narrow corridor, they struggled past where the hospital room had been before. It was gone. That route was an entrance into this Haze, not an exit.

As they got to the other end of the narrow corridor, Anna had a sinking feeling before she even touched the door. This was a mistake. This was a dead end. Still, she tried to open the door. The handle turned, but nothing happened. Looking more closely, Anna saw that it wasn't a door at all. The dark wood was as solid as the rest of the walls; the outline of the door was painted on and the handle did nothing. *What now?*

She turned around awkwardly in the corridor, Teej moaning as she moved him. He was heavy on her shoulder, and his movements were deliberate and strained. Anna started heading back the way she came. She wished Teej would tell her what to do, but he continued to grunt and groan in pain as she bashed him off the walls. The sound of the rails under their feet now sounded ominous, and she was sure it sped up a little. *Tatatata tatatata.*

Anna's hair fell across her face as she heaved Teej toward the main cabin of the train. Sweat blinded her as a wet strand poked her in the eye. His strong hands started to pull her cardigan off her shoulders as he slumped downward. With a frustrated grunt, she dropped him onto one of the wooden benches again and straightened her clothes. She looked out the window to see how far they were from disaster.

"Arrrgghhhh!" She screamed in frustration, looking around for another way off the train but finding none. This was it. They were going to crash.

No! She didn't have to let that happen. She didn't have to find an exit, she could make her own. Their fate was in her hands. She looked at Teej for a second to see if he would stop her or tell her what to do, but he was stooped over the bench with his head down. Maybe he had been hurt when she moved him. Looking away from him, she grasped the back of the seat and focused on what she would do next. She had to get them off the train. She had to smash the window, and the easiest way was to use her power.

Taking a half-step forward with both hands outstretched, her powers took effect before she even touched the glass. With a cracking, shimmering boom, the window shattered outwards into a hundred thousand pieces. Pieces so small they were like mist. One concussive blast, and the glass was gone.

A gentle breeze blew into the carriage, and the fresh mountain scent filled her lungs. It was glorious pine, grass and mountain blossoms. And now that the window was gone, she didn't feel like she was in danger. The train was still moving slowly enough that they could jump off. Looking down at the scrubby grass, she anticipated that jumping would be rough but survivable.

But perhaps the fall would be too much for Teej. Examining him now, she could see how much pain he was in. He hadn't even looked up when she had broken the window. He seemed to have gotten much worse in the last few moments, where his injuries had almost healed before. Why was he so sick now? Was something else affecting him? When she reached out to him, without looking up, he took her hand.

"Teej, we need to get off. We should jump off the train before we crash, right? Are you okay?"

"Yeah… No. I feel really weak. Sorry, Anna."

She shook his arm to get him to look at her. "Come on. You can do it! We just need to jump."

Teej looked up slowly and their gaze locked. He gave her a brief, firm nod. His eyes were hollow, his cheeks gaunt and his mouth twisted in pain. She would have to help him jump. Pulling him to his feet, she almost dropped his body as the train suddenly lurched forward. She grabbed the back of a chair to steady them. It was beginning to accelerate.

"We have to go now. Can't wait any longer."

She heard the urgency in his voice. He was right. Grabbing and pulling with all the strength she had left, she hauled him up. As his arms went around her, and his weight fell across her chest, she bent her legs then kicked them both forward and outwards as hard as she could. They toppled from the waist high window together, and as they approached the ground, she turned her body to hit first. With their arms around each other, they fell forever. Turning slowly through the air, the world spinning around them. The sound of the train went on and on as they dropped. It lasted for minutes. Hours. They seemed to float. The ground was a patient antagonist that would hurt them both, but only when it was ready. It was almost as if the train had tossed them away, like trash.

Tatatatata. Tatatata

They landed hard. Smashing down heavily on her spine, Anna's head snapped backward and hit the dirty grass with a muffled thump. She skirted the edges of unconsciousness, her vision narrowing as the world faded to black. She held on.

Teej's limp body seemed to bounce off her own like she was a trampoline, and although she tried to hold him, he slid out of her arms. He flew away from her, sliding across the dirt and grit until coming to an eventual stop six or seven feet away. His ragged form was lifeless.

It wasn't until Anna tried to take a breath that she felt the pain. All the air had been knocked out of her lungs, and she gasped and gaped as the panic rose inside her. She breathed out desperately, but when she tried to breath in, her airways closed. She rolled onto her side and tried to calm herself. She wanted to shout for help, but no words came. Pushing down her fear, Anna started to catch her breath. After what seemed like an eternity, she could take a little air into her burning chest. When her spotty vision finally cleared, she sat up and surveyed the damage.

Sticky blood dotted her cardigan, but she wasn't sure where it came from. Examining her dirty hands and elbows, she found only scrapes and cuts, nothing that would generate so much blood. She started to lift her skirt to look for wounds when she heard a cacophonous crash. Metal and stone and dirt and rock all crashing and collapsing and smashing against each other. She turned slowly and painfully, and her breath caught again in her throat at what she saw.

An obscene tower of ruined, bent metal teetered where the locomotive had been subsumed into a massive pile of other trains. Hundreds of carriages, piled like toys, scattered across the side of the hill, stacked four or five high in some places. It seemed like the first crash, many years ago, had been at the entrance to a tunnel.

They looked like models from this distance, around a quarter of a mile away from the nearest debris, and some of the smashed carriages toward the front had been ruined for years. Rust and dirt encrusted them. Here and there, smoke and small flames twinkled in the wreckage, but nothing else moved. Most of the carriages had tipped over, but they were empty of people or cargo. She and Teej were the only passengers.

With imminent danger out of the way, Anna examined her wounds more carefully. Her cardigan and vest top had rolled up to her shoulders when she hit the earth, exposing the flesh of her torso to the ragged ground. As she lifted her clothes to get a better look, she saw that all along the left side of her body, she was bleeding. The skin was scraped raw, like something you would see in a butcher's shop. Tears came to her eyes, and her mouth dropped open in an appalled gape as she pawed at the injury. Pulling at leaves and patches of dirt stuck to her bleeding side, she was only beginning to feel the pain. The shock had protected her, but now she found that moving pulled at the wound and made it bleed more.

Anna reminded herself that there was no one to help her. She had no friends or family here, and Teej depended on her. She had to stay calm. She was on her own. *Surviving is going forward. Out and through the other end.*

She turned her torso a little, then lifted her left elbow up. There was blood, but it wasn't gushing or spilling on the ground. Calming herself, she pulled her clothes down over the mess. Though the wound was nasty and needed cleaning, it wasn't life threatening. She could tend to it later. For now, she had to push herself onwards. She had to check on Teej.

Aware that he wasn't moving, Anna nervously shuffled over to him. He'd slid far across the dirt and grit, leaving a rainbow arc where his body had scraped across the ground. She hoped her body had absorbed most of the impact when they'd hit the earth together.

"Not…dead." he muttered, still not moving.

"Me neither." As she got closer, he turned slowly onto his back. "Don't move. You might have damaged your spine or something."

"I haven't."

He slowly sat up, and she crouched next to him, nervously looking him up and down. He seemed to have come off better than she had. His green sweater and tan trousers were filthy, but his only obvious wound was on his head where some blood ran down to his chin. She wiped it away with her sleeve and considered his eyes. Sometimes they seemed blue and sometimes green, but right now, in the clear mountain sun, they were gray. And sad. He wasn't looking at her.

Suddenly aware of the silence and clear air, she turned to see what captured his attention. He was staring into the distance, beyond the wreckage. The landscape was stunning. Mountains and trees surrounded them. The scale of the snowy peaks dwarfed everything, even the mammoth train terminus behind them. It was dilapidated, but at some time in the past, it must have been grand. Although the mountains made the tall building look much smaller, it was long, stretching halfway to the horizon in either direction. They'd landed nearly dead center of the imposing arched entrance in the middle.

Across the face of the terminus were double doors as far as she could see. Hundreds of them, with green windows above each. The smashed windows and worn graffiti only slightly impacted the faded opulence of the building. Intricate cornices and a smooth, domed roof were missing only one or two black slate tiles. Below their feet, twenty or thirty sets of overgrown tracks crisscrossed the ground snaking off in all directions. Regardless of the nearby sounds and smells of the train crash, this was a beautiful, desolate place.

"Canfranc station. The French side, I think. Or maybe the Spanish? Have you been to the Pyrenees before?" he asked.

"No. Are we really in the Pyrenees Mountains?"

"Yes. At poor old Canfranc International Station. Closed in the…sixties, I think. Because of a train crash. Now it's a desolate place in Basine. But here too, obviously."

She nodded, trying to process everything he was saying while taking in the surroundings.

"The first train went off the bridge at the tunnel. See?"

He lifted himself up on one elbow to point at the wreckage.

"But there's so many of them, you can hardly see the bridge any more. You can see the tunnel where they went through the mountains. I guess in this Haze, the trains just keep coming. Piling up, like it's in a loop. This station was where they changed from French-sized carriages to Spanish. Because they weren't compatible. That's why the station is so big. They had to—"

He was beginning to babble, so she cut him off. "Teej, never mind that. Who brought us here?"

He reached his hand out to her, and she helped him stand. He still had to lean on her but seemed to be in less pain now. "I don't know. Whoever brought us here isn't trying to kill us. I don't think. I mean, Aesthetes can kill you a million different ways, but crashing a train doesn't seem very efficient. Or poetic. I think the train was just to bring us here—the only convenient entryway to this Haze. The train is a key part of this Haze. A portal. It would have taken a lot of Vig to get us from the hospital to here, so it's a powerful Aesthete. We were in trouble before from the Doxa, but I don't think they are involved in this."

He pointed around as he spoke. All this. *What was all this?*

"Are we really in Spain?"

"Yes. I mean, probably. We're in a Haze, for sure, but we're also very definitely in the Pyrenees Mountains."

"How do you feel? Can you walk?"

He shook his head while he fidgeted with his hands, like he was holding something invisible. "Yeah, I feel…I don't know. I feel okay, but something's not right. I just can't quite figure out what it is. I can't make my Periapt."

"Your what?"

"Remember the Will, the Word, the Sight and the Sword? Your Periapt is your Sword. Metaphorically speaking. Every Metik has one, and it lets us focus our minds. With a Periapt, we impose our will on a Haze to change it. Some Metiks create their Periapt within the Haze and others carry theirs at all times. Creating my Periapt attunes me to the Haze, but for some reason, I can't summon mine here. That's never a good sign."

"What's your Periapt?"

"Everyone's is different. It's always a physical object. Garret's is a staff. The old fool likes to pretend he's a wizard. Ridiculous. Mine's a lot less ostentatious."

"Well, maybe you're just tired," said Anna, fidgeting with her ring. "But can you *tell* me what yours is?"

"I prefer to preserve an air of mystery."

"Okay, *Riddler,* let's go over to those benches in front of the station."

He pointed her toward the main entrance of the long, grand building. Canfranc Station. Right enough, in front were some old, gnarled benches. With his arm around her waist, and with more grunting and shuffling, they made their way slowly across the patchy rail tracks, the small clouds of smoke behind them whispers lost to the mountains.

twenty-one

Looking out at the mountains against the blue sky in the late evening sun as she sat on the rickety wooden bench, Anna found she was remarkably at peace. She'd told Teej he could rest his head on her shoulder, and he'd accepted. Putting her arm around him, she hadn't expected him to fall asleep on her, but she found that she didn't mind. Maybe they should be in a hurry to escape this place, but for whatever reason, she had no desire to get back to the hospital. Or to go anywhere else, really. This abandoned train station in the mountains was a wonderful escape, and she didn't want to leave any time soon.

"You're messing it up," he said.

"Sorry!" She pushed him away, embarrassed. She was startled to realize she had been stroking his hair.

"Aww, I didn't mind."

"How do you feel?"

"I feel better now; I just needed a little rest. It's nice here. I think I know who made this place."

"Who?"

"Hmm, maybe I shouldn't guess. There's probably some other stuff I can explain first."

"Please."

Sitting up and looking at her earnestly, he said, "You're doing great, you know? You're going to be okay."

He smiled at her and she nodded slightly, but she wasn't in the mood to be flattered. She felt the weight of responsibility for keeping him safe. She had fought off Mott, but he wouldn't be the last enemy they faced. The rest of the Doxa were still out there, and Anna had no idea who they were or how to fight them.

"Maybe. I guess. Teej, why did the Midnight Man come after me?"

He looked off at the mountains, struggling to find the right words. "That name—the Midnight Man—is a very recent one. Before that, he was Mott. And before that…who knows? He was powerful yet also peculiar. Some Dreamers are harmless, some dangerous, but few of them waxed and waned like he did. One year he was a confused old man with barely enough Vig to conjure some flames out of the air, and the next, he would create some huge Haze that Spiraled and hurt thousands of people.

"In his last incarnation before the Midnight Man, he was a threat. I think he was senile. Aesthetes don't have to die, you see. As long as they have some small amount of Vig, they can manipulate their Hazes to keep themselves alive. Same with Metiks and the friends of Metiks. Why watch your loved ones get old and wrinkly when you can spend some Vig in a Haze and fix their body? When you live too long, your mind fills up. We're not supposed to live forever. Human brains don't delete old memories like computers. It can happen to anyone in a Haze for too long. It can be a form of madness, though some of them claim it's actually enlightenment. Insight, or some kind of transcendence. But that's superstition. When a Dreamer begins raving about creating a god or changing the world, it's normally them falling into a mental state called Torpor.

"Mott thought like that. He fell in with the Doxa. It made sense for all the more ruthless Dreamers to pull in the same direction. They made some really dangerous Hazes. When Linda and I appeared in his Haze and tried to help him get some parts of it under control, he reacted badly."

Anna could see the story was a hard one for Teej to tell. "What was it like? How did she die?"

"It was a nightmare. Horror like you can't believe. I…I can't really talk about it. I don't know how." The sadness in his eyes matched his voice.

She touched his shoulder. "It's okay. Just skip over exactly what happened. Tell me *why*."

He breathed out heavily and continued, "We had to try and get things back on track. Hazes can get out of control and Spiral, especially when they are very ambitious. When Basine comes back, it comes back without compromise or care for those it hurts. You can't pull at the threads of reality too much without the whole picture starting to fray."

She shook her head unconsciously, but he noticed.

"I know this is hard for you to accept. Sometimes it's feelings as well as ideas; that's why it's hard to explain. You don't have the experience yet, but you'll learn and develop your Haze Sense eventually. Maybe I can explain better with an example?"

She could tell that a story was coming, and she didn't mind. The cool breeze took the edge off the bright sun, and she felt like she could stay there forever.

"So, there was a Hungarian Dreamer and pianist named Rezső Seress. Entire worlds burst forth into creation from his music. His fingers flowed like water over the keys.

"He wrote a piece called "Gloomy Sunday." Maybe you know it?"

Anna shook her head. Teej went on, "Rezső's music literally changed the world. The Haze he created Spiraled. It became self-replicating and grew exponentially, which is called a Fluxa Haze.

"The Dreamer creates a Haze by combining their Art with Vig to build something new. Like I've already told you, Vig is an energy they harvest from the world that's generated by people or places that inspire. This musician's Haze was so beautiful and enchanting that it started to pull Vig from the people who saw it. The Haze filled their senses with the smell of home and the touch of a lover. It left them enraptured; unable to do anything but listen.

"A Fluxa Haze can change the world, but Fluxas often Spiral. When a Haze Spirals, Basine snaps back and the damage done to everyone within the Haze is severe. It *hollows* people. And that was what happened. "Gloomy Sunday" took everything away from those people. It left them empty and lost, unable to think or feel. They were detached from reality, lost in the music."

"Lost? Lost where?" Anna asked.

"They fell between the cracks of a Haze and the real world, and those cracks led to oblivion. One by one, they killed themselves. "Gloomy Sunday" became known as The Suicide Song. It took away their will to live.

"A few people touched by the music were left barely alive. Their souls were carved up, and their feelings and memories were ripped from their minds. Afterwards, their lives would be filled with loss.

"Now, if a Metik had been there, it could have played out differently. A good Metik could have stabilized the Haze. Maybe it would still Spiral, maybe not, but regardless, lives could have been saved.

"Maybe that's an idealized example, and maybe this story didn't happen exactly as I told it, but the point stands. At our best, Metiks save people. We police the dream."

Anna nodded. She could do more than face serial killers or fight monsters. She could save people. Being a Metik, or an Undreamer, could be more than just surviving attacks by insane Dreamers. That was something she could feel good about. His story was something she could hold onto, even if it wasn't wholly true. It was enough to convince her to stick with Teej.

They sat in silence for a moment, and Anna's mind wandered. She thought about her mother. If Anna could have explained this all to her, she would have understood and maybe would even convince Anna to help Teej. Her mother had always protected her, but she'd also taught Anna that fighting for herself and for others was important, even if it was risky. If the Doxa wanted to hurt her, she would defend herself. Anna had always been willing to fight her external demons.

Glancing over at him, she noted that he seemed much healthier now. The respite had obviously helped him, and Anna felt better, too. Whatever the Aesthete of this Haze had in store for them, it could wait. If there was danger here, it would have to come to them. Sitting here on the old bench, looking at the mountains, Anna stretched out and smiled. The air was cool, but the bright sun warmed her skin. The cuts on her side would need attention later, but for now, she felt no pain, so she didn't move. Instead, she nudged him to continue, content to listen to the sonorous lilt of his voice as much as the words he said.

"I got a bit off topic. You wanted to know why the Doxa were trying to kill us?"

"Yeah! Get to the point." She grinned.

"Well, as I said, Mott was losing his mind. His last Haze had started to Spiral. Linda and I stopped it, but Linda didn't make it. To stop his Haze, we had to hurt him. Linda was a powerful Metik. She was *strong*. The rest of the Doxa were involved, and the fight got messy. Two other Dreamers, Drowden and the Apoth, were there too, along with a Metik named Wildey. Turns out he'd been looking for an opportunity to stab me in the back for a long time. He made the situation *much* worse. Everything went wrong. Linda died, and I made it out, but Basine came down hard. Mott's power dissolved, and then he disappeared. My mind was in shreds. I took a while to recover, and I don't even know what happened to Wildey. I think he found a way out, but if he survived, he would be even more beat up than me.

"That's when you got caught up in this. Mott managed to retain some of his Etunes. The Night Collectors were sent to kill me. Normally, they wouldn't be a problem, but I was in a weakened state and my mind was a mess. I fought them for a long time. I travelled...I don't know how far. Eventually, they tracked me to the city. When I found you, they started following you, too.

"And from there, you know the rest. Something unlocked in you that night when you were drugged. After that, you couldn't hide anymore because you were stuck Behind the Veil. The Night Collectors and the Midnight Man sniffed you out and realized you were a threat. They tried to end you before you became aware of your Praxis, but they were too late. You had already awoken."

He smiled as he said the last part, and she couldn't help but smile back. His eyes held something like pride, or maybe respect. Whatever it was, it made her feel better.

"I still don't understand how I became a Metik though. Why me?"

A voice from behind them said, "He doesn't remember."

They both spun around to see a tall, lithe figure standing on a low wall.

"Vinicaire!" shouted Teej.

"Sorry to interrupt your reverie, young lady," said Vinicaire. "And my old friend Donnel! You were clearly both having a moment."

The Dreamer's strongly accented upper-class English drawl was slick like oil. A black suit and cloak seemed to accentuate his height. His whole outfit was mildly ridiculous; a matador crossed with Jack the Ripper. A navy waistcoat exaggerated the thinness of his waist, while his puffy, ornate white shirt looked like a table cover. The wide cuffs showed off lithe, ropey wrists and long pointed fingers at the end of curled, bird-like hands. A featureless metal mask covered the left side of his face, while the right was fine featured and handsome, despite a sneer.

Holding his head high and standing sideways with one foot forward, he looked like he was posing for a photograph no one was taking. He stroked a luciferian goatee, which made his countenance match the ridiculousness of his outfit. His gaze was predatory, and his ice-white teeth gleamed.

"Don't get up, my compatriots! Take your time. Please savor your first adventure together."

Teej stood and backed away, taking Anna by the arm and pulling her behind him.

"What do you want, Vinicaire?"

"Now, now. No need to be so accusatory, my sullen friend! I only want to help." His enunciation was high camp. Like a pantomime villain. "Do I need a greater motivation than my desire to save a friend in need from a most heinous fate? And at the hands of such a petty, grubby little Dreamer. What a nasty situation that was. The Midnight Man! What a name!"

Anxious, Anna turned to Teej to see how she should react. She wanted to ask if they were in danger. Would she have to fight this Aesthete too? She couldn't gauge his reaction. He seemed as confused as she was.

"You don't help people, Vinicaire."

"No, I don't help people when they ask me to or when they expect it. And I think we can agree that when you turned around

186

there, you did *not* expect to see me. The look on your faces is priceless!"

As he spoke, Vinicaire strutted back and forth like he was on a stage. His arms made big loops in the air as he talked, like he was addressing an invisible audience. He seemed completely insane, and so patently ridiculous that Anna almost laughed.

"We are not friends," Teej said flatly.

"No, we are not, but I don't wish ill upon you, Donnel. Nor do I wish any harm for your friend. In fact, I like her very much. That's why I made this gift for you both."

"I don't want gifts. I don't need anything from you."

The visible half of Vinicaire's mouth curled into a smile. He practically pranced in front of them. After a brief pause, he restrained himself and adopted a posture of mock solemnity. "We are all so serious today! Let us be serious together then. If you had to guess whether this was your first adventure with Anna, or your last, which would you stake your life on?"

As Vinicaire spoke, Anna's stomach turned into knots. There was a parting of clouds in her mind as she started to put all the clues together. As dizziness overtook her, she struggled to answer the questions that she should have been asking before now. *How did they get here? How could Teej be talking and walking and awake?*

Suddenly, Teej turned to her, and she saw sadness in his eyes. Deep, sincere sorrow. He had just realized as well.

"Oh, Anna, I hope this was enough. I know it wasn't, but I believe in you. You can do this without me."

Anna struggled to get a breath, and her hands shook. No, this was all wrong.

Teej turned to Vinicaire and said simply, "Thank you."

The Dreamer bowed deeply, his sneer replaced with some form of sincerity. Anna's mind scrambled to figure out what was happening.

"Anna, this was both," Teej said, expecting her to understand. She didn't.

"Both what?" she said, tears forming at the corners of her eyes.

"Vinicaire gave us this one chance to work together. I'm too badly hurt. I don't think anyone can fix me, so you'll be on your own from here on. At least we got one Haze to explore and escape together. And when we get out, only you will continue onwards."

"Teej," she pleaded. "Please, no!"

"Sorry, Anna; this is *both*. Do you see? It's our first adventure together. And our last."

As he said it, Vinicaire opened a door that hadn't been there a moment before. Through the door that dissolved the Haze around them, Anna could see the hospital. The lifeless body of Teej lay on the bed. Next to him, the doctors and nurses ran back and forth in a panic. By his side, a life support machine displayed a long, flat green line.

PART TWO

The Ash Catches a Spark

twenty-two

It was a little magazine shop with the appearance of a corner store, nestled deep in the city's heart, close to everything but far from anything. Colorful sweets and bright confectionary lined one wall, dirty newspapers and sleazy magazines in plastic bags along the other. Barely big enough for four people at once, it was dimly lit by the tiny lamp on the counter. If you came into the store at night, you wouldn't be able to see anything except the items around the counter and the attendant.

Peter looked up from his book and stared into the mirror by the magazines to see a young black man with a wispy beard, gaunt cheeks and dark, sleepy eyes stare back at him. Unable to bear his own reflection for more than a moment, he looked away. He shouldn't let his mind wander. He had a job to do. In the completely silent domain that he called home, Peter was more than a store assistant. He stood on the periphery of a Staid Haze and guarded a gateway that was well hidden and widely sought.

Peter didn't really understand the nature of his job. He didn't understand about Hazes and Dreamers. Even though he guarded the entrance, he didn't know what went on inside the August Club. While his mind grasped the danger and the power of that gateway, it fumbled the details. Somewhere deep in his mind was the memory of the day he found this place, but he could no longer grab hold of that memory. Like a gossamer thread of fabric, each time he tried to grasp hold of it, it slipped through his fingers. Rooting through his memories frustrated him, so instead, he accepted his fate. He had to stay there until *they* let him come inside. Running his thumb along the edge of his book, Peter looked up at the clock. It was two a.m. He still had three hours left on his shift. Strange how he always seemed to have three hours left on his shift. He was sure the clock was broken, but he never climbed above the stack of newspapers in the corner to change the battery. What did it matter? He wasn't allowed to leave until they told him to go anyway.

Peter closed the book with a sigh. *The Stranger.* He couldn't remember reading it before, but it felt familiar, as if he had read it cover to cover. Even if the words on the page had been more exciting, Peter couldn't stop thinking about something else: the women.

Every thirty minutes or so another would walk past him. Usually just one girl, but sometimes two. They'd mostly ignore him. Some of them might look at him, but none of them would talk to him. He'd nod or try to smile from time to time, and when they turned away, he would stare. Though he wanted to speak with them, he knew he shouldn't.

They were all beautiful in different ways. Cute or demure or pretty or sexy. Every type of girl would pass through, and every one of them would scramble his thoughts like a car crash. Just as he was getting his mind back in order, another would come in, somehow more striking than the last.

The process was always the same. After a nervous glance to see if she was being followed, she would come inside the shop and walk around the counter and through the back door to the alleyway.

They'd look around nervously and then pull aside the curtain that hung over the doorway to the August Club. He'd get one last look at them before they went through that curtain and disappeared up the stairs, and he'd be left with nothing to do but think of them.

Peter scrolled through his memories, remembering the women and the outfits they wore. Most covered themselves with heavy coats, but he still caught glimpses. Blonde women in luxurious furs. Brunettes in cocktail dresses. Redheads in black leather and buckles. The club catered to every desire, and they all captured his attention in one way or another.

"Excuse me."

Peter looked up in shock. The tiny voice belonged to the prettiest girl he had ever seen. She was a little shorter than him, and he was only five foot six. She had soft pink lips and dark eyes with even darker eyebrows. Her bright, blonde hair was swept to one side and touched her right shoulder. Beneath her fur coat, he caught glimpses of pale white skin.

"Ummmm…" He wanted to say hello but was lost for words. He wanted to say something funny, so he could hear her laugh. He wanted to be charming…In fact, all he wanted in the whole world was for the girl to stay here with him. His stomach swam with fear when he thought about her leaving. Being caught in the gaze of her soft, dark eyes was like feeling the sun on his skin.

"Peter, some guy found the club! Isn't it exciting? No one has found the club in months. He'll come soon. Do you remember what to do?"

Peter had no idea what she was talking about. He looked at the perfect pout of her lips, the curve of her neck into the point of her chin, and the pale pink of her cheeks. Though she knew him, he couldn't remember her at all.

"Awww, Peter, you're getting worse."

She lifted a small, delicate hand and pinched his chin between her thumb and finger as if he were a boy. As she held him, her jacket fell slightly open and he caught a glimpse of her pale chest and the curve of her breasts. She considered his eyes, hoping to find something that wasn't there.

"I…yes. I know…"

"No. No, you don't, Peter." She briefly stroked his cheek with a soft hand. "You're too out of it, sweetie. I'll send someone else. Just go back to your book."

With a final pat, she was gone. His head full of fuzz, Peter started to sit down. Then, realizing he wanted to see her one last time, he jumped to his feet and went to the back door. All he saw was the curtain flapping over the entrance to the August Club. She was already through, and he would never see her again.

Peter sat down, deflated. Why hadn't he said something? Now he was alone again, and all the warmth of that girl was gone. Rubbing his cheek where she had touched him, he forced himself to remember how it felt. He had to hold onto this memory and keep that feeling.

Peter tried to go back to his book, but it was impossible. Frustrated, he got to his feet and paced back and forth. What was wrong with him? It wasn't like this before. He used to talk with people. With the women. Didn't he? Maybe he flirted with them? Maybe he even had a girlfriend of his own? He couldn't remember the last person he'd talked to; he couldn't remember why he was here; he couldn't remember where he was, and he couldn't remember the way home.

Peter had no memory of anything before the August Club. *The most exclusive club in the world.* Was that right? That's what he remembered hearing. He recalled someone saying something like, "Where all desires are met in the palace of the senses." Or maybe he had read that in a magazine. Peter's mind was a mess, and he knew it. His time would soon be up which meant that he was in trouble.

Being in this place, so close to this doorway, affected people. He was lost. Uneasy but unsure why, Peter started to walk toward the back door of the store. If he was about to be dismissed, he should try to pass through the doorway he had guarded so long. He should pull aside the blue curtain, walk up the stairs and enter the August Club himself. Why hadn't he tried before? Every minute his brain burned with curiosity about what was in there. Why not just go and look? Walking away from his tiny desktop lamp, past the rotating stand of comics and out toward the back door, he cautiously wandered toward the exit. Eyeing the blue curtain that hung completely still in the dusky, airless night, he inched closer, looking around to see if anyone was following.

The curtain parted, and a woman appeared. Startled, he scampered back to the till, nervously avoiding her gaze.

"You there! Peter. We need to talk."

She walked around and stood straight in front of him. He forced himself to meet her gaze. The stern woman was dressed like a domina. Tight latex gloves went up over her elbows, while her waist was cinched into a shiny black corset. A little black hat sat atop her immaculately styled brown hair, which was worn half-up and half-down, long enough to reach her lower back. She was, just like all the other women, breathtakingly attractive, although older and more formal than the rest. Her tone was serious. Officious. He flinched when she spoke. "We think it's time for you to go, Peter."

"Whe…where?" he mumbled.

"We don't care. There was a meeting, and it has been decided. Your contract is over. Thank you for your time."

The words cut him, but her demeanor was unassailable. She spoke with a kind of assurance and confidence he couldn't match. Peter was a stuttering mess, but he wanted to bargain with her while he had a chance. He had to try now, before the opening was gone forever.

"Can I…go in?"

"What? In where?"

"To, the umm—" He pointed weakly toward the back door and the entrance to the club.

"Of course not. Go home. This way is closed to you now."

Peter started to panic, like he was sinking. He had to convince her. "But I…"

Before he could mumble any more excuses, the bell rang for the front door, and a man walked in with curly red hair, freckles, threatening eyes, and a mischievous grin.

"I made it! Show me in, please," he said to Peter.

"Mister…?" she asked.

"Wildey."

"I am the hostess. Elizabeth Needham. Follow me, please."

Wildey nodded curtly then glanced at Peter for a fraction of a second. Peter felt instantly threatened. He put his head down and shrunk back into the corner. Wildey turned back to look at the hostess. "Do you need my I.D. or something?"

"No need, sir. You've made it this far. Finding the August Club is the only barrier to entry. You may pass."

He smiled rakishly then moved past them. The Hostess pointed her shiny, gloved arm at the back door, and he went out, disappearing through the curtain. The confident man had moved through a barrier Peter would never be able to cross. The hostess turned back to Peter, and he hoped she might tell him he could go, too.

"Peter, you were warned this would happen when you started," she said sternly. "Don't you remember anything? You paid this price. You found the entrance but were too weak to go in, so we gave you the chance to see the visitors, but to never enter yourself. Don't you remember? You said yes. You begged us for that chance. You knew that eventually your mind would—"

She trailed off. Peter didn't remember any of it. He had been here, in the light of the little lamp, for as long as he could recall.

"Goodbye," she said dismissively as she walked out the back door. Without a backward glance, she was gone.

Peter stood and waited, but no one came. What now? Could he just stay here to see the women? Or could he follow her now and sneak in? He decided to try.

Walking out the rear entrance, Peter missed the first step and stumbled into the back alley. Outside in the frigid air, the broken cobbled street was slick with glittering ice. Peter almost slid as he scrambled to the curtain. Taking a moment to gaze upon the gateway he had guarded for so long, he swallowed deeply and prepared to take the step he had never been brave enough to take before. He amazed himself with his own resolve. Finally, he would get in! Inside, the women would be waiting, and he could see them and maybe touch them and he would re-member himself. His hands shook and his whole body quivered as he steeled himself.

Grasping the bottom of the curtain, he lifted it slowly. Rais-ing it higher and higher, until, in a rage, he pulled it from its railing and ripped it away. It fell to the ground as he tripped backward. He sat in the middle of a deep, dirty puddle, and his eyes filled with tears. Looking down on him—unmoved and un-interested in his plight—was a cold, impenetrable brick wall.

twenty-three

Unwrapping the scarf from around her neck, Anna looked
out the bus window to see the rain start again. She
leaned against the glass, pointedly ignoring the curious
glances and blank stares of the five other passengers, and rivu-
lets ran past her face. She closed her eyes for a moment and
breathed out long and low, then opened them again and stared
straight ahead. Two seats ahead of her, an old gray-haired woman pulled a wooly cardigan closer around her shoulders. She
sniffled into a handkerchief, then balled it up and pushed it deep
into her handbag.

The hospital entrance and the parked ambulances faded off
into the gray distance as the bus pulled away. There wasn't
much traffic, but their progress through the dark city streets was
slow, giving Anna time to think about everything that had happened. It had been a week since their time in Canfranc. In that
period, the doctors had managed to stabilize Teej. Somehow, he
still clung on and during his recovery, she had gone to him every
day. As her injuries from the train accident healed, he healed
too, but much more slowly. Her path to recovery was a straight
line, but his was a crooked path, and at any time he could lose
his way.

Tonight, she had stayed as long as she could, but the doctors had made it clear that she was in the way. They'd urged her

to go home and get some sleep. Eventually, she had no energy left to argue, so she consented. On her way out, Teej had twitched as if he knew she was leaving, but she also might have imagined it. She knew, though, that past the breathing tube and the mask and the doctors running back and forth, he was still there. He knew what was happening. He was still fighting.

The doctors were vague when she asked if he would make it. They would avoid her gaze, shrug, and change the subject. An induced coma had been the prescription for recovery. It was rare for someone to survive the onset of multiple organ failure, but he had this time. The doctors were clear that if this happened again, he would not pull through. And they could make no promises that he would ever fully recover. If he did wake up, there was a chance he wouldn't even remember his own name.

The encounter with Vinicaire was stuck in her mind, too. The Dreamer was so strange. What had he hoped to achieve? He hadn't been able to heal Teej, so why bother taking them into his Haze? Teej didn't like or trust him. Anna couldn't make sense of it all. All the unanswered questions swirled uselessly in her head. She had no one to ask, and she was left with doubts about her own memories. Without Teej, she started to feel that word creep up on her again. What was the point in all of this? In anything? *Desolation.*

As her mind freewheeled through the same old questions, she looked off into the distance, and it took her a few moments to realize the bus wasn't moving. Everyone had gotten off except for one woman, who was now arguing with the driver at the front. Anna leaned forward to listen to what they were saying. All she could make out from the driver was "Not my fault—"

She looked around to try and gauge where they were, but it was too dark. She could see some houses, some trees and a bus stop, but no landmarks. This was the last thing she needed.

Getting to her feet and moving to the front, she leaned her head to the side to let the driver see her confusion while he continued to debate with the irate woman between them. Seemingly welcoming the distraction, he leaned around the woman to see Anna and said, "Lady, did you not hear me? The engine's overheated. You need to get off."

Anna nodded. "Is there another bus coming to get us?"

"I'm the last one on this route for the night. If you wait for twenty minutes, an engineer will come repair this one. But you need to get off now."

Anna shuffled past the old woman, stepping out into the chilly night air. The wind blew her jacket and rustled the trees behind the bus stop, which made the quiet residential area feel more like a forest wilderness. She walked over to the bare metal bench by the bus stop. The seat was cold and the thin, plexiglass, graffiti and dirt covered walls of the bus shelter provided little protection from the weather. The moment she sat, the doors of the bus closed, and it drove away.

"The fuck...?" Anna muttered under her breath as she was left completely alone. She rubbed her forehead in frustration, then put her head in her hands and closed her eyes.

"Hi, Anna."

Anna jumped from the seat and spun to see a girl sitting beside her.

"I am soooo sorry! I didn't mean to frighten you. Vinicaire sent me."

Her voice was honey-soft, childish with a lazy Canadian twang. She had a cute face: small with a button nose and dark brown eyebrows beneath scruffy braids of dyed pink and green hair. Anna guessed she was in her early twenties, but she looked much younger. Her green tank top and baggy shorts with thick tights hung loosely on her skinny frame and were completely unsuitable choices of attire for this cold night. Her fingerless gloves were ornamental rather than practical. She chewed loudly on gum.

"Everybody is talking about you. It's, like, so common right now to hear people say how you're the next big thing. You're so pretty, but you look so freaked out right now. Right?"

Anna struggled to respond. She wasn't sure if she should be on guard, but nothing about this girl seemed threatening. The way she talked and acted was disarmingly strange, though. As if she thought Anna was a close friend.

"I haven't told you my name!" said the girl. "Didn't mean to freak you out. I'm Elise. Sorry if I'm a bit strange right now. I only slept four hours this week, and I'm in a really surreal head space right now. All I can see is swirling colors. You know?"

She smiled as she talked, her big, dark eyes shining. Anna felt like she was talking to a fan after a concert. "Um, hi, Elise. What do you want?"

"Uh, I just *told* you. Vinicaire sent me! He is so back right now. You know? He's off the *charts*!"

Her expressions were exaggerated, a little like Vinicaire's, and she seemed both distracted and laser-focused at the same time.

"Why did he send you?"

"Oh, Anna, this is just so crazy! This is, like, the worst place to talk with you, right? A bus stop! That's so *not* Vinicaire. He should have sent me to meet you in an old abandoned fairground or on stage during one of his performances. You know? But maybe it *is* Vinicaire. *This* stage is full of the ghosts of people who watch from the corners of space and time. But they're just watching a bus stop and not some grand place. An abandoned stop that everyone passes, but no one gets off for years until you. So…"

Elise was hard to follow. Her effusive, stop-start rambling was frustrating. Anna needed someone to talk to about everything that had happened, but she was pretty sure Elise was not the right person.

"Slow down. What does Vinicaire want?"

Elise smiled broadly. "Sorry, I'm just glad to have someone to talk to. You know my parents don't understand any of this? And me and you are practically the same age. I bet your parents wouldn't give you all this trouble. But you're a Metik, so it's way different for you. You're so hot right now, you know? Did I say that already?"

"Elise, please...No, my parents wouldn't understand this either. Why do you want to talk to me?"

"Oh, right. So Vinicaire wanted me to tell you to tell Teej that he was just trying to help. He said to tell you that he would help more if he could, but to also tell you that he doesn't normally help people, and he can't heal people because that's not his thing *at all*. But Vinicaire wanted to give you both some time together, so although he couldn't, like, *fix* Teej, he could kind of bring him back for a while to be with you. That is *so* romantic, right? Don't tell your hero-man, but Vinicaire really hates Drowden and Mott and those Doxa guys. But you probably figured this out already, right? Do you have a sword or anything? I have a sword."

Elise bent over into her bag and pulled something from the shadows. She grasped a long, sharpened piece of steel. It looked like a replica katana, curved and silver with a blade that seemed to shine even in the low light, and she held it very unsteadily.

"Jesus!" Anna exclaimed as she leaned away from the girl, backing into a corner of the bus stop. Elise jumped to her feet and started swinging the blade in exaggerated thrusts and parries, killing invisible enemies while making swooshing noises.

"It's okay, Anna. I know how to use this, but a warrior—SWOOSH!—never uses her martial prowess unless threatened.

SWOOSH! Also, I always keep a knife in my boot just in case. Oh, you should get a weapon, too. Like nunchakus!"

"Elise! No, I don't want a weapon. And please stop swinging the sword for a minute."

Elise sat back down on the bench and put her sword across her lap. "Sorry, Miss Important Metik Lady," she said with a cartoonish pout. "I was being careful."

She looked up and smiled again, her moods an emotional rollercoaster. "Okay, so, Vinicaire is just...Uh! Just so amazing. He's the world greatest performer, you know. And he wants to make the abandoned spaces of the world his stage. Places where the world cries because the ground is lonely and the sky is feeling blue. Ha ha, blue! I didn't even mean that. Anyway, Vinicaire can only do those types of Hazes. That's his thing. When he wanted to help, he found a way to get you to an abandoned place, so Teej could heal a bit. Or he would have died. And while that would make some Dreamers happy, no one would be around to stop those guys Vinicaire hates."

Anna nodded. Elise was making some sort of sense. "I guess Vinicaire hates the Doxa, too. So Elise, you're a...?"

"I'm no Noop, if that's what you're going to say! I'm Vinicaire's assistant. I'm learning to be a Dreamer myself."

"Noop?"

"I'm *not* a Dreamer groupie. If I was one of those, I would just chase some Aesthete crush all day long, trying to be in their Hazes and stuff."

"Okay. So, you're...in training?"

"Exactly! So, Mr. Vinicaire wanted me to come find you, tell you that he tried to help, and ask you, in the nicest possible way, to leave him alone to do his things."

"Okay. Can I ask you about other things, Elise? Like do you—"

"You're really pretty," Elise interrupted.

Anna paused for a moment then laughed. This girl was impossible, but she was disarmingly earnest.

"Well...look, thanks. It's actually nice to talk to someone. Thanks."

"Thank *you*, Anna! It's nice for me, too. I don't get much *quality* time with Vinicaire. I like to talk with you. Vinicaire...it's not that he doesn't like you, but he doesn't not-not like you. You know? But no one likes you, really, 'cause you're maybe an Undreamer. And I don't know what that means, and people seem to think it's bad. Except me. I think you're ebullient."

"Ummm...thanks. So, how did you meet Vinicaire?"

"He was at my art school."

"Of course."

"Well, he came in as a guest speaker. I could tell straightaway that he was looking for an apprentice. He was making a play based on these paintings. Like Anna King crossed with, I dunno, some nightmare Caravaggio faces, you know. And I told him that I was a dancer and singer, and he felt the connection between us. So, then he showed me his Hazes like Jericho and Canfranc and Asenovgrad. And I knew I had to help him...I mean, learn from him. Become an Aesthete, too."

"What do you know about Drowden, Elise? And the Doxa and this guy Wildey?"

Anna wasn't sure if Elise's answers would help her, but they were better than nothing. She didn't know who to talk to, and she didn't have anything to say, so maybe this girl was better than going home and sitting in a dark room with only her thoughts for company.

"Hmm, I dunno. No one really tells me these things. I've heard people say Wildey's found his way into the August Club. Can you believe that? I would love to get there."

"The what?"

"Oh, you don't know about the August Club? It's supposed to be the hardest club to find in the world. A place where all your fantasies come true. My friend Sarah is really into getting spanked and handcuffs and stuff, so she went to this fetish club, and it was really unsatisfying. The guys were all ugly and old and fat, and she said it wasn't like how she imagined at all. So, she tried to find the August Club, but she had to solve these puzzles and…"

"So, the August Club is some weird Haze that's hard to find?"

"Yeah."

"And Wildey is there?"

"Yeah, yeah! Are you thinking what I'm thinking, Anna?"

"I don't think so."

"We can try to find it to amaze Teej when he wakes up. Although Vinicaire would never ask, I think he wants me to find it, too. I bet he would like it if I figured it out. Maybe we can take my best friend Steven, too. He's a virgin, and he's always trying to stay over, and he's totally—"

Anna started to tune out what the girl was saying. She had a pang of worry. "Elise, are you going to be okay? You're shivering. Aren't you cold? Look…do you want to come back to my place?"

Elise looked like she was about to protest, then she visibly changed tack. "Yeah, it sure is cold. Brrr! It would be great to come back to yours. I can tell you about Steven and when I caught him touching himself in my mom and dad's house. He stole my underwear and—"

"Another bus is coming. We can talk about everything—well everything relevant—when we get back. Okay?"

Elise nodded enthusiastically. As Anna stepped forward to hail the approaching bus, she wondered if she was making a mistake. Elise was her only link to the world Behind the Veil right now, though. She hoped that taking her back home would calm her down a bit, but as they stepped onto the bus, Elise continued. "Okay, sure. I mean, I don't mind sleeping with you, even if we just hug or whatever, but I'm not really into girls. Except I kind of am sometimes, but not you. I prefer girls that— *my sword*! Okay, got it. So anyway, where do you live? Is it near any good sushi places?"

Anna sighed and smiled. Ushering Elise onto the bus ahead of her, she followed, feeling a bit like an older sister.

twenty-four

Living with Elise, even for one night, proved to be both infinitely more challenging and enjoyable than Anna expected. After they'd arrived at Anna's apartment, most of the night had been spent in a largely one-sided conversation wherein Elise outlined every event that had occurred in her life, while Anna tried to probe her with questions incisive enough to learn something useful.

After a brief though surprisingly deep sleep, with Elise passed out at the end of a bed like an adopted puppy, Anna had time to make some coffee, call the hospital for news on Teej, and check her messages. The coffee helped her regain some semblance of humanity, but the lack of messages was frustrating, and Teej's condition was stable but unchanged. At somewhat of a loss as to how to proceed, Anna sat in the bedroom eating breakfast while watching Elise go through her wardrobe, passing judgment on what she found. "You need some more styles, Anna. Where's your girly stuff? Where's your sexy stuff? Where's your gothic Lolita? This is all so—" she held up a gray cardigan "…soccer mom!"

"Soccer mom? Actually, I think that cardigan *is* my mom's…Look, never mind that. Elise, what do you think I should do? I'm supposed to help Teej, but he's in the hospital. I can't do anything for him. I feel useless. Maybe I could find his friend?"

"He has friends?"

"At least one. Garret. Do you know him?"

"Nope."

"He was Teej's teacher, but he retired, I guess. He said we would never see him again."

"Maybe we could find him! Or maybe another Aesthete could help. They could heal him. I mean, some Aesthetes can do that, if he was in their Haze. Vinicaire would have done that if he could. He can't heal people though, he can only make them not die. And he can move people around. He's 'The Travelling Troubadour.' Or is it thespian? He finds ways to get to places and then performs. But that won't help us, right? Maybe we could try to find someone else to help Teej?"

"Where?"

"Uhhh, I don't know that many Hazes. Vinicaire always takes me. I've never gone without him."

"What about the August Club? You mentioned that before."

"Yeah! Let's do it! Do you know where it is, though? I don't actually know how to get in. I only know one Staid Haze. And all of Vinicaire's Corpa Hazes."

"I don't know how to get there either. What's a Corpa? And Staid?"

"Oh, come on, Annie!" Elise threw her arms in the air theatrically. "That's beginner stuff. Didn't Teej tell you *anything?* Corpa are normal Hazes made by Dreamers. Staid are the ancient ones that no one owns, and they never go away. Like Malamun and The Realm and The Moonlight Road and the August Club and Avalon and like a bajillion others. I don't know how to get into any of those. Except the ones that I do. Like…we could go to Malamun. It's such a scene place now. Just Noops everywhere, all hanging off Dreamers' arms. It's super gross. But Aesthetes *do* go there sometimes. Maybe your teacher Garret would be there? I mean, I don't think so, but maybe…"

"What's Malamun?"

"It's a bar. It used to be so cool. Vinicaire would go. He took me the first time. But he says it's full of wannabes now. Noops and washed up Dreamers. And it can be dangerous. Maybe for you it would not be such a good idea, actually…"

Anna had to get moving again. Waiting here for news about Teej was too painful. She could go back to the hospital and watch him struggle, or she could do something useful. It wasn't a choice at all.

"Okay, we could try. I mean, most people don't have any particular reason to harm us, right? Except the Doxa, and, well, they can come for us here any time they want anyway. Yeah, let's go to Malamun. Maybe we can learn something that will help us."

Elise leaped forward and lay across the bed in front of Anna, rolling onto her stomach and looking up at her with big eyes. "Yes! But you must let me dress you. You can't go dressed so…normal."

"Really? More formal? Or should I dress like *you*? Or Vinicaire?"

For a second, a shadow went over Elise face as if Anna had insulted her, but she shook it off and smiled quickly. "There's nothing wrong with how he dresses. Anyway, at Malamun they're big on expression. So, we can find something cool. Could you wear your hair back? And straighten it. With these…" She jumped over to Anna's jewelry box and grabbed a big, chunky set of earrings she'd gotten as a gift but never worn.

"Wear these with your hair back. And do you have, like, a choker? Or a collar with a D ring on it, and I'll pull you along on a leash. That would be really hot. And you need good heels.

None of your flat shoes. You should dress cyber goth-meets-Alexander McQueen. But casual."

"Sure, we'll figure it out. Let me just go wash up. then we can…put an outfit together." Anna couldn't decide if she was having fun or in a nightmare. It was probably a bit of both. As she walked out the bedroom, Elise called after her, "I'll just keep looking for things you can wear. I think you should be more of a vamp. You think? Did I mention Malamun is on the moon?"

Anna stopped in her tracks. "What?"

twenty-five

Hands shaking, head filled with static, Peter was a diffracted creature of light shone through a fun house mirror. He stood separate from the world around him. The city was a series of blocks and colors his mind couldn't recognize. It all brought a hazy sense of nostalgia, but no actual recognition. Streets, people, buildings, cars. He felt like he was seeing everything for the first time. There was a patina of shimmering wrongness around every object and person in his visual field. The world was made up of shapes clumsily cut from sheets of colored paper.

As he stumbled down the city street, eyes glazed, mouth slack with a rivulet of drool swinging with each step, no one helped him. Some would almost stop. They would almost try to help, but unsure what to do or say, they'd walk on. *Just another young, homeless black man.*

Peter's bifurcated consciousness had some idea of what had happened. On one level, he was pure instinct. He felt a rising sense of panic and confusion that manifested as a desperate, loping half-run as he traversed the streets looking for something—anything—that was familiar. On another level, he realized why he was like this. He had spent a long time in—or at least close to—a Staid Haze. The August Club. He'd been there for…he didn't know how long. Someone had once warned him that his mind would suffer, particularly his memories. He hadn't listened.

As he leaned his head on an electronics store window, his drive to continue drained out of him. A portion of his consciousness was amused by how much more realistic these moving images on the television screens looked than the world around him. Since he left his little nest in the store next to the August Club's entrance, he had deteriorated rapidly. His legs gave way underneath him, and he slid down the glass, collapsing in a pile in front of the store. He could hear voices around him, but he lacked the will to force his eyes open. He felt the shadows of people around them, but couldn't acknowledge them. There was nothing wrong with his body, but his life force was gone. The currency of his soul was spent. He had nothing left.

Slipping out of consciousness, Peter felt a strong hand on his shoulder. "I know you're lost, son. I'm going to need your help. I need you to do something. Say yes. Say yes, and I'll pull you out. Then you belong to me."

Peter couldn't open his eyes or move his body, but he could speak. Maybe one word, if he pushed himself. Like a drowning man, he was clawing at the air for anything to grab on to. This man's words were the only hope he had in a world already going dark.

"Yes," he croaked. "Yes."

twenty-six

Anna discovered that travelling to Malamun with Elise was a lot like trying to navigate a straight line through a toy shop with a toddler. Every time they seemed to make some progress, Elise would get sidetracked with something she spotted in a store window. In particular, Anna learned to dread walking past thrift shops or anywhere that sold shoes. For the first time in her life, she felt some sympathy for her own mother.

Their progress from the morning had been slow. Elise complicated every decision. Despite Anna's insistence that clothes weren't that important to her, she'd been forced into trying a hundred different outfits. When they finally found something Elise was happy with, and Anna didn't feel completely ridiculous in, Elise then declared she had to find an equally "scene" look for herself. Anna had been forced to preside over which outfit Elise should wear, and that took even longer. When they finally got underway, Elise was dressed like an anime sailor, combining girlish pigtails with a blue and white blouse and blue and white knee socks and sneakers. Anna, meanwhile, was wearing overall shorts with thick tights and sneakers, covered by her thick winter jacket. Which Elise hated.

Already that morning ordeal seemed a lifetime away. They'd been walking through the trendy West End of the city for an eternity, and Elise was calling Anna over to look in another shop window.

"What about these heels? Killer, right?

"Anna, look at this. Is it real fur? That is so gross.

"Anna, this pawn shop has ninja stars. You need a weapon. Like my sword. Anna? *Anna!*"

And on and on. It took them almost two hours to get to the supposed entrance of Malamun, and Anna's patience was long gone. Still, Elise refused to simply tell her where they were going, and instead took them on an increasingly circuitous route. At one point, Anna almost slapped the girl when she realized they'd passed the same street corner twice.

"Oh, yeah, sorry. I'm used to coming from the other side of the city. And I thought you might want to look at this little store that sells crystals and stuff."

"No, I do not want to look at crystals. I want to go to Malamun, like we agreed."

"Okay. Jeez, no need to be so rude. I think your problem is that you're not self-actualized."

"Sure, maybe that's my problem. Come on, let's go."

Half an hour after their terse exchange, they arrived at a thoroughly unpromising office building in the financial sector of the city. Peeking nervously through the windows into the reception area of the stylish lobby, Elise chewed on her chipped fingernails while leaning next to a black tiled pillar. She had stopped talking for the first time since Anna had met her.

"Is this it? This *can't* be it. How do we get in?"

"Yeah, it's through there," replied Elise. "But the reception lady is *such* a bitch. And if she thinks we're not supposed to be there, then we're stuck. We can't look like Noops. We have to be, like, *confident*. We get past her, and if she doesn't hit the panic switch, then we get in."

"The panic switch?"

"Yeah, we go in a service elevator behind her desk. But if she thinks we're Noops, then she'll hit the switch and it will just be a normal service elevator. All the Staid Hazes are hard to get into, even when you're Behind the Veil. We have to make sure they don't think we're riffraff."

"Well, how did you get in before?"

Elise looked nervous and avoided Anna's gaze.

"You've never actually been, have you?"

"Yeah, I've been! But always with Vinicaire. I came here twice before on my own, and the bitch wouldn't let me through. Maybe *you* can get us through."

Elise fidgeted. She pulled at her blouse, rubbing at an imaginary stain. Anna gasped as she realized Elise's real motives for bringing her here.

"Elise, this is why you found me, isn't it? You wanted to get in, and you couldn't by yourself."

Elise stomped her foot in mock irritation. "I saw Vinicaire less than a day ago, so I'm happy. I like to take every chance that comes along to see him because sometimes I go weeks or even months between visits. You don't know what it's like. Every day that I'm not with him is a day further from happiness. A counter of despair ticks away between each time I see him. Each day apart makes me feel worse and worse—twice as bad as the day before. I know he doesn't like Malamun anymore, but he still *might* be there. Or we might see something else good. You never know, right?"

Anna sighed. She was beginning to understand Elise. She'd seen that kind of desperation before. Elise was in love.

"Should we even be here? Is there any point in going on? Will this actually help me *at all*?"

"Oh, sure it will! I really think we can get some help here. I am doing this for you. We're friends, right? I didn't mean to make this all about me. You know?"

There was a genuine sadness in Elise's eyes, and Anna felt a twang of sympathy. Part of Anna wanted to leave immediately, but where would that get her? Anna didn't trust her yet, but something told her Elise wasn't an enemy. Teej had told her to trust her Haze Sense. Was that what was guiding her now? She decided it was best to push on. Maybe there was still hope they could find help for Teej.

"We have to try, right? What else can we do? I'm tired of sitting around anyway." Anna leaned past the column and looked in at the receptionist. "You're right, she does look like a bitch."

Elise giggled. "I could just sword her. She should get a swording." Elise reached into her backpack and showed Anna the blade she still carried with her.

"Oh, God, can you please put that away? No swording. You're more likely to hurt yourself. Let's just walk in with confidence. Like we're supposed to be there. Like we know what we're doing."

Elise nodded apprehensively. Smoothing down her clothes, Anna straightened her back, raised her head high and motioned for Elise to follow. Walking briskly to the revolving door at the front of the building with Elise crowding in after her, they stepped inside together. As soon as Anna entered the building, she felt something. A familiar characteristic tingle, just like she'd felt going into Hazes before. It signaled to her that they were on the right track. They were close.

Glancing over at the receptionist, who examined them closely through thick-rimmed spectacles, Anna nodded a curt hello, trying to look as nonchalant as possible. The palms of her hands were sweaty, and her shoes squeaked across the polished floor as they walked. Elise's nervousness wasn't helping, and she cowered behind Anna like she was taking fire from an invisible sniper. She clung to the back of Anna's jacket. Anna tried to ignore the little hands pawing at her shoulders as she walked with purpose, trying to exhibit the aura of someone who came through that reception area every day.

Halfway across the foyer, she started to suspect this was all a mistake. By the time she reached the service elevator, she was sure. It was a big metal door, the kind you would walk past but never notice, and as she pulled on the handle, she was mortified to realize it wouldn't open. Forcing down panic and trying to appear calm, she pushed the handle again with all her strength. It wouldn't budge.

"Excuse me, ma'am," she heard the reception shout.

She ignored the voice and looked at Elise with dismay. They had been caught.

"Push, ma'am. Push."

Without turning around or acknowledging the advice, Anna pushed the door, and it opened easily. Bundling herself in after Anna, Elise stumbled through, and they shut the door behind them, all the while avoiding the gaze of the receptionist.

"Which floor?" Anna asked as they nervously eyed the buttons inside the dark, entirely utilitarian elevator. It certainly didn't look like they would be travelling to the moon inside this small metal box, but Anna was still feeling the distinctive shimmer of a nearby Haze. She tensed her body.

"Let's try two!" Elise said excitedly as she jabbed the button for the third floor. The elevator juddered to life. It rattled and rocked upward. With nothing else to do, they waited. Anna turned to Elise. The girl was biting her lip nervously.

"What am I doing?" Anna asked. She didn't expect an answer.

"I don't know," said Elise. "I told you this was a bad idea."

Anna shot her a look, but her anger died when she saw Elise's smile. The elevator shuddered and rumbled under their feet one more time, then stopped. The doors slid aside to reveal the stark, white corridors of Malamun.

twenty-seven

A crisp, enamel-white brightness forced Anna to squint as the elevator flooded with light. Stark white walls and bright strip lighting made it hard to interpret the space, but it seemed like they were facing a long, broad corridor. Blue, neon strips along the edges of the path and along the middle of the walls lit the area in a cool glow. At the end of the corridor was a corner beyond which they couldn't see. Behind a podium desk, a gleaming, metallic robot waited for them to approach and glanced down at a guest list.

Thin steel arms and legs connected to a boxy torso. Each arm ended in a three-fingered metal claw, and on the left arm was a long metallic blade that looked like a weapon. The head, which resembled a security camera with a bright blue bulb on the end, was connected to the body with five or six thin pistons around a core segregated metal spine. The spine flexed like it was a snake, allowing the robot to twist around unnaturally and shine its blue light in their direction.

As Anna and Elise shuffled closer, they noticed that the robot seemed to be overlaid with some kind of hologram. It only came into focus when they got closer and viewed it from the correct angle, but a definite glow of a human figure shone around the form of the robot. Anna could see straight through to the metallic core, but a blue neon outline of a man obscured the robotic endoskeleton within. The fuzzy holographic aura was of a smartly dressed man in a suit. The features of the face were blurry and indistinct, like a low-resolution television signal, but there was no question it was supposed to be a waiter. The hologram produced a constant ambient humming noise.

"Good evening. The proprietor of Malamun, Mr. Ozman, welcomes you. We are especially proud to welcome a Metik, and hope that as you are without a partner, you will make no rash decisions about the future of this Decadan. We remind you that Malamun is Staid and is an area of cultural importance. Please let us know if we can assist you in any way."

The robot's voice was tinny but utterly human. Eloquent and sonorous, it sounded like a well-spoken butler. Or a recording of a butler. The words seemed to come from a tiny speaker built into the robot's head, and as it spoke, it gestured for them to continue past the desk. Its motions were jerky and off-putting, only vaguely approximating human movement. Overall, Anna was confused by its anachronistic retro-futurism.

Elise walked forward confidently. She glanced dismissively at the robot while addressing Anna theatrically. "Come, Anna. We don't have time to dawdle."

Anna walked after her, skirting the edge of the wall as she passed the robot while trying to keep as far away from it as possible. As they turned the corner, the white corridor opened into a vast, wide atrium. The bar was lit in blue, elongating the shadows and casting a phantasmic pallor over all the surfaces. The tables, chairs, and floor glowed with long neon strips that made the room look like a world sketched out on graph paper, but Anna was most drawn to the convex windows along the walls. These long panels of glass stretched from waist height to ten feet above her head and looked out onto a vast, gray, airless landscape of rock and dust. The moon.

"Oh my God, Elise," Anna muttered under her breath.

"What? Oh, that? It gets boring after a while, once you've been here as many times as I have. There's nothing here *really*. Just dust and rocks and stuff. And these *people*. What a bunch of posers. I know I asked before, but does this hair color *really* suit me or were you just being nice? Hey Anna...*Anna!* You're not listening. Can you use your super powers to detect any cool Dreamers? Any at all?"

Ignoring Elise's pleas, Anna edged closer to the windows on the left side of the room, dismissing the robots and the people and the drinks and the dancers. She passed by the blurry hologram butler, the long bar in the middle of the room stacked with clear bottles of liquid, the myriad strangely dressed people who regarded her with indifference, the catsuit-wearing dancer on the podium nearby, the bouncers in black suits with sunglasses, and her friend who was wandering off in search of a drink. Anna hustled past them all, her guts twisting with vertigo and excitement as she ran toward one of those windows.

Barely noticing the shiny plastic sofa that she was climbing on, Anna pressed her hand against the glass and felt its coolness on her skin. She took a quick glance through the black sky encompassing her, and tears came to the corners of her eyes as she glanced down at the small blue planet she'd spent her whole life on.

Closer to the window, a sea of gray dust pockmarked with craters showed the surface was far less smooth than she expected. In the distance, an immense canyon with smooth rolling hills of undisturbed gray dominated the landscape. A nearby hump in the dust revealed a glint of metal. Maybe a vehicle? The light across the surface was glaring and hurt her eyes, while the blackness overhead was existentially overwhelming. The scene left her breathless.

Anna was on the moon, but her mind failed to comprehend what that meant and how far she had come. She struggled to reconcile the view in front of her with the feeling that she had just stepped out of an elevator. Despite the unreality of the situation, all her senses told her this *was* real.

Elise flopped on the sofa next to her. "They sometimes turn the gravity to 'moon' setting at night. It's really cool, but other than that, this place is a drag, right? A big disappointment. I mean the people here…they're all phonies. Right?"

Anna turned from the window and slid down into the seat next to Elise. She was unable to talk, but Elise was happy to fill the silence, shouting over the ambient dance music.

"Wow, this place really made an impression on you. Your skin's all goose-bumpy and your eyes are big and intense. When I came, I didn't care about being on the moon. I mean, it's not like there are people here. Except in the bar. And what a bunch of posers! Seriously, *look* at these losers. When I was here with Vinicaire, it was cooler. But, maybe, that's just because he was there. You know, I told him this story, and he laughed so much. I think it was the funniest story he ever heard. It was about—"

Elise went on, but Anna had tuned her out. Slowly coming to terms with the view outside, she turned her attention back to the room. It wasn't crowded. A few people milled around the white and blue paneled dance floor in the middle of the space, but most sat around the edges on broad, shiny sofas with clear glass tables in front of them.

The area was dominated by a raised bar in the center of the atrium. It looked like a huge theatre organ with broad silver pipes stretching up into the ceiling. Attractive men and women with strange, pale blue make-up served listless patrons. While the bar staff and waiters all wore similar white jumpsuits with black belts and big chunky shoes that looked like oversized sneakers, the patrons were dressed in a myriad of fashions.

Elise had been remarkably insightful with the outfits she'd chosen for them both. Eclectic as her clothing had seemed when they left the apartment, everyone here was dressed in similarly flamboyant attire. Her wooly winter jacket might have been bright yellow, but here, it did more than help ward off the chill in the air, and her clean new sneakers matched the pristine white floors. She felt silly wearing the chunky silver earrings, but not as silly as everyone else looked.

Although Anna was still adjusting to the strangeness of her surroundings, she was also aware that this was fundamentally *just* a bar and these were *just* people. As Elise had suggested, the clientele here thought very highly of themselves, and they seemed to spend a lot of their time glancing around the room to see if anyone else was looking at them. While Anna had worried that they would stand out from the crowd, no one seemed particularly interested in them, which put her at ease.

She started to regain her equilibrium and interrupted Elise mid-story. "Okay. Okay, so this *really* is the moon. We're in a Haze, and it's taken us to the moon."

Elise giggled. "What are you, the narrator? Yeah, we're on the moon. We're in Malumun, the dullest bar in the galaxy. Look at that guy over there with the beard and the topknot. Fucking hell! Let's get out of here quickly."

Anna focused her attention on Elise for a second, trying to gauge what the girl was thinking. She knew Elise was mostly here to try to find Vinicaire. It was obvious now that he wasn't here. Did she care about helping Anna, too?

The main atrium was spacious, but it seemed to be all there was to Malamun. The open-plan nature of this bizarre moon base didn't leave space for anyone to hide. The only area they couldn't see clearly was the mezzanine above them, which looked barely big enough for five or six tables. A narrow spiral staircase made of clear glass in the back corner was the only way up, and Anna guessed it was reserved for VIPs. A robot stood next to a burly man in a black suit with black sunglasses, obviously protecting the entrance to the exclusive area. The robot was surrounded by a fuzzy hologram that flickered on and off like it was broken.

"Elise." Anna tugged at her friend's sleeve to get her attention. "I'm sorry Vinicaire's not here."

Elise smiled wanly, apparently relieved that Anna understood her dismay. "Ah, it's cool. I saw him a few days ago. And I bet he is glad I am hanging out with you. He sent me to talk with you, after all."

"What should we do now? Recognize any Aesthetes that can help us?"

Elise scanned the room, holding her hand above her eyes like she was looking across a desert. They both spotted the man approaching them at the same time. He walked in a straight line toward them, pushing dancers out of the way as he strode across the room. He wore the black suit and dark glasses of the security staff, and at his side was a sheath for a blade of some sort. His implacable visage made him seem even more robotic than the actual robots. He stopped dead in front of them, addressing them in a formal, impersonal tone.

"The proprietor is glad to have you as guests. He asks if there is anything we can help you with. Obviously, he wants to make sure a Metik that visits is made comfortable and not discriminated against in any way."

Anna wasn't sure about the subtext, but she was tired of hearing about this "Mr. Ozman" through his subordinates. She had a feeling she was being tested, and she didn't want her lack of experience or confidence to show.

"Mr. Ozman is welcome to come and talk with us."

There was a moment's confusion on the man's face, but he shook it off. She had planned to continue talking but wasn't sure what else to say. Instead, she looked at the man, holding his gaze as long as she could. He touched his hand to his ear for a second, revealing the tiny earpiece he wore.

"Please proceed to the member's area," he gestured to the glass spiral staircase, "at your leisure."

Anna nodded slowly and the man wandered off, leaving Elise and Anna alone again. "What do you know about this guy, Elise? Is he dangerous? Or could he be helpful?"

"I don't know much. Vinicaire hates him, but Vinicaire hates all other Dreamers. He *especially* hates Malamun. He says it's 'gauche, 60s pastiche nonsense.' But he always says Ozman's harmless."

Anna looked around and found herself receptive to Vinicaire's assessment. Malamun was initially astonishing, but there was something off about the place. Whether it was on the moon or not, it felt like a theme bar in an amusement park. There was something about the ambiance that turned her off, but she couldn't quite put her finger on it. She tilted her head to one side as she watched the bar tenders and the dancers. Other than their clothes, they didn't seem so strange, but something was *off* about them.

It came to her in a flash. These people felt *hollow*. It was because everyone here was an Etune. They weren't real; they were part of the Haze. Her Haze Sense was helping her now. Teej had told her this would happen. As she spent time in Hazes, she would start to recognize Etunes, find Hazes in the real world, and most importantly, feel the presence of Aesthetes. She could sense all that now. Upstairs, just like the bouncer said, Ozman was waiting for them. She didn't need to see him to know he was the Dreamer here. She could feel it.

"I guess he must be a pretty big deal," Elise said. "He has to be pretty powerful to claim this place. It's a Staid Haze. That means it, you know, stays. It doesn't go away like other Hazes.

It doesn't need a Dreamer to sustain it. Vinicaire says there's a lot of Vig here."

Anna turned to look at Elise. "What is it about him? Why Vinicaire?"

Without pausing for a second, Elise snapped back angrily, "Why Teej?"

Anna shrugged. "Fair enough. I guess it's not important. Shall we go meet him then? You still have your sword?"

Mellowing, Elise pointed her thumb at her backpack where the handle of the blade poked out the top. "Got it!"

Anna nodded and smiled a little. Together they stood up and strode purposefully through the bar. Anna tried to ignore the fact that everyone was now looking at them. She fidgeted with her ring as she walked toward the stairs, eyes set, head up straight.

"I have something much better than a sword though," said Elise as they climbed the stairs. "I have a Metik as a best friend."

twenty-eight

"**N**ow move your right index finger," the voice commanded. Peter strained as hard as he could, willing his finger to move. After a painful delay, it twitched to life by spasming upward. "More slowly. Try to keep it under control."

Peter tried to move more slowly this time. Still, his finger twitched erratically.

"Don't worry. It will come. You're not accustomed to your new nerve impulses yet." All Peter could see in the dark room was the powerful lamp shining down on him. He couldn't see the face of the Apoth, just the gloved hands.

Apparently satisfied that his work was done on the left arm, the Apoth began to sew up the open incision that stretched from Peter's elbow to his wrist. As the stitches closed one by one, they obscured the silver piston that looked so incongruous inside his own flesh. The gleaming metal replacing his ulna. The Apoth explained how this would make him feel better, but Peter didn't understand. He didn't have the concentration required to process the words.

The Apoth explained that he'd never attempted so many new techniques on one person before. This was an ambitious attempt to help Peter get better. The thick leather straps around his wrists, ankles, and neck, along with the strap across his fore-head, were essential to ensuring he didn't twitch or move.

"Now Peter, once we close this up, I'll get back to your neural functions. I know you're not able to think clearly yet, but I can fix that."

Peter couldn't reply, but he blinked once to let the Apoth know he understood. He could still feel a wetness on the back of his head where the skin had been peeled back and was held with clips. When the chunk of skull had been drilled out, he hadn't felt any pain, just a strangely satisfying rumbling. The Apoth had explained each step in soothing tones. It made Peter feel safe.

When the knuckle-shaped piece of bone had slid out, he'd felt a kind of release of pressure, but also a hint of panic. For a moment, he had wondered if he was losing something, but the feeling had subsided quickly. Now he felt comfortable and numb. He was still too weak and too tired to move or act, but he felt content that his wellbeing was in someone else's hands now. He just had to let the surgeon do his work and everything would be fine.

As a humming, warm, blue light ran across the cut on his arm, Peter watched in soporific fascination as the stitches the surgeon had just put in seemed to melt away and the flesh knitted back together. There was still a long, red scar on his dark skin, but it was faded like the surgery had happened long ago.

"Remember, Peter," said the Apoth, "you can't use your new, augmented body like your old one. You'll need to learn to walk again. You'll have to work hard to get back to where you were before, but that also means you don't need to be limited by how other people move or act anymore. If you stumble, you don't need to worry about falling. Falling can't hurt you now. If you need to catch someone, you don't need to get in a car. You're faster than cars. If someone is up high, you don't need to find stairs. You can jump to them. Do you understand what I'm saying?"

Peter blinked once.

"But it goes both ways. You must keep out of sight till you learn how to blend in again. Don't move around a lot when people look closely at you. They will see that you are different. And of course, you can't just make decisions like you used to. Your mind isn't just something you can selfishly command any more. You have objectives. You understand this?"

Peter blinked twice.

"What do you mean, no? Peter, you were worse than dead. Weren't you? I fixed you up, patched the damage and took out the broken parts. Can you pay me for that? Do you have the money? No, of course not, but you can appreciate the work I did by giving me a tiny portion of your *choices*, can't you? The Inductive Regress Chip I'm putting in your mind will rejuvenate you. Without it, you'll fall back into that black abyss again. Sure, you might recover eventually. We could try that if you truly desire it? Maybe in a few weeks you'd recover?"

Peter struggled to talk. He managed a few desperate words.

"No. Please…" he stuttered

"I thought so. The Inductive Regress Chip mounting is fitted in your brain now. Once I set the chip in place and the lever connects the transistors, it will boot immediately. It won't hurt." The Apoth went back to working. Peter heard noises. A soldering iron? There were a few sparks, and he could feel his head being tugged left and right a little, but there was no pain, as promised.

"Peter, do you believe in God?" The Apoth leaned forward to observe his response.

He blinked twice.

"Of course you do."

Something snapped into place in his head, and Peter felt a sudden calm come over him. A warmth inside his skull started to spread down his face to his neck down over his shoulders and through the veins in his arms like warm water inside his skin.

Peter's senses were being rewired. Everything sounded like it was underwater for a second, then there was a dullness in his head. As he struggled to hear what the Apoth was saying, he found his hearing was focused now. By consciously adjusting his aural data, he could hear every sound coming from the surgeon, and he could eliminate all other sound. By doing so, he found he could hear his clothes rustling, his heart beating, the gushing blood in his veins, the breath coming from his nose, and the rolling rumble of cartilage on bone. It was as if he was hearing the world for the first time.

Peter felt aspects of his own personality being filed away by The Inductive Regress Chip. Inessential memories and instincts were being removed. In their place, streamlined decision making processes were added which were like pipelines for thought and action. He considered fighting the sensation, but realized it was already too late, so a calmness settled over him like a heavy blanket. Peacefully, he relinquished some control. Let this genius do his work. The chip told him to trust the Apoth. It impelled him to trust.

"We're on the verge of a religious war, Peter. A war of ideologies. There's a new god rising, powered by the New Blood. It's the same New Blood that now powers you, but some people are turning their heads away from the new god. They pretend it's not happening, and they think ignorance will save them, but apostasy leads to damnation."

Peter listened carefully.

"Peter, you're to represent our god in the struggles ahead. You are The New Blood. Do you know what that means? It means you will hunt apostates or appeasers and any who deny the existence of our new god. We will thwart those who would seek to stop his ascension."

"Our god is young, Peter. So young that he is not even born yet. The old gods are in torpor, and our new god stirs in the womb. You will be one of his children, but you'll be his father, too. People believed the old gods made us, but we made the New God. We created him, and he lives in you now. The New God came from us all; from the noise we make as we bang the drum of reality. As my creations find their own voices and their own song, they sing his name. You're part of that song now."

The Apoth sounded far away, his voice transcendental. He sounded like he was quoting scripture, and each word soaked into Peter's mind. The words saturated him with purpose and strength.

Peter felt a tug inside his head as the Apoth went back to work. His voice sounded less distant and reverential now. "The Inductive Regress Chip seems to have interfaced correctly. Now it will keep rewriting your neural firmware. That means it will take a few days to settle into your new thought processes.

"You must remember that you are very different now in mind *and* body. There are some essential changes to your behavior you must observe. Most of all, you must avoid heat. Do you understand? You need to live in a cold world now. Icy coldness is the mother's embrace."

"Yes," Peter replied. He did not recognize his own voice.

"Good. Your endoframe gets very warm when it's pushed to its limits. The blood runs hot which will be exacerbated in warm environments. When you need to exert yourself, short bursts will not overheat your system. Pushing yourself too far will make the endoframe burn red-hot. People will see it through your skin. Indeed, if you push too far, you'll burn your flesh right off. It's not a serious problem, since we can always patch you up, but you certainly won't pass for human if you let it happen. And make no mistake, Peter, you are not human now. Not anymore."

"Yes."

The Apoth sighed and leaned on Peter's shoulders with his elbows. "This was a big project for me. I am tired but pleased. In fact, I can't express how happy I am. You have taken all of this so well. God sees you, and he acknowledges you. Do you feel that?"

"Yes, I feel it."

"All the hard work is over now. You'll soon be ready to go out and do God's work. Do you know what you are? You're a Pilgrim. That's what we call new men made of flesh and metal that pump the new blood through their bodies. That think with a mind that's both born and made. Out of all the new constructions, you are the most powerful and the most holy."

Peter felt a stirring pride. He wanted to say something, but wasn't sure if he was allowed to. The chip that was in his head, was now part of his mind, seemed to allow him to express the two words he most wanted to say. "Thank you."

"No need to thank me, my son, no need at all! Thank *you* for being you. I chose you because you understood Hazes. With certainty, I knew you could endure them, at least for a time. And your mind was so cruelly, gravely injured by those people who didn't care about you. And of course, because you could help me find the August Club. I believe fate led me to find you, and more specifically the will of God.

Moving around to stand in front of him, the Apoth grabbed a tool Peter couldn't see clearly.

"Just one more thing son. We need to replace those eyes. Try to hold still. Perhaps we can avoid removing the optic nerve. God willing. What do you say Peter?"

"God willing," Peter replied.

twenty-nine

His face was twisted into a thunderous scowl, with thick, bushy eyebrows above a frowning mouth. Wavy brown hair was brushed down into face-framing sideburns while a scraggly beard hung below a thinner, ragged mustache. Ice-water blue eyes held Anna in place. He wore a too-tight, tailored brown waistcoat with a pocket-watch over a stretched white shirt that looked almost Victorian in style. His ill-fitting clothes seemed ready to burst over his stocky, gorilla-like frame. Anna scrutinized the man in front of her, and she had to admit, Mr. Ozman was an intimidating sight.

His countenance was measured and still, while his body language suggested barely suppressed violence. With a harrumph, he gestured for Anna to sit. Her heart sank as she slid into the chair in front of him. Mr. Ozman's gaze made her feel small.

All the furniture on the upper level was made of clear plastic. Perfectly contoured to the shape of her body, Anna found the chair strangely comfortable and soft, but it felt too low, with him looming over her. Behind Mr. Ozman a retinue of robots and bodyguards stood at attention, while several other VIPs wore the same bright, eclectic outfits as the dancers below. In this case, though, Anna felt sure they were not all Etunes. These were undoubtedly Mr. Ozman's closest friends and guests. Everyone below was set dressing, these VIPs were "real." They sat in semicircles at the sofas and tables behind him, and they all watched her closely.

Up here on the mezzanine, Anna could see the whole of the dance floor and the bar. The nearby railings were one-way glass, allowing the important guests to spy on everyone below without being seen themselves. Clouds of dry ice and blue neon lights exaggerated the frosty ambience.

Anna was aware that there was no seat for Elise. The girl stood a little behind her, and Anna wished she would move closer. The air crackled with static and the hairs on her arms stood up, like a storm was coming. In the back of her mind, Anna repeated the same mantra over and over: *Never play their game. Their game is always rigged.*

Opening his arms in a placatory gesture, Mr. Ozman said nothing. Anna waited for him to speak, and he held her gaze until it felt awkward. Long moments passed. Anna couldn't think of a way to start the conversation, so she waited. This felt *wrong*.

"Well," he said finally, then fell silent. Anna wasn't sure if it was a question or a statement. Elise shifted uncomfortably. Eventually he spoke again. "I suppose…"

She waited for him to continue.

"I suppose…" his face twisted into a crooked, insincere mockery of a smile. "You must be very confused. I hope I can educate you. I must say, my dear, it is lovely to meet you. Maybe I can fill you in on some things you might have been *misinformed* about."

Coming here was a mistake. His tone was polite with a strong English accent, but his demeanor was leering terror. Ozman's smile seemed to cause him physical pain. His posture and the tension across his upper body suggested he would lash out at any moment. Anna wanted to glance back at her friend and see

232

if he was as unconvincing to Elise as he was to her. Were her senses really sharper now, or was he really so insincere?

Instead, she asked evenly, "Such as?"

"A huge number of things, my lady; a huge number, indeed! Considering who your guides have been so far—" He looked derisively at Elise for a second. "You must be very much lost in this new world."

Anna's eyes narrowed. In his old-fashioned brown jacket, he seemed thoroughly out of place here in this futuristic bar, but he was confident and secure. He commanded attention.

"Consider it this way," he went on. "You enter a church, and your guide tells you about the stained-glass windows, the wooden benches, the hymns, and about the bread and the wine, and you nod and listen, but no one mentions God to you. I am describing you, standing here before me, oblivious to deeper truths. Do you see that?"

Anna shook her head. This was not going well. She forced herself to remember that she was a Metik. She was not here to be patronized or preached to, and she had to make sure Ozman didn't realize how inexperienced she was. To do that, she had to match his level of authority.

"What do you know about me?" she asked.

Ozman held up a hairy, brutish finger as if to scold her for interrupting. Ignoring her question, he continued, "Although you don't know how our world works, you haven't offended us *yet*. Our most sacred rules remain unbroken thus far, and even though you took a life, we offer you clemency for that crime. Our old companion's death does not cause sorrow, at least not with me. He was once so focused and so *devout,* but he always had a weakness for the macabre. A killer of young women? What nonsense! His attempt on your life was uncouth, and you were quite right to destroy him. Tell me, is it true you burned him alive?"

Anna nodded, unsure how to respond.

"Yes, fire is how your Praxis manifests, I think? Mayhap I could elucidate the details of your talents. I am sure your teaching so far has been very poor. Indeed, I understand you were not instructed at all. Your Praxis is innate, and I find myself wondering if you know how rare that is."

He was throwing lots of information at her, trying to wrong-foot her. But he was wrong. Teej *had* taught her. At lease that Praxis was an old word for her Metik abilities. Ozman observed her closely as he talked, trying to gauge her reactions. His ice-blue eyes chilled her and locked her in place. She let him continue.

"Well, let me just say this: you have power, but you are a firearm without a safety. Without proper training, you are as much a threat to your friends and yourself as you are to your enemies. Critics like you—"

"Don't call me that," she interrupted. Teej had explained that, too. Critic was an insult leveled at Metiks, and she was determined to show him she understood.

"I offer an apology on this matter only. I didn't mean any significant offense, for you must understand we older Aesthetes sometimes use words and phrases that are now considered a little *outdated.* As I was saying, you can unintentionally hurt those around you, and we don't want that, do we? Tell me, young lady, do you know about the social contract?"

She nodded. "Yes. Look, I don't have time for this, Mr. Ozman."

He went on as if she hadn't spoken. "The social contract sets out the assumption that we all must set aside certain freedoms to allow us the luxury of living peacefully with our fellow man. Rousseau realized that if you are to live in a society, you must abandon certain natural freedoms, but as long as we all surrender the *same* freedoms, it's still fair.

"I trust you understand me? We give up the freedom to steal and murder others, and thus we are free of those threats ourselves, and in the same way, all of us Behind the Veil must give up certain freedoms, too. However, the rules we follow must, by necessity, be more complex. Grayer. You follow my reasoning, do you not?"

"What's your point, Mr. Ozman?"

"Well, young lady, my point is: you don't yet know these rules. If you did—" he leaned forward suddenly and anger flashed in his eyes. "You wouldn't be in my fucking Haze!"

Anna recoiled instinctively, predicting an attack, but Ozman relaxed back into his chair, and his fake smile returned. "And while we're at it, I have to tell you that you are laboring under a misapprehension. I am not the man you think me to be. My name is Drowden, though the ignorant call me the Occultist. The old fool Ozman was dispossessed of this lovely Decadan when he endangered our cause. Do you know what that cause is?"

Anna was reeling. The same Drowden that she had been warned against by Teej. She didn't know much about him, but she knew he was dangerous, and that he was one of *them*.

"You are part of the Doxa," she said.

"You say that word like you know of its meaning. You're stumbling around blind in a minefield, girl. Coming here, for what? To stop us? To find an enchanted potion to cure your boyfriend? That's not how these things work. A righteous war is coming, and it's going to burn up the apostates and believers alike. The one thing we don't need is your flame to add to the fire!"

"Hey, don't speak to her like that!" Elise shouted, and they both turned to her. She shook visibly.

"Best not to capture my attention, little Noop. Your clown is in trouble, too. Vinicaire is playing a dangerous game, and if he chooses to side with our enemies, we will not hesitate to use *you* to get to *him*."

Elise backed away only to bump into one of the robot holograms that guarded the stairs. She looked to Anna for help with dismay in her eyes. The circle closed ranks, and they were surrounded. Seeking to calm the situation, Anna asked him what she thought he wanted to hear.

"Tell me about your cause and what you want from me."

He continued to look at Elise with derision for a few long seconds, his face locked in a rictus scowl. Anna was shocked by his open aggression and how quickly his mask of civility faded. Returning to face her slowly, he forced his expression to soften.

"Please don't think of me as an enemy. We might never be friends, but we can share a cause, can't we? I am confident we can work together. We both know Donnel is not a good teacher. Even if he recovers, he will lie to you. He probably hasn't even told you about us, has he?"

"He told me enough."

Drowden leaned back, trying to appear casual. "Well there are some people who won't open their eyes to the proof that is right in front of them. There's a new god coming, and from Doxa he arises. The evidence is everywhere, and we are all a part of his inception. We all have our part to play, from the Aesthetes to the Etunes, and yes, even those simple souls in Basine. Even an Undreamer like you can be part of our cause, Anna. You can be part of the New God's genesis."

Anna's mind sped through possible outcomes. Was this going to escalate? Would they be attacked? She wouldn't be able to play along much longer. She thought back to all the times her dad scolded her for rolling her eyes in church. She distrusted anyone who talked about God or faith or righteous causes. She couldn't fake interest in his beliefs. They were in trouble here, and they weren't free to leave. She had to protect Elise any way she could. As she glanced around uneasily, Drowden noticed her nervousness.

"We have plenty of time to convince you. I should disavow you of the nonsense of your former companions. The doubters would bury their heads in the sand, but the table of the gods is empty. They old gods are absent. The Monarch idles in his dead city of Selmetridon, and he ignores us. While we should be preparing the way for a new savior, *your* kind is willing to let the opportunity slip by. Your kind is willing to let us continue on this path of nihilism in a world without rules and morals. A place where women cavort like—"

Anna rolled her eyes and tutted. She knew it was the worst thing she could do at that moment, but she couldn't hold it in. Drowden looked at them with wide-eyed rage. Why had she provoked him? Why couldn't she *ever* keep her mouth shut? Her Haze sense warned her what would happen next, and she felt the danger before she saw it.

Anna jumped from the chair, knocking it over as she grabbed Elise and pulled her to the ground. She was just in time. The pneumatic arm of the robot missed Elise's head by inches as Anna pulled them both to safety. If the blow had landed, it would have killed her. Elise let out a scream as they both scrambled to their feet and backed away to the nearby wall. Anna moved to guard her friend and held an arm across Elise's chest to ward off their enemies. There was nowhere to go. As Drowden stood, the circle started closing around them.

"This is my domain, stupid girls. Ozman had no idea how vital and powerful this place can be to our cause. It's built on top of Vig beyond comprehension, and you fools have no idea what is at stake here. You stumble into my domain and display such *arrogance*. Such *ignorance!*"

Three robot guards closed in around them while four bouncers in black suits lurked in the background. As the music

237

dropped off, Anna looked to Drowden, Elise, then back to Drowden, waiting to see what he would do next. The guards waited for his command.

"Kill her little friend. Show her we are serious."

He twisted his forefinger and thumb in a gesture that activated the robots. The flickering holograms changed and grew. Human images blinked off, exposing the robotic endoskeleton completely before new animalistic holograms took their place. The closest was a bear, the second an ape, and the third was a leopard standing on its hind paws. Snarling beasts of blue light intended as intimidation. The flickering holograms of the wild animals overlaid on the robots stalked them, the animal projections clawing the air and spitting and growling. The ape beat its chest, the leopard bared its teeth, and the bear opened its monstrous maw to let out a thunderous, saliva-spewing roar as it closed in.

"Jesus fucking Christ!" said Elise.

"Wait, wait!" Anna pleaded, holding up both of her hands. She turned to look at Drowden to see if he would call off the abominations, but he was implacable.

"No!" Anna shouted.

She didn't have to accept this. She wouldn't let them hurt Elise. Holding her hand up, she brought forth fire as her ring burned white hot on her finger. A second later, the bear closest to Anna burst into flames. The hologram burned up, screaming and writhing as the flames reached the ceiling, but the robot within was untouched. Anna and Elise edged along the wall past Drowden, but the robot followed them, undeterred. Her power had affected the harmless hologram, leaving the very real threat of the machine unscathed. How could she use her power to stop it? She realized with dread that she was out of her depth.

The gleaming metal blade on the robot's arm came up as it groped for them. The edge seemed impossibly sharp.

Drowden sneered. "You think we don't know how to fight your kind? We've been preparing for this battle for generations. You're beaten, girl. Step aside."

Acting on instinct and fueled by anger, Anna dropped to her knees and touched a hand to the floor. Everyone looked at her like she was insane. The robots stopped, the nearest one half a step away from her. Drowden opened his mouth to say something but no words came out. Anna turned to look at Elise for half a second, panic in both their eyes. The girl nodded.

Hesitating for only a second, she closed her eyes. This was the only move she could make. The only card she had left to play.

Drowden shouted, "Stop, you stupid girl!" But he was too late.

"Break," Anna commanded, slamming the palm of her hand into the ground. A lightning bolt of pain ricocheted through her arm as a huge burst of kinetic force radiated from her into the floor. Slower than she hoped but quicker than anyone could react, a vast network of cracks spread across the tiles. They shared a moment of dread, and then the whole mezzanine collapsed from under them.

The fall seemed to last forever, and as Anna twisted and turned through the air, her terror evaporated. There was a moment of peace as she accepted she might not survive this. At least she had gone out fighting. She hoped Elise would make it. As her mind wandered, Anna thought of the letter. What had it said? Why had she burned it? Maybe she already knew what was written inside. Maybe she could—

The crunching of bone on the hard tiles caused her world to whiteout with pain. For a brief time, Anna existed only as bright, searing light. She stopped breathing, then inhaled deeply and opened her eyes. Her mind raced to process the events unfolding around her. She had hit the ground hard, and her whole body ached. Elise had grabbed a railing and landed safely. The machines were moving in her direction. Drowden was…she didn't know where.

Anna sucked in air, and her vision swirled back into focus. She tried to get her hands under her body, but something heavy lay across her lower back. Blood ran into her left eye, forcing her to squint. Her left wrist had been twisted badly in the fall, and her whole arm felt numb. She could move around some, but the weight on top pinned her to the ground. Trying to slide from under it, she reached her good arm back to feel what it was. A heavy chunk of concrete lay across her body. All around her were large blocks and pieces of twisted metal that could have easily crushed her head. She had been lucky.

Turning around as best she could, Anna saw the patrons of the bar running for safety and flooding out the exits as two of the robots closed in on her. From around the corner, she heard Drowden's voice, but she couldn't see him.

"Just kill them both!"

Anna's body trembled as she strained to crawl free, but her lame left arm impeded her. She struggled until she managed to slide the concrete down her torso, but it fell solidly onto her thighs, and she let out a cry of pain. Able to turn properly now, she surveyed the mess behind her and watched the three robots between her and Elise. The nearest one flickered as if its hologram had been damaged. It seemed to be limping; its leg was twisted and crippled. Behind it, the two closing the distance toward her separated—one continuing its forward momentum while the third peeled off toward Elise. She was on her feet and had dropped her sword, but she clutched her knife and brandished it with fierce desperation. Her face snarled, and Anna took a moment to admire her bravery. She hoped this would not be the last time they fought together.

Pushing her hair out of her face, Anna wriggled closer to the heavy block pinning her to the ground and touched it with her ring. She struggled to focus, the pain in her arm and the blood in her eyes making it hard to concentrate, but she laid her hand on the dusty chunk of concrete and once again spoke aloud. "Break."

Nothing happened.

Forcing her eyes closed, Anna tried to find her center. She focused her will and pushed her hand down hard onto the flat surface, and suddenly, a heavy creaking noise drowned out the screams and shouts and everything else. She opened her eyes just in time to see the block split in two. The release of pressure on her legs caused immediate relief, and she scrambled from beneath the wreckage and crawled away. As she tried to get her feet under her body, she realized her legs were crippled. She pawed her way across what had once been a dance floor as the robot inexorably reached her. Anna was hurt, exhausted, and out of ideas. The robot loomed over her, ready to strike.

A familiar voice cut through the chaos. "Hey, hun, you sure made a mess of this place. Maybe I can help you tidy up a bit?"

Everyone in Malamun turned to see the bearded, scruffy Garret walk onto the rubble-strewn dance floor.

"That skinny kid Donnel asked me to keep an eye on you. Keep you out of trouble. That little runt doesn't realize you *are* trouble."

He looked down at Anna and winked. His smile seemed so out of place. Just moments ago, Anna had been sure she was going to die. Now though, Garret's smile reassured her to her very core. They still had a chance.

Garret calmly reached down to pick something up from the white, cracked tiles with a heavy groan. He looked old and tired. Hefting a solid oak staff as long as he was tall, conjured from thin air, he cocked his head to one side. He held it lazily across his shoulder with one hand, his ropey muscles obvious in his faded, tight black t-shirt. With a weary sigh, he gestured at the nearest hologram-robot to come at him. He brushed his wavy, gray hair from his face and stroked his scruffy beard as he waited for it to comply. His bare, toned arms knotted and tense, he looked unsteady but also, somehow perfectly balanced. She couldn't tell if he looked fragile or invincible.

The holograms continued to spit and snarl, but Anna's eyes were drawn to the needle-sharp blades the robots brandished. Animal snarls and the hum of static filled the air. She scrambled off the dance floor as the robots circled around Garret. She assessed the threat, then brandished her ring threateningly at her nearest enemy. Garret gave her a brief nod of acknowledgement and casually shifted his weight from one foot to the other. Elise's joined them both a second later, swiping at the air with her ludicrously small knife.

As the robots closed around them, Garret turned slowly, spinning on the spot. His movement seemed torturously deliberate, but at the last second, his staff swung around so fast it was a blur. The final movement of Garret's spin was like a whip crack, and the heavy wood crunched into the head of the bear-robot. There was a smashing, cracking noise as the head shattered completely, exploding into a shower of crystal shards. Fragments scattered around the room, showering the onlookers with microscopic pieces of flying metal and glass. Anna blinked as the dust flew at her face, and by the time she had turned back, Garret had run the staff through the chest of the panther-robot, too, spearing it in place. The bear-robot stood headless and harmless, teetering on the edge of falling. With comedic timing, it hit the ground with a heavy thud at the same moment Garret pulled his staff free from the second robot's chest.

Taking a few steps backward, Garret tossed the staff up and down a few times like he was judging its weight, then, with a quick flick of the wrist, he launched it like a javelin. It left his hands and flew through the air weightlessly, splitting into a thousand long, sharp blades of light. They smashed into the final robot, skewering it in a thousand places. Full of tiny holes, its smoking husk fell to the floor.

Garret casually reached down into the rubble at his feet and picked up another rendition of his staff, somehow reformed and whole once more. He flashed Anna a quick smile before turning toward Drowden, the only remaining threat. Scowling and red-faced, their enemy stood at the opposite end of the room strangely untouched by the dust that surrounded him. Through her blood smeared vision, Anna couldn't see Drowden's face clearly, but she could tell he exuded menace.

"You stopped fighting like this because you're too old, Garret. How high will be the toll you pay for this? What will be left of you?" Drowden's words were pure spite. Pure hatred.

"Enough," said Garret.

"You're not the best anymore. Even I could take you," snarled Drowden.

Garret smirked. "Try it."

Drowden's face fell.

"That's what I thought," said Garret. "Yeah, I've done too much fightin' and too much drinkin'. I should quit, but I confess, I got a hunger for both that won't die. If you want to go again one more time, I'm ready. What's the score at? One each? You wanna play the tiebreaker?"

Drowden gnashed his teeth. Was he weighing his options? "We don't *need* to fight."

Garret shrugged.

"I can leave with the girl," said Drowden, "if she wants to come with me."

Anna was incredulous. Was he talking about her? Drowden and Garret both turned to look at her. Were they waiting for her decision?

"Fuck no!" she shouted.

Garret smiled broadly.

"You're coming with me anyway," Drowden snapped.

"Sounds like we're going to have a problem," Garret responded evenly. He started walking toward Drowden.

The Dreamer backed away. "Don't come closer! I can bring this place to ruin with a snap of my fingers, then we all die!"

"We all die eventually," said Garret.

"I'll kill the girls!" Drowden shouted in desperation.

Garret sighed. "Get the fuck out of my sight. No one's coming with you."

The tension in the air dissipated as Garret lowered his staff. Drowden seemed to shrink away. He looked around for a second as if he might change his mind before kneeling down and rummaging in his pocket. Pulling out a white block of chalk, he quickly swept it across the ground, marking out a wide circle. Drawing three lines and scribbling a symbol Anna couldn't decipher, his design was complete.

Drowden looked up from his drawing and scowled at Garret one more time. "I think about killing you every day."

Garret smiled back. "I don't think about you at all."

Before she could comprehend what was happening, Drowden took a half-step forward and fell through the floor as if it wasn't there. The portal allowed him to escape before closing behind him.

It was just the three of them now. Everyone else had run for safety when the mezzanine collapsed. They were safe now.

"That was amazing," Elise said breathily. She didn't seem surprised by the nature of Drowden's departure, but she clutched her sword tightly as if something else might attack.

"Why, thank you," said Garret. "You should have seen me at my best! Ladies, I'd love to stay and chat and drink what's left of the bar, but I suspect it might not be safe here. Shall we get a hustle on?"

Anna nodded numbly. With the help of her friends, she got to her feet, and together they wandered back to the elevator and Earth.

Anna washed her hands and face, and the water seemed like it would never run clear. Blood and dirt stained the pristine white sink, making long streaks that looked like a network of veins and arteries in the porcelain.

She looked at her reflection in the too-clear mirror. *Not pretty.* The neon light, much like the kind you get in service station bathrooms, highlighted every bump and scar she'd ever had, but right now it told the story of more recent cuts and bruises. Her left eye was red and swollen, a grid of red cracks laid out a map across the white of her eyes. Crusted blood on her eyebrow marked where something had struck her, but she couldn't remember what. Rubbing with soap and water made it bleed anew, and by the time she had stemmed the flow, she was left with more crimson streaks down her face. Assiduously avoiding the cut, she cleaned around her cheek as best she could manage before surveying the rest of her body.

Ripping off her tattered tights, she found her legs hurt the most. A heavy black line ran across the back of her calves. It looked like someone had whacked her with a heavy metal pole. The pain was intense, but from her basic understanding of first aid, she guessed it wasn't as serious as it felt. Tissue damage and bruising, but nothing seemed to be broken. Her right ankle ached with twisted muscles or torn ligaments. The cut on her eye might also leave a little scar, and if that had been a priority for her, she might have gone to see a doctor right now. But it wasn't. She was more worried about whether they would be attacked again, and why someone had tried to kill them.

Anna grabbed the sink with both hands and squeezed till her knuckles went white. Lifting her head, she challenged herself to glance into her own eyes. To take stock of what she was and what she was becoming. To judge whether she was ready for the challenges ahead. Forcing her gaze up, she saw a frightened and battered face looking back at her. She could still recognize herself in the mirror, and she felt better.

She had to give herself a break. Everything that had happened so far had happened because she made choices. They hadn't always—or even often—been the right choices, but she had made them for the right reasons. She had tried to help people and to save lives and protect her friends. As long as she kept making choices like that, she could keep looking herself in the eye.

Anna knew she had to get back to her friends, but she found it hard to move. She stood and looked at her reflection, aware of the running water and the cool breeze from the open window. She prepared herself for any bad news she might be about to receive about Teej or about their next threat.

What series of events had led her down this path? She tried to put her memories into a sequence that made sense. Saving Sue from Dean, then watching her die. Meeting Teej, fighting Mott, Canfranc station, Malamun. *To the moon and back.* She almost laughed. Pushing herself away from the sink, Anna shook off the excess water from her face and arms like a wet dog. She wasn't going to get any answers here, and if she delayed too long, dark thoughts would catch up to her. She had to keep moving.

Going from the harsh, hard light of the bathroom to the sleepy gloom of Maxine's Bar, Anna's eyes took a minute to adjust. She spotted Elise and Garret in the corner. Neither seemed to notice her return. Garret sat with his feet across the bench that stretched along one wall, his back against the corner. He swirled the last of a beer bottle, and his eyes were half closed. Elise was lying next to him, her legs stretched up the wall by his head. She was on her phone, the soft light of its screen illuminating her face. She didn't seem to have any dirt or dust on her. Indeed, she seemed to have come through the whole experience both mentally and physically untouched. She was resilient, although Anna wasn't sure if that resilience came from her strength of character or from her feline attention span. She didn't have the concentration required to feel existential dread.

"Hey, Anna," Elise said without looking up. "We're just talking about whether you have a crush on Teej or not. Garret says you *think* you don't because it would be too predictable. I say you don't but you will develop a crush on him when you see another girl flirting with him in the future. Because that's how girls work, right?"

"I'm not sure who's making fun of whom," said Anna.

"It's me. I'm making fun of him," said Elise.

"Girls stick together, eh?" said Garret in mock offense. "Teaming up on me."

Anna smiled but didn't laugh. "Hey, Garret, can I take something to drink? Does the barman mind? I can leave some money."

"There's no bartender, honey. He wasn't real."

"He wasn't...so, is this *your* bar?"

"No. It's no one's now. Linda's family used to own it. But...not now. Don't worry, no one will come in. No one notices the place. That's how it works."

247

Anna went over to the bar, and Garret shouted after her to bring him a beer, holding up the bottle to show her which brand. As she searched the shelf for the right label, she decided to be direct with him. "Garret, why am I an Undreamer? What's special about me? I asked Teej, but he wouldn't tell me. Or didn't know."

He waited for his beer before answering. Motioning for her to sit beside him, he took a swig, draining half the bottle. Elise swung her legs around and sat up at the table, turning off her phone to give them her full attention. She was interested in his answer, too.

"The first thing to say," he drawled, "is that I'm not really the best person to ask this kind of question. I'm…tired, girls. Dog tired. Tired of Hazes, tired of Dreamers, and tired of fighting. You heard what that old miserable fucker said about me? I can't keep doing this. It's too much."

"What does that actually mean, Garret? Are you just tired, or are you…sick?" asked Anna

"Hazes aren't exactly conducive to clear thinking. You do this for too long and you get…fuzzy. Like when one of you girls is going out on a date so you try on a million outfits. At the end, maybe all your pretty dresses are still in the bedroom, but the whole room is a mess, and when you go back and look for a specific frilly skirt, you have a hell of a time finding one."

"You understand us *girls* so well," said Anna, "but misogyny aside, you mean memories get affected? Or your thinking?"

He laughed, but his eyes were sad. "Both, really. It starts with the memories, but it doesn't get bad until you do this for a very long time. Longer than the length of most people's regular spans, I reckon."

"How old are you?"

He chuckled at the question. "Old enough that I can't remember when I might have known."

She considered his words carefully. Were Hazes dangerous or addictive? Had they harmed her already?

"So, Hazes stopped you from getting old?" asked Anna.

"Doing what we do changes everything around us, hun. Nothing is the same afterwards. We live longer, and we see and do things that seem impossible, and eventually, that makes us come to think differently. And we can never, ever go back to how it was before."

Elise, who had been listening intently, seemed ill at ease. "Yeah, we can never go back. Everything's changed now."

Garret turned to her. "You can go back. Nothing special about you."

Elise's face sunk. She looked like he'd just slapped her.

"No offense, girlie. Nothing wrong with being normal, but you can step away from all this at any time. You're not like Anna."

"Apparently not! I should leave you two now and go get on with my *normal* life!" Grabbing her bag and stomping away, Elise slammed the door theatrically as she left the bar. Anna couldn't tell if she was genuinely annoyed or just bored. She guessed the latter.

Garret turned to her and smiled. "She needs to get angry from time to time. She needs someone to be mad at. It's good for her."

Anna nodded slowly, unsure how to take him.

"Are you going to be okay, Garret?" she asked with genuine concern. He downed the rest of his beer in one gulp, then wiped his beard with the back of his hand.

"Me? Nah. Probably not. I can't help you anymore you know? I'd just be a liability. You're going to have to look after yourself from now on."

He saw the sadness in her eyes and moved to reassure her. "Oh, don't worry! You're capable. Folks might say maybe you shouldn't have gone to the moon, but at least you learned something. Just keep moving forward, even if you make mistakes, because that's how you learn. Climb the ladder, and when you get to the top, kick it away.

"You need to be smarter in the future, though. It's *knowledge* you need. Your reactions are sharp, but you're going into all these fights with one arm tied behind your back. Everyone's going to outmaneuver you until you have a good teacher. You need to know what you can and can't do, and you need a teacher to help you discover that."

"So, teach me!"

"Nope. I passed on everything I know to someone else, so they could do the same. Teej will teach you. He'll make sure you're pointed in the right direction before you…pow!" He made a gesture with his fingers like a gun firing.

"We should check on him," said Anna.

"He's gonna make it, you know. They don't really want him dead. They don't even want you dead; they just want to make sure you don't stop them. Ideally, they'd love to convert you. They're a bunch of kids playing with matches, and you're a big old keg of gunpowder."

"Who are '*they*'?"

"The Doxa. You know Mr. Drowden now, or *the Occultist* as he wants us to call him. He's one of them, and the rest, ahhh…?"

He rubbed his forehead roughly with the heel of one hand in obvious distress. "I think this is mixed up in my head, hun. I don't know if I can explain it very well. They're a cult of sorts, and they're all mad as hatters. Half of them are falling into Torpor. The rest are easily led or naïve or just plain crazy. There's so few Aesthetes now; it used to be that you could dismiss the crazy ones. Now it seems like crazy is all that's left.

"The one with all the rhymes that killed girls was the leader for a while. Then it was Drowden, although his old comrade the Apoth has his own ideas. And then maybe Rayleigh? Old Grayface…Is he really letting this happen? Well shit. Let me think…"

Garret's concentration seemed to be slipping as he spoke, and his brow furrowed in frustration. Talking about this was uncomfortable for him. He was unraveling.

"You see, we're supposed to anchor all this madness with some sort of sensibility. Metiks are supposed to police the Dream. We're all a community, really, looking out for each other since the old times. Now we're a squabbling family."

"Garret, maybe you should get some rest?"

He snapped his fingers and pointed at her. "Bingo. That's a good idea. I'm going to the manager's office; there's a sofa I can crash on. You should stay here. It's the safest place for now. When your friend comes back, let her complain a bit. Listen to her and make her a drink. She'll be happy again in no time."

With that, he hauled himself up unsteadily and started to shamble across the room. He stopped at the door and turned back to her. "Oh, Anna. You asked me why you're an Undreamer. Why you are…how you are? I don't know the answer, but I think it's an important question. Here's the kicker: you're more likely to know than me. Maybe you've done this all before. Maybe you're a natural. Maybe it's in your blood. My point is, you have the answers, and I have a head full of bad ideas and unreliable memories. And I have to get some sleep."

He pulled open the heavy wood door to the office and was gone, and Anna was left alone to think about what he meant. Pulling her phone out of her pocket, she held it like a loaded weapon. Her fingers trembled as she scrolled down the list of contacts to find the number for the hospital. She couldn't put this call off any longer.

thirty

Peter sat on the edge of the bed trying to remember what a human would do in an empty hotel room at midnight. Redesigned and improved, he had no need for food or sleep. Even when he did relax, the Inductive Regress Chip took over some basic functions. It could process his desires and beliefs and organize them into a series of intentions. It could predict and extrapolate the movements and actions of everyone he knew and everyone he had ever met, creating a simulated version of potential events when his sensory inputs were no longer processing data. It could even take in data streams from online sources and use them to build networks of influence, expanding his understanding of theological or philosophical issues or allowing him to learn new skills while his organic brain was "offline."

Sleeping and resting were only vestiges of his old, lesser form. He also had no need to watch television or read magazines or newspapers or books. The Inductive Regress Chip was constantly pulling information from all data sources on earth. It evaluated and processed the things he might need to know, directly accessing his thoughts and memories to input knowledge. It was like having an assistant inside his head that organized and collated and curated his thoughts. Of course, it was also like having a supervisor that kept him working, chastised him when his attention wandered, and castigated him when he was lazy or lost focus on his mission.

But already that "supervisor" was becoming invisible. As Peter relinquished control and decision making to that internal dictator, he felt his old compulsions melt away. How could idle distraction compare to the sense of satisfaction he derived from following his internal deity? That supervisor's desires were becoming his own now. He was being subsumed.

So, sitting on those crisp, white bed sheets, Peter did nothing. Nothing obvious anyway. To an external observer, he would look like a deactivated robot, or a man having a nervous breakdown. Sitting motionless, straight-backed and staring into space, he was a piece of furniture, but inside his locked body, his mind continued to race. Processing data and reconfiguring itself.

The most difficult adjustment for Peter was the potentiality matrix overlaid on his reality. In his old life, he had lived in the moment. Looking back, he could barely comprehend how limited his perception of time had been. Now his senses extended far beyond the present, as did his thoughts. He existed as a smear across time now instead of just a point. No longer a moment, his width in the fourth dimension was about sixteen seconds. Eight seconds into the past and eight seconds into the future.

That adjustment had not been easy. At first, he had been paralyzed. Too much information flowed into his mind. Disconnected from time, he had tried to move his hand in the past and been confused when he couldn't. He had turned his head in the future, then had been surprised when it happened seemingly of its own volition moments later. Intentionality was no longer about "what" and "how," it was also about "when." He was queuing up actions for the future in order that they would occur without the slowness of normal human reactions. More than a man in a moment, he was a series of processes stretched out across a timeline. This was the power and the complexity of the Inductive Regress Chip at work. It changed everything about how he thought and acted. His old mind was still there. Peter was still there. But now that mind's output was just one aspect of his thinking. It was one more resource his new, higher functions could access.

At its most basic level, the potentiality matrix affected his senses. He no longer saw individuals and moving objects in their current positions. Instead, every entity that existed in his mind had associated location and velocity and potentiality for movement. When he saw someone walking, he saw them not only as an individual in a location, but also as a long, broad smear of where they had been and a series of paths of light showing where they might go. Those paths wavered and changed as the potentiality matrix processed trillions upon trillions of calculations about how their muscles would move their bodies. Everyone was a wave of possibility now, and the chip took in trillions of points of data about their surroundings, their personalities, and their past actions to calculate the decisions they would make in the future, too. For Peter, each mind was a pilot in a vehicle made of soft meat, and his advanced neuroprocessor housed within his metal endoframe made him feel like the rest of the world moved in slow motion. Each second of each minute, he felt his brain adjust to the Inductive Regress Chip, getting faster, sharper, and more accurate.

He replayed his first mission in his memories now. The pictures scrolled past in his mind like a slideshow, his memories as perfect as a video recording. It had been so simple. *Kill without detection.* The details had been left to him. He could choose his victim and method, but he had to kill someone that day, and he had to do it smartly—in a way that he would never, ever be caught. He remembered how abhorrent it had seemed at the time. It was only yesterday, but time flowed differently for him now. He had been a whole different person back then. He was still struggling to comprehend his expanded understanding of space and time, and still struggling to control his new, improved nervous system without looking like a machine, but he had succeeded. Even now, thinking back to how he felt when that mission was completed, he experienced the thrill of it anew. It made his teeth tingle and his head swim with pleasure. It had been perfect.

Going through that footage again, Peter analyzed his actions critically to identify where he had made errors and where he could improve his performance. He had chosen a victim that would help him prepare for the day when he would face the Metiks. The chip in his head had suggested he would be tasked with deleting an Undreamer in her early twenties, so his simulated mission should target that same demographic. His victim had to be a young woman.

Stalking that target had been curiously satisfying. Thought compelled him to kill the girl, and he didn't feel guilt or revulsion. In place of those negative emotions was a detached satisfaction, the kind he would feel while tidying his record collection or deleting old files on his computer to make it run faster.

He'd viewed her impassively and emotionlessly for a long time. Waiting outside the public library where she worked, he made his move at the end of the day when she was closing up. She pulled the shutters down as he watched her from the bushes across the street. He'd taken in so much information about her in those first few seconds. She was in her early twenties, with an athletic build and a plain demeanor. She wore sensible work clothes: a medium-length skirt and dark tights with a puffy jacket and scarf, and she carried a bulky handbag stuffed with folders and books. She was the perfect target.

While his expanded senses and abilities conferred many advantages, stealth was not necessarily one of them. Peter's endoframe made him faster and stronger than anyone else alive, but it also made his movements cumbersome and stiff, and his gait was unnatural. If anyone saw him on a dark night, his peculiar movement would mark him out as someone to be avoided, and he hadn't mastered the art of moving silently with his new frame. His strategy for stealth had to include keeping his distance and tracking his prey.

Thankfully, those were two goals he could achieve. His extended senses meant he could track a target from very far away. By switching between night vision and heat vision, he could keep his target in sight. His preternatural reflexes and expedited decision-making processes meant he could compute the perfect routes and paths to intercept a target in a fraction of a second. When he was in danger of being spotted, he could get out of sight long before his potential prey had turned their gaze toward him.

An apex predator, he had achieved his goal with clinical simplicity. The swiftness with which he had descended on her, the way he had muted any possibility of a scream, how her head had snapped to one side, rigid and grotesque. It was something the human part of his mind would never forget, although he could delete the footage from the robotic part of his mind if he wanted to. But he wouldn't.

The drop of blood on the lips, the sudden cold emptiness in her eyes. It had seemed neither ugly nor beautiful. Rather, it had been bleakly poignant and revelatory. Murder and death were just another event in life, no more or less special than any other. No special taboo need be attributed to them. The taking of a life didn't change anything for him. He didn't feel worse or better. He didn't feel anything.

As Peter forced himself to lie back onto the clean white sheets of the bed, he thought of his creator. The Apoth told Peter he was no longer a man. He was something new. He called Peter a "Pilgrim." There were many like him, but he was the greatest of them all. The fastest, most advanced, most dangerous, and the most faithful.

thirty-one

The old house by the lake was ten miles from the nearest town and a hundred miles from home. Anna had spent many of her childhood summers here, but in her memories, it didn't seem so bleak. The surrounding woods were eerily still, while the house itself creaked like a galleon on rough seas. It creaked in the wind, it creaked in the rain, and it creaked with every step Anna took from the hall to the bathroom or the hall to the bedroom. Even now, in the unnerving gray stillness after the storm, the house continued to creak.

Anna sat on the padded shelf by the windowsill reading her book, but she couldn't concentrate. Having read the same page six times, she decided it was time to give up. She'd been hiding Teej here since she sneaked him out of the hospital, and now she wasn't sure what to do next. When he had woken, he'd told her they needed to find somewhere to hide. Since that first day of lucid consciousness, he'd gotten much worse. Anna had thought when he escaped the coma everything would be okay, but it had been a false dawn.

Laying the book on her lap and sighing, Anna decided she couldn't take much more of this. Six weeks now, and no change. Teej showed no sign of either recovering or regressing. Anna was impatient. She had to move forward. Having him here in this house—in this state—was bad for her.

The summer house was now tidy and clean, and as she moved through the open-plan living room and kitchen to the bedroom where he rested, her accomplishments here still made her smile. It had been dilapidated. The first two weeks had been satisfyingly hard work as she'd split her time between cleaning, dusting, renovating, nailing, rewiring, and looking after Teej. Her present malaise had only set in when she finished tidying and repairing. With only one goal to work toward, completing that goal left her aimless. The immaculately clean summer house had changed almost overnight from a project to a prison.

The house had come back to life, but Teej had not. It was hard for Anna to remember what he had been like before the accident. In truth, she didn't really know him very well, but she remembered his easy, natural charm and his kindness. All of that was gone, replaced with broken, faltering speech, confusion and even undirected anger. He was out of his coma now, but he wasn't himself. Helpless and desperate, he would rage and flail under the bed sheets, fighting enemies that existed only in his mind and his memories. She wanted to reach him, but it was like he was trapped at the bottom of a well, shouting up to her and only a few words found her. Everything he said and every sign he gave her only asked for one thing: help.

She would hear him during the night. "Help. Help me. Please, help me." She would usually find he'd kicked the covers off the bed. Feverish and covered in sweat, his arms and hands would curl up like he was grasping invisible demons, and she'd have to pin them down. He would flail wildly, but if she murmured to him in soft tones and told him that he would be okay, he would eventually calm down. Slowly, he would lapse back into sleep. Even then, when he plunged back into the black waters of unconsciousness, everything was a nightmare. He'd toss and turn, and sometimes words would come out. "Linda." "Garret." "Wildey." Once, she thought he said, "Anna."

And it was exhausting. Their adventures seemed like a distant memory. Lady Almeria's garden, werewolves in the mist, and Canfranc Station seemed so long ago. In truth, Anna had begun to doubt any of it had ever happened. Her mind was beginning to rationalize everything away. Sitting in front of a bleary television as the long nights dragged on, she would find herself wondering what was real. She pondered the reality of Etunes, Aesthetes, and Hazes. Could they be a shared delusion brought on by stress, strain, and *everything* she had been through? It made sense if this was all a paranoid delusion. Anna had read about coping mechanisms and denial, and the literature seemed to describe her present situation very well.

Looking after Teej each day and seeing no real improvement in his state, she wasn't getting any closer to understanding him. The feelings for him stuck with her—feelings of concern, mainly—but she found that concern was hard to sustain. Day after day she found herself resenting him just a tiny bit more. He couldn't talk to her, and he couldn't help her. Caring for him was not helping her escape her own dark thoughts. Instead, he was anchoring her to a mundane existence where she fed and bathed him, but had no interaction with him. The crushing weight of responsibility made her weary and bitter, and with no one to talk to, it gave her far too much time to think. The old feeling crept back upon her: *Desolation*.

When the loneliness threatened to overwhelm Anna, she found herself second-guessing all her choices: going to Malamun, reconciling with Sue at the hotel. Even her decision to hide here in the cabin while Teej recuperated felt like a mistake.

Escaping the hospital seemed essential at the time, but now she felt trapped here. She had been certain the doctors couldn't help him, but she was equally certain that she couldn't help him either. All she could do was bring him here—where they might

be just a little safer from their enemies—and hope he would recover.

Perched on the edge of her window seat and swirling a
smear of red wine in the bottom of her almost-empty glass, Anna decided she couldn't do this forever. When Garret had told
her to get away from the city, she had been excited. Smuggling
Teej out of the hospital had left her feeling elated. She had been
sure that here, in this sanctuary in the woods, far from anyone
and anything, he would come back to her. But she was still
alone.

Garret was gone now. He was "broken" too, but in a different way. Unable to help them anymore and often struggling to
make much sense, he told Anna that he was dangerous to be
around. He called himself a liability. Like the explorer that sac-
rificed himself for his friends, he walked out of the tent and into
the snow. She didn't know where he'd gone, but he'd reassured
her that he would be all right. She'd almost believed him.

And Elise had left after Garret. She'd disappeared after their
time in Maxine's Bar. At first it had seemed like Anna might
never see her again, but she'd gotten a message a few weeks
ago. Apparently, she was with Vinicaire again. She was in training. That's what Anna understood of the message, anyway;
although, as always, it had been hard to follow the girl's logic.
Anna had been glad to get the message and relieved that Elise
still thought of her. She was a strange friend, but she was perhaps the only one Anna had left.

Perversely, her mother seemed happy that Anna was here.
With a boy. Their phone calls were light and full of stories Anna
plucked from thin air: boat rides and barbecues and late-night
movie marathons with the new man. Obviously, her description
of events didn't bare much relationship to the truth, but now, at
perhaps Anna's lowest point since she first met Teej, her mother

was happiest. How good Anna had gotten at lying to her loved ones.

Suddenly aware of the utter silence accompanying her reverie, Anna decided she better check on Teej. The television had gone into power-saving mode, and it had taken her several long minutes to notice. Outside the cabin, the stillness was complete; even the wind and rain were gone. The silence was too hard to bear; she slurped the last of her wine and pushed herself off the padded shelf with a harrumph.

Pushing open the flimsy balsa-wood door, Anna's eyes took a second to adjust to the gloom of the room. It smelled stale, even though she had cleaned it thoroughly, and the dim lamp next to the bed failed to illuminate the shadowed corners. Startled, she realized Teej was sitting up. After he'd slept the whole day, she hadn't expected to see him like this. She started to move toward him, but he spoke, and she froze in place.

"Anna, I'm sorry."

For the first time in almost two months, he seemed lucid. He recognized her, and the words pinned her where she stood.

All her ennui fell away. Tears of relief came to her eyes. His face was pure anguish, gaunt and tired, but for the first time since the accident, his eyes held a light again. A light she recognized, faint and distant, but it was there. He was back.

"Lie back down, Teej. Everything's okay."

"No, Anna…How long since the train?"

So they really had been on that train. "You remember that? A long time, Teej. It was Vinicaire's Haze."

"Yeah. I remember it. Then *nothing*."

"Really? You've spoken to me. You weren't making much sense."

"My thoughts were…scattered. It's not just the injury; it's the Hazes. They cause nightmares, headaches, and far worse. How long has it been?"

He looked haunted. There was a profound sadness in his soft eyes. She wanted to hold him. "Weeks. The doctors were confused by your injuries."

"They couldn't help with what was wrong with me. When the Haze that killed Linda Spiraled, it ripped away parts of my mind. Memories of people and places are scars inside my head now. Those take a long time to heal." He pointed to his head as he spoke.

Anna pushed on his shoulders to make him lie down, but he was rigid. His pale skin felt clammy, and she winced when she saw the bruises on his bare chest.

"You need to calm down." she said, keeping her voice low and steady, although she started to feel his panic resonate with her.

"I haven't been honest with you," he said cryptically.

"What about?"

"About *memories.*"

She paused to give him time to explain, but his attention seemed to shift. He was looking past her, over her shoulder at the open doorway.

"Well?" she prompted him.

He was about to answer, but then she felt him tense and try to stand. He grimaced in pain. Something was wrong.

"No. Not now. I'm just back. I'm just coming back!" he shouted.

"What are you talking about, Teej? Calm down and talk to me."

His desperate eyes found hers. "Since I'm awake, he can find us. Together like this, here, it's not safe. Runes! Did you see any written on the walls? Or the floor?"

Teej's eyes darted around the room. He groaned as he leaned over the end of the bed to look at the ground. "Under the carpet. There!"

She looked where he was pointing. A thick woolen rug lay at the foot of the bed. Anna dropped to her hands and knees and grabbed the rug with both hands and began to tug. It was stuck. The legs of the bed pinned it to the ground. This didn't seem like a priority, but he was insistent. Grudgingly, she pulled it harder, and it slid from under the bed, creating a little dust cloud as it came.

Pushing herself back against the wall, Anna threw the carpet to one side to see what was there. A dusty wooden floor. "There's nothing there. What's the problem? What are we looking for?"

She started to worry that this was just another stage of delusion. What if he wasn't really back with her and was still lost within his own mind? He seemed to sense her fears.

"I'm not crazy. Drowden's work is here. We're in danger. Don't you sense it? We need to make sure we don't look at any of his Runes."

"If we're not supposed to look for them, why did we pull up the carpet to try to find one?"

"We can't walk over them, either. That's even worse. There are different types of runes, and each one has different effects. Some are activated when you look at them, others when you cross their threshold.

Anna eyed him skeptically. His sunken cheeks and dilated pupils made him look hollow and gaunt. She believed him, but she also wanted him to calm down. He still wasn't in a fit state of mind, and if they were attacked, she would have to be the one that fought. She needed him back in bed, safe and lucid. "Teej, why don't you lie back? You're still not well. I can check the house for 'Runes.'"

He looked at her with a pained expression, still struggling to process everything that had happened. "What have I missed?"

She tried to smile. "Quite a lot. Why don't you sit down, and I'll try to explain everything?"

His expression was distant, but he nodded almost imperceptibly and lay back in bed. He was in his pajama bottoms and had been covered with a thin blanket but had wriggled out of it. Anna could still see the scars on his body, old ones as well as new. He'd been in many, many fights before the most recent one.

"Let's just talk for a while?" she suggested. "You need water. Can I go get you some? What should I watch out for?"

As she pulled the covers over his shivering form, he pointed vaguely as he spoke.

"Yes water, but look out for runes. Patterns drawn in chalk. If you see any, just don't step on them or look straight into them.

"Okay. No starring at runes. Got you; sure. I'll be back in a minute." Anna hustled out the door, cautiously but quickly moving through the living room to the bathroom. She scanned the surfaces—the floor, the walls and the ceiling—looking for any signs of disruption. Everything was exactly as she had left it.

Anna pushed the bathroom door open anxiously, letting it swing on its hinges as she scanned the room. White tiles, bath mats, colored shampoo bottles, and a clean sink with a slowly dripping tap. Standing in front of the mirror, she poured the water, taking a big glass for herself and drinking it in one gulp. She put her hands on the edges of the sink and looked at herself, forcing the figure that looked back at her to answer some hard questions.

Anna took a moment to critique her own resolve. Had this skinny, red-haired girl looking back at her really been so willing to give up on the man who needed her? Her eyes were watery. Why? Why was she letting herself get upset? Now was not the time for tears, even if they were tears of relief. Now she had to be resolute. She had resented Teej while he was unconscious, and she hated looking after him. If she had been stronger none of this would have happened.

But she *had* endured. Anna *had* looked after him, and now he was back. Not wholly himself, but no longer the moaning, pitiful creature he had been just hours before. He was coming out of the tunnel and back to the light with her guidance. She hadn't attended to him with quiet dignity, but she *had* stayed with him, and now she wasn't alone. He was back.

The cool white interior of the bathroom felt familiar and safe. The figure in the mirror had been through a lot and was stronger for it. Anna could face these challenges and overcome them. So what if she had some doubts and was tired? So what? She was human. Nodding at the resolve in her reflection, she murmured, "Good enough, Anna."

She only noticed the Rune in the mirror at the very edge of her peripheral vision. Above the shower curtain next to the bath, there was a white chalk mark of messy lines with concentric circles and a spiral. Like a spider's web, it made her feel a kind of revulsion, but a fascination, too.

Turning instinctively away from the mirror, Anna immediately realized her mistake as the Rune took hold of her. The rumble under her feet told her this was a Haze. The Rune was tugging at her consciousness, compelling her to stare into its center. For a second, she resisted its power, then with the inevitability of gravity or the passing of time, she turned her gaze to the spiral and felt it take hold. She tried to turn away, but her muscles wouldn't obey her commands. The symbol seemed to turn and twist before her eyes. The hazy, wavy lines spun inwards like a whirlpool. Anna's consciousness became detached, as if her mind was caught in a riptide. The feeling was terrifying and exhilarating. She tried to resist the familiar twinge of the Haze, but it was too late. Anna commanded her head to turn, but

266

her neck muscles were locked. She tried to close her eyes, but they opened wider. She felt the room spin as the Rune took hold.

No sound came from her open mouth, no matter how hard she tried to shout. The words were sucked away into the spiral, too. It seized her physically as well as mentally. Her clothes pulled upward toward the rune, as if caught in a sudden breeze. She was lifted into the air and carried across the room. With a hard slap, her body hit the bathroom wall, her cheek crunching against the cold tiles. The symbols swirled and twisted faster and faster. She was stuck in place, pinned against the wall. Her legs scrambled below her, trying to get a foothold on the ground to pull herself away. She kicked the air uselessly. Her screams came out now. She hoped Teej would hear her and come, or maybe the scream would stop this force or dispel the rune.

To her horror, the wall began to change consistency. It softened, as if the hard white tiles were melting. They felt like cold, dense clay, and though it was heavy and thick, she was being pulled into it.

Her right hand was the first part of her body to be swallowed by the wall. Anna struggled but couldn't pull it free. Next, her legs were sucked in, and as she tried to use her left hand as leverage to push herself away, it too sank into the sludge, swallowing her to the shoulder within seconds. With all her strength, she pulled her head back, but as she did so her torso was absorbed. As she was slowly consumed, she called out once more, but another sudden tug swallowed her even deeper. Her right eye was forced closed as her face sunk into the wall. She thought she saw the bathroom door open, but too late. With a sucking noise, her whole body pulled inside, and the bathroom was gone.

Rejected by the portal, Anna's ring fell from her finger. Her final sound was the faint echo of it clinking across the bathroom floor.

thirty-two

At first, all that existed in Anna's world was the metronomic drip-drip of water. From that drip, the world began to form around the sound. Next, light broke through the darkness as she forced her eyes open, but not much light. Then touch came with the dampness on the heels of her hands, on her knees, and across her shoulders with her wet hair. Dampness saturated her bones and seeped into everything—the air, her clothes, and the cold, hard rock where her body rested. Forcing her eyes open further, she watched a stagnant puddle of water burst into concentric circles from a steady drip. She watched for a moment and tried to comprehend where she was and what had happened.

Coaxing her mind to focus on the situation, her first concern was the numbness. She should be cold and shivering, but her body was numb. Her arms and legs wouldn't move at all. She could move her neck a little, but when she turned more than a few inches, she felt a mounting pain.

Anna took a long, deep breath, taking note of how her chest felt. Were there sharp pains? Internal damage or broken ribs? Her chest swelled, then she blew out slowly. Her vision came back into focus, and her head started to clear. Still, her neck ached, but she found she could twitch her left leg slightly. That was a good sign. Without moving her body, Anna shifted her eyes to scan the surroundings as best she could. Her vision was still adjusting to the gloom, but she was unnerved to realize she couldn't see the sky, although the cool air blowing across her cheek told her she was outside. By turns, she came to realize she was in some huge, cavernous space. Although she couldn't see the ceiling, she could feel its weight above her blocking out the sky.

The rocks under her were slick. Her hair was splayed out in front of her face. Blustering winds raked over her body, only to disappear seconds later, replaced with eerie stillness. Even when the wind wafted across her, the air smelled stale and sodden. A splash of the puddle water in her mouth made her gag and spit. It tasted like dust.

When the winds abated, she could hear the dripping from all around. Occasionally, a creaking noise sounded like it came from a bridge or other wooden structure. Then the voices, far off but coming closer. Whispers in the darkness, they seemed to echo all around, and they were getting louder. She struggled to identify which direction they came from.

Anna tried to turn her head again, but blinding white light exploded in her nerves. Frustrated at her own helplessness, she let out an angry grunt and tried to move her legs. She managed to bend her right leg up to her side, but that was all.

The voices had almost reached her.

She discerned two voices, belonging to two women…or a girl and a woman. They sounded worried. The higher voice of the girl asked questions, but Anna struggled to pick out any recognizable words. Then they stopped. Anna became aware of someone close to her, standing over her. A shadow fell across her view, but she couldn't turn. They stood behind her, and she was powerless. All she could do was talk. *Maybe* she could talk.

"I…" Anna's voice croaked out before any real words could escape. She swallowed, tried to cough, then said, "I'm hurt."

There was no point denying it. If someone wanted to harm her, she couldn't stop them. She hoped they would help if she asked.

"Can you help me? I think I fell."

The stranger's response was guttural and threatening. "Trick, is it? This how you took ma other young? Friends waitin' fer us in the shallows? Poolin' us down?"

Anna couldn't catch the accent. Snarky and barbed, it was overtly aggressive. Clipped and with rounded Rs. Almost Scottish, but not quite. It was archaic somehow. Where was she? Who were these people?

"Wait a sec," said Anna as she struggled to turn. "Could you help me?"

"No touchin' ye, hen. No ma problem. Yer done for." It sounded like the woman would leave, but then the other, younger voice spoke.

"No, ma! She's no bad. Look at her clothes. She's just a new wan. Somebody chucked her down here. She's came down through the up way, not up fae the down way."

Now Anna was completely lost. She had a vague idea of what they were talking about, but it took her brain a few seconds to restructure their words in a way she could understand. The accent wasn't the only difficult part of deciphering their speech; their words ran together as if they only ever talked to each other.

She could feel her arms now, and even move them a little. Her aching neck was still what worried her the most. At first, she had feared she might have damaged it or injured her spine. Now, she allowed herself to hope the damage might be less severe than she first thought.

Keeping her neck still, she waved with one arm while the other gripped her aching shoulder. "What are your names? Mine is Anna."

As she spoke, she managed to get her arms to her chest and push herself up a little. Finally, with a massive effort, she lever-

aged her body and turned, falling on her side. She screamed.
Stupid, stupid! Her neck was in agony. Resting on her side, and
lifting her arm to support her, she was finally able to see them.

"Sorry sight, you are. Body broken and right soppin' wet."

Anna decided she wasn't in imminent danger. Although
they were shadowy and ill-defined against the dark rocks, they
both looked less threatening than they sounded. Perhaps they
wouldn't help her, but they seemed too timid to hurt her. In fact,
they seemed frightened of her. Frightened of everything, like
nervous forest animals. Their eyes darted around, scanning for
invisible predators. Anna mused that perhaps that was a bad
sign.

"You're awright. You're no hurt bad. It just happens when
you get 'ere."

Pushing her feet under her, Anna managed to sit up and almost nodded in agreement before remembering her neck.
Feeling was coming back to her arms and legs, and with that
feeling came increased awareness of how cold she actually was.
Her clothes were soaked through. Still, she was glad of that
cold. It told her she was alive and recovering, and recovering
faster than normal. Perhaps her paralysis had come not from an
injury, but from some other force. Perhaps the process of getting
"here" had done this to her, wherever "here" was.

The girl came closer and reached out a hand. Anna didn't
react, but the woman grabbed her and pulled her back. "What,
Maw! We should help 'er!" the girl said.

"Don't you run away fi me! You hear me?" The woman
pulled her back farther.

Anna could see them better now that she was sitting. Their
clothes were practically rags. Tattered strips of cloth that could
have been dresses or tunics in the past, but were now unrecog-
nizable. Their hair was long and ratty, too, but their skin was
clean. Their feet were wrapped in cloth sandals of some sort,

and both had hand wraps made of stained, ripped fabric. The makeshift gloves were wet, so they couldn't be for warmth. As Anna looked downward and saw how high up they were, she realized the gloves must have been for climbing.

Pushing the girl to stand behind her, the woman regarded Anna. "Anna. Funny name. Think I know where yer fae. Same place as that madman. The scientist. Yer clothes are like his."

"What are your names?" asked Anna.

"Am Fee. This is Shar. She's ma wain. Her dad's no here anymore."

Anna nodded slowly, both to respond to Fee and to test the pain in her neck. It seemed to have abated somewhat.

"And where are we, Fee?"

"The Realm. You mean *where* where? The Sump. Or you mean *where* where where? Well we're near the wharf and the Black Water."

Anna struggled to understand what Fee was talking about. The Realm? The Sump? The words felt familiar, but her mind couldn't hold onto them. A Staid Haze?

"Upset somebody, so ye did, or you'd no be here. This is where the lost things go. The lost things that are never to be found. Come on." With that Fee turned and started to walk away.

The girl ran over to Anna. Her eyes were bright, filled with excitement. She held out her small, dirty hand wrapped in rags. "I can help ye."

"Thank you," said Anna, getting to her feet. The girl tried to help her, but Anna was more encouraged by the moral support than the physical. Shar was skinny and weak and Anna couldn't put any weight on her, so she had to stumble through her first few halting steps alone.

"Thanks for not leaving me behind, Shar."

"That's all right. You canae leave anyone behind here, anyway. There's naywhere to go!" Shar's words hung in the air.

thirty-three

If Anna had known how difficult the descent down the cliff face would be, she might have stayed on the plateau. Looking back where they'd come from, she could see a precipitous platform hundreds of feet above the ground. The rocky outcropping had provided a natural shelf, but the climb down was precarious and painful. Halfway through the journey, she collapsed, leaning on an outcropping and sucking in air while appraising the damage done to her bruised arms and legs.

Her brief time in the Sump had been brutal. There was a vague, natural pathway they followed down, but it was littered with sudden drops and uneven ground. Worst of all, all the hand-holds and walls were slick and slimy. Anna slipped repeatedly and gathered more cuts and bruises every time she put her hands out to save herself. Twice she lost her footing, rattling her weakened right knee on the ground.

Her endurance was being sapped away. The humidity seemed to fill her lungs with dirty water. Lightheaded and faint, the coldness seeped into her bones, and she had begun to shiver. Worryingly, halfway down she could no longer feel the pain in her hands and feet. They'd gone completely numb again.

Shar and Fee had stopped to wait for her, but Fee looked irritated and Shar looked bored now. Every now and then, Fee would go from mild irritation to sudden alertness as she scanned the environment, searching for invisible threats. Anna followed them as best she could, locking her eyes on the back of the girl, her messy, curly hair a beacon she followed. While the girl moved easily across the rocks, the older woman was slower and seemed to be in pain. Still, both easily outpaced Anna who struggled to keep up.

As they descended, Anna tried to get an idea of her surroundings. They were in a huge cave, the ceiling so far above them she couldn't see it, and she could just make out their destination. A collection of little wooden huts and doorways carved into the bare rock lay at the foot of the incline. Stretching ahead of them, a cluster of buildings lay along the bank of a long, dilapidated wharf. Most of the cave was filled with still, black water. While the wharf was to her left, the cave opened to the sea on her right. There were no ships right now, but obviously this was some form of harbor. There was space for no more than two or three boats, and she could only see the opening through the inky blackness because of the silver moonlight that shone across the water. It cast an iridescent skin on the surface, like a slick film of oil. The air filled her lungs with dampness and her nose was full of the scent of decay. This place oppressed her senses.

As she pushed onwards—the uneven ground scraping at the soles of her soaking sneakers—she tried to hold her breath. The fetid taste in the air made her want to spit.

"No used tae a bit of work, your majesty?" Fee chided.

"I'm fine. How did I get here?" asked Anna. She was interested in any answer Fee could give her, but she also needed a break. She hoped asking some questions would delay their descent long enough so she could catch her breath.

"Dunno how I got here. Dunno how long I been here. There's no way out, afore ye ask. Hurry up, now. No safe here. No safe at all."

Clearly Fee was in no mood to answer questions, so with heavy resignation, Anna pulled herself upward and continued down.

"I was at my home. And then I was…there was a portal. And I woke up here." Anna could see that her story was of no interest to Fee. She continued stirring the foul-smelling stew on the makeshift stone stove. It didn't smell like something anyone would ever choose to eat.

"Uh huh."

Clearly, Fee wasn't even listening to her. She decided to talk to the girl instead. Shar stood slightly behind her mother, peeking out at Anna from under her arm.

"Tell me about this place?"

"This is me an' mum's place. It's the nicest wan on the whole row."

Anna looked around. It was too dark to see much, but the "place" was little more than a room hollowed out of the bare rock. The floor was flat and smooth at least, with benches carved into the cold stone walls. Every surface was covered in threadbare rugs that looked a hundred years old. It somehow smelled like dust and dampness at the same time. From the low ceiling, just above her head, dangled stalactites that would be a hazard for anyone a few inches taller.

"It's very nice, Shar."

"Liar," snapped Fee with genuine anger and without turning around. Anna flinched, but Shar didn't notice. Apparently, this was how her mother reacted to being patronized.

Unsure how to mollify her, Anna ignored the outburst and said, "The Realm? The Sump? That's where we are? Tell me about them."

Shar looked up at her mother for some signal, but none came. Shrugging, she continued, "Sump is where we are. The fancy folks call it Avicimat, but we regular folk call it the Sump cos that's what it is. From the water to the tops of the rocks. If you go oot to the water and swim far, it's where nowhere people are. S'where dredges are. Then after all the dredges, it's just nae things. And up past the rocks, if you climb far, there's crags, but no people. Crags are worse than dredges, but they don't look as bad, but if you get close, they're worse. But I think dredges are more scary cos they grab you and pull you doon."

Anna tried a smile of reassurance, but she found it wouldn't come. Instead, she tried to make her grimace less obvious. She didn't know what to make of the girl, but she was sure her description of the hazards was honest.

The room was cold, but the stove produced a little heat. There wasn't really a door, rather a heavy blanket hung over the larger of two holes that led out to the main cave. The smaller hole was at the height of Fee's shoulder and about a foot in diameter, and it let the smoke out as well as the cold in. Even "inside," it was damp and wretched. Anna felt sympathy for these two, but she felt more for herself. Her neck still ached, and as feeling returned to her hands and feet, she noticed all the cuts and scrapes she'd accrued.

Also, there was something beyond her physical pain and discomfort that unnerved her about this place. She could feel a deep malaise. Perhaps it was her Haze sense picking up on the hopelessness of the Sump, but she knew the longer she spent here, the harder it would be to leave.

To make herself feel better she kept talking to Fee and Shar. "I was attacked, you know? Someone sent me here through a portal. I'm…" Anna hesitated, unsure of the wisdom of what she was about to say. "I'm a Metik."

There was no reaction from Fee. "Is that a type of sailor?" asked Shar. "Sailors go on boats, mum says. But not the boat that comes. No one ever gets on that wan."

"No, I'm not a sailor. A boat comes? Is that how we get away from here?"

Fee slammed a heavy cast-iron ladle on the counter and they both jumped. "No one leaves. No one thinks 'bout leavin', and no one ever talks 'bout leavin'."

"Sorry, I…" Anna didn't know what else to say. Looking at Shar again, Anna asked, "Is there anyone else here?"

"No' anymore, but there used to be. Most of 'em are dredgy now. Simyon and old man Kentuk and our neighbors the Kollies. And…" she looked up at Fee again, but the woman just kept stirring. "There's the scientist, but we avoid 'im. He's right weird."

Anna didn't know what to ask first, but the little girl's blue, piercing eyes showed enthusiasm for the discussion. She wanted to help Anna. Her mannerisms were off-putting, but Anna found herself warming to these two strange people, or the girl at least.

"Dredges? What are those?"

"They live doon under the water. Well, not at first. First, they're us. Then we get sad. Then we want to go under the water. Hunners of 'em down there now."

Anna shivered. Somehow what the girl said made sense. Eventually, the despair forced the people here to give up. Throw themselves into that cold, dark, bottomless water. The word came into her mind once more. *Desolation.* She forced it back down.

"Who is this scientist, then?"

It was Fee that turned and answered this time, sadness and mild irritation on her face.

"Never shut up, do ye? Blether blether. Aye, well, better tell ye, then after yer questions we'll eat, and that'll shut ye up. This

278

scientist is crazy. He's from your place, I think. You'd be better aff avoidin' 'im. When his sky boat don't work, he'll go dredgy. I've seen it happen a hunner times before. Trying tae get oota here just makes the dredge come on ye faster. He's got nae chance, hen."

Anna nodded and tried to smile. Again, it was too hard to force it. There was a push back when she tried to show any positive emotion here, as if a heavy weight pressed back against her, but she was glad of the woman's advice. Or at least she was glad of the human contact. She couldn't imagine being here without these two. They might not be able to help her, but having someone else anchored her to reality. They helped her suppress a worrying, niggling desire that she'd only just become aware of, but had felt since she got here.

The desire to walk to the edge of the water and keep going.

"I'm going to look around," said Anna. "I'll be close by."

Fee grunted. "Eat the stew first."

Reluctantly Anna waited for the wooden bowl to come to her, then took a watery spoonful of gray-brown meat, put it in her mouth, chewed, and tried as hard as she could to swallow. It tasted like rancid meat brewing in sewer water.

"Almost as bad as my mom's cooking."

thirty-four

Feeling stronger, Anna sat up and pushed aside the thin blanket. Having managed half an hour of restless sleep, she rubbed the crustiness from her eyes and decided to go exploring. Stepping carefully over the sleeping forms of Shar and Fee, she pulled her cardigan closer around her body and walked outside into the main cave.

The entrance to Shar and Fee's den was about fifteen feet from the wharf, and black water lapped gently at the thick timbers of the wooden pier. Amidst the faint fluttering of bat wings, a steady drip of water echoed throughout the quiet cave.

Walking past deserted caverns and little rock houses, Anna thought about this place. It seemed to mute her powers, making her Haze Sense fuzzy and making her feel weak. This Staid Haze wasn't controlled by a single Dreamer and was resistant to change. Anna doubted she could escape without some help. Would Teej find her here? Was that a hope she could hold on to?

Moving through the darkness, she relied on her hearing to guide her. Past three empty houses, she came to a fourth with a thick animal fur hanging over the doorway. Pausing outside, she wondered whether she should investigate. She flinched when she heard shuffling inside, but she inched forward and put her hand against the thick material.

The scratching stopped, and there was silence. She breathed in deeply and pushed aside the curtain.

The scent of ash and dust was overpowering. Anna almost gagged, but putting her hands over her mouth, she forced herself to look around. Tucked in the corner and huddled under a tattered piece of cloth were three clustered, shivering people. With their legs and arms wrapped around each other, they were a single mass of emaciated skin and bones.

Flesh hung loosely from their twig-thin frames, while their weather-beaten skin was thin as paper. A few wisps of long, gray hair hung limply from their heads. None of them looked at her. They cowered from the light. A man, a woman, and a child, or they had been at one time. What was wrong with them? What did this place do to people?

Anna called out, her voice straining to break through the oppressive blanket of stale silence, "Hello? Can I help you?"

They started to moan. Low at first, but escalating to a continuous wail of pain and anguish. She recoiled.

The man turned toward her, agonizingly slowly, and the bones of his spine cracked and creaked as they rubbed against each other. Black, empty eyes looked out from a skull visage. She had seen those eyes before: the Night Collectors and the Midnight Man.

Anna suppressed a scream, clamping a hand over her mouth. She swallowed it down deep inside her chest and slowly backed away. Was the thing still alive? Did it think? It looked like an animated cadaver. With one heaving, creaking movement, it raised its right arm and gestured for her to leave. She edged back, keeping her eyes on the pallid creatures the whole time. They settled back into a huddle. Moving away slowly, she let the door covering flop closed and crept backward into the cold cave.

Shivering and unnerved, Anna half-ran into the darkness. The skeletal face wouldn't leave her mind. Why had she forced herself to look inside? She went as fast as she could through the gloom, aware that she might stumble into danger, but desperate to get away.

Anna stopped at the water's edge. With her head down and arms clenched close to stay warm, she wandered along the edge of the wharf. The slick, black water sloshed up and down the rotten wood of the pier. Finding a rocky ledge close to the dock, she used her sleeve to dry it off as best she could then perched on the edge to look out across the bay. She needed a moment to appraise her current situation and decide what she should do next.

When she thought about Drowden choosing this place as a prison for her with deliberate malice, she felt like she'd been punched in the gut. This was a Haze, but it was more solid than any other Haze she had experienced. She hadn't tried to use her Praxis here, but she was sure it wouldn't help her. Her will to even try was disappearing. Her powers were somehow shackled or blocked by an invisible miasma that rose out of the water. The force pulled at her senses and held a morbid appeal. The desire to just step over the edge into that water was growing. She knew where those thoughts led. *Desolation.*

Anna tried to come up with some sort of plan, but too many questions swirled around in her head. Why hadn't Drowden just killed her? What should she do? What was happening to Teej right now? When her thoughts came back to him, she felt a growing panic. *She* was supposed to protect *him.*

No time for panic. When she escaped, she could help him, but now she had to think. She had to figure out what was happening. Now was not the time for weakness or recklessness. She had to recover, find out more about this place, and figure out how to get back. That would only be possible if she didn't think about him and what might be happening back at home. With great effort, she took her fear and her concern for him and forced it to the back of her mind.

Getting to her feet, Anna looked behind her. Her eyes were becoming accustomed to the pervasive dark and could pick out more details now. To her far left, a network of paths and tunnels led up to the rocky platform where she had first appeared. That route could be explored later. Straight ahead, a small trickle of steam wafted from the dwelling where Shar and Fee lived. A faint light flickered inside. Hopefully they could give her more information. And to her right, the home of the three lost souls was ominously quiet. She shuddered when she thought of their cries of sorrow. There was nothing she could do for them.

Anna's head was clearer now. Her body felt a little stronger. She would explore this place and find a way out. There was hope, she just had to hold onto it.

thirty-five

"You have to take me to him! I've tried everything else."

Fee shook her head and refused to face Anna. She couldn't be convinced. Exasperated, Anna turned to the little girl and asked again, even though she knew what the answer would be. "Shar, can you take me?"

"My maw says I canae go without her. Sorry, auntie Anna."

"I told ye no' to call her that!" snapped Fee.

"Sorry, maw."

This had gone on for days. Or weeks? Anna couldn't be sure anymore. She thought back to a time when she had hoped to escape. When the Sump had seemed like a temporary setback. That seemed like a long, long time ago. Now, any hope of escape felt faint. The scientist was her last lead and her only remaining option.

In her first few days in the Sump, Anna explored the wharf and the surrounding cave system. She climbed as high as possible past the platform of her arrival through rocky paths and caves. Each path she explored led to a dead end. At the highest points, she saw the creatures that Fee and Shar called "Crags." They were monstrous birds, uglier than crows and with serrated beaks, and though they did not attack her, they would not let her pass. Cawing and screeching when she neared them, they blocked passageways and caves. When she navigated around them and sneaked past, she found all routes led back to the same familiar spots. Climbing offered no hope of escape. All paths led back to the Black Water.

Back on the ground, there was no way to escape, either. The caves and dwellings around the dock were mostly deserted while a few contained the huddled and desiccated creatures. Fee and Shar called them Dredges, although that term was rightfully reserved for the ones that had succumbed to the Black Water. These poor souls were in the last stages of life, wasting away to walking skeletons until eventually the pull of the water would be too much for them. They would shamble out of their homes, arms stretched forward like they were being led by an invisible hand, and walk soundlessly and hopelessly into the water. They would be swallowed without a sound.

Anna had seen two of them go into the water the night before. They had barely a glimmer of life left. One of them had been aware of her presence and had turned its head almost imperceptibly toward her, but there was no recognition in the eyes. No soul left.

This was to be her fate, too. And Fee's, and Shar's. This happened to everyone here. Anna had come to realize that this was the reason for Fee's pragmatism. She had seen it happen so many times before. Fee wanted to keep herself and her daughter alive as long as she could, and in her own way, Anna came to realize that Fee was trying to save her, too. She cared, but caring about people in the Sump wasn't about giving them affection or attention, it was shepherding them away from the real danger. The hope of escape.

The Sump was a slipknot around your neck. The more you struggled, the tighter it held you. Yet *still* Anna struggled. She searched for a route out of the place. She had walked as close as she could to the cave entrance, but it was impossible to get out without going into the water, and she would never forget the existential chill she'd experienced as she got close to the mouth of the cave. The dark water went on for as far as she could see. It went on forever. The sea was infinite, stretching to the horizon with the perpetual glow of the moon casting a silver sheen across its surface.

And that moon never set. There was no sun in the Realm, or not in the Sump anyway. This was a world of perpetual night, both inside and outside the cave.

Anna's final plan for escape had been the most fruitless of all: using her powers to fashion an exit. As an Undreamer, she should have been able to dismantle this Haze. If it was too powerful, she should have been able to dismiss portions of it. She should have been able to tear down walls, break her way through locked doors and dissolve any barriers that blocked her path, but she found her Praxis spluttered out here.

She had practiced on an old wooden chair from one of the abandoned dwellings. Taking it out onto the wharf and focusing all of her will on it, over and over she had chanted "Break," "Burn," and "Dust." Nothing had happened. She had touched it with her ring finger—just as she'd done against her enemies before—and willed it to burst into flame. Still nothing. Hours of work, and the most she had managed was a small network of cracks, but even then, it had taken all her concentration and will, exhausting her completely, and it got her no closer to escape. Instead, it had made her feel more desperate. The one thing that was special about her made no difference here at all.

And with that failure, she had explored every option. There was nothing else to do, *except* meet with the scientist.

As Fee slid another stained, wooden bowl of steaming, foul-smelling stew across the table toward Anna, she pushed it to one side and continued to press the old woman for more information.

"Can't you just tell me about him again? You said he was from the same place as me?"

"Aye. Naw. Look, can't ye just eat yer stew?"

The old woman sat down at the heavy, wooden table across from Anna, and Shar joined them a few seconds later. The girl greedily wolfed down a big chunk of the meat Anna still couldn't identify. She never, ever asked Fee where she got the ingredients.

"I can't stay here, Fee. This isn't…Look, I don't want to offend you, but this isn't living. I will help you both, if I can. There must be a way to escape back to the real world. Basine, or whatever you all call it."

Fee ignored her, sliding the stew back across the table and motioning for her to eat. The old woman's ratty gray hair obscured her face as she leaned forward and slurped the liquid with a rusty spoon. Anna sighed with resignation as she realized Fee wasn't willing to talk right now.

"Please, miss, can I have some less." Anna muttered under her breath petulantly. Fee ignored her. For a moment, Anna considered eating with them, but the thought of sitting here one more minute was too much. She got to her feet and stormed out the door. "Fuck this!"

Outside, the cave seemed darker and colder than ever before. The wind whipped around Anna as she pushed the palms of her hands into her eyes to stem the tears. She stood sobbing soundlessly for a few minutes before she realized she wasn't alone. Shar had followed her out and looked on in fear and concern from just beyond the doorway. Anna tried to stop crying in front of the girl but realized she couldn't hold back her own sorrow. Instead, she was honest with her.

"Shar, I can't take this. I'm so dirty and hungry and tired and this *dread*. I can't make it go away, Shar. I can't make the dread go away."

Anna knew she shouldn't be saying this to the girl. Shar wouldn't understand, and she couldn't help. She had to be protected from all of this. She was just a child, but still, Anna couldn't hold in the outburst anymore. She admired the old woman's stoicism, and she was in awe of Shar's resilience, but she couldn't match their endurance. They could survive this place without hope of escape, but Anna could not. Maybe if her own mom was here. That was wishful thinking, and Anna pushed thoughts of home from her mind.

How could they make it through one more day? Perhaps because Fee did such a good job of sheltering Shar from the harsh realities of their situation. Maybe Shar had no memory of her time before the Sump. Certainly, neither of them was willing to talk about their lives before they came here.

"I could tell ye—" The girl was reticent, but she looked like she'd made a decision. Her bare foot fidgeted against the slick rock, and she coiled her ratty hair around one finger distractedly.

"Tell me what? The scientist?" Anna turned to look at the girl. Behind her knots of tangled, curly hair, there was a twinkle in her eyes. Excitement or playfulness, or maybe hope?

"Yeah. He's real close. You would find him anyways. Eventually. Ma knows; she just likes ye. She doesn't want you to find him cos it will make ye worse."

"I like you both, too, Shar, but I need to get home. I don't want to be here anymore."

The girl frowned suddenly. There was a sadness in her eyes. She stiffened. "You'll leave us behind."

"I don't want to leave you! I want you to come with me to a better place."

Shar sneered with a cruel smile. Anna had never seen her like this before. "Ma was right about you. After the scientist, you'll be in the water soon."

Anna stood straight and met the girl's gaze directly. "I will not. I will not leave you both. You hear me? I just won't."

After a stern look from Anna, the girl looked away, ashamed. "Okay. Fine."

"Now, where can I find him?"

"Ye know the cave by the water near the waterfall, where the big stream comes in? He's there. You go under the waterfall, and there's another hoose. It's through a wee crack in the wall, on the right. He might be Dredgy already though."

"But that's so close…"

"Aye, but ye cannae find it unless you know where tae look. It's tae the right in the wee passage."

"Okay. I'm going there now. I won't be long, okay. Don't tell your mother."

Shar rolled her eyes. "She already knows."

Anna nodded once, then started on her path along the shore. She took three steps before turning on her heels, running back, and hugging Shar. The girl's curly hair was soft as she pushed her face into Anna's chest. Anna held Shar for a moment, saying nothing, but promising herself she wouldn't leave this girl behind.

And then she was running again. It wasn't far to the waterfall. It normally took five minutes to get there. If it meant she had a chance to escape, Anna would get there in three.

thirty-six

The sounds of the echoing, windy cave faded into the distance, and Anna felt like she was hearing silence for the first time. The passage below the waterfall was longer than Shar had said. It snaked around and down, and as she moved away from the twilight of the cave, she lost light as well as sound. The tunnel was barely as wide as she was, and with only one way to proceed, she had no choice but to push on. The claustrophobia twisted her stomach in knots, but she felt a thrill of excitement as well. Any change was good. Any path to potential freedom was worth exploring, and this was the last one left for her. She would follow a tunnel like this for a hundred miles if it led her out, in the end, to somewhere new.

As she pushed on, her dark-adjusted eyes began to perceive a faint glow. A light, far off in the tunnel, like a single line of dark gray on a canvas of black. She pushed on toward that light, inching sideways through the bare rock of the cave, despite the increasing risk that she might get stuck. It was getting narrower, and her progress had slowed to an awkward shuffle.

Then noise came. She felt it before she heard it. Vibrating through the rocks that pushed in on her from all sides, it was a vague, steady thudding. It would pause every now and then, and there was a curious rhythm to it. She could imagine someone hammering then stopping when they got tired.

As she pushed onwards, each step Anna took increased the brightness around her. The single line became a crack in the darkness that widened until it became a doorway. Accustomed to the gloom now, she had to slow down and squint at the entrance ahead to avoid hurting her eyes. Sliding to the end of the tunnel, a great weight lifted off her chest. By the time she reached the entrance, she was out of breath with relief and almost blinded by the intense light. She stumbled through the doorway, momentarily unable to perceive where she was, but overwhelmingly glad to be there.

She heard him before she saw him. A comical voice— friendly but perturbed, kindly but confused, and with a slight lisp. "Oh. Oh, dear, dear. Thith is not what I expected at all. Oh no, not now. Not a good time. Not a good time at all!"

As her eyes slowly adjusted, she noticed how different it felt here. The air smelled better. Not fresh, but the staleness was different. The pervasive odor of ash and dust was gone, and the scent of moldy parchment was in its place. It was musty, but not as sopping wet as the cave, and with an unpleasant but very faint smell of urine. The smell reminded Anna of a very old bookshop run by a very old man. It wasn't pleasant, but it was better and crucially, it was *different*. Anything different was good.

And it was warmer here, too. Not warm enough to remove the chill in her bones that felt like it had become an innate part of her soul now, but enough to remove some of the numbness from her fingertips.

Books were piled high on unstable shelves all around her. The towers of texts stretched to the ceiling, some of them falling apart, others looking relatively new. They were bound in every shade; some had gold writing on the spines while others had faded titles. Wedged between each volume were manuscripts, papers, and binders. The floor was blanketed in loose notes from pages that had fallen or been pulled from the shelves.

Anna was in the narrow part of the oval-shaped room, and it opened into a huge hall in the middle. Above them, a large glazed dome stretched hundreds of feet tall. It looked ornate and Victorian. Faded murals depicting flower gardens wound around oxidized brass fixtures, and the bookcases stretched all the way to the very top. To the left and right of her large, movable ladders—the kind you saw in ancient libraries in movies—climbed nearly to the ceiling.

In the center of the room, clutching a gleaming brass hammer in one hand, stood the scientist. He seemed to be working on some elaborate steam-powered device. Shiny copper pipes and valves stretched up over eight feet in height. The central tank looked like it was for distillation and was big enough that Anna could fit inside. All around that central tank, heavy pipes and metal tubing connected smaller stills. It puffed and pumped water and spluttered.

He noticed Anna standing in the doorway, and pulling on a heavy lever as tall as a person, the scientist brought the noises to a stop and the machine slumbered again. Toweling his forehead with a dirty rag, the scientist slid his glasses to the tip of his long, pointy nose to regard her more closely.

The old-fashioned round spectacles looked expensive, but the fluffy sideburns that flanked his rosacea-dappled cheeks were messy. He looked like he was in his mid-sixties but could have been younger and tired. Heavy bags under each small, beady eye and a furrowed brow made him look like a friendly grandpa covered in smile-lines. His bald head was shiny and sweaty, with tufts of white, wispy hair sticking from either side like antennae. He was dressed in a puffy white shirt with fancy cuffs tucked into smart trousers with leather suspenders.

He continued to look at her closely, keeping his distance but regarding her with intense curiosity.

"Hello. Sorry. Am I disturbing you? I'm Anna. I'm…" She trailed off, aware that he was looking at her as if she were utterly insane.

"You're the scientist, right? I have been looking for—"

"You've been to Malamun!" he shouted suddenly.

"Yes. How do you—?"

Climbing off his tiny step ladder, he scuttled away from his machine and toward her, his rotund form waddling from side to side as he approached. She recoiled, holding her hand up as she backed away. She had experienced too many nasty surprises recently to let anyone invade her personal space, regardless of their intention.

"Back up!" she shouted. "Get back!"

He instantly stopped in his tracks, chastened. He looked guilty or confused. She found it hard to read him, but his demeanor resembled a schoolboy that had been caught doing something wrong.

"I wasn't going to touch you. I don't touch."

She kept her hand up but tried to reassure him. "Okay. Just *stay* there. I'm sorry for interrupting you. Are you the scientist?"

He mumbled something inaudible, stopped himself, then started again. "No, young lady. I'm…well, maybe they do name me thus. I suppose I might be. My name is Professor Ozman. Pleased to meet you."

She tried not to react, but her heart jumped. Mr. Ozman. The real one this time. Was it a good sign that she had found him here? Probably not. He was still a good ten steps away from her, but he held his hand out in greeting.

"Sorry, I'm a bit cautious these days," she responded, keeping her distance.

"Quite understandable, Miss…?"

"Just call me Anna."

"Miss Anna, it is."

293

"Just Anna."

"Very good. Well, welcome to my workshop," he said as he gestured behind him with his dirty rag.

Anna edged closer, and he motioned to two chairs at the back of the room. She had to admit, they looked comfortable. Most tempting of all, they sat next to a little round table with a steaming teapot. She desperately wanted to drink anything that didn't taste of ash. As she wandered toward him cautiously, she said, "Thanks. I have questions."

He smiled for the first time. A gentle smile, but his eyes shone with a hint of fierce intelligence. "As do I, Anna. As do I."

thirty-seven

In the orange glare of flickering light bulbs strung along the vertiginous bookshelves, Anna and Mr. Ozman discussed the routes into the Sump and if there was a way to escape. In all cases, Ozman was very difficult to pin down. She couldn't tell if he was intentionally obstinate or quirkily unfocused. Insight blended with madness.

He confirmed that they had both been sent here by Drowden. When he spoke of the man, he was full of revulsion and referred to him as the Occultist. Ozman hated the other Aesthete even more than Anna did. He also explained how he had been thrown out of the Haze he once called home: Malamun. He had maintained and managed that place, although he admitted it was an old Staid Haze that existed long before he took over tenure. It was a place of great power, filled with unharnessed Vig. And he hinted at some greater purpose that Drowden was working toward, but he held the man in such disdain that he refused to talk about it.

Ozman spoke in riddles, his answers often circling back to where he began. He was evasive, and his distracted demeanor allowed him to deflect questions he didn't want to answer, but he was intensely interested in her experiences of Malamun. When Anna tried to speak about almost anything else, he changed the subject back as quickly as he could.

Shifting on the old chair, which was at least more comfortable than the cold, wet rocks she had been on since arriving in the Sump, she wondered how to get the information she needed from him.

"But how long have you *actually* been here?" Anna asked.

"Hmmm, tricky. You don't know much about affairs Behind the Veil, clearly, but you at least know about the prohibition against manipulating time."

She didn't, but she let him continue.

"Well, although we Aesthetes can't manipulate time, there are tricks that a Haze can play on your mind to make moments expand across the fourth dimension. I am sure you have noticed the sun does not come up here in Avicimat? That is one such trick. When there's no sun, how does one count the days?"

"You must have some idea, though. Years or weeks or days?"

"Well, *yes.*"

She rolled her eyes in frustration. He regarded her with obvious consternation, wrinkling his nose and pushing his little round, silver spectacles up his face.

"Fine, you don't want to talk about that. Tell me how you made this place. And tell me what the machine is—no, wait. Don't get into all that again. I had no idea what you were talking about before. Tell me what it *does.*"

"Well, this place is the work of my geas. I perambulate my filtration devices in such a way that the evaporated coagulate forms these machines, pulling the moisture from the air and separating the essential ether. The Orgone Energy pools in the lower chambers of this vessel and with the correct—"

She cut him off. "You're a Dreamer, so you created all of this stuff. It's all part of your Art. Okay, I get that, even if you won't say it."

"Well, it's certainly an uncouth way of looking at Mimesis, young lady! I am an imagineer of the highest caliber. A subgenius of Slack, but there is something to what you say. Once I had crafted my workshop into existence—"

"Crafted? What fro— Actually, never mind. Just tell me what your device does. Will it help us escape?"

Anna couldn't hide her impatience. If he could help her escape, she had to know, and she had no time for more new terminology. She needed a way out, not a lecture.

"At the moment, no. It needs more work…" He trailed off, before suddenly regaining his enthusiasm. "It even has space for two, so we shall both be able to get back to our own homes of initial residence!"

"Four. It needs to fit four, so we can take Shar and Fee."

He changed the subject quickly. "You see, my device is a reformulation of the Cloud Buster. In this case, it uses Orgone to propel us. The accumulated energies will coalesce into a capsule of pure immaterium around us. Protected in a cocoon of plasminated Orgone, we will be able to fly through the barriers above."

"The barriers above? You mean the big rock ceiling over our heads?"

"Yes, indeed; quite rightly so!" He chuckled to himself. "That ceiling shall not impediate our imminent escape at all!"

"So, we're below ground now? We can escape *up* that way?"

"No, not at all! We are at a tributary of reality, flowing away from what you would call Basine. We are nowhere and also worse than nowhere. We are in that Realm, the most Staid of Staid Hazes, created by the ultimate Ancestral, Gwinn himself. And within that Realm, we are in the dumping ground. Avicimat is the place wherein all the detritus of all the worlds comes to rest. Although here in the bay, we're in a tidier little corner of that wretched place, but no less hazardous to our health and the potentiality of our future survival."

The Sump, in the lowest corner of The Realm, was just a prison. If the walls of a normal Haze were like paper to Anna, the walls in the Sump were like cold, hard steel. She had to keep his focus on escaping. With his residual power, he was the key to her cell. Her ticket out of here.

"I guess it doesn't matter where exactly we are, but if this is a Haze, then there must be an Aesthete controlling it, right? Can't we just find the Dreamer to find a way out?"

Ozman slid his glasses to the end of his nose and appraised her through them. It was an affectation he used whenever she asked him a question he found distasteful. "No small task. Quite impossible, I'm afraid. This is as Staid as it comes. That means there is no Dreamer. The most powerful being here is Gwinn, the Monarch. You don't know of the Monarch?"

"No."

He sneered a little, his countenance shifting to snarky. He was judging her, and she was showing her ignorance. "Or *God*. Have you heard of *God* perchance?"

She rolled her eyes and replied acerbically, "Yeah, he's not a close personal friend, though."

"No need for the sarcastrisms, young lady. Anyway, the Monarch is the," he wrinkled his nose in displeasure again, "all powerful. Many, my deluded brother included, once considered him to be a deity of sorts. Such is his power. I *must* say that such attitudes are relics of a bygone age amongst my people. These anachronisms are something distasteful that most of us have left aside. My brother's dawdlings with his 'New Native Power,' a ridiculous attempt to cling to theistic inanity, really showed me how deluded we can continue to be, even in these more enlightened times."

"Dreamers aren't religious then?"

He chuckled disdainfully, but his eyes darkened. There was no humor in the sound he made. "They certainly *shouldn't* cling to such antiquated concepts. If you were to check their skulls for crenulations, you would find those religious members of my brethren would exhibit the characteristic bumps of pious credulousness."

He talked like this constantly, shifting tone from playful to disdainful, using words that either he didn't understand or that didn't actually exist, and yet he revealed more than any other Metik or Aesthete had so far. She got the feeling that within his ramblings were nuggets of genuine insight, but separating knowledge from nonsense was difficult.

"You were telling me about the Monarch...?"

"Ah, yes! The Monarch, King Gwinn. Well, my point is that he, though much diminished in recent times, was at one time sufficiently potent as to be mistaken for a deity. Those amongst my brethren who looked for such spiritual verisimilitude were willing to espouse him as such. Looking for a figurehead for their spiritual bumblings, they venerated him, and that went badly wrong, and now he wants nothing to do with them. Nevertheless, he is not someone we can approach, interact with, or should even talk about too loudly. Make no mistake, young lady, he is the most potent of us all."

When Ozman talked of King Gwinn, his voice broke strangely.

"He's the most powerful Aesthete?"

He sniffed and tutted at the question. "No, my dear. Rayleigh is the most powerful *Aesthete*. The Monarch is—oh, this is too infuriating. Who is your teacher? He must be reprimanded for allowing you to wallow in such ignorance. You know not of Ancestrals or Gwinn or The Fahl. Or how we came to be."

"Okay, okay! I know I don't exactly understand everything. Just tell me. He won't help us get out of this place, will he? We can't go to him and ask?"

Ozman huffed as he shuffled away to poke at his machine again. Snapping at him made him withdraw like this. She had to contain herself.

"Sorry," she said, and he nodded without looking back at her.

He rested both hands on his machine and sighed heavily. "We are very much in the Sump. We are at the very lowest reaches, but *his* domain is wider. This Realm is different from Basine, but it is more than a Haze too. A Staid Haze. You know this type? Staid Hazes have no originators and need no Aesthete to maintain them. Quantifiably there is no doubt that scientific rationale says The Realm is a Haze, but it is not *exactly* like a Haze. Within this land we call The Realm, Avicimat is the re-minder of all the things we throw away. A receptacle for the things we no longer regard with our senses or energate with our thoughts. And into the Sump, nothing comes out. Thus, it is a most *efficacious* place to dispose of an enemy."

"And Drowden sent us both here. So, can't we go back the same way we came in then?"

"Well, that's a thoroughly ignorant suggestion! But never mind that, we simply must talk about the Occultist taking my beloved Malamun. Tell me again what happened there, and you are sure you did no damage to my lunar residence?"

"Yes, it wasn't damaged at all," she lied. "But I've told you what happened there. Can't we focus on why this happened? And how we get out?"

"I do not find this repetition of the petty schemes and mach-inations of the Doxa benefits us. You do not understand my accurate recitations of their motivations, and I lack the patience to explain them again."

300

Anna held back her frustration. "Just *indulge* me. Drowden, or the Occultist, took Malamun from you and sent you here. Why?"

"Malamun was my home. Mine! Only I could plan an expedition to such a remote locale, overcoming the obstacles of solar rays and the disturbed ether fields there. And further, to create such an eclectic menu with delights from the seven corners of the world!"

"Okay, sure. But why did the Occultist want Malamun in particular?"

"To harvest it, I suppose. The Doxa need Vig to accomplish their ridiculous plans."

Anna thought back to her encounter with Drowden on Malamun. He'd mentioned that there was a source of Vig there. Something ancient that he could use for, well, she didn't know what.

"So, it was a strategic move? Drowden took Malamun from you for Vig. Did you fight him?"

Getting suddenly defensive, Ozman was caught off balance. "We don't all have Undreamer abilities to defend ourselves, young lady. I tried! Or I would have tried if he had given me a chance. Any Aesthete knows it's bad form to enter another's Haze. Terribly rude, but he had planned it all from the beginning. He really does have that weasely, low intelligence of the working class! You know the sort; lacking the manners or insight of a true gentleman, and willing to stoop so low that he gets what he wants.

"By the by, he came to *my* home, and he knew I would be powerful there, with it being *my* Haze. He inculcated himself with my brother, John Murray Speare, who calls himself the Apoth now. We used to be part of The Association of Electrizers, but my dear brother left that—and me—behind. The Doxa knew exactly how to get to me, and with Rayleigh looking the other way, there was no one to protect me. No Metiks, of course! Mind you, to my reckoning, this is *exactly* the kind of thing Metiks should be helping us with. And they brought Mott with them, too. I believe you must have met him. I detected his taint on you as soon as you came in to my workshop."

"Yeah," said Anna through pursed lips. "I met him. The Midnight Man."

"What a preposterous name! But yes, I believe we are referring to one and the same."

This was starting to come together. Finally, Anna felt like she was on the verge of some fundamental understanding. Not just of the world Behind the Veil, but of the motivations and conflicts between its residents.

Drowden had conspired with Ozman's brother and the Midnight Man. For what reason she didn't know, but together they dispossessed Ozman of Malamun to gain its Vig. She was slowly realizing the subtle economies of this new world. If Vig was such a crucial resource for these Aesthetes, it was no wonder they were willing to fight for it. Even kill for it.

"Why didn't any Metiks try to stop Drowden? Wouldn't they help you keep your Haze?"

He rolled his eyes again. "This is exactly my point! Why do we have these meddling, interfering Metiks if they cannot protect us from the feckless, the unscrupulous, and the covetous?"

"Do you know the Metik *I* work with?" she asked.

"Yes," he said simply. His expression was blank.

"Well? What do you know about him?"

"You cannot learn a thing you think you know."

"What's that supposed to mean?"

"Why speak of him if you won't believe what I say? I wonder why he is not here with you now."

Ozman was being evasive.

"Are you friends?" Anna asked. "Or enemies? We have far too many of those already."

"I wouldn't commonly attribute friendship to Metiks, but were such a thing possible, Donnel might be seen as such. Certainly, we share ideological viewpoints. Our dislike of idolatry is similarly strong. Our willingness to avoid violence."

"So, you and Teej…Donnel worked together? Against the others?"

"I wouldn't say that, no. Some call him 'the diplomat.' He's always been the most reasonable of your kind. Some call him a toothless tiger, but not me. I see sense in avoiding violence, and he has a genuine regard for the innocent souls in Basine. I can respect that. Needless to say, my brother and his ilk have no such compunction."

For a moment, they were silent. Anna watched him closely. He was fascinating, but no matter what Ozman talked about, there was an air of defeat about him. She felt it impossible to avoid pangs of sympathy for the little man, but at least he could give her information. If he didn't have the reserves of strength to use that information, she did.

They sat in silence for a few moments longer. Anna wasn't sure what to say next, and Ozman seemed distracted. He looked back at her from his brass and chrome machine with a look of dissatisfaction on his face.

"Professor Ozman, do you know what happened to Teej's last partner? Her name was Linda."

Ozman took a moment to respond as he ran a hand over his balding head in embarrassment. "What? Another Metik? Oh, I'm sorry, young lady. I was a million miles away. No, I'm afraid not. I don't take much to do with Metik business. And, please don't take this personally, but there is a…stigma. Not that Metiks are bad or anything. It's just, well, I am a most open-minded and forward-thinking man amongst my kin, but even I try not to mix with your kind."

She wrinkled her nose, more at the condescending attitude than this strange new form of discrimination she was experiencing. He noticed her reaction. "No, no, it's not like that! I don't think you're inherently bad, but your kind are anathema to our work. You can undo in a second what we take a lifetime to achieve. Even being here, your presence undoes a fraction of my work. You understand?"

She did. As an Undreamer, she inhibited his Art. She could dismiss his work with a wave of her hand. She felt its flimsiness. In comparison to the rest of the Sump, his machine was like tin-foil in a world of cold, hard iron. She had power over Dreamers. That's why Drowden wanted her to help him. They might all resent her, but they could all use her. She was a weapon, and in this ideological war that seemed to be developing amongst the Aesthetes, she was just another asset.

"I understand. You all hate me, but you can use me."

He looked at her with some sympathy, then shrugged and turned back to his machine.

Anna wasn't ready to let it go yet. "What is this schism between the Aesthetes? What does the Doxa actually want?"

Ozman sighed heavily then started to recite a quote she had heard before, but many of the words were different. "God is dead. God remains dead. And we have killed him. How shall we comfort ourselves, the murderers of all murderers? Who will wipe this blood off us? What sacred games shall we have to invent? Must we ourselves not become gods simply to appear worthy?

"Nietzsche had a way with words, didn't he? The Doxa take that sort of nonsense very seriously. The religious predilection so common amongst the simple folk in Basine was something many of us were also attracted to. Not me, of course, for I am a man of science, but my other brethren struggled. Their work depended on the deities you know from your highly numbered cable TV channels, and they feel the world needs a new one. And my…my own brother has a candidate. His 'The New Motive Power' is one possibility.

"Drowden has another potential messiah, and there are others still. When we group all of that madness together, we call it the Doxa. The group and their ideology both share that name. Within their group, they compete with each other for sure, but they form a loose coalition. Surely it will break apart in time over the innate ideological differences and the petty rivalries, but for now, they hold enough power to conscript others. They are formidable.

"And so, they push forward, pining for a fight, playing a game of power and allegiance. They threaten and cajole, and those who believe we require no new deity or that it's not our place to impose such a thing on the plebeians, well, we end up in places like this."

Ozman's shoulders slumped and his mood had darkened, and it was having a physical effect on the workshop around them. The books started to crumple to dust, literally flowing off the shelves like little powder waterfalls. The machine behind him started to corrode, the bronze oxidizing to a dull green color. The chrome sections were taking on a red, rusty hue. The plush seats they sat on now felt bare and uncomfortable, the springs poking and straining against the thinning fabric.

"I think perhaps it's best you take your leave, young lady," said Ozman. He sounded strained. Some of his facade fell away, and she felt like for the first time, he was being completely sincere with her. "Perhaps just a few days more? Go and check on your friends. I doubt they will survive, but I shall endeavor to take them with us. That is, if our fate holds any hope of escape. Pip pip! Where there's a will…"

She looked around sadly. He was right; she was making things worse. "Okay. Okay, I'll go. Is there anything I can do? Can I help?"

"No, no. Come back in two days. And Anna…"

"Yeah?"

His eyes went dark for a moment. "Stay away from the water."

thirty-eight

Tick. Tick. Tick.

Peter's internal chronometer went three whole cycles before the Inductive Regress Chip fell into a decision condition and set out a course of action. That was far longer than normal. Its slow, deep processing routine highlighted to Peter how important this mission was. He had to do this quickly and silently. There could be no mistakes.

By overlaying potential routes and trajectories onto the world in front of him, his programming set out exactly how he would capture the girl with the pink hair. Based on the data available, this plan had a high probability of success. In a few minutes, she would be his captive, and he would escape. No one would know who took her, and no one would be able to track him.

Peter had followed her from the mall through the city center, keeping his distance the whole time. Now they were in a quiet part of town. The slate gray sky hinted at more rain, forcing most sensible people to retreat home. Close to the train bridge and the trendy bars that were all closed in the quiet early afternoon, this was the best place for him to make his move. His timing was perfect, and he could tell from her body movements and heartbeat that she wasn't aware of him. She didn't realize she was in danger.

As she moved from the busy city center to the quieter, cobbled, winding streets near her apartment, she neared his ambush location. She carried two bags of groceries. Tins of chickpeas, fresh orange juice, individual packets with cheesecake, and bottles of fruit cider. Even those were factored into his plan. His mind played out the steps of the attack, calculating how the items would fall on the ground. He saw how the tins would roll on the street and how she would drop the bags. It made no difference, no one would hear them.

Three more ticks, then he would move. In less than a second. His mind played out the simulation one last time. His muscles were already engaged, the slower neurons of his organic brain primed to fire earlier than the much quicker quantum calculations in the Inductive Regress Chip.

Even as he took the first movement in his attack sequence, he had to adjust for a new person entering his line of sight. Peter's perceptions widened and scanned the environment, using sound to triangulate where the disturbance was coming from in the time before he could turn his head. It was a man. Someone very good at hiding in plain sight, but Peter was aware of him now.

As his view shifted, four whole cycles went past.
Tick. Tick. Tick. Tick.

His plan had already adjusted. He must eliminate this new target, too. This witness needed to be removed from the equation. The Inductive Regress Chip resolved the algorithm and created a new process. He could not stop, his programming compelled him to continue. He would capture this girl, and he would kill this man.

Eventually, Peter's head turned enough for him to see the new target. Warning signals flooded his consciousness as this was no regular target. His Inductive Regress Chip highlighted this man as a grade one threat. The highest ranking possible. His goal did not change.

The man's name was Donnel. He was a Metik, and he had to die.

thirty-nine

With a terrible, inevitable inertia, Teej fell through the door into the bathroom a fraction of a second too late. She was gone. All that was left of Anna was the ring she wore on her left hand, which had slipped off and fallen to the floor.

"No! Dammit. No!"

In a moment of utter anguish, Teej smashed a heavily clenched fist into the mirror. Holding it there for a second, the cracked shards of glass didn't fall but little ruby drops of blood did. Overcome with rage, his head hung heavy while his mind raced. What could he do? It was too late. *Too slow, Teej, too slow.*

As he pulled his hand away from the mirror, several long, broken fragments fell and broke into smaller pieces in the sink. He put both hands to his face and, before he could stop himself, tears rolled down his cheeks. Sobs of immense, soul-wrenching disappointment and rage. How could he let this happen?

Gripping the edges of the sink, he forced himself to look up at that cracked reflection.

"Think, you idiot, think! What now? Come on!"

The broken reflection offered no suggestions and held no hope. Teej's face was haggard, his cheeks gaunt and his eyes glassy and weak. He'd smeared his own blood on his face, and his mouth drooped at one corner like a stroke victim. He didn't recognize the man he saw, but he recognized the expression of failure written across that face.

He had been outmaneuvered so easily. Though still weak and groggy with a head full of fuzz, he should have guessed this was always going to be Drowden's next move. The Occultist only had one card to play: his portals. He could send anyone to any place in the whole Firmament as long as he caught them off guard, and Teej had allowed him to take Anna.

As soon as Teej fully awoke, Drowden had become aware of them. It would have been better for Anna if he had stayed unconscious forever, and better still if he had died. She could have moved on, but in waking, he had failed to protect her or prepare her. Now he was left broken, and still he felt responsible for saving her. He *had* to help her, because this was all his fault.

Drowden had been swift and decisive. Either he had captured her and was trying to inculcate her into their cult, or worse, he had already given up on recruiting her and killed her instead. Teej reassured himself that though Drowden was ruthless, he wouldn't kill someone he could use later. That didn't mean Anna was safe from imprisonment or torture though.

His mind continued to race. How could he track her down? Drowden would be in hiding. There's no way Teej could find him. If he had captured Anna, their only hope was that she manufactured her own escape. She was strong and clever and more resourceful than any of them realized. Drowden and Mott had all underestimated her, and they would continue to do so. She was a novice Metik, but Teej saw how naturally she used the Will and the Word. He had never seen anyone like her. Perhaps there had never *been* anyone like her. They all thought she was some confused Noop tangled up in a world she didn't understand, but she could still surprise them all.

311

So, he held onto the hope that if Drowden had taken her, she still had a chance. They would still be underestimating her because they didn't know her like Teej knew her.

With a heavy pragmatism, Teej promised himself that if he could do nothing to save her, then he would avenge her. He would kill Drowden. If that happened, he would become everything he promised himself he would never be. A killer and an assassin—the kind of Metik Wildey was.

He had to act as if she were still alive and imprisoned. That was Drowden's MO after all. Drowden's best move would be to surprise Anna and imprison her rather than fight her. If he pulled her into a pre-made Haze of his own design, she could hurt him. Drowden was aggressive, but he wasn't brave. His best hope of success against her would be to take her somewhere she wouldn't be able to manifest Praxis easily. *The Sump!*

Teej looked down at his bleeding hand for a second. What was he going to do? *No one ever comes out of the Sump.* That was its only constant, defining feature. The place where lost things go that are never to be found.

It was a legend and a whisper among Metiks and Aesthetes who used it as a curse. No one really talked about going there, although they all knew it was possible. Certainly, Drowden could access it. His Art allowed him to open portals to anywhere, which was why he was so dangerous.

But who else could get there? Garret? He was perhaps the most powerful Metik alive, and certainly the Metik most likely to help Teej. But the old man's mind was broken, and he was fading out of the world. Supposing he could even *find* his old mentor, should Teej risk asking him for help?

As he picked small flecks of broken glass from his bleeding knuckle, Teej weighed his options. No, even if he could ask Garret to help again, the old man couldn't do it. Maybe he would know of a way *into* the Realm, and maybe he could even get them to the Sump, but he couldn't get them *out*. It was a prison for the hopeless. Nothing ever got out.

Vinicaire could get him there. They called him "The Explorer" with good reason. He was a Dreamer with an interest in the lost, forbidden corners of the Earth. He looked for hidden places to stage new productions. If the Sump was a place—and it surely was, albeit one that was hard to find and impossible to escape—then Vinicaire could take him there. And Vinicaire had helped him before.

But how would they get *out*?

Teej looked up at his reflection again. The cracked façade held some desperate hope. His subconscious mind found a slippery idea on the edge of probability and grabbed onto it. Vinicaire could send a person to the Sump…or he could send a *thing*.

Teej's face became a mask of steely conviction. There was always a way. He had caught the faint thread of hope, not that he could save Anna, but that he could help her save herself. Now he just had to find Vinicaire. Even that first step would be impossibly difficult, but he had to try. If he failed, Anna would be lost forever.

forty

Teej held the Fetish tightly in his white-knuckled fist. The powerful relic had been given to him by an ancient, reclusive Dreamer called Pinapune. Although it looked like a simple silver spoon, it was imbued with Pinapune's particular talent: tracking. She had been the greatest hunter and tracker who ever lived. Long ago, Teej had received this gift for helping her gain control of a Spiraling Haze. Perhaps a rifle or even a hunter's hat would have been more fitting, but Pinapune had a sense of humor. The silver spoon might have been a sideways allusion to Teej's privileged upbringing, but it was nonetheless a useful tool. By simply clutching it and thinking of a particular individual, the Fetish would direct him toward that individual.

Of course, as with many gifts from wayward Dreamers, Teej had at first assumed it was useless. His skepticism had proven ill-founded when it had successfully helped him track down an old friend a few years ago. He was hoping it could do the same for him now.

Although effective, it was an imprecise tool. If he maintained concentration and continued to hold the person in his mind, it would get warmer as he got closer to them. The effect was subtle, and the mental energy required to use it was considerable, but there was an arcane intelligence to the item. By holding it over a large printed map of the city, he had been able to feel a tiny change in its temperature when he held it over specific areas. Taking a taxi to the sleepy, gentrified South side of town, he had a general area to search. Jumping out of the car with very little idea of where he actually was, he followed that lead.

But that had been three hours ago, and since then, he had been wandering around quiet streets, past coffee shops and trendy clothes stores and through empty parks with little indication that he might be closing in on his target. The spoon remained warm but never got hot. He was close to *something,* but he also seemed to be wandering in circles. After three hours, he had been wandering long enough to begin to doubt himself. His initial enthusiasm for his plan had given way to trepidation and doubt. Would Vinicaire help him? Was Anna in The Sump? Was Vinicaire even capable of *getting* to the Sump? Was Teej just an idiot wandering around with a spoon?

He'd questioned his own sanity more than once before, but Teej never felt more foolish than when he was forced to rely on the tools of Aesthetes. As a Metik, he was inherently skeptical and cautious. As dangerous or powerful as Aesthetes could be, they were just as likely to be ridiculous or ineffective. For every genius he met, there were five madmen and a hundred fools. Although he knew Pinapune was in the group of geniuses, he was beginning to doubt himself.

Putting the Fetish in his pocket for a moment, he paused to examine his surroundings. He'd meandered past the city center through the tall office buildings south of the river, and from there he'd continued into the narrow, cobbled streets near the railway. The early evening sun was dipping below a low bank of clouds, and the wind whistled through the sleepy streets. The cool, comforting air turned chilly, and Teej was forced to button his coat.

Standing at a crossroads, Teej saw a corner shop, a boarded-up restaurant and a long, narrowing street that went under a railway bridge. Coming up the hill toward him, he noticed a skinny girl with multi-colored hair, and it was at that point he felt the heat in his jacket pocket.

It was her.

Teej scrambled for the spoon and fished it out of his jacket. Clumsily pointing it at the girl, it became so hot he had to constantly move it between fingers to avoid burning himself. He was sure it was her. Somehow, in some way, she was the key to getting to Vinicaire.

Teej put the spoon back in his pocket and relaxed his thoughts. It had taken him as far as it could. From here, he had to follow the girl to find Vinicaire. This was still a tenuous lead, but he had to try.

Aware that he had to keep his distance, Teej pulled his phone from his pocket to look less conspicuous. He examined her with sideways glances, but she was still a distance off. An art student maybe? She was scruffy but stylish. Her multi-colored hair was messy, tied back to reveal a slim, attractive face with big, spacey eyes. Her slender form looked awkward, and she had a childishness that would make her attractive to someone like Vinicaire. Teej had no doubt this girl was Vinicaire's "type." A Noop, she was probably there at his beck and call, available any time he needed some wide-eyed, attractive girl to accompany him on one of his productions.

Teej weighed his options. His relationship with Vinicaire was unclear. The Aesthete had helped him recently, but in the past, they had been at odds and even fought occasionally. With the recent conflicts between the Aesthetes, everyone was taking sides. Teej had been out of the game for a while now, so he guessed the rivalries had escalated and the schism deepened.

Perhaps the Aesthetes' political maneuvering had erupted into all-out war during his absence, so he had no idea how this Noop might react to him. Would Vinicaire have warned her about him? Would she run from him or attack him? Normally, he wouldn't feel threatened by a skinny girl, but he knew better than to judge her purely by her innocent appearance, especially in his weakened state. Aesthetes could equip their Noops with all sorts of arcane weapons and teach them basic Mimesis if their will was strong enough.

As he deliberated, Teej became aware of the lingering malaise in his muscles. As a Metik, he was hyper-aware of his own body and what he could ask it to do. At that moment, all he could feel was the thinness of his upper arms and the heaviness in his legs. His conditioning was gone. Muscles had wasted away as he lay in the hospital, and his reactions had slowed. His edge had dulled, and he was a fraction of his former self.

And worst of all, it wasn't just his body that had been damaged; his thoughts were slower, too. He was paralyzed with indecision, and he knew why. Partly, it was a lack of confidence in his ability to handle any situation, physical or mental, in this diminished state. The memory of the fight hindered his decision as well. He remembered the feet stamping on his head and fists slapping wetly on his bloody face and skull as he dripped red over the cold, gray floor outside Anna's apartment. For the first time, flashes from that night came back to him. The best part of him had been beaten out.

He was lost in thought and caught in the headlights of indecision, when the girl looked right at him. "Teej! You're Teej!"

How could she know him? Teej was instantly disarmed. Was she an ally? Maybe she even knew Anna already? He started to move toward her, but as he took a step, something shifted in his consciousness. His Haze Sense told him they were in danger. An Etune untethered from its Haze was coming at them. It was strong enough to wander around in Basine. A rare threat, but one of the most dangerous he could face. Outside of a Haze, he had few powers that could stop it. Though he could feel it come closer, he didn't know where it was.

The girl ran toward him. She looked hopeful, her expression warm and her eyes filled with recognition. He knew she was Behind the Veil, though. He sensed the Vig within her, accumulated from time she had spent outside of Basine. It was like an afterglow. She was a Noop for sure, and she wasn't a neophyte, but she didn't realize the danger they were both in.

Teej started crossing the road to meet her, but as he took the first step, he identified the threat. Teej couldn't see it yet, but he could sense the movement of the Etune behind the low wall to his right, moving to intercept them. The ground rumbled with more Vig than he had ever felt outside of a Haze.

The girl's expression changed. She had spotted the attacker, too. From where she stood, she could see the Etune, even when Teej couldn't. He started to run, but his muscles were slow to react. It was like moving through water. His senses still dull from the accident, he nonetheless felt a shapeless dread.

The girl started to turn, perhaps to run, and at the same time, the attacker took to the air. Teej had never seen anything like it. It leaped ten feet over them, and the fight began.

It looked like a slim black man in a long coat, baggy shirt, and loose jeans. Teej's Haze sense penetrated through the façade, and within the man was a frame of metal and circuitry, Vig-infused actuators, and a mind augmented with some form of advanced computer. Unfeasibly fast and ruthlessly efficient, Teej recognized the Etune as one of Dr. John Speare's Pilgrims. The Apoth had created these strange cyborgs before, but never with such potency.

The Pilgrim sailed through the air, and at the apex of its leap, Teej appraised his enemy. The long coat fluttered in the air

318

but couldn't hide the potent, lethal limbs that were poised to strike. Even without Teej's expanded senses, and discounting the fact that the Pilgrim was ten feet above the ground, it would be clear to anyone that it wasn't human. Its skin glowed with long, orange lines illuminating the surface of its arms and hands. The one flaw in the Apoth's design was the Pilgrim exerted high amounts of heat. In this case, the Vig within made the internal metal literally burn through the flesh. The Pilgrim was imbued with a deadly fire that would consume it, but not before it eliminated its target.

It was disarmingly fast. Even as Teej shouted out, he was almost too slow. Almost. The potential damage the creature would do to the girl couldn't be quantified. She could be dead a thousand different ways if he didn't stop it.

"Stop!" Teej's use of the Word was weak, but it was sufficient. As the Pilgrim hit the ground in front of the girl, it froze in place, poised with malice but standing completely still.

She stumbled back and fell awkwardly. The Pilgrim's arm was raised and ready to strike. It would have killed her instantly if Teej hadn't been there. That arm could pile-drive her body through the ground, but the Word held it in place.

The Pilgrim turned its head to look at Teej. The eyes were dead and empty, the humanity within utterly subsumed by the machine.

Teej walked toward the Pilgrim, hand raised in warning. He held it in place as best he could, focusing his mind and keeping the Word foremost in his thoughts. As he got closer, the Pilgrim spasmed unnaturally. It didn't understand what was happening. It probably didn't even understand what it was. Unaware of its own nature, it struggled to reconcile its situation. Meanwhile, Elise scrambled away in confusion, backing up to the shutters of a nearby shop front.

Now that Teej was closer to the creature, he could see the innate *wrongness* of it. At one time it had been a man. His Haze sense penetrated the human exterior to the robotic eyes linked to the neural processor. He could delineate where parts of the man's organic brain had been excised completely. Within that body, he could see the metal polymers grafted onto the bones, the replacement circuitry where the nerves should be and the lymphatic system, replaced with a vascular network that pumped liquefied Vig around the body, maintaining this abomination's presence in Basine. It was as insidiously clever as it was obscene. For a second, Teej felt a pang of sympathy. The soul of this thing had been brutalized.

Teej's concentration slipped for a second, and the Pilgrim was like lighting, closing the distance between them in a blink and raising its arm to attack again. He shouted, "Stop," just in time.

In that tiny window of opportunity, the creature had moved ten feet and was within striking distance of Teej. It was uncomfortably close now. He could feel the heat coming from the burning orange lines etched across its arms. Where the open sleeves of its shirt rolled back, he could see the scorching metal glowing from within its skin. He could smell the cooking flesh.

Gesturing for the girl to get behind him, Teej backed away from the smoldering enemy. It was frozen again, unable to move but regarding them with cold fury as it shuddered and twitched.

"What's your name?" he asked the girl, only half listening. He had to hold this creature as long as possible.

"Elise. I know Anna. You're Teej. I saw you when you were sick. What *is* that thing?"

"No time. Listen to me closely. I can't stop it."

"Run?" she asked, already halfway down the street.

He nodded. "Run."

320

forty-one

The cold penetrated Anna's bones. The wind had died away for the moment, but in its place was an icy, pervasive chill. Like frozen fingers curled around her spine, holding her to attention. A vague feeling of loss tugged at the edges of her mind.

She had been searching for Shar and Fee for a long time now. Their home was empty. The stagnant stew had gone cold in the pot. All around her was silence. The still black water was like a sheet of polished black glass. It waited for her.

Anna leaned on one of the wooden posts by the wharf. Looking up at the cave ceiling, she could see no evidence that they might have travelled the high paths. It was the only place left to look though. She was sure they hadn't gone that way, but felt she should push herself to look for them, and the only place left to look was up there. Or down *there*.

Anna moved closer to the edge of the wharf to gaze in macabre fascination at the water that was slick with a layer of oily iridescence. Where the moonlight found the surface, little rainbows rose and fell with the gentle tide. The closer she got to the water, the more intense the sense of dread and fascination. What if she just went in? Took one more step? It seemed like the only thing left to do. She'd explored everything here. There was no other escape. The only way left to go was down.

Even playing with the idea made her feel a curious excitement. She wasn't going to do it, but when she considered it, even for a second, her body felt a little bit alive again. It reminded her of a time before being here, when choices meant something.

Awareness of the danger snuck up on her. Now she found herself looking into that water, and it was impossible to move away. Stepping back was simply too horrible. To step away from the water was to face the Sump again. To go back to Ozman and his hopeless invention and to find Fee and Shar and see them devolve before her eyes, the skin wasting on their bones, their eyes glazing over, their thoughts melting away.

She couldn't look at Ozman's machine anymore. It was a doomed endeavor and a madman's folly. It was almost worse than no hope; it was a fool's hope. He would never get them out of here.

The black water contained all sorts of tiny ripples she hadn't noticed before. Mini-whirlpools and concentric circles expanding out, creating networks of arcs and curves across the surface. The black water was constantly moving, even though it seemed still.

There was a warning in her mind, faint but insistent. *You've pulled yourself out of the water before, don't let it take you now.*

With heart-wrenching difficulty, Anna pulled herself away.

She took a step back from the edge, tripping as she did and falling heavily on her backside. Her tailbone found bare rock and pain shot through her spine. It hurt so badly, she gasped and felt her eyes get wet. There was no point in shouting out, no one would hear. Instead, she just cried. Not only because it hurt, but because she realized how close she had come to ending it all. The pain of the fall slapped her back to reality.

The water had almost taken her, and it had felt good. She could still feel its pull. It took all her strength to hold herself

322

there, away from the water's edge. All she wanted was to go back to that edge. To glance into the little ripples on the surface. Her senses pleaded with her for just one more look, but she resisted. She shouted aloud to no one and to everyone and to the black water, "I won't do it! Never again!"

As those words came out, she felt her resolve harden. The will-to-life returned, just a little. Maybe it was part of her Metik ability. When she spoke, the words conveyed power, both to change the world around her and, as she'd come to discover, to change herself. Maybe if the insidious reach of the black water was getting inside her head, her Metik abilities could dispel it for a time.

Anna didn't know for sure if that was true or if she was finding the strength to withstand the despair, but she did know that shouting made her feel better, so she shouted again, "I'm never going out that way!"

The words rang hollow as her voice shook, but she found strength in being able to say them. It was a small victory, but staying away from that water for even a few hours more seemed like a success of sorts. She had to look for Shar and Fee, and if she couldn't hold onto them, she had to get back to Ozman and help him. She seemed to be the only one of them with any hope left. Perhaps that was why the black water called to her so loudly.

Looking for some remnants of the former, stubborn Anna, she picked herself up and shouted to no one in particular, "If some crazy Dreamer or Metik wanted to suddenly appear and mess everything up right now, I'd be fine with that!"

forty-two

Turning into the empty alleyway, Teej immediately realized he had made a mistake. They should have kept running. Standing in a wide passageway filled with dumpsters, pallets, metal cages full of cardboard boxes, and dirty puddles, he noted with grim resolve that this was a dead end.

They'd run halfway down the alleyway before seeing that the only possible exit was fenced off. A mesh gate topped with barbed wire warded off the stock delivery area for the back of a large store. As they turned to go back again, the Pilgrim rounded the corner.

The creature's clothes had burned away. Singed rags were all that remained. Much of the human form had slewed off too, the fat bubbling and melting away while the crusty black surface that had once been skin popped and fizzled. The face was a mixture of bone and gleaming orange metal. Even at a distance, Teej could feel the heat radiating from the emaciated thing. It was a blackened golem; a dark, smoldering ember of death.

Teej continued trying to hold it back with the Word. As it chased them through the empty streets, he'd stopped to shout repeatedly, but each time it was less effective. Each time it weakened him. He pushed out all his Will in an attempt to slow the Pilgrim down, but like an implacable foe walking through a storm, the creature slowly pushed through each barrier. For every step Teej could push it back, it took two more forward.

And though he was weakened and caught off guard by the creature, Teej still couldn't understand why it wouldn't stop. He'd never seen an Etune this powerful before. Even when Etunes were mundane in appearance, they rarely lasted in Basine for more than a day or two, and that was when directly controlled by a nearby Dreamer. This creature was far from mundane. An abomination, it seemed to have almost endless Vig to call upon. Teej was shredding through its energy stores with his Praxis, forcing it to expend more and more Vig, but still it had reserves to push onwards. And he couldn't sense any nearby Aesthetes. If he could, perhaps it would be possible to attack the Dreamer and dispel the Pilgrim, but whoever was pulling this puppet's strings was either far away or very good at hiding.

As the creature continued its remorseless advance, it leaned forward and pawed at the air between them like it was fighting invisible enemies. Teej stood firm and poured all his strength into his Word. "Stop! Come no closer."

Elise looked ready for action. Impatiently, she hopped from foot to foot, ready for a fight. He was impressed with her resilience and how fast she ran. Maybe if she had left him behind she would be safe by now, but she had shouted encouragement and run by his side. They should have split up. Instead, he'd led her down this dead end. Folly upon folly.

He sensed Elise move to one side but couldn't turn his attention away to look at her. She was rooting through one of the piles of garbage looking for something. After a few more agonizing moments of holding the Pilgrim back with all his strength and almost bringing it to a standstill, she appeared by his side. She carried a piece of rotted wood with a nail sticking out the end and brandished a trashcan lid like a shield. Teej didn't know whether to laugh, but he cracked a thin smile.

"You hold him while I bash him with this, yeah?" said Elise.

Teej shook his head, "No. Stay behind me."

"We are so fucked," said Elise, still bouncing nervously.

She circled away from him to one side until he couldn't see her anymore. Suddenly, the Pilgrim lurched forward, taking advantage of a lapse in Teej's concentration. He managed to stop it again, but it was just a few steps away now, and they had nowhere left to go. One more slip and it would be on them.

It was too fast. Even now, looking like a charred, smoking piece of coal covered in rags and scorched black flesh, hunched over like it was crippled, it was still much faster than any human. He could feel the heat radiating from its glowing core. Sweat beaded on Teej's forehead as he wondered how the creature would finish them. The heat alone could be lethal if it got any closer, but it had machine strength they couldn't match either.

Teej cursed his weakness. If he'd had a few more days to recover, he could have stopped this thing. The Pilgrim was strong, but no Etune could last forever. Regardless of how much Vig it contained, a decent Metik could drain it away. He wasn't strong enough right now though, and that frustrated him more than anything else.

"Teej, I found a way out!"

He couldn't turn to her, but he backed away from the Pilgrim toward the sound of her voice. Glancing sideways, he got an impression that she had found a door. He turned to see her pry open a wooden panel behind piles of dirty trash and old, soggy cardboard boxes. The thin wood buckled as she pulled it. It was chained on the other side, but she was managing to squeeze herself through the gap between the door and the wall.

"Come on, Teej!" she shouted as she slid through.

The distraction was all that the Pilgrim needed to break free.

The deathblow came, but Teej's old training saved him. He dropped to the ground and rolled out of the way as the creature smashed a solid metal arm through the door and part of the wall, filling the air with shredded wood and dust from the crushed bricks. Momentarily blinded, Teej lost sight of Elise.

He rolled to his feet, his head spinning. He was sluggish, but even if his conditioning was gone, his reflexes were still there. He'd trained for most of his life, in a hundred different forms of martial arts, acrobatics, and athletics, with Aesthetes and Metiks. His body might be failing him, but all those years of knowledge stuck with him and, in this case, kept him alive. His instincts were intact. Now he would need them as his Praxis had failed completely. The Word was useless, and the Pilgrim was free to come at them with everything it had.

Teej backed toward the wall, waiting for the creature to make its next move. It seemed slower now. Behind the Pilgrim, Teej thought he could see Elise lying on the ground, but it was too dark to be sure. The backhanded forearm blow had smashed concrete and dust off the wall as well as splitting the door in two and destroying the top half of the wooden doorway. Perhaps she'd been too close and had been knocked backward, or maybe he was mistaken and she had escaped into the darkness.

Teej crouched, poised to dodge, depending on how the Pilgrim came at him. He could run to the left and try to get out of the alleyway, but he wasn't sure how fast the thing was now. Perhaps it was running low on Vig or the accumulated heat was slowing it down, or perhaps it was feigning weakness. Either way, his old legs felt too tired to run, so he decided to fight.

The Pilgrim lurched forward suddenly, propelling itself with one leg while swiping for him with the opposite arm. Teej tucked and rolled, his shoulders thudding heavily on the ground.

As he struggled to find his feet again, he realized what was wrong with the machine. Somehow, one of its legs had seized up. Perhaps the heat had caused the joint to fail. Teej felt the solid metal arm fly inches over his head and recognized the potency of the attack. The weight and speed of it. If that arm had connected, it would have gone through him like he was made of paper.

Before Teej knew what he was doing, his training took over. He pushed out a front kick, thrusting his hips into the attack to generate as much power as he could. Old lessons drilled into him by martial arts masters throughout the ages paid off now. He pushed his momentum into the kick, focusing all his energy forward and out. The Pilgrim tried to avoid his attack. No doubt its reactions and abilities in combat far exceeded his own, but the lame leg slowed it down, and his heavy blow landed square in its chest. Even in his present condition, the kick was delivered with such precision and technique that it would have completely floored a human opponent, but the Pilgrim's weight was misleading, and although he managed to push it backward into the wall, he knocked himself backward, too.

Teej fell heavily onto his backside once again and suddenly felt immensely vulnerable. He could only watch in horror as the Pilgrim fell back against the wall before instantly pushing itself off to come back at him. It was relentless. Teej tried to scramble his legs under his body, but they simply wouldn't move quickly enough.

And then Elise leapfrogged past him, smashing the solid wooden plank into the Pilgrim's face at the exact moment it stumbled forward. As it reeled backward, she jumped over Teej into the path of the killing machine. She fought like they stood a chance, and she hit it so perfectly and forcefully that it seemed for a moment that they might actually prevail.

The Pilgrim had attempted to sidestep the attack as it came forward, but with its damaged leg, it only managed to turn into the blow. The wood splintered over the very top of its part-mechanical, part-organic skull. Flecks of ash and chipped, scorched skin flew from its face as it fell backward. Elise's whole body shuddered at the point of impact, and it was a mighty, awesome strike. It would have killed a normal man. Teej wanted to cheer.

Elise continued the attack, smashing the heavy post down again and again as the Pilgrim fell. Each dramatic thud echoed percussively through the alleyway. It was a terrifying noise, but no matter how hard she hit, she was still attacking a piece of solid metal with a piece of wood. She kept it prone with the barrage of attacks, but she was doing no real damage. There was no way she could defeat the creature like this.

Again and again she lifted then dropped her weapon, hammering the Pilgrim into the ground. The skinny girl was quite something.

Stumbling to his feet, Teej struggled to reach her and help. Her face was flushed with the heat of the creature as well as her exertions, but as she raised the plank of wood above her head to swing one more time, Teej saw the threat too late. The Pilgrim's hand reached out for her leg. With a terrible inevitability, its metallic fingers curled around the exposed skin of her pale ankle. Time seemed to slow, and there was a moment before she realized what was happening. Steam bubbled up from her cooking flesh. Teej couldn't help her. A knot of dread twisted in his stomach as he waited for the scream.

A horrifyingly loud snapping noise echoed like a gunshot, followed by a rumbling crunch as the metal claw sunk deeper into the flesh and ground the bones.

Even then, when the scream came, it wasn't a cry of pain but rather of surprise. Elise fell backward, but the creature clung to her, smoke rising from its vice grip as it crushed her bones to shards. The Pilgrim pulled itself closer, climbing over her and raising the other arm across her head in preparation for the killing blow.

Jumping faster than he thought possible, Teej bounded at the thing, grabbing its metallic wrist and wrenching back with all his strength. Instantly, the flesh of his hand began to char and burn, but he didn't let go. Searing pain whitened out his vision, and for a second, he felt the Vig fail in the Pilgrim. Finally, its reserves of power were waning, and he felt something stir within himself, too. His Praxis was there, and a residual memory of the potency he once held came back to him.

As Teej held the creature, his Haze Sense penetrated its exterior, and he could feel the obscene nature of the thing. He knew he could hurt it now. Channeling all his Will, he focused on that piece of burning metal in his hand.

The metal began to cool. He couldn't really feel it—the skin was burned too badly now, the nerves destroyed—but he could sense it, and even hear it. A low reverberation as the metal crumpled. The Pilgrim noticed his attack too late. It tried to pull away from Teej, but he held onto the creature just as firmly as it held Elise.

"Let her go," he commanded.

Instantly, the Pilgrim released her. Elise scrambled away on all fours, her shattered ankle leaving a bloody trail as she went. She wailed as she crawled to safety, long dark lines forming from the tears in her mascara, but Teej couldn't help her yet. He still had to deal with the Pilgrim.

He twisted his wrist, and the creature's arm snapped off in his hand. He had converted its essential material, maybe changed it to something brittle, or cooled it so much that it crumbled in his hand. He wasn't sure which, but he felt elation. He couldn't drop the broken limb; the flesh of his hand had burned and melted into it. Instead he smashed it against the ground until it came free. As he pushed aside the horror of his wounds, he prepared to finish this fight. He could face this creature without fear now.

With one broken arm and one malfunctioning leg, the Pilgrim tried to get away from him, but Teej pounced. He locked his burned hand on the creature's shoulder and pushed it to the ground with a heavy thud. As it flailed at him with its functioning limbs, he held it tightly.

With a tone of righteous anger, he said, "You will stop fighting. You will stop struggling. You will *not* hurt us. You have failed. You hear me?"

Teej's voice trembled, and he spat the words, the exertion of the fight taking its toll on him. Despite that toll, he felt stronger. Today would not be his last day.

He held the Pilgrim down as he spoke, both hands pushing it into the ground. Its glass eyes housed in the bone-and-metal skull starred at him emptily like a horrific puppet. He held its gaze.

"I have been a Metik for longer than you can know. I have been a Metik for longer than you have been an *idea*. I have destroyed a hundred things like you before. A thousand. And I will kill a thousand more if your master keeps sending them. Understand?"

The creature could offer no reply.

"Now go," said Teej. "Know that I have beaten you. Use whatever small amount of time you have left to make peace with your own nature. If that nature represents a debt that must be repaid, then settle the account with your maker. Let your ruined soul be a flame that burns only him."

As Teej finished speaking, he released the creature. The Pilgrim recoiled, its ruined limbs propelling it awkwardly away from him as fast as it could...as if *he* was the monster. As it

331

backed against the wall, it grasped onto the solid stone and started climbing backward like some grotesque spider. With its one working arm and leg, it found spaces and divots between the bricks as it climbed two stories, then three, then four, creating little showers of dust where it smashed and grabbed holes to lift itself higher. In moments, it climbed onto the rooftop and out of view. It was gone and two injured, tired people were left. Teej had no idea what it would do now, but it couldn't hurt them again. He doubted it could live long in that state with so little remaining Vig.

Fighting through waves of fatigue, Teej made his way over to Elise. She was wailing in pain, but she was conscious and trying to speak between sobs.

"It hurts." Her voice held a note of pleading.

"I'll get you help immediately. But Elise, you must tell me something. Do you know a man named Vinicaire? Can you get to him?"

She seemed to calm at the mention of his name. She gave him a weak nod though her face was a mask of pain.

"Okay. That's good. We need him. Anna is in a lot of trouble."

"Teej, my leg. My leg!"

"I know," he said as he reached down to her, pulling a handkerchief from his pocket and laying it across the wound. The damage was substantial. Little fragments of bone poked through the skin. Teej couldn't believe she was still conscious.

With the blood momentarily out of sight, Elise breathed in raggedly. She was struggling to say something, so he moved closer to her. "Anna?" she said. "Is she in trouble?"

"Always." He calmed her with a hand on her forehead. "Don't worry, though; we can save her. Vinicaire can access the lost places. He can help us send her something."

She opened her eyes and, for a second, it was as if she had forgotten her pain. "What?"

Teej smiled a little but didn't answer. "Come on. We get you to a doctor, then I'll tell you."

Sliding his arms under her slight form, he lifted her easily. He was tired, but she was skinny and limp, and his desperation gave him purpose and energy. Would his plan work? He still had no idea.

forty-three

With a weary sigh, Anna decided that if death were to come, she would treat it as an escape rather than a defeat. No reason to cry now.

What need is there to weep for parts of life? The whole of it calls for tears.

She'd already taken her first steps into that black water. She'd taken off her battered sneakers and filthy socks and dangled her feet over the surface. Playing with the idea of sliding off the old wooden pier and falling in, she'd rocked on the edge like a petulant child. Instead of pushing herself off though, she swirled her toes around in little circles, watching the whorls and ripples with childlike fascination. It felt warm and comforting, and though it called out to her, she coyly teased the water. She bit her lip and pretended to be shy. "No, I can't come in just yet. Maybe later. I can't decide if I want to yet. I'm not sure."

Anna could feel the voracious hunger of the Black Water. It had already taken Shar and Fee, she was sure of that now. She'd looked for them everywhere, from the crags up high to the rocky caves nearby and the tunnels below. They were gone. The water had closed in over them. It took everyone, eventually.

It almost had Ozman, too. His work had become increasingly manic. If she was blind to the oppressive, malign force that affected everyone in the Sump, she might think he was desperate and urgent, or on the verge of a breakthrough, but she saw through the façade. He was working faster and harder because he knew all hope had already faded. He was keeping busy to avoid the reality of the situation. That reality was simple: no one ever escaped the Sump. Whether Metik, Aesthete, Undreamer or Etune, this place devoured everyone eventually. They were all washed away by the Black Water in the end. Souls dissolved here.

Anna could remember the exact moment when her last hope faded. Unable to find anyone else, she'd run back to Ozman's little sanctuary. She didn't know what she'd hoped to find. A spaceship or an elevator to the real world? Instead, all that was left was a sad, grease-smeared man bashing away at an old brass storage tank with a wrench.

Over the last few days, Ozman's powers had gradually faded, and as they left him, his creations regressed. The books on the shelves had crumbled to dust, the chairs had collapsed into rotted wooden planks, and their "escape ship" had become a rusted heap of metal. It was a bluish-gray corroded pile of junk, and yet still he labored on it. Did he see the same failure as she did, or did this pile of scrap metal look different to him? Anna knew that deep down, he felt the same doom; he just hadn't faced it yet.

And that's when hope left her. In that moment, she accepted that she would die here. The only conflict left now was whether she would finally face that old pain. *Desolation.* For the first time since the accident, some of those memories came back to her. She remembered how blue and lifeless his face was when she pulled him out of the water. She remembered touching his face and saying his name, although she hadn't said that name since. How much of her had died that day, too? It was all locked up in her mind, and she'd only survived by vowing to never remember any of it. The memories found her here in the Sump, though. She couldn't run from them here.

Those old memories didn't feel like her own anymore. They were old Anna's memories, before Teej took her Behind the Veil, before she had started studying again, and before the drinking and the breakdown and the time she'd burned all the pictures and thrown away everything of his except for the letter and the ring.

No, she didn't have to go back to those memories. That was her final comfort. She would never have to deal with those thoughts. They could die with her. That pain could no longer terrorize her by creeping into all her happy moments and ruining them, because she would be dead soon.

Anna wondered absent-mindedly whether she should go back and check on Ozman one more time. She was still morbidly curious to see what state he might be in, but she was also nervous that seeing him might spark some faint hope of escape. Sorrow, despair, pain or death she could endure, but disappointment was what she feared most. If even a tiny flicker of hope arose to be extinguished, then it would be too much for her. Better to stay here, by the edge of the black water, and look at the ripples till it was all over.

Even if she wasn't prepared to go back to old Anna's memories, she could remember more recent events in her life. She could daydream a little before the long night.

Anna replayed those strange memories now. Garret defeating Drowden, Lady Almeria and The Night Collectors, Teej's smile, Elise and Malamun, killing the Midnight Man. It all seemed so prosaic now that it was almost amusing. She thought of the fear that Mott had inspired in her, and laterally, the triumph she'd felt when she'd beaten him. Her triumph had made her feel stronger and safer. Back then, she'd thought the worst danger was over. She couldn't remember being that confident, potent version of herself. The Anna that kept fighting was lost.

Shuddering in the cold, she closed her mind off and shut her eyes. Running her fingers through her straggly, matted hair, she hummed a tune her mom used to sing to her as a girl.

Anna remembered her first experience in a Haze, wandering through the dark woods, trying to find her way home. It had been terrifying but exhilarating even when she was fighting for her life. Being in a Haze was an addictive experience in hyper-reality. Only one visit had her hooked. Teej had that same quality. He stuck in her mind. His little smiles and the knowing looks he gave her, the bad jokes and the teasing, it was all addictive. She remembered when he stirred coffee and looked up at her warmly and when she'd fought off the werewolves and he'd clapped his hands with joy. When he held her.

It had always been about Teej. With her thoughts now free to wander wherever, she let her mind drift away on flights of fancy. What would it be like to kiss him? Would it bring back all the old hurt, or would it wash some of that pain away? If Teej held her, would she forget? And how did he feel about her? He made her feel special, but was that just his way with women? Did he feel the same about her?

Maybe if she'd had more time to learn from Garret and Teej, they could have prevailed against the Doxa. Maybe Teej could still stop Drowden. The Dreamer was ruthless, a religious zealot blinded by righteous zeal, and Anna had felt the cruelty of men like him before. Teej was something else though, better than Drowden, but stronger than him, too. Teej was worth fighting for.

As she struggled to slide her fingers through a big knot in her hair, she wondered if there had ever been a real chance of escape. If she had reacted quickly enough in the first few moments, would she have been able to get back through the portal

Drowden had used to send her here? Or if she'd gotten to Oz-man sooner, before both of their minds got so foggy and their powers drained away, would they have been able to complete his machine and use it to escape?

It was impossible to know. She was left with too many hanging questions. All that she could do now was fantasize. Maybe Teej would arrive and save her. Or maybe Garret would jump up out of the black water, staff in hand, flash her one of his charming smiles and tell her to follow him through a secret passage that would take her home. Or, while she was engaging in wishful thinking, maybe she could turn back the hands on her watch and go back in time. Back to before the Sump and before Teej and before she fell in the river and it would all be just a terrible dream. And her husband would stroke her hair from her face, kiss her forehead, and tell her not to worry. When he did that, it always made everything a little bit better.

It didn't really matter. The Sump was *in* her now. Desolation had infected her to the core. They were one and the same. Different names, but the same feeling. They would always catch her. Even if she were to escape, this place would find her again. She was part of it now. It held her mind and would never let go, even if her body somehow escaped.

Anna was unnerved when she slowly began to realize her reverie was being interrupted by something new. On the horizon, she was dimly aware of a speck steadily growing. It took a moment before she was sure it wasn't her imagination. Something really was coming into the bay. For the first time since she got here, something new was happening in the Sump, and it raised a lump of fear in the back of her throat. She couldn't go back to uncertainty. She was content that her fate was already decided. She had no fight left. Why did this have to happen now?

Standing slowly, Anna squinted to see something gliding across the water. It was moving quickly and silently, and it seemed to be coming straight toward her. Even as it grew, the darkness clung to it, and Anna found it hard to make out any details in the moonlight. The black shape felt threatening though, like it was accusing her of something. Shame mixed with fear as she shuddered in the cold. Anna didn't want any living thing or person to see her again. She just wanted to sink away. Why did this *thing* have to come now?

If it had come a day ago, or even an hour ago, it might have been a welcome sight. Or at least something she could deal with, but now it only exacerbated her distress. She couldn't face it. Turning away, she refused to look at the black shape. She sunk down onto the wet rock by the pier, curling into a ball and hugging her knees as she closed her eyes tight.

In her mind, she heard her mother's voice. Soft and tender, a whisper in her ear. "Anna, honey, you can't keep the darkness away by closing your eyes. You must open them and let them adjust. Then you see that the darkness is just a different kind of light."

It wasn't the voice of the mother she had now, worn down by life, her sharpness and wit eroded by time. It was the voice of the mother whose lap she had lain upon as a girl. The mother who taught her about people and the little lies they told. It was the mother who still wrote poetry and wasn't afraid to share it with the world. It was the mother who had a quick word for the ignorant and the cruel, and a slow, kind word for the people they hurt. The mother who made her strong enough to face anything. Even this, even now.

Smoothing down her ruined clothing—now little more than rags of cloth—Anna lifted her head, coughed a little to clear her throat, sighed, and then steeled herself for whatever she would face next. Taking the time she needed to prepare, she found a calm, quiet corner of her mind. She raked through her memories for words that would make her strong. Camus came into her thoughts, and she spoke the words aloud.

"In the depth of winter, I finally learned that there was in me an invincible summer."

Yes, that would do. She turned around.

Bobbing gently back and forward on the black water, a long sailboat sat silently by the pier. It was almost close enough for Anna to touch, and it waited. Though it was dark gray and looked heavy—almost as if it was made of stone—it sat high on the water. The tattered sails might have been white once, but were now gray-brown shreds of cloth. Standing in the center of the boat, holding the mast with one inhumanly thick arm, was a ten-foot-tall monster.

Its face was long and goat-like, with tight flesh pulled over a prominent skull. Slit eyes barely visible beneath a drooping, heavy hood with a furry body, mostly hidden beneath a long cloak. Anna found it hard to judge the scale of the creature, but it stood far larger than any human. Dominating the deck, it towered over her like she was a child. Obscured by shadow, partially illuminated by moonlight, it loomed still as a statue, only slightly twitching and straining its arm muscles as it gripped the mast with one massive hand. With the other, it clutched a long spear, its shaft as thick as a lamppost with a jagged obsidian spike at the end that looked like it could skewer an elephant.

The arms drew Anna's attention. Rusted metal and thicker than her body, they held ghastly potency. The interwoven cords that made up its limbs slid over and across each other as the creature moved, like massive snakes twisted together. Beneath the sunken cheeks, a gaping, fang-filled mouth wheezed. Though several teeth had been broken or chipped, they remained razor sharp. She couldn't help staring into that mouth, wondering what this creature ate. People like her, she guessed.

Though terrifying, Anna was strangely reassured by the overt horror of the creature. As opposed to the existential dread of fading to nothing in the Sump, this creature looked more like the kind of enemy she had faced before. Capable of breaking her body, not her soul. She wasn't sure if it could speak, but she had questions.

"Hello." Her voice trembled, but she swallowed down her apprehension and started again. "Hello. Are you…is there a way out of here? With you?"

Her voice didn't carry far into the emptiness of the huge cave. She didn't know if the creature heard her. It didn't seem to react at all. It just stood, rocking slightly from side to side on the water within the heavy boat. Skeletal fingers flexed around the shaft of the spear.

Long, uncomfortable moments passed. Anna didn't want to repeat herself but was unsure if the creature had understood her. Although it remained utterly still, its eyes followed her as she shuffled nervously from side to side.

When it spoke, the voice was clear, accent-less, and authoritative. It sounded ancient, and it made her feel like a child.

"I am Charon." His voice was deep and resonant.

She waited for him to say more, but he simply stood there, looking at her. Was he waiting for her response?

"Hi, Charon. I'm Anna."

Charon slowly lifted his spear a foot or so off the ground, then brought it down again. The action was slow, but when it hit the deck, a dull thud echoed throughout the cave and shook her insides. The black water splashed up the sides of the boat. Was he trying to get her attention? Or intimidate her? She stood resolute, consciously straightening her back and looking straight into his dark eyes.

"You are the last one," he told her simply.

"What do you mean?"

"You are the last one here."

"No, I'm not. Shar and Fee and Mr. Ozman. Are they…?"

"You are the last one."

She sighed because she knew he was right. They were gone. She was the last one. Still, she pushed him for more information.

"They were right here, though. And Ozman is back there, in the cave."

"He is not," Charon replied simply. His voice was emotionless and resolute. He looked at her directly and spoke. "He has gone to the water. You are the last one."

"When only one soul remains in Avicimat," he continued in his flat, emotionless tone. "I come for them. To give them a choice. To make a deal or to offer them mercy."

She eyed him with suspicion but forced herself to move one step closer to him. She wanted to prove—to herself as well as him—that she wasn't scared. She didn't want to appear intimidated. Her fate might depend on how this creature regarded her.

"What deal?" she asked. She hoped she sounded defiant.

"Come with me instead of letting the water take you."

"Where? That sounds like a good deal."

He looked straight ahead now. His gaze went over her, and his mouth barely moved as he spoke. He stretched out a massive arm and pointed out the cave entrance to the moonlit sea.

"I will take you to die in a better place. And so when you pass on, the water won't take you. Your soul will leave your body in the Holy Realm of King Gwinn. Instead of here, in this accursed place."

She turned away from him and bit at her fingernails, her mind racing. As she understood it, King Gwinn's lands were huge. They spanned not just the Sump but constituted a whole world in its own right called the Realm, but those lands were not

342

her world. Not the *real* world. And why did she have to die? Surely the creature hadn't travelled all the way here just to kill her?

"I want to go home," she said flatly, her voice trembling as she realized how weak and plaintive it made her sound.

"That is not a choice open to you. Nor is survival. I will bleed you here but sail you to the other side.

"When your final breath leaves your lungs, you will be looking up at the azure sky of Selmetridon."

His tone was matter-of-fact. Was this a test, or an idle threat? She feared it wasn't. She feared that her best option really was death. Death elsewhere; perhaps it was an offer she should accept.

No, she would not let this monster kill her. Not without a fight. Anna couldn't face her own fears and nameless dread, but she could face this creature. She could fight, regardless of the hopelessness of her struggle. This couldn't be the end. *Never play their game, their game is always rigged.*

"You will not harm me. You will take me home."

"I will not."

And with that, there was silence. An impasse. What could she say now? What could she do? Charon's eyes held her, showing no sign that compromise or bargaining would help her. His voice did not waver or falter, and what remained of her Haze Sense told her that he was immensely powerful. She had no powers to speak of here, but even if she did, he would likely be an insurmountable foe. This was his domain.

"I won't let you harm me. I will destroy you if I have to." Her threat seemed ridiculous.

Charon remained silent for a long moment. What was her goal here? Fight him? Better to punch a mountain or wrestle the sky or pour away the sea. This was her worst plan so far.

"I do you a great honor by offering this to you. I can leave you, or I can take you."

Did he sound impatient now? Angry? Anna stepped to the edge of the boat and looked straight up at him. The hull came to her waist, and his head was so far above hers that she was looking straight up. She didn't know what she was doing, but with no real power to threaten him, all she could do was bluff.

"I will make you take me, or I will destroy you. I am an Undreamer. I can…Undream you. Now, I need to know, can you take me home? If not, you will take me out of this place, but you will not harm me. Am I clear?"

Charon slowly crouched, and involuntarily, Anna jumped backward. He moved at a glacial pace, but he was so tall and heavy that when he shifted his massive red-black cape, it created a breeze that blew his scent in her face. A curious mix of cinnamon and rot. She recoiled, ready for his attack. Even crouching, he towered over her.

From the deck of the boat, he picked up a heavy hook with his free hand while he continued to lean on the long spear. It groaned and scraped across the surface of the vessel as he lifted it. Heavier than a car, taller than a house. As he straightened his back and stretched up again, she was in awe. His pale, skull-like visage held no sign of compromise. He spoke slowly, a rumble that vibrated her whole body.

"I come here to show you a mercy. No one ever leaves Avicimat unless their soul is ready to rot. That is the purpose of this place. To offer no hope.

"But there is succor. One might escape to die in a more peaceful place. Such mercy is beyond your comprehension. And the water is already in your head. Were you not ready to let it take you? I come to offer you this gift, and you threaten me?"

His tone didn't shift, but she felt the anger in him. It was terrifying. He would not be intimidated. She was certain he would kill her now.

Her bluff was called. Still, fighting was the only choice she had. She winced as she said, "If I defeat you, will you take me home?"

Again, she had that familiar feeling: out of her depth, making mistakes. Facing an ignominious death, she was thankful that no one was here to see her make a fool of herself by challenging this giant goat monster to combat. Charon tipped his head to one side like he was appraising her as a potential opponent.

"You hold no threat for me, Undreamer. I am an Ancestral and you are weak here.

You are weak *anywhere*.

"I would relish a real opponent. My role here is tedious. But slaughtering you would do you no honor, and bring me no satisfaction."

"Don't be so sure," she responded. Before she knew what she was doing, she was climbing into the boat. Scrambling over the hull, she clumsily half-fell onto the deck. The abrasive surface, like concrete, was rough and wet. She must have looked ridiculous, but still, she got to her feet and faced him. Anna stood directly in front of Charon. Although he was huge, the boat was spacious inside. Perhaps if he attacked her, he would be slow. She could even dodge and move around on the deck for a while. Maybe he would get tired. *Yeah,* she chuckled to herself, *maybe he'll fall over the edge or have a heart attack.*

"You are willful. In this place, the strength to fight is sucked from the bones of the hopeful. Yet you resist. Maybe in some other world this match would be a good one."

She nodded at him, hopping from foot to foot like she was about to start an exercise class. "Ridiculous situation," she muttered. "I can't believe I'm going to die like this."

As he turned around to face her, the whole boat rocked. Large waves splashed over the edge as he adjusted his massive feet, shifting his weight from side to side.

Taking in a deep breath, she prepared herself. About to run at him without a plan other than surprise, she suddenly became aware of a glint on the deck. A beam of moonlight illuminated a blinking object each time the boat rocked on the water. Something small and completely out of place.

She looked up at Charon, and it was clear he saw it, too. Their eyes locked for a second, and they both froze, then everything happened very fast.

They moved in unison, Anna diving forward at the same moment Charon took a giant stride that rocked the boat. Unbalanced by the shift in weight, Anna almost fell as the deck tipped to one side. Scrabbling across the ground toward the shining object as fast as she could, she was only dimly aware of what was happening above her. She went down on all fours, her knees and hands slipping across the slick surface, before springing upward again and sprinting straight ahead. A whoosh of air went over her head, and she felt something brush past her hair. Charon had swung his immense spear, but she'd ducked under it as she'd stumbled. His attack wasn't fast, but the inertia behind it was enormous.

Expecting another attack to come any second but unwilling to question her own instincts, she tucked and rolled across the deck and smoothly scooped up the glowing item.

Her ring.

It almost slipped out of her hand again, but she grasped it close to her chest.

As Anna slipped the ring onto her finger, she looked up to see Charon poised to strike. She craned her neck backward, and his huge form blocked out the light. It felt like a wall was about to fall on her.

Charon swung downward with stomach-wrenching momentum, and Anna had no choice but to run toward him to avoid the massive blade. He dropped to his knee as she ran past to one side. The spear slammed into the hull with a dull thud that shook through her legs and momentarily bounced her into the air. She scrambled back to her feet, but Charon was reacting more quickly. He slid the hook across the ground with a heavy scraping motion that produced a shower of sparks as he lashed out at her. Again, she slipped past the blow without realizing where it was. It missed the back of her legs by inches as she twisted and stumbled.

The boat tipped in the water, and for a moment, it seemed poised to capsize. They both struggled to retain their footing. Twisting her body to get away from Charon, Anna's toe found a divot in the deck and she tripped heavily, landing on her backside. She struggled to catch her breath as foul-smelling water splashed all around her. Drowning again.

Above her, Charon put his colossal arms out to balance the boat. For a moment, neither of them moved.

Splayed across the deck on her back, Anna realized she couldn't escape the next attack. There was nowhere left to run; she was cornered. She watched Charon slowly turn, his movements labored. Was he winded? It didn't matter now, there was nowhere left for her to go. He pointed the tip of the spear at her and thrust it forward.

Anna wasn't afraid now. *The ash caught a spark.* Some vestige of her power was in that ring. She'd always known it had helped her focus her powers. Teej had called it a Periapt. It didn't hold any power by itself, but it unlocked something inside her. It gave her a frame to hang her powers on, a lens to magnify them through. While the Sump had drained her will, the ring seemed fresh and not yet tainted by this place. It was a symbol of the Anna from another time, before the Dark Water saturated her. The ring reminded her that this was a Haze that could be changed and shaped. She did *not* have to accept her fate. If she died here, it would be because Charon defeated her, not because she surrendered. *Sometimes the flame splutters back to life.*

Anna slammed her hand onto the deck before looking up at Charon. With his spear poised to skewer her chest, he hesitated.

"How long have you had this boat?" she asked as the fire burned in her veins. Her body trembled with restrained power. Her ring glowed white hot, but it was a controlled exertion of her Will. It would burn anything or anyone she desired, but on her own skin it felt cool.

Charon didn't lower his weapons, but he didn't attack either. "Beyond your reckoning of time."

Anna lifted her hand, and as Charon looked on aghast, she smashed it down onto the deck of the ship. Shocked by her own power, she scrambled backward on all fours as a network of huge cracks spread across the ground below their feet. Within seconds, water bubbled up at the point of impact. Just a little spurt at first, but the damage was clear. One more blow and the whole boat would shatter. She lifted her hand again, even though it was now bruised and sore. Her small finger might have broken, but she couldn't feel the pain. She was elated by her strength. She would not be threatened, nor was she a victim to be saved. Anna was an Undreamer.

"Take me home or the Black Water takes us both."

She heard hesitation in his voice for the first time. "I cannot take you where you need to be."

"You will take us *somewhere* or we will stay *here*. Forever!" she barked.

"Selmetridon can be our destination. I can offer nothing more."

"That's no good." She raised her fist again.

"I will take you to Selmetridon, and you will come to no harm. On that you have my word."

She shook her head.

He put his hand up to her in what might have been an imploring gesture. "Woman!" he said. "Into this water we *cannot* go. You know not what I am or what this means—"

"Shut up," she cut him off. "Take us out of here. If you try anything, I will smash this boat. I swear to God I will do it, then what happens is on you."

The giant lowered his weapons slowly and deliberately.

"And don't call me woman. My name is Anna."

The monster nodded acquiescence. Placing the hook down carefully to avoid further damage of the boat, he pushed the bottom of the spear into the water and used it to cast off from the dock. They began to glide away. Anna breathed a sigh of relief.

Once the boat started to move, she was shocked how far they travelled in just a few minutes. They skated across the surface like the water was ice. Anna kept her hand held high, ready to strike the deck again if he made any moves against her. Every muscle in her body was tensed. Knee-deep in dirty water, she couldn't feel any pain as adrenaline coursed through her body, but she knew it would come.

They sailed soundlessly out of the cave, and Anna's mind reeled. The wharf was fading from view. Her heart continued to pound in her chest, but she allowed herself a moment to breathe and calm her nerves as she watched the Sump fade into the distance. Were they really leaving? Although Charon pushed the long spear into the water, the boat seemed to sail itself. They were approaching the cave mouth before he spoke again.

349

"Be calm. I have agreed I won't harm you. My word is steel."

The water continued to trickle through the cracks soaking her, but the hull was so huge and deep that they weren't in immediate danger. She kept her hand ready to strike, but she adjusted herself to rest her tensed muscles. Charon's dark eyes and inhuman face looked down on her impassively, subtly shifting the boat to steer it straight as they approached the exit.

Out into the vast, dark sea, Anna felt both the pain in her hand and a sense of dread for those she had left behind. She glanced behind her to see the quayside and the cave fade into the darkness. The moonlight didn't penetrate far into the gloom, but she saw the outline of high cliffs and jagged rocks fade as they sailed onwards. So, that was the Sump. Avicimat. An unassailable prison; a trap no one had escaped. Until now.

Charon ignored her, so she allowed herself a moment to think. Was Ozman really gone? And Fee and Shar? The Dark Water had surely taken them, but a knot twisted in her stomach when she remembered their faces. Had she really tried to save them?

No, there was no way they could have escaped. She had brokered this pact with Charon somehow, but her own chances of escape remained slim, even now.

The air was changing. It was colder but clearer. Anna felt like she was coming out of a thick, invisible fog that had been choking her. Killing her so slowly and so subtly that she hadn't noticed it. Now that she was out of the Sump, the cold breeze rejuvenated her, and her head started to clear.

"I do not know how you have that item of power," Charon confessed. "I do not know how it got into my boat." He didn't look at her when he spoke, and she detected a hint of genuine confusion, although his voice remained disinterested.

"Me neither," Anna said. "How long until we get to Selma-whatever?"

"I do not know how you judge time. As long as we have known each other."

She decided further talk wasn't going to help her. Sliding toward the front of the boat, still holding her ring prominently as a warning, she looked out at a still sea of refracted silver moonlight. Where would she end up? She found that she absolutely did not care anymore, as long as it was away from here.

It was hard for Anna to judge how far or how fast they went in the leaking boat without a visual frame of reference. The mist rolled toward them in waves, while the water was glacially still. The moon was a brilliant white coin in the sky, unnaturally bright and large. The sky was pricked with a million tiny stars, and when she looked up, Anna could even see broad, gassy nebulae in green and blue and the occasional white glint of a quickly passing meteor.

Charon's huge arms worked like a machine, his broad strokes impelling them forward with metronomic regularity. Anna sat huddled in the corner of the boat, tired and spent. She knew if she let her guard down, he could kill her easily and quickly, but she trusted him. Perhaps it was her Haze sense, or perhaps she believed simply he would keep his word. Either way, she briefly considered closing her eyes. Perhaps that was a step too far. She spoke to him to keep herself from drifting off.

"What *are* you Charon?"

"How can it be that one so ignorant can live when so much wisdom is dead? It is a wonder you know to put your socks on before your shoes."

Anna inched forward to look at Charon more closely. Though he faced away from her, she thought he twitched.

"Are you making a joke?

"This journey with you across these waters is a joke."

Anna leaned back and twirled her ring on her finger. It was still hot to the touch. "Are you an Ancestral? A big, grumpy Ancestral?"

For a moment, it seemed like he might turn to face her, but he kept rowing.

"I am. Both ancient and eternal, I am a fixed point in the Firmament. A piece of solid granite in the ever-changing rivers of realities."

Anna grunted, unimpressed. Leaning over the side of the boat and looking out across the water, she made a promise to herself. "When I get back, I'm going to kill Drowden."

She didn't expect a response from Charon, but she got one.

"You are an infuriating woman."

Anna laughed. "You know, of all the people that have tried to kill me this month, I think I like you best."

Far above her, Charon's shoulders twitched again. Could that be a chuckle?

"You heard what I said?" she asked. "I promise, I will kill the man who sent me here."

Charon nodded slowly. "Of that, I have no doubt."

forty-four

In a world of fog and shadow, two figures stood on the shore of an endless silver sea. A pale moon shone bright in the cloudless sky.

Anna's perception of the two figures was vague and disturbed, viewed through the lens of exhaustion and despair. Sitting on the edge of the sinking boat, hand still held aloft ready to strike, albeit limply now, she struggled to process everything that had happened. Who was this giant boatman that loomed over her? Where was she? Was this the end of her journey? She had no answers, and she was too tired to make sense of anything.

As they bumped up to the shore, Anna couldn't see more than a few feet in any direction and almost all color was drained from this place—an eerily featureless fog world. The thick gray sky stretched to the silver sea. The powdery sand that greeted them on the beach look like smooth, flat concrete, but it glittered and sparkled in moonlight that somehow shone as bright as the midday sun. Even if she had been fully awake and alert, this place would have felt like a dream. No place had ever felt less real.

On the shore, hands reached out to take her as she raised her own arms pitifully. The first figure held her shoulder and guided her out, but it was when the second person clutched her that she felt a pang of familiarity. The strong hands that held her gently but firmly were his. Teej's.

Anna wanted to smile or say his name, but her bones were lead. Her mouth wouldn't work. It was all she could do to keep her eyes open. As soon as Teej held her, she allowed herself to go limp.

She was in his arms, just like she had dreamed. A sweet, foolish dream. In the distance, she heard Teej speak, but she was too tired to understand the words.

Maxine's Bar is hard to find, not because it's hidden, but because it's veiled in banality. Huddled near a quiet corner of a quiet street, a dirty sign hangs over a heavy door and a food menu is printed outside that door. The prices are all wrong and the food descriptions are partially worn away. The stairway descends to an entrance that smells of stagnant water and mold. It's unpleasant enough that the only people who go beyond the stairs are those who already know what lies inside.

Stumbling down those steps, the Metik carried the sleeping girl. When a shaft of sunlight broke through the rain clouds to shine on her face, her nose twitched and her eyes almost opened. She stirred as the rain stopped.

He soothed her, "It's okay. We're safe. I can help you hide. They won't find you. You don't need to fight anymore. I can take you *home*."

It took a long time for the words to penetrate Anna's awareness. When she realized what he was saying, panic rose in her. She didn't want to go back home. She wanted to be with him.

At that moment, she would have told him everything if she could. She wanted him to know. *It's a wedding ring. I was mar-*

ried, and he wasn't happy. He jumped in the river, and I tried to save him. The current was too strong. There was a letter, and I was afraid to read it, so I burned it. I was killing myself slowly. I wanted to die, until I met you. I am ready now. I am an Un-dreamer.

But she didn't say any of that. Instead, a familiar phrase came back to her, and the words made sense now. She said them aloud, hoping he would understand.

"Sometimes the ash catches a spark…"

Teej smiled. "…and sometimes the flame splutters back to life."

glossary

Aesthete (Dreamer): An artist so pre-eminent in their field that their Art can change the laws of reality and create a possibility space known as a "Haze."

Ancestrals: Precursors of the Aesthetes, these ancient and powerful beings have mostly disappeared or fallen dormant. Their nature and origin are contentious theological and philosophical debating points amongst Metiks and Dreamers.

Apoth (John Murray Speare): A member of the Doxa and a powerful Aesthete that creates monstrosities known as Pilgrims through unnecessary surgery. Brother to Mr. Ozman.

Art, the (Mimesis): The ability held by Aesthetes to create Hazes.

August Club: A secret nightclub/brothel where every fantasy can be experienced. It is a Staid Haze that is almost impossible to find.

Banille: The pressure that Basine exerts on a Haze. Banille will cause any Haze to eventually collapse.

Basine: The "real" world. Everything outside The Realm that is not inside a Haze.

Behind the Veil: A term used to describe awareness of more than just the Basine aspect of reality. When a person is Behind the Veil, they are able to perceive Hazes and are conscious of their experiences within them.

Black Water: An expanse of malignant, hungering water located at the base of The Realm, spreading from the depths of the Sump to the silver shores of Selmetridon. The Black Water swallows "all lost things that will never be found."

Charon (the Boatman): An Ancestral that seeks out the lost and hopeless. He never provides aid, but will offer an end to suffering to the last person alive in the Sump.

Corpa Haze: A Haze that is sustained by the energy of an Aesthete. A Corpa Haze is temporary, but it will influence Basine when it resolves.

Crags: Razor-beaked creatures that exist in The Realm, especially high in the caves of the Sump.

Crit Command (the Word): A verbal command issued by a Metik that compels anything within a Haze to obey. One of the four powers of the Metik (the Will, the Word, the Sight and the Sword).

Decadan: Archaic term for a Haze.

Doxa: A loose collation of Aesthetes united in their desire to bring about a theological change to Basine by creating a new deity.

Dreamer: Colloquial term for an Aesthete.

Dredges: Lost souls trapped in the Sump, these creatures are emaciated and have lost their humanity to the Black Water.

Drowden (the Occultist): A powerful, precocious Aesthete and the de facto leader of the Doxa. His Art flows from arcane symbols and occultism.

Endless Gray Sea: The sea that exists around everything in the Firmament. The end of every journey.

Etune: A living being created within a Haze. An Etune can be a person or animal, but when a Haze ends, they disappear from Basine.

Fetish: A physical object imbued with Vig, exhibiting residual behaviors from the Haze where it originated. A Fetish can seem supernatural to people in Basine.

Firmament: A term used by Aesthetes and Metik to describe "everything," including Basine, The Realm, all of the Staid Hazes, The Moonlight Road, the Endless Gray Sea and anywhere else that may exist.

Fluxa Haze: A form of Haze which is self-sustaining, pulling Vig from those who experience it and growing exponentially. Fluxa Hazes can change the nature of Basine, but they often Spiral and are always disruptive and harmful to reality. Fluxa Hazes are very rare, the most recent occurring hundreds of years ago.

Gwinn (King Gwinn, the Monarch): An Ancestral, and the unofficial ruler of the Firmament. By far the most powerful being active in The Realm, he has lapsed into apathy and torpor. His absence from Basine has loosened his influence on the world, and some now doubt whether he still resides in the holy city of Selmetridon. His nature, origins and intentions were once hotly debated amongst Aesthetes and Dreamers, but he is now rarely discussed or mentioned.

Haze: A possibility space created by an Aesthete where they use Art to change the rules of reality. Their power within the Haze is determined by their natural abilities and the amount of Vig they can retain and channel.

Idyll: A place where Vig is present in large amounts. An Idyll is often a place where people will feel inspired. Idylls are essential resources for Aesthetes and are often contested or fought over.

Kanna Island (Avalon): An ancient Staid Haze. Its origins are a mystery, and no one knows who created it. In the Firmament, it is close to—but not part of—The Realm.

Malamun: A Staid Haze that appears to be located on the moon. An ancient and potent source of Vig, Malamun is currently a run-down bar and nightclub, but it has existed in different forms for as long as any Aesthetes can remember.

Metik: An individual with the ability to change the Hazes created by Dreamers. Their abilities are sometimes broken down as "The Will, the Word, the Sight and the Sword."

Mott (the Midnight Man): An Aesthete and a founding member of the Doxa. His Art is based on writing, in particular macabre poetry about murdering young women.

Muse: An individual whose presence generates more Vig than normal. Muses are typically very inspiring people.

Night Collectors: Etunes created by the Midnight Man. They are large monsters that capture and suffocate their victims in constricting bags.

Noop: A derogatory term for a person who is neither a Muse nor an Aesthete, but who is nonetheless Behind the Veil and spends their time in the company of Aesthetes. A kind of groupie.

Ozman, Mr. (the Scientist): An Aesthete, formerly the proprietor of the bar on Malamun. His brother is The Apoth.

Periapt (the Sword): The weapon and tool used by a Metik within a Haze. The term "the Sword" is symbolic, and the Periapt can be any item. Often a Metik learns to produce their Periapt within a Haze, while other Metiks will retain a physical Periapt imbued with some Vig and associated with an emotional memory from their past.

Pilgrim: An Etune that has continued to exist after the resolution of its Haze. Pilgrims are anomalies and typically don't exist long as it requires large amounts of Vig to sustain them.

Pinapune: An Aesthete and old friend of Teej.

Praxis: The process by which the Art (Mimesis) is modified and co-opted by a Metik.

Rayleigh (Old Grayface): A powerful and old Aesthete, and the acting leader of the community. Although Dreamers as a whole are too anarchic and disparate to universally recognize his authority, they all respect his judgments and few would contradict him.

Realm, The: The generic term given to a large, mostly empty world ruled over by King Gwinn from his throne in the Holy City of Selmetridon. Whether it is a Staid Haze, a shadow of Basine or a different reality entirely was formerly a contentious issue amongst Aesthetes and Metiks, but it is now seldom visited or discussed. No one knows exactly how big The Realm is, but it encompasses many distinct regions including the Sump, the Silver Shores, Selmetridon and many regions beyond. There are few remaining open gateways into The Realm from Basine.

Selmetridon: A sprawling, seemingly uninhabited Holy City in The Realm. Home to King Gwinn, it is now difficult to reach Selmetridon from Basine.

Spiraling: A term for when a Haze collapses, causing harm to people and damage to Basine. Fluxa Hazes are the most likely to Spiral. Many Metiks interpret their duty to be the prevention of Spiraling Hazes.

Sump, the (Avicimat): A huge cavern and network of underground tunnels and chambers at the lowest level of The Realm. The Sump is where all lost things go that will never be found. It represents both a prison for enemies and a place of exile.

Staid Haze: A Haze that is no longer affiliated with a particular Aesthete, and that endures far longer than a Corpa Haze.

The Will, the Word, the Sight, and the Sword: The four primary abilities of Metiks. They in turn represent the willpower to change a Haze, the ability to command Etunes within a Haze, sensitivity to the flow of Vig, and the Metiks Periapt (weapon).

Torpor: A form of apathetic madness that affects the minds of very old Aesthetes and Metiks. It is characterized with a disinterest and desire to disengage from Basine, and muddled, incomplete and incorrect memory formation.

Undreamer: A rare and powerful form of Metik that has limited ability to change Hazes, but great potential to destroy them.

Vig: The fuel Aesthetes use to create their Hazes. It can only be detected by those who are already Behind the Veil, where a unique sense allows them to experience it as a kind of air current or invisible light.

Vinicaire (The Travelling Troubadour/Thespian): An Aesthete whose Art flows from acting and performance. He holds a deep love for abandoned places and hidden stages.

acknowledgments

Most of all, thanks to the best dad. My dad.

Thanks mum and sis for telling me you were proud. It kept me going.

Thanks Evelyn for all the books you shared that got me into fantasy.

Thank you Hannah, Emma, Carrie, and everyone at Owl Hollow. I couldn't wish for a better team. We did it!

Thank you, Gary, for being my best friend and for everything you did for this book. You helped more than you know.

Thanks Nikola for your friendship and feedback.

And, of course, thank you Nana.

Thomas Welsh is the winner of the Elbow Room fiction prize and has been published in *404 Ink* and *Leicester Writes*. He received an honorable mention in *Glimmer Train's* Very Short Fiction award, and his story "Suicide Vending Machine" is featured on the *Pseudopod Podcast*.

His work has qualified him for induction into the Fellowship of BAFTA, and he has been published on major sites like *Kotaku, Unwinnable Magazine and GlitchFreeGaming*. He loves Neil Gaiman, Ursula K. Le Guin, Roger Zelazny and dark fantasy stories where women save themselves! He lives in Scotland with his wife Nana.

Follow Thomas at

calmdowntom.com

#AnnaUndreaming

CPSIA information can be obtained
at www.ICGtesting.com
Printed in the USA
LVHW03s2019190618
581244LV00005B/1107/P